Firehearted

Sabrina Chase

Cover art by Les Petersen

ISBN: 0-9852704-9-7
ISBN-13: 987-0-9852704-9-0

Also by Sabrina Chase

Firehearted
The Last Mage Guardian

THE SEQUOYAH TRILOGY:
The Long Way Home
Raven's Children
Queen of Chaos

ACKNOWLEDGMENTS

Many thanks to the critical group-mind of STEW, eagle-eyed editor Deb Taber, detail-oriented proofreader Roger Ivie, and hordes of patient beta readers. But thanks are most especially due to Lee McCormick, who read the short story and *insisted* there was more. Here's the rest of it, Lee.

S. Chase

CHAPTER 1

The two Naguri advanced, backing Erith up against the line of trees at the edge of the clearing. He edged a step to one side, aiming for the bare patch of ground under the largest tree. As long as they didn't push him too far back to get a full swing, the footing would be better there than on the trampled snow in the clearing.

"These are not Harali lands," said the one with the bear-claw necklace.

"They aren't Naguri lands either," Erith replied, unobtrusively resting the point of his sword on a tree root. His injured arm tired quickly, and he would need all his strength to survive the inevitable fight.

Motion caught his eye. Another man was approaching the clearing at a run, and he felt his stomach twist. *Son of the Dark Woman, there are three of them!* Maybe he wouldn't survive this after all. The two facing him had not yet seen the third, though.

"But maybe you have kin here in the Spirit Mountains? I thought it just a rain-tale, that the Naguri were bastards of the bolgash…."

Erith leaped back as the Naguri lunged, slamming into the trunk of the large tree behind him. Heavy, wet snow slid from the branches onto his enemies, giving Erith precious time to raise his stiff sword-arm while they clawed snow out of their eyes. He struck with all his remaining strength at the larger of the two, the one without the bear-claw necklace. His sword connected solidly and the Naguri screamed, twisting in agony.

Erith struggled to free his stuck blade before the bear-claw Naguri could attack, and felt his foot slip in the new wet snow. He went down hard, pain lancing through his knee, and jerked back as a knife blade sliced through the air where his head had been. Wet drops of blood sprayed his face, tasting of bitter metal, and he waited for the pain to follow, but it never came.

He heard footsteps and heavy breathing behind him, and he fell to the ground and rolled. He felt the third attacker slam into his ribs and stumble over him and onto the body of the slain Naguri. Erith staggered to his feet, nearly stumbling himself on the splayed legs of a deer, its belly split for gutting.

That's where the blood came from, Erith realized. They'd been hunting when they had seen him and attacked. That explained why the Naguri were so far away from their lands, not that it helped him now. He'd thought he'd be safe going this far north.

The third Naguri tugged his tattered cloak and dropped it to free his arms. Erith glanced about, hoping to find some means of escape, but his enemies were on him before he could put any plan into motion.

Erith was the better fighter, but they were two and he was already weary and injured. He could feel his battle rage weakening as he fought, desperately trying to just keep their blades away. He gasped for breath and saw it white in the cold air.

I am a warrior of the Harali—I will not die in fear! Erith gritted his teeth and lunged. The bear-claw Naguri stabbed him in the side, and Erith grunted with pain but managed to grab the hand with the knife, pulling it out and twisting until the blade was in his grasp and free to slash across the man's neck.

Then he felt the crushing blow of the third Naguri smash into his leg, and agony overwhelmed him. Erith felt himself hit the ground hard. He had no more strength to lift his sword, and now he was unable to run.

He scrabbled as best he could with his one working leg away from the approaching Naguri, who had a snarling grin on his face and his sword raised high. Erith felt the dead deer's stiff hair under his hand.

"Where would you go, then?" his enemy taunted. "Your people are far, and we are many."

"Not my people any more," Erith gasped. He shifted his hand further, seeking. "Kill me, and you please them."

He saw the momentary confusion in his enemy's eyes. It was just enough time for Erith to grab the still-warm entrails in the deer's belly and throw them under the man's feet. The viscera were slippery and the ropes of intestines caught around his ankles, tripping him as he struck with his sword. Erith let go of his own sword and grabbed the man's arm, pulling it up and away and stabbing with the knife, rolling over and pinning the Naguri with his weight until the man stopped struggling.

Erith took deep, gasping breaths until his heart calmed. Then he wearily took the knife and cut strips of cloth from his dead enemy to bind his wounds. The stab wound in his side was ragged and bleeding sluggishly, but the slash in his leg was a more serious problem. It took time, sitting in the cold snow, before he was able to slow the bleeding. Then he carefully crawled on one knee to the gear the hunters had left. A leather-wrapped spear gave enough support that he could walk, painfully. Nothing else was of any use to him, besides a handful of dried meat and berries in one of their carry-bags. He simply wasn't strong enough to carry more than his sword.

Erith hobbled over to the dropped cloak and picked it up. It had fur trimming, even though it was ragged, and if the only way he could go now was toward the mountains, he would need the warmth.

He staggered on for some time before he realized he was leaving a trail of blood in the snow. Erith was tired enough that he thought for a moment about how to remove it before shaking his head. Even if the Naguri knew where he was going, they would not pursue him. Among the people of the High Plain, the phrase "to go to the Spirit Mountains" was another way to say "to die."

He stopped for a moment, breathing heavily, and looked back the way he had come. The clearing where the Naguri had set upon him was lost in forest; the High Plain, farther away, was only visible as a bright, distant haze in the light of the setting sun.

An icy breeze found its way through a rent in his tunic, and he pulled his stolen cloak closer as he resumed his climb. He had to keep moving. Every time he stopped it was harder to get moving again. He had been running—and fighting—for longer than he could clearly remember now.

Fighting was all he had left. He could feel a broken rib grinding every time he leaned his full weight on the spear to climb, and lightheadedness made it even more difficult to keep his balance—and he could not afford to fall.

Erith knew he was only delaying the inevitable. The dead-white sky held the promise of yet another winter storm, and he was in the Spirit Mountains. Well, he had traveled wounded before. And as for the spirits… the legends spoke of them, but surely even a bolgash or a bloodraven would be somewhat daunted by a sword.

His hand clutched convulsively on the hilt. They had come close to taking it, at the *turos*. His one slender hope of survival…which would be useless, if he did not find shelter soon.

Erith continued on even as the pale sun set. There was no shelter anywhere; the trees were sparse and thin, scattered among boulders and the mountain's jagged stone. The night became one long delirium of travel, forcing one foot before the other. He wasn't aware of when he had dropped the spear, only that it was gone. He wasted precious time trying to find something to replace it.

After struggling slowly to the top of a ridge, he found a curiously carved tall stone. Near it was a pole with a ragged piece of cloth at the top. Erith tried and failed to think of any people who were supposed to live in the mountains. The pole would make a useful replacement for the lost spear, and it looked long-abandoned. He squinted, staring at the deep colors of the sunset. Was that a trail of smoke far ahead, or a dark edge of a cloud? It was faint, or maybe he was dreaming again.

The pole helped him go faster, and he descended the ridge back into forest. He headed for the direction he had seen the smoke trail. Real or not, he needed a goal. Even in the dark he kept the vision in his mind, using the moonlight to locate landmarks he had seen during the day.

At one point he roused from his waking dream and slowly realized something blocked his way. Small twigs scratched his face and snagged his hair, and he caught the tangy scent of fresh sap. He blinked and took a clumsy step back. A tree. He would have to go around it. Why was it there? He shook his head to clear it and looked about.

The tree was on the edge of a pleasant glade, with a few low bushes clustered around a tall, weathered boulder. Golden light washed over the glade, enough to show that one bush still bore a single, many-petaled flower. A small part of his mind wondered at the flower blooming in midwinter and the bright golden light that shone although the moon had set and the sun had not yet risen. He trudged on.

When Ronne emerged from her quarters, Kashan was already stretched out in front of the main door. He heaved to his feet as Ronne approached, barely letting her reach the door latch in his impatience. Ronne glanced outside, closed the door behind the snowtiger, and sighed. The sky was dead grey, which meant yet another storm was coming.

She went to the storeroom next to the kitchen. There was only one barrel of grain left—she would have to ration that; once it was gone there would be no more. She reviewed the rest of the supplies, thankful that much had been deemed too heavy to remove. Firewood was plentiful. She might go hungry, but she would be warm.

At least she could hunt. Otherwise, her situation would be much more dire. Ronne wondered if the court had thought of that when they had exiled her, or if they really hadn't cared if she starved. How many years could she live like this, if needed?

If a storm was coming, she should walk the bounds. She could take the hunting javelins as well, in hopes of fresh meat. One last check of the perimeter before being stuck inside with nothing to do but stare at the walls. Kashan would be bored, as well.

Ronne took her light armor from the stand and fastened it, taking care with the worn strap at one shoulder. She stepped outside, closed the door firmly, then placed her spined helm over her braids and strode out into the frozen landscape.

The rising sun gave light but little heat, and Erith slowly realized he could not last much longer. His leg had gone numb. This made movement less agonizing, but it was a sign the cold was beginning to win. He had to find shelter immediately or he would become wintermad, thinking he was warm while his body froze. Frowning, he squinted at the rising sun. Perhaps he was already wintermad, for hadn't he seen the light of sunrise long before?

He looked about blearily, trying to focus. The narrow, rocky ravine he stood in was bare and exposed, with a bitter wind racing the length of it. He could see the tops of trees in the distance, which meant a valley below. Leaning heavily on the rock walls, he made his way slowly down the ravine and around an outcropping.

He stopped short. A huge beast with thick, black-striped white fur was visible no great distance ahead. It moved with power and grace, shoulders shifting as it paced on broad paws over the snow-covered ground, the long tail curving down and up again. None of the legends of the Spirit Mountains had mentioned a demon like this one.

Some small sound must have alerted it to Erith's presence, for the heavy, round-eared head turned in his direction. As soon as it saw him it gathered itself and sprang over the snowdrifts in large bounds, the open jaws revealing a formidable array of teeth.

Erith backed up, trying to draw his sword, but his cold-stiffened hands only pulled it free from the scabbard to let it drop. His wounded leg buckled beneath him, and he fell heavily to the ground. Erith saw his sword spin away, just out of reach. The creature slowed its rush and padded intently towards him, making a strange *wuffing* noise. He made one last effort to reach his sword, pain racking his body, and felt his hand just touch the hilt as the world went dark.

"Kashan!" Ronne paused, then called again. "Kashan! Where are you?" She hoped he had not gone too far. The building storm looked like a large one.

She climbed a pile of boulders at the edge of the forest to check on the outer boundary marker, which was just in sight from that location. The flag was not visible, and she frowned. She would have to go all the way out there and raise it if it had fallen, but there was no time for that now. The storm would catch her halfway.

Then she saw scuffmarks in the snow, with streaks of pale red at the edges. Ronne drew her sword and moved cautiously, no longer calling to the snowtiger. The tracks were meandering and hard to read. It was possible they were from a wounded animal, but unlikely.

She followed the dragging tracks until Kashan appeared in view in an icy ravine, crouched over something lying in the snow. When he saw her, the snowtiger gave a chirruping call. Ronne walked with care on the uneven, icy ground. Her boots were far from new, and when they wore out she was not sure what she would do to replace them.

"What have you been hunting, warrior of twenty daggers?"

She stared at Kashan's "prey." Six feet and more of plains barbarian lay sprawled in the trampled snow, clad in a ragged woolen tunic and trews. He also wore a tattered, fur-trimmed cloak and boots even more worn than her own.

Had Kashan attacked him? She would have heard something, surely, and Kashan appeared more friendly than aggressive. Yet there was blood on the snow, and one leg of the trews was dark with dried blood.

She came closer, raising her sword. When she stood beside the man, she nudged him with her foot. His outflung arm fell away, revealing a face as pale as the snow beneath him and more bloodstained rents in his tunic. The only color he possessed was in his flame-gold hair. Another, more forceful kick produced no response.

Ronne went to one knee beside him, pushing the curious Kashan aside. Something—or someone—had wounded him badly. Who? Why was he here? The plainsfolk never came this way; their lands were far to the east.

A cursory examination revealed the man still lived, but barely. She sat back and regarded him, feeling her face return to the formal, expressionless mask she had worn for so many years, even as her mind wrestled with unaccustomed thoughts.

She was a swordnoble of the Empire. Her duty was clear. Any threat to the safety of the Empire could not be permitted. But how much of a threat was he? He was alone, and dying as she watched.

There were those who would have left the man to die. Killing such a one had no glory, and their duty would be fulfilled. With her…gift…the Imperial Court had never believed she did not seek glory. Well, the court was not here to judge.

Many of his wounds were not fresh. He had been traveling injured for some time, and over difficult terrain. Respect was due such courage, even if he was a barbarian. It was a cruel death to die of cold, unworthy of a warrior.

She raised her sword to give the unconscious man a deathblow. As she struck, Kashan butted his head against her and she lost her balance, the blade landing harmlessly in the snow. Annoyed, she waved the snowtiger away and prepared to strike again.

She looked down at the man's face and hesitated. Lines of pain had not yet been erased by unconsciousness, and he had a gaunt and careworn expression. Now she saw dried grass poking through holes in his boots, and a rip in his tunic that had been crudely pinned together with a small twig. How long had he been wandering like this? Perhaps he had been abandoned by his people, even as she had been abandoned by hers.

Her thoughts continued their rebellion, and she lowered her sword, looking at the golden emblem on the blade.

He will die even if I aid him. Surely it will not violate the Code to watch a barbarian die in the comfort of my house.

A single snowflake spiraled down from the leaden sky, landing finally on the man's bright hair. She stared at it until it was joined by another.

He is far from home. I will give him a place to die.

She stood and sheathed her sword, then called Kashan from a hole he was investigating. With some effort, she managed to balance the barbarian's limp body on the snowtiger's back. Pausing only to retrieve the man's fallen sword, she led Kashan and his burden down the steep slope from the ravine into the glen below.

Erith dreamed of carrying a flame and some nameless, heavy burden. If he had had a destination, he had long forgotten it; all that remained was the knowledge that to stop was to die. The cold, lifeless dark seemed to press in on the faint, flickering flame in his hands.

As the flame faded, his burden grew heavier, and he knew he could no longer continue. Just as he was on the point of collapse, the quality of the darkness changed. It was warm and comforting, and surrounded him like a soft black fur. He nodded in understanding. *It is the Dark Woman, not her Son, now.*

Vagrant sparkles drifted in thin swirls around him. One of the tiny crystals passed through the flame he held and the flame flared, burning brighter. He moved to catch more of the glittering dust, unsure why he did so, but as the flame grew more intense he remembered more. A feeling lurked in the back of his mind that there was something he should be doing, something he should be saying, but he could neither remember what it was nor open his mouth to speak.

Now his flame blazed like a new sun, and he thought he could see vague shapes in the distance. The ground he stood on was solid grey stone, with slight undulations in its surface. There was nothing living in sight, and for some reason that disturbed him.

He began to move forward again, toward a dark projection on the stone plain. Moving was difficult, but this time the air itself resisted him—he felt light, as if he were floating, and his feet found little purchase on the ground.

As he drew nearer, the number of floating crystals increased. The feel of the ground under his feet changed too, and he looked down to see the rock crumbling where he had stepped, footprints of shards far behind him, then gravel, and just behind him, sand.

Now he could see that the figure before him was human, and from it streamed thick, glittering waves of crystals. Although his flame was blinding in intensity, the figure remained shrouded in shadow. He had to get closer, to see who was there, but it was impossible to move. Surely this was what he was seeking. In disbelief, he realized the person before him was chained…and suddenly everything vanished.

Erith woke to the small crackles of a fire burning in a huge stone hearth, half-remembered echoes of his strange dream reverberating in his head. He stared at the fire, bemused. A fire had not entered into any story of the afterlife he had ever heard.

He wasn't sure what he had expected. All the tales of the people of the plains said the spirits of the dead rose to the skies, and if judged worthy, remained to be visible as clouds. His clan, convinced of his guilt, would have said Erith was doomed to the other fate—to be cast down to earth as rain to try again. He knew his kinfolk would be careful to avoid going out in a rainstorm for some time, fearing his vengeful return. But he was not guilty, he knew that in his soul. So where was he? What was he?

When Erith attempted to rise, he abandoned all speculations on the afterlife. A dead body's wounds would not affect a cloud-spirit, so he must be alive after all—but he was very weak. His effort left him exhausted and barely clinging to consciousness, but after the first wave of pain subsided he began to wonder what had happened to him.

He lay on a makeshift pallet of folded blankets, covered by a faded quilt. His wounds had been bandaged. The fire burned in a large stone hearth, with iron hooks descending from above and an iron pot supported by a long-legged tripod over the coals. The room was also built of stone, the largest such room he had ever seen. Even the *turos* was not so large. He could see a sturdy wooden table with a pitcher and some bowls on it, and other gear that made it seem this room was merely a cooking place. It was nothing like the hide-and-cloth tents he knew from the plains.

Movement glimpsed from the corner of one eye made him turn his head, and he froze. The fearsome creature he had encountered in the ravine was there, and it ambled over to where he lay motionless with shock. Ice-white eyes surrounded by a mask of black stripes regarded him intently as he stared back, hardly daring to breathe.

A door banged open and a tall woman with dark, intricately braided hair entered. Her arms were full of logs, which she placed in a box by the hearth. The creature, meanwhile, had left him to lean up against her, making rumbling noises. She reached down and stroked its head, a smile disturbing the severe beauty of her narrow face. Brushing bark and moss from her arms, she turned to the pallet, freezing when her eyes met his.

Erith saw, with a chill of fear, her unnatural grey eyes, almost as light as those of the creature. Were they just different forms of the same spirit? Her angular face remained impassive, but her eyes blazed momentarily with anger and astonishment, and, most strangely, something akin to fear.

"What kind of spirit are you?" he whispered, his voice hoarse with pain.

One eyebrow rose. "There are no spirits here, man. Although not long ago you seemed certain to become one."

Her voice was cool, and she spoke the language of the plains with a slight accent. He stared at her, wordless. If not a spirit, what was she? Her form was human enough, but her face was strangely angular and her skin light brown in color. There was also something in the way she held herself and the way she moved that jarred. She wore a lethal-looking sword and spoke as one accustomed to command. Her plain swordbelt was worn over a tunic of a nondescript brown color but intricate weave. Instead of a skirt, or even trews, she had long, soft leather boots over knit hose.

"But it attacked me!" he said, incredulous, looking at the beast as it sat beside her. "Now it pays me no heed."

She regarded him for a moment before replying. "Kashan is a snowtiger, a predator of these mountains, but has no need to hunt half-dead barbarians to survive. You are of the plains?" He nodded. "Why did you come here?"

Erith grimaced. "My enemies fear this place…and I didn't have anywhere else to go. My name is Erith, once of the Harali. I am outcast." He shifted a little and winced. "I would have died without your aid. I owe you life-debt."

"You owe me nothing," she said shortly, and turned away.

"I owe a debt to whoever aided me, and I will pay what I owe."

"Then you must repay Kashan," she said, indicating the snowtiger, "for it was he who found you and carried you here. I have done nothing but stop you from bleeding on my floor. You owe me *nothing*."

She went to the fire, lifting the lid of the pot on the tripod. An appetizing smell of spices and meat wafted out. Erith had not eaten well since he had left the *turos*, and he stared hopefully at the stew she ladled out.

She looked at him, then at the stew. Her mouth thinned, and anger flared in her eyes again. Abruptly, she placed the bowl by the pallet. "Eat, then, if you are hungry." She filled another bowl for herself and did not look at him again.

Rather than risk spilling any, Erith left his stew on the floor and spooned it up as quickly as his weariness would permit. It was thick and richly flavored, and he could have eaten the entire pot. The woman left the room with her bowl in hand, and Kashan followed. Watching her leave through the fog of pain and fatigue, Erith wondered why she was so angry. She acted as if she were being forced to help him against her will.

He looked down at his now-empty bowl and shook his head in disbelief. She had brought him to this place, warmed and bandaged him—and had almost refused to feed him. He wondered where the rest of her clan was. There was nothing to indicate the presence of anyone besides herself and the…snowtiger. A very dangerous animal to keep about. Perhaps the rest of the clan had fled in fright. Shrugging, he pulled the quilt closer and returned to the oblivion of sleep.

Ronne sat in the dusty stillness of the empty greathall, her uneaten stew congealing in the chill. She stared, unseeing, at the moonrose banner hanging at the end of the hall. The golden flower glinted faintly in the gloom.

How could he still be alive? He had been too badly wounded to survive, she'd seen that quite clearly. By the time she had found him he had nearly bled to death. And now they could say she had fed and healed an enemy of the Empire.

He is hardly an enemy of the Empire all by himself, outcast. If it makes you feel any better, consider him a prisoner. It is not dishonorable to feed prisoners. And how is the court to find out? It may be a year or more before someone is moved by idle curiosity to see if you are still alive. It is most unlikely the barbarian will wait so long to betray you. In a year's time, there may be no Empire.

It was only custom she had broken, not the law of the Code, but it still could be used as an excuse to justify her death. She laid her head on her arms, suddenly tired. *Why must he choose my posting as the place to escape his enemies? Why should I care if there is one barbarian more or less in the world?*

Kashan, concerned, nosed her shoulder. She reached out a hand to stroke his head. Outside the outpost walls she heard the first banshee wails of the storm skim high.

<h1 style="text-align:center">CHAPTER 2</h1>

Erith took a deep breath, winced at the sudden sharp pain in his side, and lifted himself up on his elbows again. With both arms and one leg he could make his way very slowly across the stone room—the *kitchen*, she had called it, in her own tongue. In a few feet he reached a wooden bench, and with effort and stifled groans, managed to haul himself up to sit on it.

He looked around while he rested, panting but trying to take shallow breaths to prevent the pain from returning. Erith wasn't sure why he still hurt so much. He'd already checked his injuries, and every one of them had healed completely over with a smooth pink scar. Even the scabs were gone. Had he been unconscious for so long? The weakness remained, however, and the pain when he moved. If he kept moving, or trying to, the pain seemed to lessen.

Light came through square openings high in the wall. Motion caught his eye, swirling white snowflakes that moved with the wind until they reached the edge of the square opening—and stopped. He felt no wind, either. Magic? If so, it was magic that kept him warm. It had been a long time since he had been able to enjoy the warmth of a fire. It was almost enough to make him forget he might be safer out in the cold and he was unable to get there.

Then again, he seemed to have lost his sword. Erith closed his eyes, trying to remember what had happened. He'd had a spear, also, that he had taken from the Naguri. No, he remembered not having it later. There had been the smoke he thought he'd seen in the distance, the ravine with the snowtiger…no, before that. A glen, an ancient boulder, a flower that glowed….

He shook his head and sighed. He had trouble remembering what had really happened and what had been ghosts of his mind.

His stomach growled, reminding him why he had crawled to the table in the first place. The contents were disappointing: two bowls, both empty, and a pitcher with only a finger's thickness of water. Erith drank it anyway, wondering at the plainness of the pottery. Then he saw a small, withered rootlike thing that had been hidden behind the pitcher.

As he reached for it he heard the door creak open, and he turned quickly around. The giant black-and-white striped beast nudged the door wider and ambled through. Erith slowly shifted away to the far end of the bench, hunger forgotten. The snowtiger turned his head towards Erith and Erith froze, his heart hammering. The snowtiger slowly padded over, making a soft wheezing grunt. The huge head with the ice-white eyes leaned closer, sniffing. Erith leaned away, not daring to breathe, and felt the wood bench start to tip.

Arms flailing, Erith landed hard on the stone floor, all of his injuries screaming with pain. When the wave of agony had retreated, he opened his eyes, only to see the snowtiger's face inches from his own, whiskers tickling his chin. He saw a trace of dried blood on the muzzle. Sheer terror held him motionless. He had no weapon, no strength—he couldn't even reach one of the bowls on the table to throw, and it would likely only make the snowtiger angry.

A cold, damp nose nuzzled him once, twice—then he felt more than heard the snowtiger moving away. When he could look again, Kashan was stretched out in front of the fire. The snowtiger yawned, revealing an amazing array of teeth, and then lowered his head on his massive paws. Erith waited until the snowtiger's breathing slowed, then cautiously and slowly moved away. He had to be careful, for any noise would make Kashan lift his head and look his way, but he finally reached the room's stone wall. Erith felt better with a wall at his back, even if it was colder here.

Fatigue eventually overcame his fear and discomfort, and he dozed fitfully, awakening with a start, and then subsiding when he saw the snowtiger had not moved. Then the sound of a distant door slamming shut woke them both, and moments later the woman entered the room.

She looked tired, cold, and wet, and carried a deer haunch in one hand. Kashan heaved to his feet to greet her while she glanced over at the empty pile of bedding, then over to where Erith huddled against the wall. Her lips thinned.

"Finally awake. What are you doing over there?"

"The snowtiger…."

She shook her head, sighing. "I told you, barbarian, Kashan will not harm you." She hung the haunch over the fire on a big iron hook.

"You may be safe from him, but I would feel better with my sword to hand," Erith muttered.

"Prisoners are not allowed weapons," she said, her face like stone. "And what good would it do when you cannot even stand, much less hold a sword at the same time?"

Some of the words she used were strange to Erith, and sounded Southern. The mention of the sword reminded him of the question that had been troubling him.

"My sword—did you see it? Was it in that ravine? I thought I remembered it…but I don't remember everything."

She shrugged. "There was a badly-forged piece of iron near where I found you, if barbarians call that a sword."

"Is it still there?"

She didn't answer, but went through another door. From the little Erith could see past the table and benches, it led to a smaller room with barrels and things hanging from the roof beams. She came back with more of the withered roots in her hands and dumped them on the table. Her expression was stormy.

"What does it mean, *prisoner?*"

That made her look up. "Your people also say…captive?"

Erith blinked. Had she seen the gold clanmark around his neck, then? The term referred to a person of status captured in a raid, such as an older chief no longer fighting. "For ransom? I am an outcast from my people. My father is chief of the Harali, but he has disowned me."

"No. You crossed our boundary into Imperial lands and the penalty for such an attack is death."

Erith stared at her, appalled. "But you gave me food!"

"Of course." Now she looked puzzled. "I have never starved a prisoner. That is something a barbarian would do."

"We would never do something so shameful!" Erith protested, sitting up and then wincing before leaning back against the wall. "Share food with someone within the walls of your own tent," he hesitated, looked at the rock walls, and shrugged. "They are your guest. It is shame to harm them while they remain with you."

She folded her arms, looking down at him. "What do your people do with those who surrender in battle, kill them in cold blood?"

"Surrender?"

"Say they will not fight." They stared at each other, her face reflecting the puzzlement Erith felt.

"If they are your enemy, you fight until one of you dies," Erith said slowly. "Why would we take in an enemy who might have killed a kinsman?" He thought more on what she had said. "Are you going to kill me?"

"Perhaps." She collected the withered roots and put them in a metal pot, adding water from a bucket and hanging it beside the deer haunch over the fire.

"Why do you wait? It can hardly become easier for you than now, when I must crawl on the floor and cannot even die as a warrior with a sword in my hand," he said bitterly. Then he glanced up and saw her face. It looked frozen.

She said, "I have not decided what to do with you. But if I do decide on your death, I will give you your sword first."

Erith closed his eyes, suddenly weary. "Thank you," he said softly.

Ronne opened the big ironbound door, grimaced at the snow still falling from the sky, and closed it again. She'd never seen so many storms so close together. There was barely enough time to hunt between them, although the deep snow also hindered the deer and made them easier to track. If not for that, and Kashan's help, she and the barbarian would be dangerously close to running out of food before spring.

The other problem with the storms was that there was nowhere to go. The barbarian—*Erith*—was bored and talkative. Even Kashan's presence wasn't enough to keep him subdued now.

Are you going to kill me?

Ronne sighed and leaned her head against the cold iron strapwork of the door hinge. What was she going to do, if not kill him? Forcing him to leave in the storm, still weak, would be a death sentence. Keeping him here would be equally dangerous to her if anyone found out. She could not see a path that kept to honor.

She raised her head. She was *tier sanas*; the most dishonorable thing would be to deliberately hide her actions. If punishment came, she would accept it—and maybe the barbarian would heal and go when he was able. It was always possible Erith was lying about being an outcast, but she had seen the old wounds and ragged clothing. Subtlety was not a barbarian trait, and it would not occur to them to send a spy with such a careful disguise.

The great hall still felt cold, even with her heavy cloak. Ronne took it off and spent as much time as she could in swordpractice, but eventually she had no choice. She had to return to the kitchen or freeze.

She eased the door open. Kashan and Erith both slept before the fire, the barbarian curled up against the snowtiger's back. Ronne moved with care, hoping to avoid more conversation, but Kashan's head lifted and he heaved to his feet to greet her. Of course the barbarian woke at that. Ronne grimaced, then forced all emotion from her face.

"Were you hunting?" Erith asked groggily.

"It still snows," Ronne snapped, warming her hands at the fire.

"Does it always snow so much here?"

"I have not seen it so before." Ronne rummaged in the wall of drawers at the far end of the kitchen, where she kept various scraps of leather and kit. The strap on her armor was in imminent danger of breaking if she didn't mend it.

"Do you…do your people take many prisoners in battle? Do you make them slaves?"

"Slaves? Of warriors?" Ronne glanced at him, surprised.

Erith shrugged. "I have heard of some clans, if they are completely defeated and their chief killed, sometimes the women and children are taken. If you don't have a use for prisoners, why do your people want them?"

Ronne thought for a moment, wondering how to explain. She found a piece of leather cord that might work and shut the drawer. The barbarian waited, looking at her with an open, slightly puzzled expression in his green eyes, which did nothing to soothe the irritation she felt. Why was he so stupid? Why did his questions make her question what had always been done?

"We keep prisoners to exchange with our enemies. If they have captured some of our people, we can get them back." She sat down at the table with an iron nail she had pried loose to use as an awl, and turned over her armor.

"How would you not know your warriors had been in danger and gone to aid them before they were captured?"

"In the dust and confusion of a battle between armies? Even the commanders don't always know what has happened until the next day. Our armies have thousands of soldiers."

A brief silence. "What is *thousands?*"

Ah. She had used the Imperial word unconsciously, not knowing the barbarian one. Maybe they didn't have a word for such a large number.

"A thousand is…ten hundreds. A battle between armies numbering thirty thousand each is not unknown."

She saw his eyes unfocus, trying to imagine. "It would fill a valley," he said finally, hushed. "How would you move? How would you have room to fight? The largest battle our tales speak of was between three clans, and it only ended when every sword had shattered."

"Having seen the quality of the metal in your sword, that would not have taken long," Ronne commented, trying to find a place to attach the leather cord.

"My sword was made by the same smith who made my father's! Other clans would trade with us for his swords!" Erith said, sitting up and glaring at her. "What would you know of such things?"

Ronne stood, drawing her sword and advancing on him. Erith swallowed and looked suddenly even more pale, but Ronne noted he did not cower.

"See for yourself." She held the sword out on the palms of her hands, the nightdark metal gleaming.

His eyes grew wide. "The metal is black! And smooth…but it looks like water has been on it." Erith moved his hand in a waving motion. Then he pointed at the golden mark on blade, near the hilt. "What is that?"

"The crest of my family." Ronne shifted her weight, ready to move back if he tried to put his grimy hands on her sword, but Erith continued staring at the crest with a furrowed brow, as if seeing it troubled him.

"It looks like a flower."

"The moonrose. A thing of myth, supposed to be a test of true blood. The old tales say it glows with magic."

That got her a startled look. "Truly?"

"Only barbarians and children believe in magic," Ronne said with scorn. To her surprise, Erith showed no sign of anger at her reply. He stared at the crest again, as if he could make it answer him by will alone.

"I have never heard of a glowing flower," he said slowly. "Why do I feel that I have seen it before?"

Ronne jerked her sword away and slammed it into the sheath. "Do you want to live or die?" she snarled. Her sudden reaction startled Erith, and herself as well. He hadn't done anything, but all her instincts screamed that he was dangerous. Lying on the floor, unable to attack, unarmed. *Dangerous.*

Erith watched her without moving a muscle, his breath fast and shallow.

"When the snow clears," Ronne said, wondering at the strained tone in her own voice. "If you can leave then, I will not stop you."

The rock walls had just enough roughness for his fingers to grasp to give him balance. Erith reached for another handhold, and forced his stiff leg to move. He could walk now, if he had something to steady him.

Not good enough. I must stand alone to leave. More likely, he would need to be able to run. Ronne's mood could change again—as it had when he finally asked her name.

Kashan sat and watched him, tail tip slowly twitching. Erith had become somewhat accustomed to the snowtiger, but not to being steadily observed. Like prey.

He took another step toward his goal, the door on the far side of the wide fireplace. He needed to know more about this place, especially the way out. To get there, though, he'd have to cross an open space with nothing to hold on to for at least two steps.

Erith shifted his weight to his bad leg and almost immediately felt it start to spasm and collapse. Desperately, he stumbled, flailing his arms for balance. Kashan stood, looking interested, and came to investigate.

"No, stay back! Stay—" Trying to avoid the snowtiger, Erith felt himself falling, his outstretched hands landing on Kashan's back. The fur was thick and wiry, and warm. His full weight rested on Kashan, but the snowtiger didn't seem to mind.

With an effort, Erith managed to stand upright again, but this time he kept one hand on Kashan's shoulder. With a few more shuffling steps, he made it to the doorway and clung to it. Kashan rubbed against him, nearly making him fall again, but when Erith didn't move, the snowtiger wandered away again.

Erith opened the door. It was not a passage to the outside, but a room with no other openings, full of wooden barrels and big ceramic jars. Ropes of dried roots and herbs hung from hooks in the ceiling, but most of the hooks were empty. Erith, curious, lifted the lid of one of the wooden barrels. It was half full of grain. The jars held some kind of liquid, perhaps oil. Only two were not empty.

He had just finished checking the fifth empty barrel when motion caught from the corner of his eye made him look up. Ronne stood in the doorway, glaring at him with her jaw set.

"What are you doing here?"

"I need to move, to strengthen my leg," Erith protested. "Are these all your food stores?"

Ronne didn't answer. "Get out of there. If you need more room, use the greathall."

Erith struggled out past her forbidding expression and looked where she was pointing, at the other door. He would have to cross the entire length of the room to get to it, with hardly any support along the way. Kashan was nowhere to be seen. Erith gritted his teeth. He was going to fall. Was she deliberately trying to humiliate him?

He slowly moved towards the far door, using the wall as much as he could. He heard Ronne approaching and turned his head, wondering incredulously if she would offer to help him, but she walked past and out the door without so much as a glance his way. Too impatient to wait for him to fall?

Then Ronne returned, holding a dark wood staff with metal bands at each end. "Use this," she said curtly. "Keep moving as long as you are able."

The staff was solid and smooth and felt cool in his hands. It was much easier than trying to use handholds to support himself. He finally reached the far door and opened it.

At first he thought he was outside, and that it was night. Then he saw the bare flagstone floor and more tables and benches, similar to the ones in the kitchen. The room was huge, easily big enough to hold three clan chief-tents, and the roof was barely visible in the gloom high above.

"How big is this place?" Erith wondered aloud, seeing his breath faintly white in the cold.

"Keep moving," said Ronne.

Erith did, sore leg nearly forgotten as he explored. A big door, studded with metal and bearing large leaves of metal along one side—that must be the way out. Everywhere, fastening the huge wooden beams and in the furnishings, was metal. More metal than he had ever seen in his life. Were all Imperial buildings like this?

By the big door was a stand that he mistook for another person until he got closer. A strangely shaped metal head, with spines extending from the top and sides, and what looked like a lumpy, stiff shirt that gleamed dully. More metal.

He limped down the long side of the hall, followed by Ronne. At the end was a raised platform with a single chair; behind it, on the wall, hung a long silk banner with the same familiar flower he had seen on Ronne's sword. He had counted ten long tables on his way, and he could see another ten matching those on the far side of the hall. They were dusty, as was the floor except where they were walking. He saw footprints in the dust that went beyond the platform, but of only one person—and a few pawprints as well.

"Where are the rest of your people?" he asked, finally. Had there been a plague?

"They left." Ronne was looking out at the empty tables, too.

"Why didn't you go with them?"

"It was forbidden." She bit her words off with precision, as if they tasted bad.

Erith tried to remember what the ravine had looked like. He had thought it was empty of habitation, except for that one thin thread of smoke.

"None of your people are nearby, are they?"

She smiled without humor. "This is the most isolated outpost in the Empire. That is why I am here."

He stopped, leaning on his staff and breathing heavily from exertion. "Why do you stay? It is colder than the tongue of the Dark Woman's Son up here, you are alone, and the stores I saw—is that really all the food you have?"

"That is all that remains," Ronne said. Her expression was not as hard now; instead, it looked grim and tired. "I cannot leave without permission. I am *taien*." She noticed his confusion and explained, "It means something like 'warleader' in your speech."

She can't really be a warleader, Erith thought. *A sword doesn't make a warrior, and what man would follow a woman?* "Do you have food for the winter? Even if you stop feeding me, it doesn't look like enough."

"I do not starve prisoners," Ronne said, and turned back.

Erith followed. His leg was becoming painful. "It isn't any better if you starve with me," he said.

"If the snow ever stops, I can hunt. By spring, a cart with supplies is supposed to arrive." She turned and gave him a look. "You had best be gone well before then."

Erith said nothing. They had reached the big ironbound door again, and Erith gave more careful attention to the metal shirt on the stand. He'd heard of armor, but it was rare among the plainsfolk. A warleader might have armor. He blinked. Whoever had made the armor had definitely made it for a woman, and—he stole a glance at Ronne—a woman of Ronne's size. Why would armor be made if it was not expected to be used? There were dents and marks of blows on it as well. It had seen battle. That would mean Ronne had too.

Ronne moved through the steps and passes of the Path of Small Turnings, stifling the feeling of irritation when the inner door opened and Erith, followed by Kashan, entered the greathall. She wasn't sure, after so many months alone at the outpost, whether she liked company or not. Now that the barbarian was mobile, she needed to keep track of him. It was good that Kashan appeared to find him fascinating. She shook her head. The snowtiger definitely missed the soldiers and all the attention they gave him.

She extended her awareness to the sounds they made, maintaining a mental map of their positions as she continued her swordpractice. She might as well make use of the intrusion. The barbarian was healing fast, and only leaned slightly on the staff now.

The faint tapping of wood on stone stopped, and Ronne altered the pattern enough to turn and see why Erith was no longer moving. He stared at her, then suddenly looked away and continued walking when their eyes met. He did not stop again, and Ronne finished the Path.

Back in the kitchen, Ronne took the scrap of soft leather that always hung by the fire and carefully wiped the blade of her sword, removing any dampness that might have gathered in the cold greathall. Erith came in and sank down on a bench, wincing a little.

"It is finely made, but too slender for battle," he said, nodding his head at her sword.

"And yet I have fought with it in battle many times," Ronne said, raising an eyebrow. "What else do you know that is not true?"

His pale face slowly turned red. "I also have fought a time or two. A blade like that would break too easily. Especially against armor."

Ronne shrugged. "It would seem our smiths are better than yours. And the smiths of my family are the best in the Empire. Only they have the secret of the darkmetal." She thought for a moment, considering the truth of the matter. "A two-handed battle sword is larger, but with skill a lighter sword is just as deadly and can be wielded longer. We must be able to fight as long as there is light to see by."

Erith looked at her doubtfully. "Your ways are…different."

A gentle way of saying he didn't believe her, but no matter. There were questions she should ask, before he left, to follow her duty—even if by letting him go she could be accused of failing it.

"You seem certain your enemies will not follow you here."

"Through all that snow?" He opened his eyes in surprise. "The Naguri never give more effort to any task than they must. Besides, these mountains are considered haunted, full of spirits and monsters."

She remembered how fearful he had been, thinking she and Kashan were spirits. "Then why did you come here?"

Erith shrugged, frowning. "The Naguri were real, and I had to escape them. Going to a place they feared would give me a better chance, and I was wounded and slow. But also…" his voice trailed off. "There was something else. It doesn't make sense to me now. Something I've forgotten…."

Ronne felt the same small stirrings of disquiet that had made her want him to leave in the first place. "So your people will not come this way, unless their enemies chase them?" Erith shook his head.

That was good to hear. The rest of the Empire might be invaded, but not from her demesne. It would be even better to know that the rest of the plains barbarians never heard about the existence of an outpost with only one Imperial swordnoble to hold it. "When you leave, where will you go?"

From the look on his face, Erith had not considered the matter. "Somewhere the clans do not. I had thought I was safe where the Naguri found me, so maybe there is no place like that." He shifted on the bench, stretching his arms. "My leg is nearly healed, but I will need to be stronger to fight. You spar with shadows in there," he said, jerking a thumb back in the direction of the greathall. "Why not spar with me?"

His expression was innocent of guile, but there was a small smile at the corners of his mouth Ronne didn't like. She wasn't sure if he thought he could trick her into handing him his sword, or that she would refuse out of fear.

"Why not, indeed?" she said, returning a bland smile. "A change will be welcome."

The departing troops had seen no need to take the few wooden practice weapons, and they were still in one of the big chests that lined the greathall. Kashan jumped up on a table to watch. He remembered the practice weapons and had loved watching the soldiers. Erith scowled when he saw them.

"What, toys for children?"

"Practice weapons, suitable for wounded barbarian prisoners that have forgotten what I said about returning swords," Ronne said coldly. She unfastened her swordbelt and hung it on the armor stand. "Now, do you wish to spar, or will you go back to sit by the fire like a toothless elder?"

A muscle twitched in his face, but he remained silent. When Ronne picked up the long wooden sword and the shortblade, he did the same, looking disgusted. His first blows were halfhearted, as if he expected the wooden weapons to break. Then, when Ronne deflected his sword with her shortblade, she saw the stirrings of anger in his eyes, and the next blow had some muscle behind it.

It was different, facing an opponent who was taller than she was, and rare. Her father was taller, by a few fingers. Erith's height was no help to him while his balance was so poor, however, and Ronne considerately stayed on a single flagstone and did not take advantage. If he fell hard and injured himself again, it would take even longer to get rid of him.

Now Erith was definitely angry. Ronne realize she had only been using her shortblade to deflect. She hadn't intended to insult him so, even if he was an incompetent barbarian. She attacked, landing a solid blow to his ribs.

"Guard yourself!" she snapped. "Use the shortblade."

"We use…shields," Erith gasped.

"You don't have one," Ronne replied, hitting him in the ribs again. He stumbled. "What happened to it?" Another blow.

"Didn't have it…with me…when outcast."

Ronne raised an eyebrow. "So, perhaps you should learn a defense to replace it?" An overhand blow this time, to his shoulder, followed by a glancing tap to the side of his head. "Pay attention."

His anger was gone, but he still fought doggedly on. Ronne was reluctantly impressed. Erith was getting beaten like a drum and hadn't touched her, but he still tried. *No skill, but endurance in the face of reason*, she thought. This must have been how he had dragged himself over the mountains half-dead.

To continue in this manner was cruel and useless. Ronne slashed at the hand holding the shortblade, causing it to fly spinning in the air. Kashan leaped from his table and chased it as it slid across the floor. Erith gripped the longsword stubbornly in both hands, his long bright hair coming loose from its tie and falling across his face. Ronne twisted to avoid his blow and smacked his knuckles, hard, with her weapon's hilt. The wooden sword dropped, and when he tried to reach for it, she stepped on it and struck him on the side of the face with the flat of her blade.

"Do you yield?" Ronne asked coolly.

For a long moment he glared at her, his face crimson and his breath ragged, then he sighed.

"I yield." Erith staggered to the nearest bench and collapsed on it, dropping his head in his hands. "Only to avoid the shame of being killed by a woman with a stick, but I yield."

Ronne nodded, satisfied. He did not sound like he would willingly attack any Imperial outpost in the future, so duty was again fulfilled.

Then he lifted his head. "I don't understand," he said finally, his brow furrowed.

"Do I need to explain further?" Ronne asked, moving forward with her sword raised.

"No, no—I was beaten, I know that," he said, waving one hand. He drew a quick, hissing breath, then held that wrist carefully. "I just don't know how. Unless it was magic—"

Ronne laughed. "No magic, barbarian."

"I'm larger and stronger than you."

"Yes."

He looked at her, radiating puzzlement. "Then how could you win?"

"I fight better." Ronne gave him a bland look. "The aurochs that draws a cart is stronger than you, so why does it bear the yoke?"

"You speak in riddles."

Ronne walked over to him and handed him her wooden shortblade. "Stand up."

Erith stood, watching her warily. He flinched when she raised her sword.

"I'm trying to show you something," Ronne said, making an exasperated noise. "I won't hurt you unless you do something unusually stupid. Now hold the shortblade like so." She demonstrated with her hand, holding it chest-high and angled up. "As my blade comes down, meet it with the edge, then turn the blade."

Erith swatted at the wooden sword as it slowly descended. Ronne allowed her weapon to move aside and snap back. She let the blade rest on his shoulder.

"No. You are not dealing with a fly. Think instead of a heavy branch that you must move aside but cannot break." This time, his shortblade deflected her sword to the edge of his shoulder. "Better. Again." This time she moved faster. Erith stumbled, but still managed to deflect. "Once more."

Ronne struck hard and fast. The blade hit the table behind him with a hard crack and Erith glanced at it, startled, then at her.

"You see. You were tired and weak, yet you defended yourself."

Erith turned the wooden shortblade over in his hands as if he had never seen it before. "I will likely fight again wounded and alone. It would be good to know your way of fighting," he said slowly. He gave her a hesitant look. "If you are willing to teach me."

"If you are willing to learn," Ronne said, surprising herself, "I will teach you."

CHAPTER 3

"No, the rough wood writing case," Alland tes Arhi directed the servant, who replaced the ivory set he had reached for instead. "I will seek inspiration in the Winter Garden." The servant bowed.

Alland adjusted his outer robe so that the sleeves flowed lower and the neck was open wider, revealing the rich pattern of the underrobe—pine branches over a woven design of mountains. It was not only suitable for writing seasonal poetry, it provided just enough reference to his clan and status to not require, according to the complex court rules, actually wearing his clan crest.

He left his quarters, moving with studied idleness in the expected corridors and halls, exchanging greetings with those he encountered. The servant followed silently. There were few robenobles in evidence to greet, this not being a day with a formal Audience or any required event, and the time late enough that personal entertainments or assignations were already taking place.

Alland did not receive many invitations to personal entertainments at court. Some of this was certainly due to the distrust felt by the Imperial coterie for the Arhi family, but that could have been overcome sooner. No, the current difficulty he found himself in was all due to Ronne. It was not easy to learn the full truth of the matter without appearing…concerned, but it appeared that his sister had managed to make powerful enemies. A rumor had reached him that she had skirted the edge of insulting the Emperor, but without being immediately directed to serve him in a final and fatal manner. There were some who would consider her current location a fate worse than death, but the fact that she still lived indicated to one conversant in the ways of the court that killing her directly would bring more of some scandal to light than convenient. A slow, forgotten death in the mountains was a much better way to deal with her, especially if no communication was permitted.

The central hallway of the outer palace intersected another main hall and widened at a place known as the Higher Ascent. There were more people here; visitors to the palace frequently waited for their summons or for information they were not permitted to go further within to obtain themselves.

A group of swordnobles caught his attention briefly, then fully when a woman left the group and came towards him—a woman he recognized. Narat tes Olon, whom he had not seen since she had left the court after the completion of her year-service. She gave him the greeting of association without the formal gesture of intimacy, since they were no longer *kalasen*. Narat was his favorite, since she was the only year-service swordnoble woman who had not sought him out merely to learn more of Ronne's dangerous talent.

Narat had changed. Tiny lines of strain were visible near her eyes, and she was thinner. "I did not think the Face of Fortune would grant me your presence, Radiant One," she said with a small smile that made her look more like her former cheerful self. She concealed it well, but he had known her long enough to know something was wrong.

"I go to the Winter Garden to be inspired by the subtle changes of this season. White-petal wine matches it in subtlety, but should be shared," he suggested.

"I go to experience the season more directly, as I travel through the night," Narat said dryly. "I have brought certain dispatches, and only wait for answers to return. It gladdens my heart to see you." Her expression became suddenly serious. "Only say I gladden yours, and I will detain you no longer."

"Gladdened, and comforted," Alland said, now completely puzzled. She spoke as if she still held him dear. They had parted friends, but nothing much more. "I will wish you fortune and glory, if you permit." He kissed her cheek and felt her hand touch his wrist, pressing something long and cylindrical against his palm and forearm under the long sleeve. He kept his face calm and unemotional as he folded his hand around it, concealing it from view. They bowed, and Alland continued on his way to the Winter Garden.

Narat had looked relieved as he left. He would have to wait to see what she had delivered him, since there were too many unfriendly eyes in this section of the palace.

Finally, he reached the Winter Garden. He indicated the bench he wished to use, and the servant brushed it clear and left the writing case open. Alland sat and pretended to admire the twisted rock sculpture and bare branches while he waited for the servant's footsteps to fade. He was fortunate that poetry was so highly regarded, and considered so pure and fragile that the mere presence of a servant was held to contaminate it. Otherwise, he would never be without some court spy. Of course, a low-ranking robenoble and tes Arhi would never be permitted a personal servant loyal to him alone.

Alland carefully took out the cylinder Narat had given him. As he had hoped, it was a message rod. It had no seal or crest on the surface, and only a single piece of paper inside. He held it on the writing case as if it were a blank sheet and opened the ink, dipping a quill while he read.

The situation of the Southern border worsens and grows grave. More of the tribes have come, far more than the reports will say. Do not trust any word of treaties; hear the words of all I might send, and keep your counsel close as I know you always do. Should you hear what I should know, send in your turn by this messenger and tasse *will be yours.*

Despite his increasing worry, Alland smiled. No signature was necessary; the tone and reference to *tasse* cakes were enough to identify his father's voice.

Well. He might have to contrive a slightly scandalous renewed relationship with Narat to conceal any messages he would send—but perhaps that would cause too much notice. Perhaps he should appear to wish to renew it, but secretly urge Narat to politely refuse him? That would provide many opportunities to seek her out, and the amusement it caused observers would hide the true nature of the meetings. It would endanger all his careful plans for building alliances—such as a certain court lady known to be fond of seasonal poetry—but his father had never asked him for help before. If a commander in the field was not being given necessary information, matters were serious indeed.

Alland folded the message in half, concealing the words, and began composing a love stanza. The quill should show use, after all, or it would occasion comment. He had already written his seasonal poem in the comfort and warmth of his quarters.

After a week of practice, and more bruises, Erith felt more at ease with the shortblade. Now Ronne was trying to show him how to use it in the attack, but it was taking much longer to learn. He felt his temper fray as the session continued. He had never fought like this, hardly ever making a simple, direct blow. It was hard to imagine anyone fighting this way.

He'd been eager to try, confident in his newly-won skill. Ronne had even indicated his quickness in learning the defense was unusual, at least until he'd laughingly asked if he'd done better than she had.

"Barbarians cannot understand the Path of Swords, and you will never learn it," she'd snapped. He was beginning, gloomily, to agree with her.

His slowness did not improve her temper. "You strike like a falling tree. Move!"

Erith lashed out with the stupid wooden sword, but Ronne had spun away. He lost his balance and nearly lost his grip on the weapon. "Son of the Dark Woman!" he swore.

"And hold your anger in your hand. When you let it go, your opponent has the advantage."

He stared at her, breathing hard and wiping the sweat from his forehead. "Anger fuels the fight and strengthens the arm in battle."

Ronne raised an eyebrow. "That must be why the plainsfolk always lose against us," she said coldly.

Erith bit back an angry reply. The last thing he wanted was for her to continue to see him as an enemy. He wasn't sure he could hope for anything more than tolerance from Ronne, but he had to stay alive until he could leave.

He took a deep breath and realized it didn't hurt to do that anymore. He still limped slightly—especially, like now, when he was tired. The meals were not large, but much more regular than they had been for months, and much of his strength had returned.

Maybe he should leave now.

As soon as the thought crossed his mind he felt cold. He could leave, but he didn't want to—why? Ronne wasn't friendly, but she hadn't threatened him for days. Erith was even starting to get used to Kashan, and to dare to give the snowtiger the head-scratches he loved.

A sudden painful thwack on the side of his head jolted him. "Pay attention," Ronne said. Erith took up the guard position again, watching her carefully. If he wanted to stay, he had to earn the privilege. Ronne would only continue to teach him if he showed her he could learn. He wanted to learn, wanted to show Ronne that he had skill. It was hard, though, when every time he faced her he saw contempt in her grey eyes.

He should think of something else. Something other than how clumsy he felt. Ronne was never clumsy. Even when she practiced alone, her motions had a deadly grace that caught his attention. A flowing motion that changed, but never stopped. He had hoped to see it again, practicing with her, but—

This time he caught the blur of motion from the corner of his eye. Without thinking, he deflected her blow with his shortblade, and equally without thinking let it continue on in an upward curve, turning away while holding his sword-arm against his chest and then thrusting it out.

Ronne stood motionless, staring at him. For a brief, panicked moment Erith thought he had hurt her, then he remembered. She had turned aside like she always did, and he was only holding a wooden weapon.

Had he finally done it right?

"I did not teach you that attack. How do you know it?"

Erith scratched his head, shrugging. It hadn't felt like he had done anything but allowed the movement to complete.

"It just seemed to want to go that way," he muttered, aware of how idiotic he sounded.

"You sound like Zeltan," Ronne sighed. She gave him another hard, considering look. "Maybe there is a better way through your thick skull. I am teaching you *dal ria*. It means 'first step' in our tongue, because it is the first thing a new soldier learns with the sword. You, though, have fought with a sword before. Defend." She moved slowly in an attack. Erith, puzzled, responded with the appropriate defense. Ronne held her position as his shortblade touched her sword. "Now, how would you attack from here?"

Erith froze, confused and struggling to remember the flowing feeling he had felt just before. He closed his eyes. The attack came at him so. He moved so to block it. Fumbling, he tried to continue the motion—and his eyes flew open as he recognized what he was doing as one of the attacks Ronne had tried to teach him.

Ronne smiled. Stunned, he realized he had never seen her smile before.

"There. You have set your feet at the beginning of the Path."

Ronne propped her head on her hands, leaning her elbows on the rough kitchen table, and wondered why she felt a sense of unease. It was late and she had not yet lit any lamps—the kitchen fire providing the only light— but that wasn't it. She was a little tired from the hours of practice, but nothing unusual. Kashan slept soundly before the fire, curled on his side with dream-twitching paws. Erith sat beside the snowtiger, one arm around his updrawn knees and the other idly stroking Kashan's head. He stared silently into the fire, his face bleak.

Maybe that was what had disturbed her. Ronne realized suddenly that since they had returned from the greathall, Erith had been uncharacteristically silent. Not a single question. Had she offended him? Ronne frowned. Erith would be more likely to explode with anger if offended, not retreat into silence. She had pushed him hard today, but so had she the weeks before. Today he had, for the first time, earned her praise. Why would that make him unhappy? Especially after all her freely expressed scorn.

She glanced over at Erith. His strange hair glinted like metal in the firelight, and his expression was somber. Not sad, but as if he faced a hard fight. She shrugged and turned away. A barbarian's troubles were not her concern.

Ronne found herself staring at him again. Something was wrong. Her instincts niggled at her thoughts, refusing to be quieted but not providing any insights. She thought back over the practice session, trying to find a reason. She still did not believe Erith was offended.

Perhaps he should be, she thought suddenly, remembering what she had said. Remembering one irritable comment in particular, which had now been proven wrong. Ronne clenched her jaw. He was a barbarian! Did it matter what she said to him? Barbarians had no honor, no skill, no value.

But that was not completely true. Erith had honor, it was just different in form from hers. He was learning the same skills she had learned. Erith was a barbarian, and she was *tier sanas*, and it mattered what she said. To anyone.

Ronne stood and left the room, still arguing with herself. No one would know if she did not say anything—except her. It was not his custom—but he was learning hers.

When she reached her quarters she had to light the lamp hanging there to search the chest that held her few remaining belongings. At the bottom of the chest was a small, sheathed shortblade that she rarely carried, as her favorite fit her hand better. She still felt reluctant to give it up, but she had nothing else suitable.

Ronne walked slowly back to the kitchen and held out the knife on the palm of her hand. Erith looked up at her, surprised, and reached out only to hesitate before touching it.

"It is a contrition gift," Ronne said quietly. "It is our custom, if a swordnoble has spoken wrong of another, to make a gift when this is admitted. You have shown you can learn the Path of Swords; I was wrong to say you could not." Slowly, he reached out again and took the knife.

There, it was done. Ronne turned to leave again, wishing the way of honor was not always so hard.

"Wait!" Erith scrambled to his feet, disturbing Kashan, who sighed and dropped his head back down on his paws. Erith looked worried. "This isn't...are you still wanting to kill me?"

Ronne bit back her immediate response. She took a moment to remember what he was referring to. "I only said if I was planning to kill you I would give you your sword first. That is not your sword."

Erith took a deep breath, glanced at the shortblade in its sheath, and gave a quick, nervous smile. "No, it isn't." He gently pulled the knife free, freezing when the black metal became visible. "This is of your family's make."

"Yes."

"Why do you give such a thing to me?"

"Now that you know *dal ria*, you may find it useful to have a shortblade that is not made of wood."

Erith shook his head. "I know how you value your weapon, and take pride in its forging. This is too much for a few angry words."

Ronne was silent for a moment, thinking of how she could explain. "A contrition gift should be valuable. It conveys the sincerity of the apology, and the cost is a reminder for the future to refrain from...angry words."

Erith sheathed the shortblade and tucked it with care under his frayed belt. His eyes still held a troubled expression.

"My…the people of the plains also have a custom. We give pledge-bonds, to seal an oath. It is the most valuable thing owned, and forfeit if the oath is broken." He pulled a thong free from around his neck. A hammered gold disk hung from it, cut through in a design of a stylized wolfhead. "This is my clanmark. All that I have left of what I was. It shows I am of the Harali, and the son of a chief. What oath can I swear so you will believe I will not fight you?"

For a moment, Ronne was too stunned to speak. "I have no reason to think your word would not be sufficient," she said finally.

"No. You do not act only for yourself here, you have said so before. What oath would satisfy your people?"

Ronne closed her eyes and sighed. "Nothing you could say would satisfy them. They do not know you; you would just be another barbarian in their eyes." She opened her eyes and stared down at the fire. It was low, so she put another log on it. Why was she so tired?

Erith still held out the golden clanmark, the line of his jaw slightly more visible with stubbornness.

"You should not give up the only tie you still have to your kind," Ronne said, turning back to face the fire. Kashan stretched, yawned, and subsided again, oblivious to the dangling object above him.

"They don't feel bound to me anymore. It is only a memory, and painful in remembering."

"It is still yours, and the only thing you value." This time when she glanced at him his gaze met hers, and she could not look away. For whatever reason, this was something Erith wanted badly. And what reason did she have to refuse? The alternative was to say she did not trust him or his oath, and start the whole angry cycle anew.

"Swear allegiance," Ronne said, and her voice was rough. "I will keep your pledge-bond until you ask for it, and so release you."

"By the Bright Man, by the Dark Woman, I will fight your enemies and aid your clan; I will accept no other binding, nor bond others that work against you; I will keep your secrets and hide them with my own." Erith placed the clanmark in Ronne's hand. With one finger still on it, he said, "Blood and bone, all given."

Ronne closed her hand around the gold disk. It was heavy. Gold from a barbarian, who had no understanding of what it meant to an Imperial. She felt a bitter smile tug at the corners of her mouth. Barbarian gold. More honorable than gold from the Emperor, defiled with the blood of assassinations. Gold that Talorgen had been given more times than she could count. They would definitely kill her for this insult, if they discovered it.

She pulled the thong over her head. The wolfhead design looked stark against the weave of her tunic. *Face of Justice, let this time be different!*

Well. She had made her decision, why persist with half-measures? It felt strangely right to do dangerous things, all of a sudden. Ronne went to the edge of the hearth, causing Kashan to look up sleepily. The fire was a little warm, but she would be quick. Grasping one edge of the mantel, she leaned in and reached up as far as she could in the rough rock chimney until she felt a cloth-wrapped bundle wedged between two large fieldstones. Grabbing it, Ronne spun away, checking her tunic for any sparks or burning.

"Your sword," she said, and handed it to Erith. This time she left the kitchen before he could say anything.

CHAPTER 4

Erith took a cautious step, and then froze. Kashan sank his head even lower, the tip of his tail twitching. Just as he saw Kashan's muscles bunch to spring, Erith spun quickly behind a tree. Kashan crashed into the bushes behind where he had been standing a moment before. A startled bird flew out with grass dangling from its beak, and Kashan, distracted, watched it fly away.

Even as he slipped in a patch of mud, Erith still managed to reach out and tug Kashan's tail before the snowtiger could turn around again. It was a relief to be out of doors, in the fresh air. Snow still covered the ground, but much of it had melted, enough that it was possible to finally go hunting.

As the mock-battle raged, Erith saw Ronne appear in the outpost's open doorway. She carried the short, slender spears she called hunting javelins.

"Behold, the brave spirit-wrestler!" she said, looking amused. "Is this how you would deal with a wild snowtiger?"

He looked up, grinning, adroitly sidestepping Kashan's pounce. "If I had no other choice, why not?"

"Why not, indeed?" Ronne peered up at the sky. "We should go. The days are still short, and the deer range far for food this late in winter." She handed him his javelin, and they set out.

Erith alternated between studying the ground for tracks, watching Ronne, and wondering how he was ever going to hunt anything with such a short spear. Ronne had said it was to be thrown. It did feel light, and the head was finely made, with a long shaft. He tested the edge, and swore under his breath so Ronne would not hear. It was certainly sharp enough.

The sun had crested and begun its downward path before any sign of prey appeared, and it was Kashan that alerted them. He slowed and sank down, belly dragging in the snow, his muzzle slightly open and nostrils twitching. Ronne and Erith stopped and began to copy Kashan's slow and stealthy movements.

Ronne caught Erith's eye and tilted her head slightly to one side. Erith edged away, and after a few more steps finally caught sight of a group of four deer, browsing ravenously on a stand of bushes. The few branches out of reach, on the top, showed the fat buds that had attracted the hungry deer.

Erith was hungry too. He picked his target, a young male that was closest and had his side facing Erith. Slowly, he brought the javelin up as Ronne had shown him, muttering a brief prayer to the Dark Woman to conceal him and give his prey a quick death, and threw with all his strength.

The javelin missed the deer, skimming over its back, and hit the bushes behind it. The deer all spun and leaped away, eye-whites visible, but one suddenly crumbled to the ground with a crash. Ronne's javelin had caught it just under the shoulder.

"That worked well," Ronne said, looking down at the deer with a satisfied expression. She looked up at him. "The javelins require practice. You will have many chances to do better," she said after a moment.

Erith merely nodded, not trusting his temper. He had come close, but not close enough. He retrieved his javelin from the middle of the bushes and went back to help Ronne gut the deer. His mood improved as he realized that, if nothing else, he would eat well tonight, and the dark gleam of his new shortblade reminded him how much he had already learned. The javelins were just one more new thing. He would learn them, too.

Kashan nosed insistently over Ronne's shoulder until she tossed the entrails to one side for him.

"Does he always hunt with you?" Erith asked.

"Usually. Sometimes he strikes first, sometimes I do. Between us, they rarely escape." Ronne sliced deeper. "There is something I do not understand. You fight better than the plainsfolk I have encountered in battle. Why did your people cast you out so eagerly? Your kind do not live peacefully with one another, and a skilled warrior would be valued."

"Because I would not use my skill to put my clan in danger." Erith sat back on his heels, wiping his blade on the deer's hide, then with a tuft of dry moss.

"How so?"

Erith grimaced, remembering how hard it had been to explain. He still saw the anger and contempt in his father's eyes. "A raid was being planned, a raid for cattle. My father and brothers and their warriors all wanted to attack the pens of the Naguri when they were away, engaged on a feud battle with another clan. It was true, the Naguri had more cattle than we did, but we had enough for our needs!" He gestured in frustration. "We might, with luck, take a few and escape in safety, but the Naguri would surely follow later. We would have to fight a second time to defend what we had stolen. The Naguri had more fighters than we did, so we might even lose our own cattle. The risk outweighed the gain, and when we met in the council *turos*, I said as much. So they named me coward."

He swallowed, remembering. "I drew my sword, forgetting in my anger this was forbidden in council. There was no hope after that. I had always been thought too strong for a youngest son, too dangerous to be trusted, and finally they had an excuse for what they had wanted all along. My father exiled me that moment."

Erith got up stiffly, looking about for a suitable sapling to use as a carry pole.

"Was it your own clan that wounded you?" Ronne sounded shocked.

"No, the Naguri. The raid must have succeeded. It did not matter to them I had not been there; it was my clan, and that was enough."

Ronne had cut strips of hide from the deer, and they used these to bind the legs. Threading the carry pole between them, they hoisted the deer to their shoulders. Erith stayed deep in his dark thoughts as they walked back to the outpost, until a question occurred to him.

"Are you an outcast also? Did you anger your clan? Is that why they do not come to you?"

Ronne gave a short laugh. "I angered the Emperor. In truth, I do not know what my family thinks of what I did. They were forbidden to have any contact with me."

"What did you do?" They were going down a steep slope, and Erith had to carefully place each foot on the snowy ground. He felt the carry pole shift as Ronne shrugged.

"I suppose you could say I accused the Imperial Court of cowardice," she said. "I am a swordnoble: one who leads and fights. Of late, the court has preferred to pay its enemies for peace rather than rely on military defense. The nobles of the robe have never felt entirely comfortable in dealing with the nobles of the sword. When they are forced to call on us for help, they feel weak and ineffectual. Which they are," she added. "I tried to show them the dangers of such a policy, but without success. That is, in part, why I was sent here, to guard a secure border, to a desolate outpost. I am in disgrace with the court."

"If you were in disgrace, why did they send you here? Surely it is an honor to guard the border."

"You will have noticed I have nothing to guard it with," she said dryly. "This place had a garrison of over fifty soldiers. The *taien* who came to take them away told me of a great force of barbarians massing on the southern border. That was six months ago. The danger has been growing for years, and they have been blind to it. The end is only a matter of time."

"And you will do nothing?"

"There is nothing I can do." Her expression was carefully controlled, but he thought he could detect anger and bitterness in her voice. "I have warned them before, and now.... It is treason for swordnobles to leave their posts without permission. Should I attempt to return to court and alert them to the danger, I would be in chains within the hour and executed within the day. My enemies will not listen to anything I say, and will prevent those who support me from assisting or defending me. And there would be…consequences for my family."

"Maybe things have changed. You have no way of knowing. When the supplies come, the people who bring them could tell you."

Ronne said nothing for a while. "There should have been supplies sent in the fall. They never came. It would not surprise me if they do not come in the spring, either." She sounded tired.

"Is there fighting already, then?" Erith asked.

"More likely my enemies at work. It would please them greatly if I died here with no effort on their part."

Light began to fade from the sky, so Erith was glad to see the steep roof of the outpost ahead. Back inside, he cut thin strips of meat to cook quickly while Ronne prepared a more substantial haunch for later.

"Your Empire would be angry with you if you left this place, even if you have no food. Won't they be angry with you for rescuing me?"

"Yes."

"Enough to threaten your family?"

"Yes."

Erith looked at her, puzzled. "Then why did you do it? I have no claim on you; my people and yours are enemies."

Silently, Ronne poked at the fire with a piece of wood. Erith began to think she wouldn't answer his question, and wondered why he had been stupid enough to even ask.

"My *omlior*—that means 'surface thought'—was that you would die no matter what I did," she said slowly. "But you lived, and healed, and I asked myself the same question. There were *nadlior*, bone-thoughts, hidden thoughts that were the real cause. I am chained here. I cannot help my family or even speak to them without putting them in danger. I cannot save the Empire even if I sacrifice my life to do it. But I could save you. An enemy, perhaps, but a brave one. I had to save *something*," Ronne snarled. She flung the piece of wood on the fire in a shower of sparks.

Erith had found her contempt daunting before, but her anger and pain were even more upsetting.

"I don't have to stay," he blurted. He saw her startled look, and made haste to explain. "You are forbidden to leave, but I could go and come back. With food."

Ronne raised an eyebrow. It was a mocking expression, but at least she wasn't angry any more. "From where? Your people cast you out, on the point of a spear to judge from your wounds."

"There must be someone I could travel to, some of your kind," Erith said, determined to find a way.

"Perhaps. I doubt they would be happy to see an armed barbarian, even one come in peace."

"I could disguise myself as one of you."

Ronne stifled a smile. "If you go at night, wearing a hood over your bright hair—which none of us have—and stoop down like an old man to hide your great height, and dye your pale skin, and they are half blind, yes. But what would you say to them that they would understand?"

Erith blinked, suddenly realizing what she meant, and laughed. "I had forgotten. I thought all would be as you, speaking the language of the plains."

"I learned it from questioning prisoners," Ronne said, her face hard. She sighed and turned back to the fire. "I suppose you should learn some of our speech. Enough that if Imperials do come here, they will not kill you out of hand."

"Or so I can trade for food."

She shook her head, smiling. "Or trade for food. In the middle of the night."

Alland eased his door open and carefully looked up and down the hallway. It was empty. He doubted very much it was unobserved, but since he had given the impression in his servant's hearing that he was going to an assignation that evening, they would expect him to be discreet. A pity he could not dress in a manner less fashionable and more suited for climbing, but that would definitely occasion comment.

The bathing rooms were a favorite destination, so none would wonder if he was seen there. Sometimes he had to wait in the shadows for the servitor to leave for more oils or to send for hot water, but tonight he was lucky. No one was in the antechamber, or in the smaller room with the rock wall, planted with delicate ferns and most importantly, open to the sky. It was not yet warm enough for this room to be in demand, but he would have to think of another way when the weather changed.

Using fine silk ties, Alland caught up his robes in a manner that would not crease them and carefully began to scale the rock wall. Certain childhood skills had proven unexpectedly useful. Once at the top of the wall, he had access to all the lower roofs of the Imperial Palace. He still had to be careful not to disturb anything that would fall, or to allow motion to attract the attention of those below, but it was a much easier way to get around unobserved.

He reached the meeting place early, and Narat was not there. He settled down to wait, shivering. Echoes of the dream he'd had earlier, that had woken him in terror, made him start at any motion. The night was clear and quiet. After a while, though, the chill worked through his court robes and Alland became restless. Where was Narat?

The meeting place was a small, flat section of roof, hidden from an outer courtyard of the military section by a steep, higher roofline. He crept cautiously to the ridgeline and looked over, hoping to see Narat's arrival below.

He saw dark shapes moving silently in the courtyard, which had strangely few lamps or torches. There was enough light, however, for him to see a huddled shape on the slope of the other side. One hand was visible, and blood streaked its surface.

Alland carefully pulled himself up to lay at full length along the ridgeline, then edged his way over. It was Narat, dead but still slightly warm. She had one hand clutched to her chest, and when he shifted her, the hand fell free from the wound it covered.

He flinched. In the slashed wound was tucked a message rod. He forced himself to remove it, ignoring the sticky wetness and the metallic smell that turned his stomach. Narat had died to get here, and knew he would come to find her and the message. He owed her memory that much, at least.

They intend to take Ynduria. Do not trust the palace captain, he is in their pay. Find the nearest alar *contingent; they must defend the Emperor at all costs.*

The chill in his body turned to ice. Narat had been killed, which meant the unnamed enemy was already here—or the corrupt palace captain was involved. The shadowy shapes in the courtyard had a new meaning. Pulse hammering, Alland realized he had not seen a palace servant or anyone else for some time. He'd thought he was just lucky....

The *alar* contingents were encamped outside the Imperial city. He had to get out of the palace and warn them—somehow persuade them he wasn't mad, that they had to move inside the outer gates and defend Ynduria.

Then he saw a flickering light at the far end of the palace and caught the scent of smoke. He was too late to save the palace. He would have to escape to even save himself.

Alland managed to slide back from the roof ridge without alerting any of the shadows below. He desperately ran across the lower roofs, searching for a way out as screams filled the air and collapsing walls tilted and shifted the tiles he ran on. There was nothing he could do except bring help.

At last he saw a way down to a kitchen yard, where barrels had been stacked. Haste made him clumsy, and one of the barrels fell with what sounded to him like a deafening crash, but no one came to investigate. The smoke was getting thick, so he soaked one sleeve in the water trough and held it over his mouth. Where was the side gate from here? Everything was on fire and he couldn't get his bearings.

Alland ran with desperate speed through the burning outbuildings, despite the acrid, smoke-filled air that seared his lungs and blurred his vision. It seemed that the world was ending in fire and the screams of the damned. *I should write a poem about it*, he thought, fighting the obscene urge to laugh. Half-seen shapes loomed threateningly in the distance, and he dodged aside, stumbling down a shallow flight of steps he hadn't seen in time. *Find a knife, or even a staff. I am a tes Arhi, I can at least make it more difficult to kill me.*

Who had done this? Had the barbarian hordes managed to destroy all the military might of the Empire so easily? How had they managed to come so silently to the Imperial capitol and destroy it with no warning?

This same thought repeated relentlessly in his mind as he fled for the gatehouse. All about him, the buildings blazed and bodies lay strewn on the ground. A sudden crack made him look up. He flung himself away, but he knew he would not be able to avoid the burning roof beam as it fell.

Sardis looked about carefully, then continued on down the columned walk past the gatehouse. She thought she had heard a cry, but this section of the outer palace was deserted except for the dead. The troops had done their work well.

She looked at her sword and frowned. Perhaps too well. Ash from the burning building mixed with the blood on her blade, making a sticky mess. *I suppose there is no tidy way to destroy an Empire.* She saw the edge of a robe under a fallen beam, and hacked a piece of the fabric loose. It was good brocade, heavy and finely woven. Just the thing for her purpose.

She scrubbed at the stubborn stain, admiring the fabric's design. Why did it seem familiar? She looked at it again, and then looked sharply at the fallen beam. Sword ready, she jumped over it to the other side. Now she could see the beam had pinned someone when it fell, someone wearing a court robe with the full sleeve of high rank. A sleeve of which she now held a piece. She knew that crest. "Tes Arhi," she snarled, and with a burst of energy heaved the smoldering beam aside.

She knew who it must be. The family didn't have that many representatives at court and only one of that rank, but it took her some time to recognize the blistered, bloody face. She stared at him, her hand going involuntarily to her cheek, where the three deep scars puckered the skin, and nodded, satisfied. It was a good beginning.

Now she did hear a voice, one she recognized. She dropped the scrap of fabric on the body and moved with haste, wondering if she could at last get rid of the bulky barbarian furs over her armor. Surely the disguise was no longer necessary. And why did the Southern Horde have to wear so many of the damn things, anyway?

There he was. He seemed annoyed, and she hurried to his side. The fight had taken longer than they had planned, and she wanted to give him some good news. "The palace is taken, Talorgen. And there are no survivors. No danger of word getting out."

"Oh, there are survivors. But they are prisoners, and no threat to us now." He seemed pleased at the thought, and her anxiety lessened. He headed back towards the inner palace, and she followed.

They entered the hall of the Lesser Presence, and Sardis felt an almost automatic boredom. There were times when she had to viciously suppress guilty thoughts about what they had done, but this was not one of them. Regardless of the outcome, she would never have to attend another formal court function again.

"I was able to fulfill the Emperor's last…commission," Talorgen said as they walked. "Not only is tes Siadek dead, but her heir as well. A pity I will not be able to accept the gold of the glorious thanks of the Empire, but doubtless the Emperor would find my methods somewhat lacking in honor."

"That the Emperor requests gives all honor," said Sardis without thinking, and then felt her face go hot as Talorgen gave her a mocking, malicious smile.

"And did he thank you for *your* services to the Empire, by chance?" he asked.

Sardis was silent, remembering the sick feeling when she had seen the Emperor's face for the first time. Was it still the same day? So much had happened…. She and her soldiers had slaughtered the Imperial guard and broken their way into the innermost chambers of the palace where few of even the highest rank were permitted. The bodyguard had put up a fierce resistance, but at last the Emperor stood alone, his deformed, vacuous face never changing its expression even as she struck him down. He had made no effort to defend himself. *Perhaps he did want to thank me, poor monster.*

They passed more richly-clad bodies, some showing evidence of looting. They would have to watch that. The troops still needed discipline; this was only the beginning. "Why do we want prisoners?" Sardis asked, her thoughts coming back to that troubling piece of information. "We can hardly use them for bargaining now."

Talorgen laughed, and there was an unpleasant undercurrent in his laughter that made Sardis shiver.

"You must have forgotten, then. There are services the most loyal of my people would not perform willingly."

She felt her face twist as she realized what he meant. *He's still serious about those things…unless he just likes to watch them feed.*

She realized he had stopped and was frowning at her. He must have seen her grimace of distaste.

"Why so dainty now? Death is nothing strange to you, even if the method is more…intimate." He smiled and moved closer, taking her chin in one hand. Sardis took a deep breath, feeling her heart beat faster.

"It doesn't seem worth the…the extra effort," she managed. "It is just another kind of animal."

"Oh no," he said softly. "Very, very different. In return for a…home, and their special kind of food, they give power. Magical power." He stopped, his eyes searching her face. "You don't believe me."

"Magic doesn't exist, except in tales for children," said Sardis, worried. She didn't like this turn of events. If the troops ever heard him, they might think his mind was wandering.

He released her. "Oh, it exists. You can have it too, if you have the courage to grasp the opportunity. It is not for the weak of will." He turned about slowly, his nostrils distended. "Ahhh, there it is. Come, I will give you a demonstration."

He started walking toward the end of the hall, and turned to the left after stepping through the giant golden doors of the Higher Presence. They passed the remains of a ceremonial meal, the light, puffy *nimmo* cakes still floating in the pool of green wine that ran down the center of the table. Sardis plucked one out and took a taste as they went by. *And candied aroe, too. What were they thinking? Did anyone bother to tell them they were being attacked, or did they simply not care?*

Without any hesitation, Talorgen went up the stairs at the end of the room that led to the high walkway used by the Emperor on his rare court appearances. The floor was paved in tiles of gemstone, carved to look like flowers and flowing water. A figure huddled on the ground not far from the stairs, and Talorgen headed directly for it.

"You missed one, my devoted Sardis," he said in a dry voice.

The court lady lifted her head at the sound and raised one bloody hand imploringly. The other was pressed against the ghastly wound in her abdomen. Her delicate, sheer overrobes were soaked with blood, and Sardis could see the trail where the woman must have dragged herself along the walkway, seeking a hiding place.

"She'll be dead soon enough," said Sardis, annoyed.

"How very true." Talorgen smiled. Sardis stepped back, suddenly afraid. "Your appearance is a disgrace," he said to the court lady. She sobbed in terror, realizing her danger. "I really can't allow this sort of thing."

The court lady screamed as a blinding flash of light enveloped her. Sardis felt a wave of heat, followed by the stench of burning hair. All that was left of the woman were a few black cinders and the end of one of her long, trailing scarves, still burning fitfully.

Sardis gaped, blinking in disbelief. *It really works. The magic—it is real.* Then she realized Talorgen was starting to collapse, and she hurried to support him.

"It takes…some time to get accustomed to the effort," he said, leaning on her. "I was distracted by the blood. Now do you believe?" She could only nod numbly. "They can do other, even more wonderful things. But it would take too much for me to destroy all our enemies this way. You must take one of the creatures yourself; we will need more power to subdue the *alars*. Now, will you?"

She hesitated, but only for a moment. How could she refuse him when he wanted it so badly? "For you, anything," said Sardis, touching his cheek. He smiled in satisfaction and kissed her. *And if it will also destroy Ronne tes Arhi, there is little I would not do.*

CHAPTER 5

"The soldiers found him," Ronne said, slowly and carefully, making sure to speak each word fully. "He was crying and hungry, and there was no sign of his mother. Snowtigers give birth early in the spring."

Erith took a breath. "No saw other snowtiger?"

Ronne repeated the question, with the correct grammar, and shook her head. "We saw no others, then or since."

"You say—you *said*—you were angry."

"Yes." Ronne paused, remembering. "We were soldiers with a duty. Kashan was just a pet, then. I did not want them distracted." She had to translate the new word for Erith, then continued. "The soldiers feared my anger, but Kashan did not. If I stayed anywhere long enough for him to find me, he came. When he grew to his full size, he broke the door to my quarters once, so he could sleep beside my bed."

Erith grinned. "Good is so strong for you, not against."

Ronne leaned back and picked up her mug. "You are learning Middle Speech very well, but you need more practice speaking it. Now, you tell me a story." She had to smile at his expression of sudden worry. "This was your idea, remember? How are you going to trade for food without talking to anyone?"

"What I say you?" Erith sighed, resigned.

"It is, 'what shall I tell you?' and anything at all. Tell me…tell me why your people dislike rain."

Erith rubbed his chin, thinking, and then started the tale of the hero Varot Henth, a mighty warrior who had killed one hundred enemies, and then when they returned from the afterlife in a terrible rainstorm, fought them all again. Ronne listened, corrected mistakes or provided new words, and thought. She had expected Erith would soon tire of the exercise, but he hadn't. She noticed that once he heard a word or phrase he rarely forgot it. It was all the more strange that his people apparently regarded writing as the secret of shamans and smiths, and he had never learned the letters of his own language.

"So, everyone you kill might come back in the rain?" Ronne asked when the tale ended.

Erith shook his head, smiling a little. "Only if not enough brave." He grimaced and made a gesture as if he were removing something inedible from his mouth. "Brave *enough*. That is why the Hundred had to bargain with the Son of the Dark Woman and the Daughter of the Bright Man to return for revenge."

Ronne started to notice the pangs of hunger were becoming more insistent. They couldn't put it off forever by drinking water. "It's your turn to cook," she told Erith.

"Cook what?" he grumbled, but got up anyway. The snow had given way to rain, not as cold but equally effective at preventing them from hunting. Kashan didn't like the wet weather either, and it had been a long time since their last full meal. She heard Erith rummaging around in the storeroom, the rough scrape of the heavy barrels as he heaved them about with ease.

Then she heard him swear, sharp and loud. He emerged from the storeroom with a double handful of rotten, oozing lumps that looked like they used to be the last of the tarpa roots, the one food they had left if they didn't have meat.

"They went bad at the bottom," he said. "There is only one good one, and it is small." He showed her the black, smelly mass.

"What's that?" Ronne pointed. What looked like a small green bud was visible on the side of one root that was not as rotten as the rest. "Is it… growing?"

They looked at each other, considering the implications.

"I suppose they must have grown somehow before," Erith said slowly, reverting to the language of the plains for this new topic. "How is it done with your people?"

"Farmers plant them, of course," Ronne stated, and tried to remember anything else about farming. "I have seen them, they dig up the fields for these roots. But is that all there is to do? What do the plainsfolk do?"

Erith shrugged. "I was the son of a chief, not a farmer. All I knew was food was gathered somehow. I should have paid more attention."

It was a very small root. Ronne did not know much about farming either, but she was sure they would need more than what one root could provide, and it would take more time than they could afford to wait. "You may have to go trading sooner than I thought. See if there are any more like this in the stores," she said, and went to leave the kitchen.

"Where are you going?" Erith asked.

"To find you a disguise—and see if we have anything worth trading."

Sardis slowly pulled herself up yet another collection of boulders, breathing heavily for a moment at the top. Talorgen was still ahead, apparently finding the rocky path easier to traverse. For a brief moment she wondered if he was just playing with her, then she shook her head. He'd gotten his power somehow, and he was quite insistent she get it too. She looked around the barren landscape. They were climbing a mound, almost perfectly symmetrical, surrounded by ravines. The mound was located in the south of the Empire, in a sparsely occupied region that was rarely visited. Now she knew why. Nothing grew here, and the dust smelled sour.

"Come, we are almost there," Talorgen said, and beckoned. Sardis cast a look at the top of the mound, still some distance away. "No, not there. Beyond the outcrop."

Where he pointed, a bulge of grotesque stone disturbed the slope's symmetry. The stone looked both twisted and rotten, the grain disturbed. When she reached it, Sardis examined the stone closely but the surface was continuous, with no opening apparent.

"How do we get in?"

Talorgen caressed the twisted stone, smiling. "They had me hide the entrance. Only one with power can open it, and the only source of power is within. Clever, no?" He closed his eyes, face grimacing with effort. The stone's twisted grain twisted further, like an animal writhing in pain, and slowly flowed away. The opening it revealed was rather small, just large enough to crawl through. Dry, acrid air flowed out from within. "I will go first, or the guardian may strike at you."

Sardis wriggled down the dark, narrow tunnel on her elbows, cursing when she encountered a sharp stone. "How in the name of the Face of Secrets did you find this place?"

"When I was sent to kill Venet. He was clever and had the usual routes watched, so I came this way. The guardian contacted me when I made camp nearby."

The tunnel opened into a wider space. Sardis stood with relief, looking about. A faint light covered all the surfaces like frost, just enough to see by. The stone here was solid and protruded in long fins and ridges from the ceiling and walls. In the center was a rough black plinth, slightly hollowed at the top. Inside were five small stones, identical in size and appearance.

"There. That is what we have come for." His voice was almost reverent.

Sardis approached the plinth. Everything here was almost, but not quite, natural. Each thing alone could be explained away, but together they spoke of purpose and intent. Someone had *made* this place.

"Who put them here?" she asked. She touched one of the stones with her fingertip. It felt completely ordinary. The suspicion this was all a trick returned.

"An ancient people, long gone, whom even time has forgotten. The remalks were their weapons."

Talorgen took a stone flask from the satchel he carried. It had the same frosty sheen as the cave walls. "Let us begin." Taking the stopper from the flask, he poured a thick, dark fluid into the hollow where the stones lay. "It is not living blood, but it is enough to wake them. Your remalk will require feeding once you have…housed it."

Sardis stood beside him, staring down at the plinth now full of blood. "That is a remalk?" Talorgen had told her very little of the things, beyond their unimaginable power. Magic power.

"No—an egg. They require a body to live in. It will be bound to you, and you to it." One of the stones began to change. Pores opened on the surface, which was becoming wrinkled. "Good, you have been found acceptable. Now take it. Swallow it. Take it inside you." He had a strange, intent smile on his face. She had seen it before, but only in his bed.

He wants this. I want this. I will rule beside him, I will destroy Ronne tes Arhi. Why do I hesitate? Sardis grabbed the remalk egg and put it in her mouth. The taste of blood nearly made her gag, and the egg was rough and dry still. She fought to swallow, then reached in to take it out to try again.

The egg moved. It stuck in her throat, wriggling and alive, and she choked. Still trying to pull it free, she turned desperately to Talorgen for help. He was smiling.

"Too late to change your mind. Your only choice is to accept it or die, for it has chosen you."

Her vision started to darken at the edges, and her knees buckled. In a sudden burst of strength, Talorgen grabbed her shoulders and shoved her down on the plinth, pinning her legs with his own and pulling her head back with a vicious yank on her hair. With the other hand, he jabbed stiff fingers into her mouth.

Pain exploded in her throat, spreading like hot iron down her chest as the egg descended. Sardis gasped as her airway opened again, and the pain increased to an unbearable level. She could not even scream. Gradually, she became aware that she was collapsed on the floor, sobbing. The agony of her raw throat made it difficult for her to concentrate on anything, but she became more and more aware of the scent of blood. It was wrong, somehow. Like the smell of brackish water.

Then she started to notice other things. Her vision was sharper, clearer, and the previous soft glow of the walls was now a bright illumination that let her see faint, worn symbols on the rim of the plinth bowl. She could hear a slight breeze whistling by the entrance and smell Talorgen's scent. With fascination she stared at a moving presence that floated above the plinth, and knew it was the guardian. Power prickled on her skin. Slowly, she regained her feet, feeling incredibly weak, as if she had been sick for a month.

"Water," she tried to say, but all that came out was a croak. Something to soothe the fire in her throat, to restore her. Talorgen shook his head.

"You are not thirsty, my dear. Not for water, anyway." He turned her around to face the tunnel and gave her a push. "Perhaps now you know why I brought that useless servant with us on such a mission of secrecy. He thought he was simply carrying our supplies, not that he was part of them."

Sardis did not understand at first, but the creature inside her did. The wracking pains of hunger became the only focus in her world, an overwhelming desire. Living meat. Warm blood. Spirit and soul. It waited for her outside, at the bottom of the mound.

Sardis lunged for the tunnel.

Erith tucked the handful of rock sorrel in his makeshift pack and debated taking more. It would be wilted by the time he got back to the outpost anyway. He looked around, noting the landmarks for a return. If he could bring some of the plants back, alive, maybe they could plant them with the tarpa root. A few handfuls of greens would not be enough to feed them both, but it would help.

He hadn't found much more than the sorrel. A few nuts, some he didn't recognize and hoped were edible. He'd left snares at likely places to check on his return, but he was determined not to do that until he had found a useful amount of food.

He looked around for Ronne, then shook his head. For some reason, it felt as if she were missing when he knew she had not come with him. They had decided it would be better to divide their efforts, and she was the better hunter. Erith was not restricted to the boundary of the outpost, so it made sense for him to explore the mountain slope. Kashan, of course, went with Ronne. He sighed. Being alone seemed harder now.

Erith shrugged his crude pack back in place, nothing more than a folded blanket tied at both ends with a rope, and moved on. Parts of the mountainside looked familiar. Perhaps he had come this way when he was escaping the Naguri, numb with cold. He couldn't remember much of that journey, or which parts were real and which delirium.

The sun had already passed its highest mark and he still had not found anything more. There would be no point to setting more snares now; he'd be lucky to get back to the outpost by nightfall. Time to take a different route: along the foothills and then up the steep slope. Erith climbed, scanning the ground as he went. Deer tracks, followed by something with paws like a snowtiger but smaller. The fresh carcass of a fawn indicated the predator had succeeded.

Erith frowned. This place looked very familiar, and there was something strange about it. There should be light…. He stepped with slow caution into a small clearing. Slanting late-afternoon sunlight cut through the trees. No, it should be…softer. All in one place. He stood and stared at the weathered rocks near the center. He *knew* he had seen them before. A small bush grew next to them, covered with leaves with deep-cut edges. He looked closer. A flash of white-gold caught his eye, and he reached in to lift the foliage away—slicing the side of his finger on an unseen thorn. He swore, then smiled. A beautiful flower, many petals cupped in a bowl shape.

It shone like the moon in my dream. Erith shaded the flower with his other hand. It shone just as brightly as it had in the full sun. How strange. He wondered how it could do that. It had to be the one he dreamed—only he hadn't dreamed it after all. What else did he remember that he'd thought was just delirium? He closed his eyes, trying to chase the memories. A chained figure, floating, drifting sparkles—no, that had been after Kashan had found him.

Something else nagged at his mind. It wasn't just from his long journey up the mountain, dying of cold. He'd seen something like it, but when he was warm.

He drew in a breath. The crest on the banner in the greathall. Ronne's family crest. What had she called it? Moonrose. Magical, and therefore a myth. He could bring it back for her, and perhaps the novelty would distract her from the fact that it wasn't edible. Carefully, he reached past the thorns and picked it. It still glowed faintly in the shadows.

Darkness fell while he was still some distance from the outpost, but the moonrose provided enough light for him to see his way if he didn't go too fast. He took the opportunity to check the snares. One thin rabbit was all he found, but it was better than nothing.

No light shone from the outpost windows when he reached it. Erith pushed open the door, which softly bumped into Kashan, who had been lying behind it. The snowtiger got up and sniffed him with interest, especially where the rabbit was lying in his pack.

"Get your own," Erith said softly. If Kashan was here, Ronne must have returned. He could cook the rabbit now and wake her when it was done. He went into the kitchen. By the light of the glowing embers in the fireplace he could just make out Ronne, slumped asleep at the table, her head resting on her arms. Shadows accentuated the angles of her long face and deepened the gold color of her skin. She looked exhausted.

The remains of some unfamiliar animal were still on the spit. Good, then he didn't need to cook his scrawny rabbit right away.

"Ronne. Wake up. I found something you need to see," Erith said. Ronne didn't stir. Carefully, he reached across the table, intending only to shake her arm to waken her and draw back before she reacted. He wasn't sure if she would wake startled and violent.

He wasn't fast enough. One hand grabbed his arm in an iron grip as her eyes snapped open.

"It's just me, Erith!" She blinked at him a moment, then sighed.

"You are late returning," she said, her voice rough with fatigue and sleep.

Erith smiled. He had been tired, but now he felt restored. "I found something. Look!" He held the moonrose out to her. Her grip on his arm tightened for a moment, then relaxed. The expression on her face was one of pure, wordless astonishment.

"Is that a…a moonrose?"

"I was hoping you could tell me. It is your legend, not mine."

"Impossible," Ronne breathed, but she reached for it anyway. Her fingertips brushed his, and he laid the flower in her hand.

The instant the moonrose touched her, it blazed with light. A slow smile of delight and wonder spread across Ronne's face, which faded when she looked up at him.

"What's wrong?"

Erith shook his head, trying to find the words. "I dreamed about a glowing flower when I first climbed this mountain, half-dead. At least, I thought I was dreaming, but then I found it and it was real. I also dreamed of…holding a light. And it blazed up, just like that, when I stood before someone wearing chains. I couldn't see their face…but you've never worn chains, have you?"

"No. I've never worn chains," Ronne said slowly, staring at him. She took a deep breath, seeming to realize that she was still holding his arm, and let go. She cradled the moonrose in her hands, smiling a little as she gazed at it. The golden light bathed her face and made her skin look like pearlshell.

She is so beautiful. A cold wave washed over Erith. He felt tiredness descend on him like a sudden weight. Beautiful and dangerous. What had he gotten himself into?

He sat heavily on the bench.

"You should eat, and rest. It is only a few hours to dawn." Erith nodded, not trusting his voice at the moment. Ronne got up and left. She stopped at the door and turned. "And Erith…thank you." She lifted the moonrose.

He watched her go in silence. He'd given her her legend, and she was pleased. It was enough. He took out his shortblade and cut off a hunk of meat, having just enough energy to chew it before collapsing with a groan on his pallet. Kashan padded in, nuzzling Erith's face in his usual request for a headscratch. Erith complied, then pushed the snowtiger's head away when he nuzzled him again. "Let me sleep, spirit-monster," he muttered.

Then he looked at his hand. Something was missing. The long scratch that the moonrose thorn had left was completely gone. He couldn't even see the scar in the dim light of the fire. The scratch had been deep and annoying and kept opening up whenever he used his hand on the trip back, bleeding sluggishly. Had the moonrose cured it? No, when he shook Ronne awake he had left a little smear of blood on her sleeve, and he remembered hoping she wouldn't notice—she was fastidious about such things.

He rubbed his finger. No pain. It was like the injury had never been there. He fell asleep trying to figure it out.

CHAPTER 6

Ronne opened the big ironbound door to let Kashan out, and checked the sky. The early morning chill had already gone, and the signs showed it would be a clear and sunny day. She needed to go hunting again, but first she would walk part of the bounds. The deer would not be moving so early anyway, and she had neglected her duty for too long. Besides, she felt restless, uneasy. For some reason, the moonrose troubled her thoughts.

She stretched, then went to the armor stand by the door. Donning her traveling armor and fastening the buckles, she looked at the heavy spined helm, sighed, and reached to pick it up.

"You don't like it?" Erith stood in the kitchen doorway, watching her. "Why wear it then?"

She grimaced. "No, I don't like it, but that is no excuse. My father's *samhal* always says 'bad armor worn is better than good armor left.' " She had heard it so many times her voice echoed Zeltan's inflections instinctively. "I intend to walk the bounds, the line of the outpost, what I am sworn to defend. My armor, my weapons are part of that duty. I must always be ready to fight. Once, I left my weapons when I thought I was in a safe place. I will not make that mistake again." She stepped outside. Erith followed.

"What happened?"

"I was in Ynduria, with some of my father's troop. We have enemies—and I knew Sardis, an enemy of mine, was there, but I disarmed in my quarters. It would be…foolhardy for one noble to attack another in the Emperor's city, so I thought I would be safe. I was not attacked, but one of my people was."

"Attacked…and killed?"

Ronne looked out through the trees into the distance. "No, I succeeded in disarming her in time. But my method was crude, and I marked her." She drew a finger up and across her jaw and forehead. "Her family demanded blood-debt, but she was not killed or maimed, just scarred. She was only of the third line of a ruling house, so they could not say we were of equal status. My father paid *wergild*. But then Sardis had an even greater reason to hate me, so that when the original cause was removed, nothing changed."

"And what was that? Why did she hate you?" Erith seemed concerned.

"A man." The old anger and disgust returned full force, and she wondered how she found herself speaking of it again. She walked faster, pretending to ignore Erith's questions. A quarrel over Talorgen's affections. Ronne made a face. What a worthless thing to fight over.

Erith had long legs, and caught up with her after a moment. "You said…enemies," he said.

"My family has always had enemies," she replied, glad he had found another topic for questions. "The tes Arhi are considered young upstarts in the Empire. Our *alar*, our holding, is only six hundred years old. The oldest *alars* have been in existence for nearly two thousand years. They resent our new status, they resent that we have the best swords in the Empire," she tapped her hilt with one finger, "they resent our independence from the court. Our lands are far to the north and west, backed against a range of mountains. Not easy to travel to, especially for robenobles with little physical endurance."

Erith grinned. "Very useful. You said your enemy was armed, but you were not. How did you defeat her?"

Ronne was silent, trying to think of what to say that would not make him even more curious. Her chest felt tight. "There was a cowl of chainmail on a bench nearby," she said. "I used that." Zeltan had told her, when she came…back. How fortunate he had been the only other witness. "I don't remember exactly how I did it; it happened very quickly." She hadn't remembered anything at all, but Erith would not notice her careful phrasing. In some ways he was still the blunt, straightforward plains barbarian, no matter how well he spoke Middle Speech. "If you wish to go with me, ally, get your sword."

He nodded, smiling, and ducked back in the outpost. Ronne headed out, her heart pounding. Give him something else to think about. Don't let him wonder. Talk about the tart leaves he had found, and how his people used them. Anything but talk about her peculiar curse.

Erith rejoined her, and to her relief did not bring up the subject again. She started to relax. He made the outpost much less empty, and it was not by size alone. Although his height took some getting used to. It was a strange feeling to have to look *up* at someone, since she usually loomed over everyone except her own family.

They walked north along the ridge in companionable silence for some time, eventually stopping at the crest that overlooked the mountainside to the southeast. "I can just see a glimpse of the High Plain. Why didn't they build the outpost here?" Erith asked, breaking the quiet. "They would have a much better lookout."

Ronne grimaced. "When you have felt the autumn windstorms, you will know why they preferred a more sheltered site." The view was beautiful, she had to admit. The early morning forest was quiet and still, a light breeze whistling over the rough outcrops. Not a sound disturbed the peace. Erith was still staring out in the direction of the High Plain, an expression she could not read on his face.

"Are there those you miss, among your people?"

He sighed, shaking his head. "Few wished to be seen befriending me, when it was clear my father's favor was not given. No, my only friend stands here."

"*Mersaa beytin suer*," Ronne said, before she realized what she was saying. Erith raised an eyebrow. "It means, your friendship is gold," she translated. "That is High Speech, the language of the court."

"Do I need to learn that too?" Erith said, grinning.

Ronne contemplated the thought of Erith at the court of Ynduria, and had to bite her lip. "No need at the moment. If they do not send supplies for another, say, five years? Maybe then I will send you to petition the Emperor."

He laughed. "You would wait so long? We will be long dead of starvation."

She shook her head, mock-solemn. "It will take at least that long to teach you the protocol. If you were to—"

A voice shouted distantly, from the direction of the outpost. Ronne snapped her head around, then jumped up on one of the outcrops. She could just make out the clear space in front of the outpost. People— soldiers, only two that she could see. They were too far for her to see any crest or other distinguishing mark. One raised a hand to her mouth and called again. Calling Ronne's name.

Ronne jumped down, her heart cold and sharp like she was going into battle. Perhaps she was. Erith stared at her in confusion.

Erith. For a moment she saw him as *they* would see him, a barbarian and nothing else.

"You must leave. Now." At least he had his sword with him. He had nothing else worth risking a return to the outpost. "Those are Imperials down there, and they are seeking me. You must leave before they see you."

Erith didn't move. "They will know I have been there. Or will you lie to them?"

"It will not matter if they know of you if you are too far to chase," Ronne said, exasperated. "Now go!" She shoved at his chest. She might just as well have pushed the mountain. Fear tightened her chest. They must not find him. Erith would die, and that was not permitted.

"You said you would be killed if your people knew you sheltered me. I swore allegiance to you. Do you think I would leave you to this when I am the cause?"

One part of her mind wondered at how calm Erith seemed. The rest was frantic. "I release you from your oath!"

He folded his arms over his chest. "I won't let you."

The voice called again. It was getting closer. She still didn't know how many were here. If it was a troop, there could be more than twenty, and it would be difficult for Erith to evade being seen even if he did run.

Ronne snatched the helm from her head and thrust it at Erith. "Hold this, walk behind me, and *say nothing!*" she snarled. Face of Pity, why was he being so stubborn?

She turned and strode toward the outpost, and after a brief hesitation, Erith followed. But even as she began to move, two figures emerged from the trees. Both were armed and armored, and one, with a shock, she recognized.

"Zeltan? You should not be here." Her father's *samhal* looked haggard, and his beard had more streaks of white than when she had last seen him. More worrisome, he had not given any evidence of noticing Erith. If a six-foot golden-haired barbarian could be easily ignored something was very wrong.

He came forward and gave her the bow of respect, hand before his face, and her heart grew cold. Zeltan only did that for her father.

"I bring news of glory," he said, his voice rough.

Yes, it was bad.

"Your lord father and your brother Medar have died with greatest honor in defense of the Emperor. We come to bring you back, that Arhi may have a Sword for its defense."

Ronne struggled to speak, then turned abruptly and went to the edge of the outcrop, where she stood and gazed at the forest beyond. Both dead? Dead in battle. It must have gone badly, then. The shock made her numb and distant. When she felt she had her countenance under control, she faced Zeltan again.

"I may not return," she said, her voice empty. "I am under Imperial ward and bond to stay."

"There is no Emperor left to bind you, nor court to condemn," Zeltan broke in, his eyes bright with unshed tears. "Ynduria is destroyed and desolate. The southern hordes slayed and robbed, then burned. When all was burned, they toppled walls. There is not one stone left standing on another."

"Were there..." she began, then her voice wavered. "Were there no survivors in the court?"

"Alland lives, but with the mark of the passing of the Many-Faced. A burning roof beam fell on him; his face is scarred. It was he who told us of Ynduria. The Arhiia…" he hesitated. "Perhaps three in five survive, and many are wounded. The land is full of unrest. There are rumors that warlords have emerged, as in the Time of Blood." He looked at Ronne. "You must return! Have you no care for your folk, for the honor of your line? Or have you forgotten all you were, abandoned here?" Zeltan gave Erith a cool, dismissive glance.

Well. She was beginning to think her ruse had made Erith invisible, but Zeltan never revealed anything unless he wished. Since no swords had been drawn, she was doing better than she had hoped. The female soldier, whom she did not recognize, wore a stony expression that did not bode well. That would not matter if she could convince Zeltan.

"This is Erith ne'Haral. He is outcast from his people and has sworn allegiance to me."

"You would make *this* your helmbearer? Do you think your people will accept this in silence?

"If I remain here, my decision will not trouble them," Ronne said, her voice like ice.

"We are running out of food," Erith murmured. Ronne darted a warning glance at him, and he gave a small shrug.

"It is he and his kind that destroyed Ynduria, and you think to bring the same to Keris Kera? It is protection from him we are needing."

"Unless Ynduria fell before midwinter, Erith cannot be held responsible, for he was here with me. He left his people because of their ways. More importantly, he is my helmbearer. I have spoken," Ronne said softly, staring him down.

Zeltan narrowed his eyes at her, angry and defiant, but then dropped them in the face of her commanding gaze. "*A'liata,*" he murmured. Then he looked up again, pleading, "Do you not want to come to Keris Kera?"

Ronne smiled sadly. "I wish it so much I fear it may lead me wrong." She was silent for a moment. If there was any chance the Empire could be restored, her presence as *alaran* of Arhi could provoke a war. But if the Empire was destroyed in truth, it would not matter—and what other catastrophe could have taken both her father and brother in battle? "Now is a poor time for such talk. I will give my father and my brother fire, and think on what you have said."

There was only one other soldier at the outpost, a young man. He stammered out an excited greeting, flushing at Ronne's curt response and then paling as he caught sight of Erith. Ronne moved with purpose to the back of the greathall. When she saw Erith hesitate, she motioned him to follow as she opened the door to her quarters.

Ronne searched through a small, heavily carved chest for the fire bowl and the leather net pouch of scented *kama* wood twigs. She had thought to barter them for food.... A wave of grief washed over her, and it was an effort to bring her thoughts to what must be done next. Erith. He had to understand what was happening, what he needed to do.

"What we do now is a kind of mourning, not unlike your chief-wakes. All you need to do is follow me with my banner." She closed her eyes, swaying slightly on her feet. Her voice was faint and strained. "To be silent, to be still is to show respect. I have called you my helmbearer, and in the eyes of the others what you do and say reflects on me. Have care for my honor, even when you have no care for your own."

"I will be silent," he said. His face was somber.

Ronne was relieved to see the young soldier had already mounted the banner on its pole. She had forgotten to order it herself. After she gestured to Erith, the soldier reluctantly handed the banner to him. She had a vague recollection of the soldier's face, but she couldn't remember his name. It was not important, not now.

She left the outpost and went back to the rocky outcrop, followed by Erith and the Arhiia soldiers. Placing the bronze bowl on a boulder, she filled it with the aromatic sticks of *kama* from the net bag. She struck hard with her flint and steel, and chanted the old, familiar words as the flame caught, ritual steadying her. "Fire to you, to light your way/Flame to you, to warm the dark...."

When the smoke from the bowl was thick, she took out her shortblade, grasped the blade, and pulled away sharply. Holding her hand above the bowl, she let her blood drip into the fire, mixing with the fragrant woodsmoke so her father and brother would know it was she who mourned them.

She remained kneeling and motionless as the last fragments burned, and thereafter, thinking of a world without her father, her brother. No one spoke or moved. Only when the sky itself flamed with the sunset did she rise and silently return to the outpost.

Ronne went directly to her quarters and shut the door behind her. Erith removed the banner from its pole with care and replaced it on the wall. He looked at the closed door, wishing he knew how Ronne was faring, wishing there was something he could do.

The three Arhiia soldiers hurried in and out of the greathall, moving their gear inside. From the door, Erith watched the strange, leggy pack animals mill about in the yard, loosely tied up. The Arhiia called them *lenghur*. They had not brought much gear, so they were soon finished.

"She was wearing gold about her neck." It was the grim-faced woman who spoke. Zeltan looked up.

"Ayeh, I saw. It's none she had before, eh, Sebaa?"

The young soldier shook his head. "No. But who gave it to her?"

Erith turned away from the door, puzzled. *You would think they had never seen gold before.* "I did."

All three of the Arhiia turned and stared at him. Sebaa's face was pure astonishment, Zeltan was inscrutable. The woman just looked disgusted.

"Face of Pity, gold from a barbarian night-companion! The other was at least…."

"Tekbeh." Zeltan's voice warned. "Herself has said what he is. Have a care." He glanced at Erith, as if to gauge his reaction.

I seem to have been insulted…too bad I don't know what part was the insult. Ronne hadn't told him everything about the Middle Speech, it seemed. He decided on deliberate misunderstanding.

"I was the one who gave it to her. If you doubt me, ask the *taien*."

Tekbeh seemed confused and disconcerted by his calm response. She muttered an insincere apology and left to look after the pack animals.

"It's *he'alaran* now, but she'll not have told you." There may have been a glint of amusement in Zeltan's eyes, but it was indistinct and soon gone.

"What is *he'alar…?*"

"*He'alaran* is the one that takes up the duties of the *alaran*, when that one is no longer able. Her father was *alaran* of Arhi, and her brother was named *he'alaran* four years gone, but they both are dead. And of those left, all but she wear the Robe."

Well and good, if I knew what an alaran *was*, thought Erith.

Zeltan nodded to him in a not unfriendly fashion and headed for the kitchen. Sebaa watched the old soldier leave, looking up from the harness he was repairing, and when Zeltan was out of earshot, he glanced hesitantly at Erith. He seemed both fascinated and repelled, and more than a little curious.

"How did you meet with her? That is, I'm sure she did not leave, or… but how did you come here?" he asked, stumbling in embarrassment.

Erith hesitated before replying. It was his existence rather than his method of arrival that was the sore point, so there was no need to hide the truth of the matter. They all seemed to know exactly what he was. But did he know enough of the Middle Speech to explain? He had been following what they said well enough so far, but it was more difficult to speak than understand.

"I have many enemies in the High Plain, and they had hunted me to the far side of these mountains. They think this place is…." What was the word? Ah, yes. "…haunted. Full of evil things. So I came up this mountain, and Kashan found me. I was wounded, very sick, and I fell. When I woke up again, I was here."

Sebaa looked somewhat confused. "Er-it," Sebaa shook his head, and then said with care, "Erith, who is Kashan?"

Erith grinned. "I forgot, you haven't met him. He should have returned by now."

Out he went, and Sebaa followed with a mystified expression on his face. Erith called once, then again, and was rewarded by the sound of a familiar chirrup. It sounded somewhat muffled, and he saw why when Kashan came trotting up, dragging a rather battered deer. The snowtiger was immensely pleased with himself, and when Erith came up to him he dropped the deer and roared, lashing his tail. He then spoiled the ferocious effect by flopping down and washing the blood from his fur.

A small noise from Sebaa made Erith look up from Kashan's prey. His gold-brown face was completely pale, and his eyes appeared twice as large as before, but he made no move to run. A good thing, in Erith's opinion, as Kashan seemed to be in the mood for a game of run-and-pounce, and he doubted Sebaa would have appreciated it.

"This is Kashan. I would introduce you to him, but it would be better to wait until he has had his dinner. Which I believe he is willing to share with us…." Cautiously, Erith went up to Kashan's prey and removed a haunch from the doe with his shortblade. Kashan did not seem to mind, and when they had retreated, he fell on the rest of the deer with appetite.

Erith checked that the door was latched behind them when they went inside. "Sometimes he tries to bring them in, and Ronne draws the line at bloody carcasses in the greathall," he explained.

Sebaa nodded, his astonished eyes on Erith's face. "Understandable," he croaked.

That evening, Erith and the three Arhiia soldiers ate venison and rough journeybread in the greathall. It was a silent meal. Erith could feel Tekbeh's glares across the table. Sebaa darted quick glances whenever he thought no one was looking, but said nothing. Zeltan paid Erith no attention, concentrating on his meal with the focus of a warrior who knows his next may be far in the future. Tekbeh left as soon as she had finished, which seemed to remove the atmosphere of constraint.

"D'ye know where they all went to?" Zeltan's gesture encompassed the numerous empty tables and benches in the greathall.

Erith shook his head. "I only know what Ronne told me, that the soldiers were taken away and she remained. When I came here they had been gone some time, and that was one moon before Darkest-night. You say, one *month*." It was so hard to remember all the different words.

Zeltan looked grim. "Ayeh, it has the taint of court meddling on it. They're none so fond of Herself. The Face of Fortunate Happenstance was looking on her that only yourself came by."

"Kashan stayed with her." Erith stifled a grin at the look on Sebaa's face. "He should be finished by now." He got up and opened the door.

Kashan was waiting, and he rubbed by Erith with absent-minded affection as he padded in. Sebaa had evidently warned Zeltan ahead of time, for he showed no more surprise than raising his shaggy brows as Kashan wandered by. Both men were sniffed, and apparently found boring, since the snowtiger left them and wandered further through the greathall in search of Ronne.

Zeltan looked after Kashan, a thoughtful expression on his face. "You say the soldiers found him, eh? And kept him here? I did not hear of such a thing when talking to others. Sebaa, did you hear aught the like?"

Sebaa shook his head. "I heard no mention of any mascot. No one I spoke to had served with Ronne either, although it is possible that they would not speak loudly of such a thing where others might hear."

Erith was puzzled. "What do you mean?"

Zeltan returned his inscrutable gaze to him. "Why, that the soldiers lately gone hence seem strangely quiet, or did not meet with any others. And that's a thing not likely—the war called all together."

The next morning Ronne emerged from her quarters, and Erith feared from her appearance that she had not slept at all. Yet she began making preparations to leave, packing her few belongings as efficiently as possible. Erith could see that there wasn't much spare room in the lenghur packs even for the little she had. Ronne had still not told them her decision, and it seemed to Erith that Zeltan avoided asking any questions, accepting her actions as proof.

The tension affected everyone. Kashan was a constant source of annoyance, getting in the way, showing his teeth to the Arhiia when they came near, and generally being in an irritable temper.

Toward the afternoon, Erith found Ronne sitting by herself in the greathall. Her angular face was shadowed and drawn, and she did not look up when he approached.

"Those that Tselt…Zeltan called the Southern Horde, are they the Hairy Folk?"

"The *what?*"

He grinned at her surprised tone. "The plainsfolk call them that because they don't shave their faces."

Ronne considered, and Erith was pleased to see some of the empty look leave her face. "The Southern Horde are bearded, yes. Their grazing lands are near the Tiika river."

"They are the same, then." He paused, then looked at her intently. "This is something you should know. Whoever destroyed Ynduria, it wasn't them. It is their belief and custom that all stone is sacred, and they will not touch or deface it. If they know you to have stone buildings on your land, they take it as a sign of power. Even though the plainsfolk are few compared to them, we had status in their eyes from the stone *turos* we built."

Ronne gazed into the distance. "There is a strange smell to all of this. Zeltan says the troop that was here was not seen again after it left. Even if it had been attacked and destroyed, the report would have circulated. The saying is, 'to gossip like a soldier.' " She sighed and turned the cup in her bandaged hand.

"Are you going to leave?" he asked softly. Her hand clenched about the cup until her knuckles whitened.

"I will go home," she said with quiet vehemence. "Whatever the cost to me...." She shook her head in a sudden motion, then looked at him. "But you may go or stay, as you please. There is no danger to me now because of you."

"Do you want me to leave?" Erith asked bluntly.

"I will not take you where you do not wish to be," she said, her voice rough. Her gaze was locked on the cup in her hands. "That would not be the action of a...of a friend. You have seen how my soldiers think of you, and there will only be more of the same if you come with me. All I can promise in Arhi is blood and death. If there is a safe place in all the world for you, it is here. It...is not a bad place to live if you must. No one will trouble you."

It was a moment before he could trust his voice. "You call me friend. Is this how your people hold friendship? That I will let you go to danger alone? No, you won't be rid of me that easily."

"My people have little love for barbarians, and now, even less. I might not be able to shield you from their anger."

"You almost starved me when I first came here and planned to kill me. How much worse can they be?"

Looking up, Erith saw Zeltan standing to one side, waiting to speak to Ronne. He was sure some of their conversation had been overheard, but the soldier's face gave no sign of it.

Before he could speak, however, Ronne caught sight of him. "Zeltan. There are things here that should be preserved, out of sight, that we cannot carry. Have the others dig a pit in a concealed place. And be prepared to leave at first light."

Erith stifled a grin at Zeltan's relieved expression as he departed on his errand.

It was full dark by the time the soldiers had finished concealing the pit and its contents. Ronne knew they might never return to retrieve the gear she had hidden, but something in her would not let her leave a job half-done. The hard physical labor helped keep painful thoughts at bay.

She made her way wearily through the pitch-dark greathall to her quarters. The faint line of golden light under the door startled her until she remembered she had a greater treasure to bring back home, and safely. How could she have forgotten the moonrose? But in the pain of Zeltan's news, and the danger to Erith, she had.

She stopped short, thinking hard. The moonrose would be a powerful symbol, and it might also win Erith a measure of acceptance when it was known he was the one to discover it. Holding the moonrose in her cupped hands, she made her way to the kitchen. There had to be something she could put it in for protection on the journey.

The others were there before the fire, Erith sitting apart from the little group of Arhiia, who were talking among themselves. They all rose when she entered, the Arhiia with expressions of wonder and surprise as they saw what she held.

"Is that…it can't be. A moonrose?" asked Sebaa in an incredulous voice.

"A moonrose, yes. As our legends said and few believed. It was Erith," she said, nodding to him as he came forward, "who found it and gave it to me."

A muttered comment that broke off with a sharp intake of breath made her turn her head, but she only saw Tekbeh holding her side and glaring at Zeltan.

Erith, who had understood her purpose in bringing the moonrose, brought her two wooden bowls. The moonrose nestled inside one perfectly, and the other, inverted, formed a lid. Tied together with rags for further protection, it formed a compact bundle. She could carry it in her travelsack. It was too valuable to risk damage or loss on the lenghur.

"Is all prepared for our departure?" After receiving a nod from Zeltan, she asked Erith, "Do you have everything you wish to take with you?"

"He isn't coming with us, is he?" said Tekbeh, horrified. Ronne saw Zeltan also did not approve, though he said nothing, and even Sebaa looked troubled. She did not allow any of her growing anger to show—that would only make things worse. She simply looked with raised brows at Tekbeh until the soldier started to wilt.

"My helmbearer will travel with us. He will not be of much use to me here," she said with finality. It was clear the other Arhiia thought he would not be much use anywhere, but they made no more objections.

Early the next morning, they loaded the lenghur and set out on the track that Ronne had rarely taken, to the west and the boundary marker that defined the range of her former command—and the limits of her freedom. When they passed the boundary marker, she hesitated, then gritted her teeth and continued on. There would be no turning back.

CHAPTER 7

A week of travel passed in a blur for Erith. The Arhiia were determined to get back home as quickly as possible, and the route was now familiar to them. Zeltan would only consent to stop for a short time to hunt, and without Kashan's assistance they were soon reduced to the tough and tasteless rations the soldiers had brought with them.

Erith missed Kashan, and he thought Ronne did too. She said nothing, but he had seen her look back the way they had come more than once. He doubted Kashan had understood they were leaving the outpost. The snowtiger had gone with them for a while the first morning, much to the consternation of the lenghur, but then he had gone off on his own. Ronne had called to him, but he had not returned. If Kashan were with them now, perhaps Ronne would not look so grey and worn.

Erith had learned little more of the three Arhiia soldiers. Tekbeh was competent, taciturn, and loathed the sight of him. Zeltan was essentially unreadable. On occasion, Erith had the feeling the older soldier found him amusing, but Zeltan did not hesitate to inform him, in the manner of a father instructing a backward child, if he did not act as expected. Sebaa worshiped Ronne, which meant Erith was accepted as a matter of course.

That night they stopped in a valley between the last of the foothills, an area dotted thickly with brush but few trees. Erith and the others went about the routine tasks of setting up camp. Ronne did her share without a word. She seemed to be traveling in a grim fog, speaking so rarely that Erith was surprised when she suddenly said, "Quiet."

She stopped near the edge of the light cast by the fire, and when they were all still, Erith could hear something moving in the darkness: very faint sounds of stealthy movement. Ronne drew her sword and slowly moved even further away from the fire, and Erith and the three Arhiia followed suit. The noises stopped, then resumed even closer. Erith frowned. There was something familiar about them, like a large beast moving through the brush. He smiled.

"Kashan!" he called, and as Tekbeh rounded on him with a curse, a familiar white-and-black shape emerged from the darkness and blinked in the light. Kashan ambled in a casual way towards Ronne, as if to indicate it was pure coincidence he happened to be there and he was not following her. Ronne just smiled faintly and scratched his head.

"He's a rare beast, but should you be bringing him along?" wondered Zeltan, lowering his sword.

Ronne looked up. "I could not make him follow us. How would you have me keep him away?"

Tekbeh slammed her own weapon back in its sheath. "I suppose he's around for the same reason," she muttered, glaring at Erith. Her voice was low, but Ronne heard her—and went and stood before her, staring her down.

"I thought I had made myself clear. Erith is my helmbearer, and you will treat him accordingly. I have no need of disobedient soldiers."

Tekbeh paled and said nothing further. Zeltan looked as if he would speak, but he encountered a freezing look from Ronne and subsided.

Erith glanced at Sebaa, and the young soldier gave him a shrug and a grimace. Of the three, Erith did best with him, and he was not surprised when Sebaa joined him by the fire when his tasks were done. He was curious about Erith's exile and the customs of the plainsfolk. Sebaa, in turn, satisfied many questions Erith had about the Empire in general, and Ronne in particular.

"Did she give you that?" Sebaa asked, pointing to the shortblade Erith honed. He nodded.

"Is that when you gave her the gold?"

"No. That was an oath-gift," Erith said, using the closest translation to the plains term. "When I swore allegiance."

"Gold must not have the same meaning to the plainsfolk," said Sebaa, thoughtfully.

"The only meaning it has for us is wealth. Why shouldn't I give it to her?"

Sebaa looked about the camp. Ronne was on the other side, engaged in an intense conversation with Zeltan, but he lowered his voice nonetheless. "Gold can only be worn by the nobles, and the *tier sanas*—that means, 'the swords that see'—they can only wear gold that is given. They have an eye to their sword," and he pointed just below the hilt, "and are bound by the customs. Gold is given to mark bravery and skill. She used to have much gold, even though she was not popular at court. Have you seen her walk the Path? One in my barracks did." He sighed, envious.

Confused, Erith just shrugged. Sebaa still hadn't explained why the Arhiia had reacted so strongly to his gift, and he was beginning to suspect that he wasn't going to. Or were they just upset at whatever a barbarian did?

"There was some scandal," Sebaa continued, and his voice got even lower. "We never found out exactly what had happened. The rumor was she sent all her gold to the Emperor in a dirty box!" He was clearly shocked. "It was true that she wore no gold after that—but now she does. We were surprised to see it, and…and to hear you had given it to her."

He did not continue, and Erith gave it up. "How much further north will we be going?" he asked after a while. The question had been bothering him for some time.

"Many days travel," said Sebaa with a wry face. "Arhi is an *alar* on the north edge of the Empire, and Keris Kera is in the northern part of Arhi. The court put her as far from her family as they could, you see. Away and isolated."

Erith frowned. "They don't have any…demons up there, do they? Black demons?" Few of the plains traveled far from their own lands, but traders carried tales—except of the north. Erith had only heard one do so, and the memory lingered.

Sebaa laughed. "Demons? No, no demons. Do you believe in them? They're magic, not real. They don't exist."

Remembering the fear he had heard in the trader's voice, all those years ago on the plains, Erith was not so sure. The man had been very afraid of something, something real. And whatever it was, it had been far to the north.

"The moonrose is real," he pointed out. "And magic."

Sebaa stared at him, an arrested expression in his eyes.

Ronne studied the worn map and traced a route with her finger. "We must head to the east, here," she said to Zeltan, indicating on the map. "Through Oguz. It will add some days to our journey, but it is a better way to Keris Kera." The direct route went through the middle of Vaidis, and she did not even consider it. The way she had chosen was dangerous enough, if Talorgen was nearby.

The others gathered around the map, Erith and Sebaa leaving their discussion to join them. Zeltan made no objections to her plan. He had been with her in Ynduria and knew the reason for her caution. Tekbeh and Sebaa would not question her, either. Gossip would have hinted why Talorgen and the *alar* of Vaidis were dangerous to her.

Erith was another matter. He would wonder why they were taking a longer route if they were in a hurry to return and was quite capable of asking about it. They had been traveling hard and avoiding any cities or towns as they left the mountains, since the way to Arhi was closer to Ynduria than Ronne liked. Their supplies were getting low as a result.

To her relief, Erith said nothing, although his face showed his confusion. His face reflected nearly all of his emotions, and she wondered what it had been like to live in a place where feelings did not have to be concealed. She was glad he was here, glad she had something immediate to watch and worry over to distract her from the keening grief within. She refused to think about her sudden, unreasoning instinct to protect him when she had thought Imperial soldiers had come to the outpost. What was done was done, and both she and Erith would have to live with the consequences.

Sometimes she felt a twinge of guilt when the Arhi soldiers made it hard for him, but she couldn't bring herself to force him to go. At least Sebaa seemed to be getting along with him. She would deal with the rest when she was home once more.

Erith saw smoke curling from an inn's chimney in the distance, just visible in the twilight, and felt relived. Ronne had finally allowed them to approach the villages, but they had been empty. It disturbed him to see the abandoned homes, empty of people and food, and he could tell the Arhiia were also worried. Ten days now, and no sign of anyone but themselves.

The inn was not a very impressive structure; the roof was thatch, of a variety of materials, and the daub-and-wattle walls had been often and poorly repaired. The barn nearby was even more dilapidated.

"We will stop to get supplies, and shelter for the night," said Ronne.

Zeltan nodded. "In the barn, for preference. It's snug for our large company, but we need provisioning, and news is welcome." He looked at Erith, then back to Ronne. "You'll not be wanting to draw their notice, now," he said carefully. Ronne lowered her brows at him, but nodded.

"Yes, 'A silent step is worth two swords.' Erith, you and Tekbeh take Kashan and the lenghur to the barn, and stay with them." She handed him her helm.

Zeltan made a protesting noise, and Ronne lifted a hand as if to stop him from speaking. "It is more dangerous to show my rank than to go without a helm. It stays with him."

"I am doubting anyone in such a place would know the Arhi crest," Zeltan said, unconvinced.

"They will know a commander's helm, and that is enough." Ronne turned and headed for the inn, and Zeltan and Sebaa followed.

Erith frowned, watching Ronne enter the inn. What was she so worried about? He understood why she didn't want him so visible, but why would she want to escape notice herself?

Tekbeh, gloomy and silent as ever, picked up the lenghur string and led them to the barn, leaving Erith the task of convincing Kashan that he didn't want to follow Ronne. What he managed to do was convince the snowtiger that he wanted to visit the barn first. This took long enough, and by the time he had reached the barn, Tekbeh had almost finished tethering the lenghur. They wuffed nervously when they caught Kashan's scent, but they were almost used to him and soon quieted.

Erith crouched by Kashan and scratched the snowtiger's chin, looking out the loose-woven twig walls at the inn. If he had not been touching Kashan, he would have missed the faint sound of jingling harness and tramping feet, but the snowtiger's sudden alertness and taut muscles caught his attention.

He slipped out of the barn into the shadows and headed for the inn. Before he got there, a group of more than twenty soldiers passed by his hiding place. One of the soldiers carried a pole with something burning at the top, and by its light he could make out the banner device of a leafy vine. The troop came to a disciplined halt outside the inn.

Three soldiers went in, one with a spined helm similar to Ronne's. A sign of rank, Ronne had said. Erith felt the hairs on his neck stand up. *Why do I have the feeling this is very, very bad?*

The inn was even less prepossessing inside, and much more fragrant. Ronne tried to breathe through her mouth as Zeltan opened negotiations with the weevily innkeeper. For all their desperate need, she was not sure she wanted to eat anything that originated from such a filthy place.

Her attention was caught by the innkeeper's hands clutching and twisting a dishrag. She wondered why he was so nervous, then it occurred to her he must have had customers more prone to violence than payment since the fall of Ynduria.

Zeltan had just agreed on an only mildly extortionate price for provisions and permission to shelter in the barn, when they heard the sounds of approaching feet. A voice raised outside made her start.

She closed her eyes, willing away the sudden stab of fear. She recognized that voice. Talorgen. She looked about, thinking furiously. They couldn't get out the door in time to escape, and there was no place of concealment or even room to fight. *Why does the Face of Cruel Jokes love to look at me?*

Footsteps entered, stopped. "My Blade of Shadows," came the soft, detached voice. "You have come back to me at last."

Ronne was not fooled. She knew that tone; it was a dangerous sign. She turned to face him. "Talorgen tes Vaidis. You are far from home."

She could see the rebuke contained by her formal inflection was not lost on him. His eyes glittered with something akin to hunger; the smile on his face did not reach them. She saw two *taia* behind him, one whom she remembered. His face was rigid with shock as he recognized her. The other looked uneasy beneath her calm facade. *They will have soldiers with them…where is Erith?*

"You have wandered far from your border prison. Do I object? And I am not so far from home as you seem to think. There have been… rearrangements, since the tragic fall of Ynduria. In short, Oguz is now mine. How fortunate our paths should cross…but this is not the usual route to Arhi. That is your destination, I assume. What has brought you so far out of your way? Can it be possible you wish avoid me?"

Despite his evident effort to control it, his voice began to quiver with anger. *He hardly knows what he is saying—he is on the verge of violent madness,* Ronne realized. *I must find a way to calm him, or none of us will live.*

Erith returned to the barn at a run. "Tekbeh!" he whispered urgently. She shot him an annoyed look. He could see she was about to say something rude, and cut her off. "There are soldiers outside the inn."

Her eyes widened. "Did you see their banner?" She had already drawn her sword and was heading for the door.

"A vine with three leaves. A square around it."

Tekbeh muttered a brief, nasty curse. "Talorgen. Come, barbarian. You may be useful after all."

Erith gritted his teeth and followed, telling himself this was not the time to argue. They circled the inn from the rear and crept up to the tiny open window that showed the common room. Ronne, Zeltan, and Sebaa had their backs to the window, facing the commander of the troop and his *taia* with drawn swords.

He's quite an impressive sight, but I don't think he means to be friends, thought Erith. The commander had long, curling black hair, which was caught up in several gold clips and pins. His face was handsome enough, in a hawkish sort of way, but his dark eyes were hard and glittering and he moved like a predator that had scented blood. His harsh voice shook with strong emotion.

"…and so it was kindness, kindness to me, that made you leave? I think not. You mountain swordsmiths always thought yourselves better than everyone else. It is a wonder you don't marry one another to keep your bloodlines pure. How it must have irked your father, forced to accept Inar as a consort from the court."

"You will speak with respect of the honored dead." Ronne's voice was soft and menacing.

The commander laughed wildly. "Do you refer to the court, or your father? No, you had no reverence for the Emperor. You thought his gold honorless and did not hesitate to say so, did you? In a very crude manner, I might add." His eyes narrowed. "No respect for those the Emperor favored, either. That was my undoing. Too much for you to ignore, even in a night-companion. Well, my *kalasen*, there is no Emperor to offend you now. Come with me. What does Keris Kera offer that I cannot? I will take it anyway, as I have taken Oguz, so if you wish the walls of your city to stand, you must conciliate me."

Erith dropped back down and pulled at Tekbeh's sleeve. She bared her teeth in a snarl at him, but he ignored it and whispered, "We have to get her out of there."

"There are thirty-odd warriors at the door, barbarian. Do you plan to kill them all yourself?"

"Your civilized ways have curdled your brain. Or do you value this wall above your *he'alaran's* life?"

He grasped one of the supports where the mud had fallen away and exposed it. The wall was narrow here, and only two posts supported the end of the roof. Tekbeh's features expressed qualified approval, and she prodded the wall near the other post until she had a firm handhold. They looked at each other, nodded, and pulled.

A tremendous shriek and crack of protesting wood sounded as the wall fell, and dust billowed from the opening. Thatch fell from the roof. Tekbeh and Erith took advantage of Talorgen's surprise to move between him and Ronne, but he recovered and went on the offensive almost immediately. Trading blows, the Arhiia backed toward the gaping hole as shouts from outside showed that the alarm had been raised.

When he saw Ronne about to escape, Talorgen made a desperate lunge. Sebaa shouted a warning and moved to block it, but instead caught the full force of the thrust in his chest. His mouth opened silently, as if surprised. Then his hands reached out, grasping the blade that impaled him, so when he fell it was wrenched from Talorgen's hand. With Ronne and Zeltan out of the inn, Erith and Tekbeh followed them into the night, pursued by a howl of pure rage.

Ronne was sure the darker shadow against the night sky must be Erith, from the height. *At least he is still alive…Sebaa, how will I tell your father?* There were large rocks underfoot, and tree roots that sprang in lumpy lines from the hillside. Shouts and sounds of pursuit followed them.

When the rocks got even larger she leaped from one to another with desperate haste, trusting to her instinctive balance for safety. Erith made slower headway on the uneven terrain, but his longer legs made up some of the difference where the ground was clear. There was no sign of Tekbeh or Zeltan. *Face of Justice, see them safe….*

A sudden flash of light, a sharp crack, and a tree just ahead of her slowly fell with a rustling crash, the base of the tree in flames. The ground underfoot twitched, like Kashan in sleep. Ronne vaulted over the tree trunk, branches scratching and pulling where they caught on her armor.

Lightning? The night sky was clear, with no sign of a storm. What had brought the tree down?

Another flash, and this time she could see the bolt of light illuminating the area. The ground heaved and shuddered like a living thing in pain. Ronne headed up the slope, aiming for a rock ledge she had seen in the brief light. They could make a stand and fight there; it was defensible and hard to reach. As they ran toward it the ground beneath their feet shuddered again, hard. The hillside heaved up in a shower of dirt and rock and then collapsed in a terrible roar, and she fell with it. Ronne heard Erith cry her name amid the rumble of falling stone, just before something struck her head.

CHAPTER 8

The world was pale light, a face surrounded by firegold hair, and pain. Ronne slowly reassembled order from her personal chaos. Her whole body ached, her head in particular. Erith knelt beside her, holding the moonrose with an expression of frantic concern on his face that quickly changed to relief.

He helped her sit up on the pile of rubble they had landed on, and she looked around as best she could in the light of the moonrose. The light did not reach far enough to see anything above them, even when she held the flower herself and it blazed more brightly. There were no sounds save those they made themselves. It was as if the world had vanished around them.

She checked her gear. Her weapons were all present, her travelsack as well, but her helm was gone. No, she had given it to Erith before entering the inn, and he must have left it there. Erith held out the remains of the bowls that had protected the moonrose in her pack. One was broken in several pieces, and the other was chipped. One luminous petal lay in the bottom.

"I suppose we are fortunate that we all survived with such little damage. Are you hurt?"

He shook his head. "Beat up, bruised, otherwise whole. What happened?"

"The ground collapsed. We must have fallen into a cave. I doubt Talorgen will be able to find it easily in the dark."

"We fell a long way," said Erith. "We might not be able to climb out."

"A problem. We need to find a way back to Zeltan and Tekbeh." She clenched her teeth as she got up, putting all her weight on one leg. There was something not quite right about her left knee, but they could not stop now. She would just have to bear the pain until they could get out. She took one step and collapsed to the ground in agony.

She did not cry out, but it was some time before she could detach herself from the white haze of pain and respond to Erith's urgent voice. "My knee…" she gasped. "You must find Zeltan yourself. I cannot walk." Erith made no move to go, but knelt down and motioned toward her knee.

"It may not be so bad. Perhaps I can splint it so you can walk. Show me."

It was futile, she knew. This pain indicated an injury too severe to ignore. Still, she loosened the ties that held the upper part of her boot to her thigh, and rolled down the top one-handed. Erith cut her hose with his shortblade, revealing a swollen and bleeding mass. One corner of his mouth twitched, but the rest of his face revealed nothing, even as he moved her hand that held the moonrose to better see her injury.

He began to probe gently. Ronne's breath hissed out as pain lanced through her knee, and he looked up.

"I am sorry, but I must be sure of what is damaged." He bent his head again. "What happened there, back at the inn? Was he one of your enemies?"

She laughed, a short, explosive snort without humor. "Enemy…that word begins to describe him. Talorgen tes Vaidis, tes Vaidis ni Oguz, if what he said is true. I threw a stone four years ago, and now it has fallen. My armsman is dead, my people and land are threatened, all because I had poor choice in lovers. It did not seem so important at the time," she said with bitterness.

Erith shifted his position but kept his gaze on her injured knee. "I heard him, there at the inn. You…you cared for him once. He must still love you, beyond wisdom, and is willing to do anything to win you back."

"I doubt love is what he feels for me. What I felt for him," she sighed, "was little enough. I took what was offered. His face and form were pleasing, and it served to pass the time at court. It would occasion comment if a swordnoble on her year-service did not follow tradition by taking even a token lover. With my family history, it would cause an uproar," she said with a grimace, thinking of how many stories there were about Amrane and her wide-ranging affections. "Still, there were signs, and when it was clear his honor was debased, that his sword was blind, I ended it." *And got myself banished to the edge of the Empire in the bargain. But how could I look at the Emperor's gold again and not remember?*

She gradually grew aware that the pain in her knee had lessened, that it no longer throbbed in agony. Just when the pain had eased she could not recall. She looked down. Erith continued to examine her knee with careful fingers. She moved her leg experimentally, expecting a sharp jolt of pain. It never came.

Erith looked at her and stood up. His face seemed strangely haggard and drawn, and she frowned, puzzled. She pushed to her feet and stood swaying, gradually putting weight on her injured leg. She took a step. No twinge, no sudden buckling, no pain other than the general bruised feeling that covered most of her body. An icy wave coursed down her skin as she realized what must have happened. The impossible. Again.

"Do you know what you have done?" she said, her voice rough. "What are you? What did you do to me?"

He glanced at her, then away, and shrugged uneasily. "I only looked. Something must have been misplaced, and I…pushed it back. Knee-joints are tricky things."

She looked at him, searching his face for the truth. "Have you ever done such a thing before?"

He shook his head. "Our healer dealt with those matters. I have only bound wounds in battle. Usually my own," he said with an attempt at a grin.

"I have only once before seen something of this nature," Ronne said. He looked up warily, alerted by her tone. "There was a barbarian with mortal wounds. Yet within a day he had begun to heal, and within four he could stand. A curious tale, no?"

They stared at each other across the luminous moonrose. "Barbarians can be hard to kill," he said after a moment. "They are too stupid to realize they are dead, so they keep living."

"That has not been my experience," she returned, "and I have killed enough of them to know. I have also seen enough of battle to know the wounds that can be suffered and survived."

There was a taut silence, then Erith ran his fingers forcefully through his hair, sweeping it back. "I am not hiding anything from you, I swear it!" His voice was tinged with frustration. "If I haven't answered your questions, it is because I don't know the answers."

Ronne sighed. "Forgive my shortness of temper. There have been too many mysteries today, and I too dislike not knowing the answers." She gripped his shoulder in apology, and she felt the tension leave his body. "Now let us find the others."

They half-walked, half-slid down the slope of rubble, which ended at a slab of rough rock. Holding the moonrose higher, she could just make out a curving surface above. They proceeded down the tunnel, walking for what seemed like hours. Eventually it became so narrow they had to proceed half-crouched, and Ronne began to fear they would have to turn back. Then the passage widened and she saw three stone steps just at the edge of the light.

She stared at them in shock. The steps were unremarkable, except for their location in the middle of a mountain. They led up to an arched doorway in a masonry wall. Ronne saw that the floor beyond the doorway was smooth and inlaid with colored stone in an abstract design. The doorway was at the end of the tunnel; they could only retreat or go forward.

In silent agreement, they drew their weapons and went through the archway. From what she could see in the zone of light from the moonrose, the room beyond was longer than it was wide, with columned galleries on either side. The doorway they had entered by was at one end of the room, facing the longer wall. The room appeared to be empty.

As she walked out from the gallery, Ronne marveled at the skill shown in the carved stone columns. Branches sprang from the tops and flowed upward, becoming impossibly fine and slender. The gallery looked like a line of young trees, frozen in time. The wall at the end of the room, near the doorway, was covered with a jewel-like mosaic of interlacing lines and stylized creatures that emerged from the design and then became one with it again. The colors were rich and deep, sometimes changing as she moved and the light shifted. Ronne had never seen anything like it.

"What is this?" Erith's whispered voice was full of awe. Small echoes of his words reflected strangely.

Ronne shook her head. "I do not know. I have never heard of such a place, even in the oldest records." She moved cautiously down one side of the room, Erith following close behind.

She could not explain her strong feeling of unease. Perhaps it was the occasional streaks and smears of sooty black that obscured the luminous mosaics, or the lack of debris. It almost felt as if the original inhabitants were to return after a brief absence.

Ronne saw another arched doorway on the far wall, further down, and walked more quickly.

"There's our way out," Erith said, sounding relieved.

Ronne shook her head. The base of the doorway was obscured by something dark. When they were close enough, she saw the doorway was half-filled by a frozen flood of rough stone, flowing from the doorway into the room. The lava filled the passage beyond, and the doorway was completely outlined in black, wings of soot framing it.

"What's that?" Erith pointed, and Ronne saw a length of pale color lying on the floor. He bent to pick it up, and as his fingers touched it she felt a slight disturbance, like a sound not quite heard or a vibration in the stone floor. He handed the thing to her, and she saw it was a flute made of bone, beautifully ornamented with thin lines of gold inlay in the shape of vines and leaves.

Then she noticed what had been beside it. A skeletal hand lay at the end of two long, thin arm bones that protruded from the lava flow. Something stirred the dust on the floor beside it, but there was no breeze.

Ronne felt the hairs on her neck stand up. "One of the inhabitants, I think." She knelt and replaced the flute in its original location, gently touching the dusty bones beside it. "Forgive, departed, our error. We steal not from the dead," she said, in High Speech.

She rose and gestured for Erith to follow her as she continued down the hall. There had to be a way out. She felt an added urgency to leave, some instinct alerting her to danger. It took considerable strength of will not to break into a run. Erith, too, seemed to sense the additional tension in the atmosphere, turning and walking backwards a pace to watch the rear.

Ronne stopped suddenly when she saw what lay at the other end of the hall.

"What is it?" Erith whispered, and she pointed in response. The pale light of the moonrose revealed a banquet table across the short end of the hall, with further tables extending down the hall from either end. There had been food there, once, in platters and pitchers and bowls, but it was reduced to bones and dust.

Bones and dust were all that remained of the banqueters as well. They lay fallen across the tables or slumped in their fantastic, ornate chairs. Dust-covered gems glittered on skeletal arms and finger bones, and thin threads of metal gleamed through the tattered remnants of cloth that hung out of habit only on the bodies scattered there.

Two ethereal chairs stood like thrones at the center of the main table. They were made of crystalline branches woven together, and allowed to spring free as a canopy at each chair's back. The crystal chairs seemed also skeletal; there was a sense they had once, like their occupants, been alive.

What happened here? wondered Ronne, incredulous. *Who are these people, and how did they die?* And how long ago, that no record remained of them or their works?

One of the crystal chairs was empty. Its former occupant lay across the table, arms outstretched in a vain attempt to halt the approaching doom. The other chair still held an upright figure, bony hands clasping the chair arms, empty sockets still defying victorious death. A free-form rivulet of iridescent metal circled the skull.

Erith stared in amazement at the scene before them, his pulse hammering. He felt a breeze begin, which increased in speed and force. It was numbingly cold and brought shadows that moved within it. He could also see a glow of blue just at the edge of sight.

We have to get out of here. But when he turned, something moved in the shadows at the other end of the hall. Something that was only a thickening of the air, but glinted in the light. There were only two entrances to the hall, and now both were blocked. He took a deep breath and tightened his grip on his sword.

For a moment there was no sound but the increasing wind, then a thin, dusty voice was heard, blending with it. Ronne looked quickly about, and her mouth moved in a silent echo of what the voice had said. He thought he saw an expression of startled recognition on her face.

"Take this!" shouted Ronne over the wind, and thrust the moonrose at him. Reversing her grip, she tossed her sword up and caught it again by the blade, a handspan below the hilt.

What is she doing? She can't fight like that! Ronne shouted something in a language he didn't recognize, but which seemed to be similar to the one the wind had used. The voice on the wind, stronger now, spoke a short, clipped phrase.

She can talk to spirits? Erith was amazed to hear a pleading note in Ronne's voice as she struggled to communicate with the bodiless voice. It was clear her command of the language only extended to a few words and phrases. Finally, she said something that the voice repeated. He stood with her now in a circle of light surrounded by deep black shadow, although the moonrose had not dimmed. She repeated what she had said before, adding the word, "Talorgen."

The wind stopped, and the deep blue glow shone through the unnatural dark with intensity. Erith heard many voices, riding over and responding to one another like an invisible council meeting. The voices began to say a certain phrase until all said the same thing in unison. Whatever Ronne had told them, it had made an impression. Erith hoped fervently it was a good one.

A louder, imperious voice declaimed a statement like a judgment. When it had finished, the quiescent wind roused to a furious gale, knocking both Erith and Ronne to the ground, and blackness engulfed them.

CHAPTER 9

Erith could feel grass under his fingers, and a bird was singing in the distance. Somehow, this was wrong. He forced his eyes to open, and then he sat up with a gasp. It *was* grass. The afternoon sun was bright in the reddening clouds. No cavern, no ancient underground hall or talking shadows. He checked his weapons. Both sword and shortblade were there, in their sheaths.

Ronne. He twisted about where he was and saw her sprawled on the hillside a few feet away. He got up, impatiently untangling the strap of his travelsack, which had somehow gotten wrapped several times around his arm.

The slow rise and fall of her chest reassured him. He reached out and shook her shoulder. "Ronne. Ronne, we're outside."

She made a sound almost like a groan, and blinked. She sat up slowly, then rested her head on her hands. Erith felt a twinge of concern. She didn't appear to be injured, but she made no attempt to stand.

"Are you hurt?" he asked.

He almost thought she hadn't heard him, then her head rose from her hands. "I will not walk the Path," she said in a rough whisper.

"What path?" Erith looked about the hillside, puzzled. He could see nothing that even remotely resembled a path. "Where?"

"No. It is too dangerous. Why don't they understand?" She looked groggy, her eyes unfocused.

Seriously worried now, Erith reached for his waterskin. It was empty. He hesitated, debating whether he should leave Ronne in her present state. But what else could he do?

"I'm going to look for water," he said, searching her face for any sign of a response. She said nothing.

He searched but there didn't seem to be any water to find. The hillside was littered with ruined columns and blocks of carved stone, translucent white with veins of deep blue, green, and gold. He saw no familiar landmarks or openings they might have used to leave the underground hall.

Was it underneath them? How had they gotten out, when all the exits were blocked? Had the spirits somehow carried them up here?

The terrain was unfamiliar; twisted, gnarled trees were scattered over the grass-covered hillside, interspersed with large thickets of brambles. The sun was beginning to go down, telling him they had lost at least an entire day in the underground hall—or more. He found a brackish puddle in a rocky cleft and returned with as much water as he could get.

Ronne was still there when he returned, looking more alert. "We should prepare for the night," she said, when she caught sight of him. Erith felt a surge of relief, hearing in her voice that she had recovered from her strange mood. "There is no knowing what we may encounter, and Kashan is not here."

"Do you know where we are?" he asked.

"No. I can only guess we are on the other side of the mountain we were climbing when we ran from the inn. Our maps show very little of the mountains, and nothing at all of what lies beyond them."

North of the High Plain, thought Erith. "I have never been this far," he said. "But I have heard from others it is a dangerous place." Perhaps if they stayed in the hills, in the trees, they would be safe. The northern trader had said the demons rode other demons, demons of the wind, and that they preferred to travel on the open plain.

As night fell, Erith started a fire, more for safety than warmth. "I hope Zeltan and Tekbeh escaped," he said. And how would they find them again? They didn't even know where they were now.

Ronne stared into the flames, her face sad. "Sebaa did not, and he is only the first," she said quietly. "How many more? Why must others pay for my mistakes?"

Erith was silent, thinking of Sebaa and his frank, open face and friendly smile. How he had worshiped Ronne. "His greatest wish was to be of service to you," he said, and stopped, remembering how Sebaa had grabbed the sword that killed him, giving Ronne the chance to escape. "He knew what he was doing. And I don't see how you are responsible for Talorgen's threats."

Ronne shook her head. "It is my burden, and my task to end the threat he represents. And I do not disdain Sebaa's gift. I will thank him the only way I can now." She took out her shortblade and drew it along her palm, letting the blood drip into the fire. Erith took his own knife and added his blood to hers.

The next morning they discussed what to do. Ronne took a pull from the waterskin, making a face at the taste. It would be worse if they had no water at all, but not much worse. She shook her head at Erith's suggestion.

"We cannot return to Oguz. There is only one road to Arhi from there, and Talorgen will have troops waiting."

"What about Zeltan and Tekbeh?" asked Erith. "Should we try to find them first?"

"No. We cannot afford to wait. Talorgen may well decide to attack Arhi immediately, making it difficult to reach Keris Kera no matter how we approach. Did you see which way they went?"

He shook his head. "I think Tekbeh went to the barn. There were soldiers following her. What shall we do for food?" he said suddenly. "It doesn't look like the hunting will be good here, and we only have our travelsacks with us now."

He gestured towards his as he spoke, and Ronne raised her eyebrows in surprise. "What do you have in it? It looks rather full."

He pulled it forward, frowning. "It wasn't like this underground. I'd remember carrying anything this heavy. What about yours?"

It was bulging. Ronne felt her stomach tighten, wondering what they might contain. And why. The voices of the underground hall were not finished with them, it seemed.

Erith had already opened his travelsack. He pulled out a beautiful gold box with amber insets, with light glowing faintly through them. The moonrose was nestled inside. He also found a number of small, wax-sealed jars, a simple, unadorned cup of grey metal, and several brooches with the same kind of intertwined design as the walls in the underground hall.

Taking a breath, Ronne opened her own travelsack. On top were three books with metal clasps and enameled covers. She opened one—she was unable to read it, but the writing was troublingly familiar. She explored further, producing a dagger and sheath of a frost-white metal, a deep blue gem the size of an egg covered entirely with carving, and the bone flute.

From the very bottom Ronne drew something wrapped in rotting white silk. She held it for a moment, knowing what it must be. She pulled the silk away, revealing an iridescent diadem in the shape of a frozen rivulet. She could tell Erith remembered as well as she where they had seen it last— encircling the skull of a long-dead ruler. *But why have they given it to me?*

Erith reached out to touch it, and Ronne held it out to him, but as soon as her fingers left it, it ran liquid through his hands, pooling on the ground in its original shape. Only she could pick it up in its solid form.

Erith propped his arms on his knees and rested his face in his hands. His shoulders shook. "Sebaa laughed at me for believing in magic—but this is too much for me. I don't believe it even as I see it. I suppose we couldn't expect them to give us anything to eat, but why did they give us this?" he said, raising his head again. "What did you say to them?"

Ronne shook her head, dazed. "They were angry, at first. I didn't understand why. They spoke of woken evil, evil magic being used that woke them. There is an oath, the binding oath for the *tier sanas*, the sighted swords. The archivist at Keris Kera is a man of great learning. He discovered the meaning of the words, which had been long forgotten, and taught them to me. The oath is very old."

The writing. That's where I saw it before! Temaso's ancient manuscript of the oath! "What I told the voices was part of that oath, saying that honor was my light in darkness. I did not understand most of what they said in return, but I heard the words for path and proof, or testing. I thought perhaps they referred to a reason for disturbing them there, so I attempted to say that we were forced to go there by an enemy, an enemy that was in darkness without honor. They demanded a name, I told them it was Talorgen. What they said afterward I did not understand at all."

She sighed and began to replace the items in her travelsack. "I think it best we leave now. Heading north and west, we should find a familiar landmark before long."

Erith nodded and began his own preparations. "Are you certain we shouldn't wait for the others?" he said after a pause.

"How are they going to find us? We went through a mountain."

"I think they can find us," Erith responded, and she heard amusement from his voice. Ronne looked at him sharply. "You see?" He pointed. Two people—and one snowtiger—were climbing the brush-covered slopes to the south.

"Is it you, then!" said Zeltan. Erith thought the old man even seemed pleased to see him, as well as Ronne. "Fortunate Face!" He laughed, slapping his leg.

"How did you fare after the inn?" inquired Ronne, bracing herself as Kashan stood on his hind legs to nuzzle her face, heavy paws draped over her shoulders.

"Not well, at the start. We ran right to the arms of those going to support Talorgen, and we had all to do to stay alive." Zeltan gestured, and Erith could see a rough bandage through a rent in his tunic sleeve. "But then your tiger gives voice from the rear, and the young lord is screaming even louder within, and they did not know which way to turn! I am thinking it is the young lord they fear more. Tekbeh fades back and away, heading for the barn as I think, and I run off with a noise and a clatter to draw the rest. We came together again early next day, heading the way we saw you go last."

"Just took some packs. Couldn't take the armor and javelins, lenghur couldn't keep up, and they were spooked in addition," Tekbeh said gruffly. "Sorry." She looked tired and worn.

"You did right," said Ronne. "Making a second door in the inn wall was also good thinking."

Tekbeh turned a dark red and seemed to have difficulty speaking. "His idea," she jerked out, and waved a hand at Erith.

Erith's jaw sagged in disbelief. He pulled himself together as Ronne turned to him. "It…um, looked like it was falling down anyway," he explained, while his mind reeled in amazement. While not an effusive declaration of friendship, it was the first time Tekbeh had spoken of him without contempt. "How did you find us?" he asked.

"It was Kashan, in the end. We did think to go the road to Arhi, but by daybreak it was full of troops, and none of the right sort. Tekbeh found the tracks, and we followed to Kashan and then to you." Zeltan looked about, eyes squinting in the light. "It's a bare place."

"Where is Arhi from here?" asked Ronne. "We were forced to take an… underground route and have lost our position."

Zeltan knelt and began to sketch in the dirt. "The inn is here, by the border. Yon hill is there, and this is the Klevang range…this place is nigh about here," and he pointed.

Ronne frowned. "The Klevang mountains have no northern passes."

"Ayeh, none that I know of. But for truth, it is not a place well known. Could be several, could be none. We know for certain the way we came is very chancy. We are not given any good choices."

Erith was aware of a sinking feeling in his stomach. What could he tell them that they would believe? He glanced up to see Ronne looking at him, and he realized she had noticed his frowning study of the map.

Reluctantly, he said, "I was told by one who traveled widely on the plains that this is dangerous territory. This is where the Windriders come from, when they raid for slaves."

They all turned their gazes to him then, even Tekbeh. "Who are these Windriders, and what is their nature?" asked Ronne.

"They are said to have command of wind demons, and can ride them wherever they wish, but this magic turns them black with burning. It is also said that they take captives to feed these demons. I have never seen one," he continued, shrugging with hands spread, "but this is what the caravan traders say, and they fear the Windriders greatly."

Ronne thought for a moment, then sighed. "This does not change our situation. The danger is too great in Oguz. We will be able to travel more quickly on this side of the mountains, with less chance of being intercepted by Talorgen's troops. We will continue on and hope for a pass less guarded. But we will watch for these Windriders as well."

Erith was not able to change her mind. Arguing forcefully, he managed to convince Ronne to at least stay in the foothills as much as possible. They continued northward for several days, occasionally encountering other reminders of the underground hall—a ruined tower, looking like a giant swirl of thistledown; a row of stone slabs, some missing or broken, that were covered in mysterious sigils; a great gate that emerged from the earth in ripples of seamless opalescent stone.

Ronne gave Tekbeh and Zeltan a brief description of what had happened underground, omitting the voices, so they examined the relics with great curiosity as they went past. Without needing to say anything, the whole party went around the gate. As he looked back, Erith thought he caught a glimpse of lush growth and one or two indistinct figures faintly superimposed on the bare hillside. He opened his mouth to speak, but the figures vanished. *They already think I am imagining things*, he thought, and decided to say nothing.

The second night out Erith noticed Tekbeh working on something, off to one side of the fire. When she saw him looking at her she glared and moved further away, preventing him from seeing what she was doing. The next day as they camped, Tekbeh produced two hares.

"Now, how's this been done?" said Zeltan, shaggy brows raised. "Never tell me you charmed them to your hand?"

"Sling," mumbled Tekbeh, and showed the thing she had worked on the night before. Cobbled together from bits of a worn pack, it was ragged but effective.

"Sure, and aren't you a bit old for such?" Zeltan chuckled. "I never thought to see a child's toy in your hand, even when you were of an age for it." Erith had to agree, although he knew better than to say so. Tekbeh seemed to have been gloomy from birth.

"Enough," said Ronne firmly. "That 'child's toy' is all that feeds us now, unless we stop for snares. Kashan is still displeased with us, it seems."

Erith frowned. "Water may be a problem still."

Zeltan scratched his chin, looking about thoughtfully. "There's a bit of green down aways, and perhaps a ravine. A likely place to fill the skins if we're low."

The place Zeltan had indicated was out in the valley, on the edge of the group of hills they had been following. Ronne could tell Erith did not approve of leaving the thicker forest for the plain, but it did seem more lush than the surrounding countryside. When they investigated the ravine the next day it proved to have a brisk, ice-cold creek, and Tekbeh and Zeltan lost no time filling the empty waterskins.

Kashan accompanied them to the water's edge, but then he suddenly lifted his head and moved intently downstream. When Ronne followed him, she found him by a wide, open area where the stream broadened. It was muddy and trampled. Kashan was sniffing intently, tail twitching, making small noises deep within his throat.

Ronne studied the muddy area with care. It was covered by the same kind of track; a nearly complete circle the size of her spread hand. The beast must have been large to leave such a mark; Kashan's pawprints were not as big. She straightened, intending to return, when a different shape caught her eye. By the water's edge, washing away as she stared at it, was a human footprint.

She drew her sword. Stepping back from the stream, she listened carefully but heard no sound other than the water swirling past. When she returned to the others, Zeltan drew his own weapon as soon as he saw hers in her hand, and Erith and Tekbeh followed suit.

"A footprint, down further. It was fresh," said Ronne. "They must have been here before us this morning, at first light."

Searching further, they found a campfire, still warm, on a ledge above the creek. Tekbeh paced beside the tracks, scowling.

"Hard to tell how many humans; they stayed on the rock ledge, mostly. Maybe ten or fifteen of the…whatever they are. Never seen anything like it. The beasts must be immense; their stride is longer than he is tall," Tekbeh continued, gesturing at Erith. "Are these their wind-demons, that you spoke of?"

He shrugged. "I have never seen them. They could well be."

Ronne only hesitated for a moment before deciding to continue on. An unknown but avoidable threat compared with the definite danger of Talorgen—they were still better here. She took every precaution she could think of. They traveled through the night and started well before dawn the next day. They lit no fire when they camped, and ate only cold hare and some berries.

Two days after leaving the creek she saw the string of foothills was ending, with the next visible at the other side of a wide, grassy valley. Kashan had already started across, but Ronne scaled a tree to look for signs of the Windriders. From her vantage point, the plain spread flat and empty to the west. It seemed quiet and peaceful.

"Anything?" asked Erith as she descended.

"Nothing," she said, landing lightly on the ground and dusting bark off her hands. "There is a spur to the south and west that might hide them, but I see no sign of movement."

She looked at each of them in turn. They were all tired—the constant travel had taken its toll—but not so tired they could not go further. They had to chance the crossing now so they could return to the shelter of the foothills as soon as possible. "The way is clear in all directions as far as the nearest hill. We should be able to cross unseen, but let us go now and with speed."

The valley was still and empty. Halfway across, Ronne found Kashan and the remains of a small deer-like creature. He seemed puzzled that they did not stop and share his prey.

Ronne glanced back as they passed and noticed Kashan had lifted his head, listening to something in the distance. After a moment, she heard it too—a distant rumble combined with high, hawklike cries. A cloud of dust grew on the horizon.

She started to run, and the others followed suit. The cloud of dust grew larger, and she could see smaller, darker shapes within it. It moved like a storm across the valley floor, impossibly fast. Ronne could see they had no chance of reaching the foothills before they were intercepted, and she shouted to the Arhiia to form up. *Better to be ready to fight—a few feet more won't make a difference.* They had all drawn their weapons by the time the Windriders had them surrounded.

CHAPTER 10

There were bulky shadows, dark faces that hovered in the swirling dust. The faces yelled and shrieked, and from the giant beasts the raiders rode came high-pitched, drawn-out sounds as they thundered around the Arhiia. They had formed a hollow square, Erith at Ronne's left, Zeltan at the right, and Tekbeh in the rear. Ronne saw Kashan in the tall grass from the corner of her eye, his belly flat to the ground, ears back, snarling and lashing his tail.

She could see the Windriders more clearly when they left off circling and began to make darting attacks. They were black as charred wood, just as Erith had said. They wore their hair in a long, flowing crest very like the crest that ran along the necks of the beasts they rode. Their weapons were crude—stone-tipped spears, clubs with jagged inset edges. There were enough of them to be dangerous, even so.

The creatures the raiders rode were large, almost the size of an aurochs. They had longer, more slender legs, well-muscled and ending in a solid hoof. The head was long and narrow, looking strange on the large neck, with small, pointed ears at the very top. The beasts had grace and agility as well as speed, and their tails flowed out behind them as they ran.

Another attacker sped by, slashing at Zeltan, who blocked and returned the blow. Ronne felt a fierce pride in her people, including Erith. They fought and gave no sign this was a danger they had never faced before. A rider headed for her out of the milling horde and she prepared to meet it. *Perhaps a cut to the tendons of the rear leg; that would slow them down....*

A black-and-white blur erupted from the grass and launched itself at rider and mount. Kashan's claws left a scarlet trail down the beast's flank. It screamed, sounding almost human, and thrashed about violently. The rider fell when it spun about and fled.

The other animals began to catch the scent of blood, and of Kashan, and sounds of consternation replaced the exultant cries of the Windriders. The few that remained mounted had difficulty controlling their beasts, who showed great reluctance to resume the attack.

Ronne saw they were facing only eight or nine of the raiders and she smiled inwardly. *They are not so dangerous now. Once off their beasts, we have a chance against them.* The raiders, most now on foot, continued the fight. Kashan stayed in front of her, darting out at any foe that came too close. In response, the raiders changed the target of their attacks.

One of the few still mounted moved to attack Erith. Charging from the edges of the circle, the raider drew back his arm to throw his spear. Erith, occupied with one of the dismounted raiders, had not noticed the threat. As she lunged to do something, anything, the world and all within it slowed.

She felt the dreaded pricking of her skin and hot dryness in her eyes, and her heart wailed *Ah, Face of Mercy! Not here, not now!* By then it was too late. She had never been able to control the Pathwalking, to stop it when it began or even know when it would come. She could only pray that the madness would be short, and that only her enemies would suffer from it. The gates of her private hell opened.

The Center turned, and all that came to it was broken. All that moved, all stood before it, all that ran. Nothing could withstand the Center that walked the Path.

With a gasp, Ronne emerged from her trance just as her sword was about to decapitate a tall raider with a high, stiffened crest. His strange wooden weapon, inset with jagged stones, was broken and lying on the ground. The sudden transition to sanity unbalanced her and her blade clipped his crest instead, missing his scalp by a hairsbreadth. Heart pounding, she looked about, frantic and terrified, to see who she had killed.

There was a great difference, Erith decided, between a mounted raider and one on foot. His present opponent was courageous and determined, but unskilled in combat. Blocking a wild swing with his sword, he spun and lashed out with his shortblade, burying it to the hilt in the raider's side.

Suddenly there was a crack of wood, and a flying splinter scored his cheek. Glancing down, he saw a broken spear with its point embedded in the ground only two paces from him. *That was meant for me....* Turning his head, he that saw Ronne must have been responsible for the spear's destruction, and was engaged with another raider who had approached him unnoticed.

Watching Ronne from the corner of his eye as he stood ready to defend, he noticed something different, something wrong. She moved in a fluid, unhurried way, yet always seemed to be a step ahead of her opponent.

Her angular, gold-brown face had lost its habitual hard, grim expression and was slack, almost drowsy. She turned with the new attack, suddenly spinning and pulling with her sword arm. He heard a loud crack and her opponent screamed and fell to his knees, clutching his ruined wrist.

Ronne flicked her sword across his throat with the casual air of one brushing crumbs from a tabletop. As another raider came near, she used the follow-through motion of her first blow to finish her first opponent before returning to the defense.

Her eyes half closed, her weapon held loosely, she faced the tall, muscular raider as he attacked. A curving motion of her sword, graceful as a dancer, checked his weapon and then skipped away and back again over his head. The raider stood like a rock as the front of his stiffened crest fell over his face and down his shoulders, face thunderous as the gasps and exclamations of his fellows turned to laughter.

Ronne stepped back, weapon at guard, but there were no further attacks. She seemed to have lost her relaxed detachment, and Erith saw her look quickly about the field of combat, and at him, with a gaze of such fierce, desperate intensity his breath caught in his throat.

It was only later that he remembered that her hand had trembled as it wiped the sweat from her brow, that he could see her pulse hammering at the base of her throat, that her face was nearly as pale as his own. All he knew was that something was wrong, and he had to buy them time to put it right.

"Going through!" he yelled, in the pidgin tradetalk he had learned on the High Plain. "Going far! No blood hunt, we go." Another memory came to him of the caravan traders who had told him of hand gestures that had meanings like words. He thought he could remember the one for house, or hut…. He moved his fingers to make the half-remembered form.

"Heh. Rabbit, Walks-on-the-ground. You run, rabbit," said one of the mounted raiders in accented tradetalk. "Kenjah hunt you." She put the throwing-axe she held back in her baldric with the others and made the same hand gesture, inverted, and then pointed north. There were no houses there, he guessed. "This kenjah place!"

He made the sign for house again, and pointed to the north and west. "Stand, say to me rabbit!" he challenged, pointing to her with his sword and then to a spot before him. Some of the raiders chuckled then, one making a comment that amused the others.

The mounted raider made the gesture meaning bargaining, or balancing of accounts, and said, "Big rabbit?" and flashed a brilliant smile. Her golden eyes seemed to glow in her dark face, and he tried not to think about demons.

"Big rabbit," agreed Erith with irony, and pointed to Kashan. Her smile vanished, and her mount sidled nervously, tossing its head. *Let us try still more*, he thought, and drew a deep breath. Dabbing at the cut on his cheek, he showed her the blood on his hand, then made the sign for trade, inverted. *I hope I understood her correctly….*

She stared at him a while, then shouted something to the others. A period of argument and discussion followed. A few were opposed, including the one whose crest Ronne had clipped, but the rest seemed to agree to the truce. Many made a brushing motion on both sides of their faces. The raider repeated Erith's gestures then, pointing to Kashan and tilting her head, questioning.

No fighting, he agreed, indicating the snowtiger. He turned and found Ronne at his shoulder, once again her usual impassive self. "Can you call Kashan and keep him close to you? I think we have a truce of sorts, if he can be kept quiet." She nodded, and called to Kashan coaxingly.

At first the snowtiger merely turned his head at her voice, but the soft tone reassured him. In the absence of an obvious threat, he responded to her call, leaning his head against her as she scratched between his ears. Gasps came from the assembled raiders, followed by muttered comments and gestures to avert ill-wishing.

Turning back to the Arhiia, Erith discovered Zeltan trying to bandage a deep gash in Tekbeh's leg while still holding a sword. "Throwing axe," gritted Tekbeh when she saw his glance. "Faceless bastards, don't they know how to kill?"

He went to help. "I'll take care of that, Zeltan. You'll never stop the bleeding one-handed."

"It's what can be done," growled the old man. "Herself needs watching more. Get back to her! Do you trust them so entirely?"

"They are dealing with their own wounded," said Ronne, her cool voice cutting through Zeltan's angry words. "Stop arguing, and take full advantage of the truce Erith has won for us. Kashan and I will watch them."

The raiders were indeed drawing away, yet still keeping the Arhiia in view. Muttering under his breath, Zeltan rose and began binding his own nicks and cuts, most of them minor. Kneeling, Erith took up the task of bandaging Tekbeh's leg. The cut was deep and bleeding badly.

"Let it go." Startled, he looked up at her face, greyed with pain. "I can't walk on it, probably lose the leg anyway. Better if I die."

"Better for you, or for Ronne?" he said roughly, pulling the bandage tight. It was suddenly hard for him to focus. Pain and fatigue consumed him, and every inch of his body ached. *And when did I hurt my leg?* He shook his head and sat back on his heels.

"I'm not like them," she continued, waving to indicate Ronne and Zeltan. "My folks aren't soldiers or nobles. I was the first to take arms in my family. Don't got any honor to speak of. She'll think she has to wait for me, carry me, even. They need her now, back home. She's got to get there soon as she can. I'll just slow her down."

Erith felt a surprising flash of sympathy for Tekbeh. "Maybe. And maybe having you along will mean she gets back alive," he pointed out. He rose stiffly. "It's stopped bleeding, anyway. Don't move unless—"

"Erith." Although Ronne's voice was not loud, the tone caught his attention. Three of the raiders were riding off with great speed.

"Good. Fewer to worry about."

She shook her head and pointed. In the direction the riders were heading was an immense cloud of dust.

Ronne watched the horde of Windriders with a sinking feeling of dismay. There had to be over a hundred of them. It was hard to count, with the constant movement and the dust, but she was beginning to identify some of the same faces. Strangely enough, they made no attempt to threaten the Arhiia, but instead gave them a wide berth. She scratched behind Kashan's ears and invoked a silent blessing on his head. There was no doubt they owed their lives to him.

Their continued safety was her responsibility, however, and so she tried to understand the raiders' actions. The ones they had killed still lay where they had fallen. How could the truce last when they had killed the raiders' comrades? Why had they agreed in the first place?

Her musings were interrupted by two figures emerging on foot from the dust and noise, heading for the Arhiia. One was the axe-thrower who had spoken to Erith, the other a tall, proud man noticeably older than the rest of the raiders. Ronne could see a number of pale scars on his dark skin, and his left hand was missing.

Both wore the characteristic leather clothing of the raiders. The axe-thrower wore a tight vest, and her leggings were laced loosely from the knee down for cooling. The man wore a full leather shirt that wrapped in front, held closed by a broad red belt. The shirt had black geometric decorations at the seams and edges. Both wore shoes of soft leather, tied with thongs at the ankle, shoes not intended for much walking.

The two raiders came to within a spearlength of the Arhiia before they halted, despite Kashan's presence. The old man appeared not to even notice the snowtiger, but the axe-thrower eyed him nervously and kept her companion between Kashan and herself. Meeting the man's cool, determined gaze, Ronne was aware of a twinge of recognition. *This one commands.*

Erith was able to communicate more easily with the raider chief, who knew more tradetalk than the axe-thrower. They worked out names: the chief was Un'Varten; the woman with the axes was something unpronounceable meaning "Edge Singing." This they assumed from her running a finger down the edge of an axe, giving a short, sweet trill as she did so. Then the difficulties began.

"Tell them we must leave," said Ronne. The sooner they were away, the better. She did not trust the raiders' intentions. Erith and the two

Windriders exchanged their small mutual vocabulary. She could tell the two Windriders were both startled and offended when they finally understood.

"Fight us, not stay? Kenjah not good fight?" said Un'Varten, gesturing at the Windriders behind him, who were beginning to set up camp.

We fought them, and they want us to stay? Ronne thought for a while, feeling her way towards their reasoning. "The kenjah fight well. But my home and people are in danger and I must go and defend them."

Erith did the best he could with this, and Edge Singing joined in, speaking rapidly in her own tongue to the chief and making the "house" hand sign. Faces intent, they conversed for a brief interval, then Un'Varten asked cautiously, "Ancestor-house? Spear thrown at ancestor-house?"

Ronne nodded, and the faces of both raiders cleared. This seemed to be a sufficient excuse for their rude behavior in wanting to leave. More discussion followed, then a question to the Arhiia.

"They want to know if we will wait until morning. They really seem to want us to stay, and not as prisoners. I wish I knew why," said Erith, with a grimace.

Ronne sighed. "There are enough of them to enforce their will on us, and we cannot outrun them or evade them in the open here. It is beginning to get dark. We may as well stay and see how matters develop."

This answer seemed to please the raiders, and after they were assured Kashan would stay by the Arhiia, the Windriders went back to their encampment. Erith and Ronne set up a firepit near where Tekbeh lay. She had her sling out and a concealed pile of stones close at hand in case the truce broke down. Zeltan left to retrieve the kill Kashan had left on the plain, and soon they all had the comfort of being well fed.

As she ate, Ronne watched the Windriders gather about their fires with a good deal of noise and talk. At the central fire Edge Singing stood and spoke for some time, gesturing as she did so. Ronne couldn't understand what she was saying, but the words had a lyrical beauty that gave them their own weight. The others paid rapt attention to her, and to those who stood and spoke after she had finished.

Beyond their fire Ronne could see the dark, moving shapes of the riding beasts, gathered together for the night. There were many more of them than there were raiders, and she wondered why. Wouldn't one for each be enough? Did they also use them like lenghur, as pack animals?

The chieftain Un'Varten was the last to speak, and although he gave no sign himself, the glances of the others told her he was speaking of the Arhiia. Whatever he said seemed to provoke debate. He heard it with arms folded, firelight playing on his sharp-planed face. Finally he made a sharp gesture that ended the discussion, and spoke in a tone that did not permit argument. That his pronouncement did not please some of the Windriders was clear, but they said no more and soon began to settle down for the night.

What have they decided?

The next morning Erith saw Edge Singing leave the raiders' camp and head for the Arhiia. Her golden eyes were full of excitement. "You go ancestor-house horse, we bring!"

Erith translated, but he didn't understand. Neither did anyone else. "Horss? What is she saying, then?" asked Zeltan.

Edge Singing shook her head in frustration, then tossed her head up so her long crest flew about, pawing at the air with her hands and making a high, drawn-out cry. "Hooorrssse", she said slowly, and pointed to the riding beasts. "You horse, go ancestor-house. Un'Varten say."

Ronne came up beside Erith, facing the slender Windrider. "Ask her why," she said, her voice taut.

When he managed to communicate the question, Edge Singing responded with a torrent of speech that he could not catch the meaning of. Again, she made the flipping-back motion on both sides of her face, looking at Ronne, and then swiftly moved her hand edge on by the front of her crest, her golden eyes bright with merriment.

"*Cha'tral nou maneket va heyt,*" she continued, glancing at Kashan and making a clawing motion with one hand. Then, with the lightest possible touch, she placed the tips of her fingers on Ronne's shoulder. "*Cha'tral,*" she said softly, and pulled two decorated braids free from the long hairs of her crest. Holding the braids in one hand, she pointed to Ronne with the other. "*Cha'tral.*"

Shaking her head at their puzzlement, Edge Singing made a few more stylized hand signs and with one or two words of tradetalk turned away to the horse picket. Erith shrugged when Ronne looked at him.

"She says there is some ritual they must perform north of here, and then they will guide us."

Ronne nodded, her face impassive. "Do they truly talk with their hands?"

"They don't always speak the same language between tribes." He looked at her sidelong. "Are we going with them?"

She was still, and silent as stone. Then she loosed her breath forcefully and nodded. "It is a risk, but a risk we must take. If they wanted us dead, we would be. As long as we are on good terms with them, we can make up any delays by riding the…*horses*, and they will know the terrain better. But we must always be on guard. There is no reason for them to be helping us."

He frowned. "You seem to have special status with them. Something to do with the cutting of the tall one's crest. The fight before that was amazing too. I've never seen that technique. Can you teach me?"

"It can't be taught. And the less you know of it the happier I will be," she said harshly, and walked away.

Erith blinked in surprise. He hadn't seen her so angry since he had first appeared at the outpost. He remembered her face after the fight with the Windriders—she had been desperate, terrified. Of what? He doubted she was frightened by the kenjah. Not when she could fight as she did. So what had she been afraid of? *I will find out, even if she won't tell me—and destroy it.*

Edge Singing was arguing with some of the raiders at the picket line, but eventually they stepped away, pulling horses. More argument, and they brought leather pads and fastened them to the horses' backs. The horses were brought to where they stood.

The lanky boy who brought Erith his horse was expressionless, but the tall warrior with half his crest missing seemed distinctly surly as he brought a snorting grey to Ronne. Erith frowned. The warrior was Ronne's last opponent. The horse he had brought her, a grey-colored beast, seemed half-wild and unpredictable, difficult to control. He looked for Edge Singing, to see if she could find a better one for Ronne.

Ronne studied the arrangement of the leather pad and attached loops, then approached the horse with determination. All seemed well when she put weight on the mounting loop, grasping the edge of the pad to pull herself up, but then the tall warrior dropped the reins and gave the beast a vicious slap.

The grey reared with a snort and leaped ahead, thundering across the plain with a flash of speed. Erith's heart clenched with fear, and he tried desperately to think of some way to save her. A startled shout came from the rest of the Windriders. *Where is she…don't fall, Ronne!*

He could see her dark head against the grey, one leg just across the back of her horse. Slowly, slowly she pulled herself up and over. His knees felt weak, and he leaned against his own, more placid, mount. Some of the band had mounted hastily and were pursuing, but the grey was swift. He could no longer see her, she had gone so far.

It seemed to take an eternity for Erith to clamber up on his own horse, planning to go after Ronne. He had no idea how to make the beast move as he wished, or how to stop hers if he found her. Then came the thunder of approaching hooves, and she returned. Her dark braids flew in the wind, and she was *laughing*, arms spread wide and joy in her face. Erith felt his jaw sag. Had he ever seen her laugh before?

The warrior who had brought her mount stood near the horse lines, astonishment in his eyes. Ronne saw him, and the grey turned without hesitation. *Now how in the name of the Dark Woman did she do that?*

The warrior turned and ran, but Ronne caught up with him. As she passed, Ronne bent and dealt him a blow with her fist that knocked him sprawling.

92

CHAPTER 11

Ronne did not need Erith's translation to know that the Windriders were embarrassed and ashamed. Edge Singing was incapable of looking her in the eye when she rode back to the campfire, where an intense discussion was underway between Un'Varten and several of the raiders.

They brought the culprit to her when they saw her approach. Ronne was still filled with a sense of exhilaration after her wild ride. *It* was *like riding the wind. A wind I could control.* But how had she controlled it? How had her horse known where she wanted to go? It was not cooperative at the beginning, but somehow that had changed. While she was riding, communication was instinctive and complete.

Still in a benign mood, she looked down at the group of Windriders and waited for them to speak. It took some effort, but what they finally communicated surprised her. They wanted her judgment on the raider who had caused the incident. Un'Varten let it be known that among the kenjah, such dishonorable behavior—and rudeness to a guest—could be punishable by death. Ronne was not sure which offense they considered worse.

With courtesy the equal of a Linariach ambassador, he asked her if she would choose a suitable punishment since her customs might be different than theirs. Looking down at the rigid face of the captive raider, she shrugged inwardly and decided on leniency, to improve relations with the Windriders.

"There was no harm done, so I see no need for his death." She considered a moment. "If one of my people had done such a thing, I would dismiss them."

By now Erith had joined the group. When he translated what she had said there was confusion among the Windriders.

"Dismiss?" asked Un'Varten.

"Tell them to go. No longer one of the group," said Erith helpfully.

Edge Singing looked up, eyes glowing. *"Taraak!"* she cried, and the other raiders echoed her with enthusiasm. The raider being held struggled fiercely but to no avail as the others shoved him to the ground and held him down.

Shocked, Ronne glanced at Erith for an explanation, but he appeared equally astonished at the sudden violent turn of events. Edge Singing knelt by the man's head, holding a short knife of lustrous black stone. She pulled out a braided strand from his crest, decorated with beads and ornaments, and with one decisive movement she cut it free.

The captive went limp and made no further effort to escape. The other raiders hacked the remainder of the man's crest short until the hair on his head was one uniform length. Edge Singing paused only to give a stunned Ronne the decorated braid before mounting her own horse with the rest.

The kenjah sped away with the Arhiia in their midst. Looking back, Ronne could see a huddled figure alone on the plain, surrounded by severed strands of long black hair.

It amazed Erith how fast they traveled. He found it safer not to look down and see exactly how fast, since he was no better than any of the Arhiia at riding. The increase in speed had a price, however, as he discovered when he dismounted that night. Erith had to bite his lip hard to keep from crying out. From their stiff movements, he could tell the others were also sore. Tekbeh, who had been forced to ride sideways behind Zeltan because of her wound, could not even dismount by herself and had to be carried to the campfire.

Their fire had been placed away from the main body of the Windriders, so Kashan would not disturb them. The snowtiger had followed them, seeming pleased that they had picked up the pace, going off on his own occasionally and then reappearing. All of the horses save Ronne's grey still were quite frightened by him, and to keep the peace she had to ride some distance from the main group when Kashan was with them.

Erith frowned, remembering. The Windriders hadn't gone near Ronne even when Kashan was not there. They treated her with a combination of respect and awe, and a trace of fear. He couldn't understand why. Ronne had fought fiercely, but most of the credit for their defense had to go to Kashan.

He shrugged and pulled his travelsack free as one of the raiders came to collect his horse. He took his burden to where the Arhiia were setting up, glancing about the plain and grimacing at the lack of visible firewood. The nearest brush was in a gully some distance away. He would have to cover a wide area to find enough for the night, and it hurt to move at all.

He hefted his travelsack thoughtfully. He had been thinking about the mysterious gifts from the underground hall, wondering what they were and why the voices had given them to him. What if they could help? He knelt and opened the sack to search through the contents.

Ronne turned the long braid over in her hand, fingering the ornaments woven into it, and decided it was a kind of honor lock. In the earliest days of the Empire, the warriors of noble family had something similar. The traditional Northern families, including her own, still wore their hair braided to wear the gold won in battle. Now that she knew what to look for, she could see that all the Windriders had the honor lock. Edge Singing had two.

Ronne frowned. Did they think her braids meant she was that much better, even if she no longer wore gold in them? She drew in a sharp breath as she understood the meaning of another puzzle. The long tassels that hung from the raiders' belts were trophies, each strand taken from someone who would die before giving it up. She looked again at the braid she held and realized she had witnessed a killing, even though the victim still lived.

Just as she was wondering why the Windriders seemed so enthusiastic in exacting their punishment, Erith approached, walking jauntily.

"I found out what one of the jars from the hill is for," he said in greeting. "Here, try it! It makes all the soreness go away."

Ronne took the jar and examined the contents. A translucent white salve filled the container. It had a sharp but pleasant scent. "How did you know what this would do? It could just as easily have killed you, for all we know of it."

His ebullient expression faded, and he looked away. "It…just felt right."

Ronne gazed at him, wondering. "Just as my knee felt wrong? And Tekbeh's leg? That wound was going to kill her, did you realize that?"

He struggled to speak, then gave up and just nodded. Without another word, Ronne rose stiffly and walked out into the darkness with the jar. When she returned she made the other Arhiia use it as well. Tekbeh had to be helped, which did not improve her temper.

When they gathered again, Ronne announced her intention of visiting the Windrider campfire. "It will be a courtesy. And we need to know more about them."

"I will go with you," said Erith. He did not seem pleased with the plan. She had noticed how ill at ease he was around the kenjah, which was another factor in her decision.

"No, I wish you to stay here."

Now he looked surprised and a little annoyed. "How courteous is it to go and say nothing, understand nothing?"

She turned to him, feeling impatient. "How courteous would it be if Kashan decided to visit too? You are the only one besides myself who can do anything with him. Part of the trading talk is derived from the language of the plains, so it is not entirely futile."

He reddened. Glancing at the Windrider camp, he said, "They have never mentioned we killed three of them and wounded several more. They can't have forgotten; how can you just sit there as if nothing happened?"

"You aren't the only one who noticed that," Tekbeh said sourly. "It won't make a damn bit of difference where we are if they all decide to kill us. But then," she continued, "when that one got his first taste of the haircut, they all laughed at him. Maybe…maybe they fight just for themselves, and not for each other. Maybe they don't care we killed 'em."

When she joined the kenjah, Ronne was convinced Tekbeh was correct. If anything, the deaths of their comrades seemed to have raised the status of the Arhiia, and she saw others who had been wounded boasting to those who had come after the fight had ended. The mood was almost jovial, the conversations noisy and animated.

She looked around the fire and caught a glimpse of the corpse next to her. Only iron discipline kept her from shifting away from it. Her seat was clearly a place of honor, but the bowls of burning incense were not enough to disguise that the body had been dead for some time.

She wondered why the dead woman was being treated in this manner. The raiders the Arhiia had killed had been left on the plains in shallow pits, with no ceremony. For this person, a crude attempt at embalming had been performed. The legs were drawn up with the arms wrapped around them, and the whole tied together with thongs.

The Windriders had insisted she sit beside the body when she joined them. This displaced Edge Singing, who then sat behind her and attempted to translate. On the other side of the mummified corpse sat Un'Varten. Ronne was offered a very potent beverage from a skin bag. It was tart and slightly thick, and it made her eyes water. They also shared an unidentified delicacy that crunched in a disturbing way and did not sit well in her stomach. It tasted salty, with a bitter edge. Ronne sent a silent and heartfelt prayer to the Face of Justice that she not die from being polite.

Edge Singing stirred beside her. "*Ohiye,*" she said, pointing to the body. "Say you come, say *Cha'tral.*"

Ronne digested this. The woman must have already been dead when she had left the outpost. How could she have seen them? "Why don't you bury her, like the others?" She mimicked digging a pit, laying something in it.

Edge Singing looked shocked. "She *ohiye!* She big magic, eh? Put high place, spirit place." She pointed north, the direction they were traveling. Then Edge Singing began to ask careful questions. Why was Ronne so far from home? Was she kenjah like them? Did her family decide to take her back? Without Erith's help it took much longer to reach understanding, but Edge Singing was persistent.

Determined questioning on her part let Ronne begin to build a vague picture of what "kenjah" meant; not a nation or a tribe, but a status. All the raiders had been cast out of their original tribes or had left on their own.

Speaking softly, Edge Singing managed to convey that Un'Varten had been a chief of one of those tribes until he had lost his hand in battle. This somehow disqualified him, and rather than stay with another as chief he had left and become leader of the kenjah. This group of raiders was different from the others because of it.

"Kenjah out there, they *taraak*," she said darkly. "No honor good fight, just kill. Trade taken people for red cloth."

Perhaps we were fortunate after all, thought Ronne.

A number of subtle differences were apparent when they continued traveling the next day. Erith approached his mount with some trepidation, but the salve seemed to have a permanent effect. His muscles were stiff, but the excruciating pain did not return then or anytime thereafter.

Ronne's visit to the kenjah campfire had apparently broken down any barrier between the groups. Erith was surprised to see some of the raiders joining them when Kashan was not nearby, sometimes attempting to talk with the Arhiia or simply riding with them in companionable silence. Edge Singing stayed with them for the greater part of the day, and she, Ronne, and Erith struggled to converse.

Another kenjah stayed almost as long as she, but he never spoke. He just stared at them when he thought no one else was looking. Erith was almost certain he was staring at Tekbeh, and he searched his memory for any reason this particular rider would be following her, but could find nothing. He had not been involved in the fighting; he'd come with the second, larger group of kenjah.

When they stopped for the night, Erith saw the same raider in the group closest to the Arhiia's fire. His gaze never left them.

CHAPTER 12

"There *ohiye* place," said Edge Singing, pointing. A lone mountain reflected the rosy morning light as it towered over the plain. Erith stared at it as they rode on. It seemed strange, standing isolated from the mountain range behind it. The peak was almost perfectly symmetrical.

"We come this day?" he asked.

"Yeh."

He turned and passed the information on to Ronne, knowing it would be well-received. They had been traveling for five days now, and she was getting impatient.

His horse stumbled, and he struggled to keep his balance. One of the Windriders gave him an admonishing glance, and pointed to the ground, then his reins. There was still a faint clear trail visible, but the ground beside it was rocky and uneven. He concentrated on guiding his mount. A fall here would be much more painful than on the plain.

As they entered the foothills, the trail became steep and harder to negotiate. His legs began to ache with the effort of staying on his horse. Erith noticed the vegetation getting more sparse and then disappearing altogether as they approached the mountain. The ground was covered with dust and strange reddish stones full of small holes.

Erith saw the trail snaking up the steep slope of the mountain and groaned. He could never manage that. His horse was tired just from the distance they had come; he knew his size was a burden. But the kenjah did not continue up the trail. Instead, they turned off to a wide area at the base of the slope and dismounted.

He was glad to follow suit, and Ronne and the two Arhiia soldiers were, also.

"Are we stopping, then?" asked Zeltan, stretching stiffly.

"They're putting up the rope lines they tie the horses to," said Erith. "If we're going on, we are going on foot."

To one side of the flat area was a large, evil-smelling pool with white and yellow encrustations around the edge. Steam rose from the water's surface. After setting up the pickets for the horses, the Windriders began to take off their gear and clothing.

"They aren't going to make us walk up the mountain like that, are they?" Tekbeh asked, horrified.

"They are bathing in the pool," said Ronne.

Erith winced. The water must have been hot, but the kenjah made no complaint. He glanced at the pool, then quickly looked away. They also had no objections to men and women bathing together, it seemed. From the edge of his vision he saw kenjah returning, and gathering in groups. They had donned their clothing again and were marking their faces and hands with red paint. They did not speak, and their mood was solemn.

No one had indicated the Arhiia should also go through the ritual. When all of them had bathed, two of the kenjah took the wrapped mummy of the sibyl and carried it tenderly up the mountain slope, and the rest followed. When Erith stood, wondering if they should go as well, Edge Singing held up her hand to stop him.

"It's just for them," he said, relieved. It was good to rest, especially after the grueling ride.

"How I will live quietly back home I cannot imagine," said Zeltan, after a while. "I am accustomed to a new marvel every day."

Erith grinned. "Now you know how I felt at first, with everything strange and different." It was very quiet now that the kenjah had gone. He ran his hand idly through the gravel where he sat. A sharp pain lanced through his fingertips, and he jerked his hand back with a stifled curse.

The tips of his fingers were cut by a single line; small beads of blood formed along it. Digging carefully, he uncovered a shard of glassy black stone with a fractured edge.

"That looks like the stuff in their weapons," said Tekbeh, interested.

"It feels like it as well," groused Erith.

"There is a great deal of it here," Ronne commented, standing at the base of a hillock on the far side of the pool. They found that almost the entire pile consisted of shards, some so thin they were transparent. Erith also found evidence of work on the stone: broken knives and arrowheads, a discarded axe handle that had split.

Erith's interest soon waned, and he wondered how much longer the kenjah would be away. Tekbeh was restless, wandering around the pool, finding interesting bits of the black stone. Although she still limped, it did not prevent her from making her way to the far side of the small valley and beyond.

"Her wound is healing with miraculous speed," said Ronne, giving him a thoughtful glance. "I would not have thought she would be walking so soon."

Erith shrugged, not knowing how to respond. "All I did was check it, to be sure it wasn't infected," he said after a moment. He knew Ronne was right. Tekbeh's leg shouldn't have healed so quickly, especially since they had been riding hard all this time. But what had he done to help?

When Tekbeh returned, she brought something with her. "This one's a different color," she said, holding the shard up for them to see. "All the others are black, but this one is green, with yellow bits."

The first of the returning Windriders came into view as Erith and the others examined her find. The kenjah who had been grave and silent now talked and laughed among themselves.

"Take you ancestor-house now," said Edge Singing with her characteristic brilliant smile, coming up to the group of Arhiia to see what was going on. When Edge Singing saw what Tekbeh was holding, her jaw sagged in surprise. She fired a rapid spate of her own tongue at Tekbeh, who just shook her head in bewilderment. "Where you get? *Ch'o tre*...is stone for magic. How you find?"

Erith translated, and Tekbeh pointed to a knoll down past the spring.

"Are they angry?" she asked Erith.

"I don't think so," he replied cautiously as the Windriders went off with great excitement. He didn't understand why they hadn't known about the green stone—unless they had not come here before.

Tekbeh was left holding the shard and looking puzzled. She glanced about and saw the raider who often rode with the Arhiia without saying a word.

"Here, you want this?"

His hand extended reflexively at her offering gesture, and she dropped the stone in his open hand and turned away. Erith saw the raider stare at her as she limped back to the Arhiia, an unreadable expression on his face. Why was he always watching her? Erith wondered if he should warn Tekbeh.

After a while the other raiders came trooping back, a few lucky ones carrying some of the green stone. As they went to the horses, one of them noticed the man holding Tekbeh's stone and spoke to him, gesturing as if he should go get more. The other frowned, speaking one word in an emphatic, determined voice, and then put the stone in a small leather bag that hung about his neck.

Erith was astonished. He had begun to wonder if the man was unable to speak at all, and judging from their expressions, the other Windriders were also surprised. One said something that made the others laugh, and they pulled their crests at the quiet rider, pointing toward the group of Arhiia. *Something to do with us, or what Tekbeh did*, Erith guessed. *But they don't seem angry*. The other kenjah were teasing their comrade, he realized, and a glimmering of understanding flickered through his mind. He grinned to himself, imagining the reaction when the object of the Windrider's interest figured it out herself.

The kenjah that split off from the main group consisted of five in all, including Edge Singing and the quiet man who often rode near them, whose name was Kemar'sto.

The farewells between Un'Varten and Ronne were brief but sincere. She gave him a long dagger from their meager belongings, and Erith knew that any weapon of metal would be greatly treasured by people using stone weapons. Un'Varten, in turn, gifted the Arhiia with the mounts they rode.

"Is merit, fight honored one. Better merit, fight beside honored one," he said, just before they left the main camp. "We meet more, fight beside you."

Ronne thought about Un'Varten's parting words as they set out for the distant range of hills to the southwest, towards what she hoped would be the other side of the Arhii mountains. She had wondered about the kenjah's callous disregard of their comrades' deaths. But to these people, outcast and landless, honor and glory were all they had, and personal bravery the only wealth.

They bore the Arhiia no ill will for killing their attackers; the kenjah would have done the same in their place. Indeed, they seemed to think fighting with her was a great honor. Was it just Kashan, or was it also the Pathwalking? If so, she could no longer say her curse brought no good. But much was still owed in the balance. *It was the Pathwalking that caught Talorgen's eye—he thought the evil like his own.*

They found a notch in the foothills carved by a rushing, ice-cold stream two days after leaving the kenjah. They followed it to the crest of the ridge, and as they descended, Zeltan shouted, "Smoke! In the valley, down the way!"

Ronne urged her horse to greater speed, conscious of a feeling of anticipation. If only this proved to be Imperial territory! With the aid of the horses she was confident she could get to Keris Kera before Talorgen and his troops. Kashan bounded ahead for a while, then darted off into the underbrush on some urgent mission of his own.

By afternoon they had reached the valley floor and were heading towards the center, where the smoke had been. Suddenly Zeltan reined in. "Is it likely that every house did their baking today, and burned it all?"

Ronne and the others stopped, too. There was black smoke where he pointed, more than should come from any village, and the smell of burning was strong.

Ronne frowned, looking down through the forest. A pale, huddled lump was visible not far away. The trees were spaced widely enough that she could ride away from the path, so she went closer. The lump proved to be the body of a young man, dressed like a farm laborer in a light-colored smock. He had been cruelly hacked with a sword, so deeply that his head was almost severed from his body.

Why? She stared at the body in disbelief. The man's eyes were still open, his face frozen in an expression of terror. Why would anyone want to kill a simple farmer in such a manner?

She drew her sword, and the other Arhiia followed her lead. The man was far from his village; most likely he had been running away from whoever killed him. "Tell them to be ready to fight," she told Erith, nodding at the Windriders. She saw their eyes brighten when he relayed her instructions, and they strung their bows and hung their spears ready to hand.

She led the way as they continued cautiously towards the source of the smoke. She saw another body, this one an old woman. Her staff was still clenched in a gnarled hand, and she lay in a pool of blood.

A sudden noise from the forest made them start, and Zeltan cursed. The kenjah nocked arrows and turned their horses to face the threat. More thrashing, and a wounded lenghur stumbled out of the underbrush. Its flanks were heaving, eyes wide with fright. It fell, then struggled to its feet again and fled.

This is insanity. Face of Mercy, what is happening here? She saw a road through the trees, in the direction of the village. As they followed it, bodies became more numerous, and Ronne felt a cold, growing anger. All appeared to have been fleeing the destruction, and had been killed regardless of age or condition.

"What has happened?" Erith said, in a voice barely above a whisper. "Is this…are we in Arhi now?"

"We are in the Empire. But this is not what I expected to find. I have never, in any field of battle, seen this kind of abomination," Ronne replied through clenched teeth.

A group of bodies partly blocked the road ahead. When she was close enough to identify them she had to close her eyes to try to contain her fury. Several children were grouped around the body of a powerfully-built man, evidently a smith from his leather apron and the heavy hammer still in his hand.

She leaned closer. There was blood and matted hair on the hammer. The smith had fought back, defending the defenseless, and the murderers had not escaped unharmed. She felt a stab of red-hot joy, all too brief. *So you took some with you into darkness. It is well.*

Fumbling for her almost-empty purse, she managed to open it one-handed and take out a half-telat coin. It was small, but it was the only gold she had to give. "Honor given for honor earned," she said in High Speech, and tossed the coin on the smith's battered body.

Slowly, she raised her sword above her head in witnessing, and just as slowly lowered it. "What the eye sees may not be concealed!" she said, hearing raw emotion in her voice. Beside her, Zeltan wiped tears from his eyes with the heel of his hand, and Erith and Tekbeh looked on in horror and shock. The faces of the kenjah looked as if carved from black stone. She rode on.

When Ronne reached the village she discovered the source of the smoke —it had been torched. The carnage was even greater here, and she began to fear there had been no survivors. The destruction was thorough; only one house was even partly intact.

She felt a light rain on her face, and frowned at the grey sky.

"It will be a storm shortly," said Zeltan. "Shelter would be good to have, even though there's little there," he continued, nodding towards the house.

It was an ordinary enough structure from the outside, but better built than the usual peasant hut. The owners had been wealthy enough to build a rough stone foundation, and stonework continued halfway up the walls. Even the roof was not completely destroyed, as the burned section had collapsed into the house interior. Ronne doubted there would be room enough for all, but it was better than nothing.

Erith was the first to enter, sword in hand. His recoil was so sharp and sudden that Ronne, following him, slammed into his back. "Son of the Dark Woman!" he cursed, lapsing into the tongue of the plains in his shock. Ronne stiffened when she saw what had caused his reaction. She moved him aside and stepped carefully into the house.

Blood was everywhere: soaked into the dirt floor, spattered on the walls, and the sharp, metallic smell was overpowering. Three bloody human skeletons were left behind—two tossed in heaps on the floor, one lying on a rough wood table. They were fresh; blood still gleamed red and wet on the bones, and they had been picked so clean only small shreds of flesh still remained. It could not have been many hours since the people had been alive.

A mark on a skull caught her attention, and she tilted it with the tip of her sword to put it in better light. She tasted bile in the back of her throat and swallowed convulsively. The skull had been chewed on by something with many small, sharp teeth.

When Ronne emerged from the house, Erith could tell she was shaken. "We will find shelter elsewhere."

Erith had already mounted his horse, and none of the others showed any inclination to argue. They had seen enough of what was inside. Following Ronne, Erith rode out away from town in the increasing drizzle.

He was alert and ready for any attack, but none came. He wasn't sure what he was looking for. Nothing human had killed the people in the house, ripping the flesh from their bones. Still, he kept seeing the skeleton lying on the table. As if it were a meal.

He peered through the rain, trying to see if any shelter was ahead. Something on the edge of his vision caught his attention, and he stood up a little in his stirrups to get a better view. "There's something on that hill."

Edge Singing cocked her head at this, and she swung her legs up and under her, rising gracefully to stand on the back of her patient mount.

"Yeh! Is house, maybe. No fire," she reported after staring in the direction Erith had indicated. She resumed her seat with a subdued comment in her own language.

"She says only walls keep out evil spirits," translated Erith when Ronne looked at him in question. "Shall we try it?"

"Yes. It is hard enough to see that it may have escaped the destruction."

It was getting dark, and Erith agreed completely with Edge Singing's desire for walls. He was relieved to see the house was still intact, at least from the outside. It was curiously constructed of large timbers that still bore their original bark in places, so even when they were quite close the house blended with the forest.

No lights shone, no sign that anyone lived there. They dismounted silently and approached the door. Erith eased it open and glanced inside. No scene of butchery met his gaze, just a clean, ordinary room with simple but sturdy furniture. It appeared unoccupied.

He entered, and Ronne followed him in. She looked about, then nodded silently at the stair in one corner. It led to a sleeping area under the roof, which was also empty. Erith descended the stairs again. They were steep, and he put a hand on the stone chimney running beside them to steady himself.

"It's warm," he said, surprised. "Someone had a fire going here not too long ago."

"Did they escape, then, or were they killed with the rest?" wondered Zeltan.

"They are not here now, and it is nearly dark. We will have to stay here, and like the kenjah I will feel better to have walls between me and whatever walks the night here." Ronne pulled the tiny attic window shut and latched it.

"There's a cattle-shed, looks like," called Tekbeh up the stairs. "We could put the horses there. Don't want them killed either."

"A good plan. But we will check it first," said Ronne.

Erith followed her through the increasing rain to the rough structure, and they pulled the big door open. Only various farming implements were visible in the gloom.

"Zeltan! Bring a light from the fire!" Ronne took a step inside.

Erith heard the faint sound of something descending rapidly, and he shouted a warning. Ronne struck instinctively, and with blinding speed. Erith heard a resounding crack of breaking wood.

"Agh! Not the shovel!" said a male voice in an aggravated tone.

A tall, lanky body lunged from the shadows with a broken wooden handle, only to be stopped cold by a rake that suddenly rose up and struck him on the head when he stepped on it. The man fell in a welter of tools, rope, and clay jars. He struggled up with much flailing of arms and legs and confronted Ronne again. "G-go away."

He trembled with fear, but he still held the broken handle in a determined grip. Erith thought about taking it away from him, then decided against it. The man was no threat to anyone but himself.

"We have no intention of harming you. There has been altogether too much of that here." Ronne stepped back from the doorway and lowered her sword.

The man, a shock of ragged white hair falling into his unusually pale face, looked at her in glowering disbelief. "They were Imperial soldiers, too! Supposed to protect us! Not hunt us down, and…kill, and…." There were tears on his face.

Imperial soldiers. Erith glanced at Ronne, and saw the surprise he felt reflected in her expression.

"We had nothing to do with that horrible slaughter," Ronne replied, her face grim. "Tell me who they were, and I will give you justice."

The pale man hesitated, doubt in his eyes. A soft voice spoke from the darkness. "Duanoch, she is good."

A slight figure came towards them, one hand against the shed wall, the other held out before her. Erith barely repressed a gasp when the girl turned her face to them. He had never seen anyone so pale. Her skin was whiter than the man's, her hair pure white with the faintest wash of gold. Even her eyes were one expanse of sightless, opaque white.

For all that she was blind, she turned to face the Arhiia and took a step toward them. This was too much for the man. "Bryddhe, get back! How can you possibly know what they are?"

"I know," she said quietly, but with a certain dignity. The girl approached Ronne and held her hands out as if she were warming them at a fire. "You are so very bright."

And what does that mean? wondered Erith.

"I am Ronne tes Arhi, and these are my armed and the kenjah, who travel with us. We came to this place to take advantage of your walls, not tear them down. We will protect you with all we have. Does this satisfy you?"

The tall man put his arms around the girl, trying to draw her away. He looked up, and Erith was surprised at how young his face was.

"Don't let them touch my sister," he said, his voice breaking.

"We will not permit them to harm either of you."

At this point Tekbeh arrived with a lamp from the house, and Erith was able to see more of the interior. The shed had not been used for its original purpose for some time. It had been taken over by a collection of tools, pots, and strange contraptions spread over several narrow benches. A hole in the roof had been cut crudely for a small forge.

"How are all the horses to be fitting in here, then?" asked Zeltan, doubting.

"It'll be tight, but consider the options," Tekbeh said dryly. She headed out the door to start bringing them in.

"Horses?" said Duanoch, "what is this?"

Ronne looked back over her shoulder. "An animal to ride on. The kenjah have them. Come and see."

"Kenjah?"

Erith watched curiosity war with fear in Duanoch's face, and curiosity won. Still holding his sister, he made his way cautiously out of the shed. His eyes got very big and his mouth opened in surprise when he saw them. All but the nearest were obscured by the rain and the failing light, and the dark-skinned kenjah were almost invisible in the dark.

"How can you ride them? They are so big…do they bite?" He reached out to touch the nearest one, Ronne's grey. A delighted smile grew on his face, and he stroked the beast softly.

Bryddhe, encouraged by her brother, put out a hand to feel the marvelous creature. Duanoch patted the horse's shoulder, just as Kemar'sto emerged on the other side.

"Aaah!"

They both yelled in surprise, and it was hard to tell who was more startled by the other.

"What's that!"

"One of the kenjah," said Tekbeh over her shoulder as she led two horses through the doorway.

Erith, with assistance from Edge Singing, tried to convince Kemar'sto that the supernaturally pale person was an ordinary man. "Not warrior!" he said, pointing to the broken handle Duanoch still held. Then he gestured to his tunic. "No blood! Not kill down there."

Neither was entirely convinced at first. Then Tekbeh came for Kemar'sto's horse, and Kemar'sto suddenly transformed from a stone-faced warrior to a man completely fascinated by his footwear. Erith grinned at Duanoch's expression of astonishment. Then he saw Kemar'sto watch with approval as Duanoch gently guided his sister through the crowded, muddy yard to the house. They both seemed less apprehensive after that.

It was not long before the horses were safely installed in the shed, along with Zeltan and three of the kenjah to guard them. Erith was glad to return to the house, and to bar the door shut against the night.

Duanoch built up the fire, and then rummaged around for bedding. Descending from the attic with an armload of blankets, he tripped and fell down the stairs with a crash. Erith was surprised by Bryddhe's calm reaction once it was clear Duanoch had not hurt himself; the blankets had softened his fall, and Erith realized it had probably happened many times before.

"What *alar* is this?" asked Ronne as they ate.

"Oguz. We're on the very eastern edge."

"Have you heard the Empire was at war, and Ynduria destroyed?"

"No." Duanoch's expression was one of complete shock. "It's rare that news gets here, and I don't go down the hill much. Not many talk to me when I do. Our mother…some said she was cursed, with white hair. They think we're unlucky too."

Ronne looked at him intently. "Who did it?"

Duanoch's cheerful face fell. He seemed to trust the Arhiia, but the horror of what had happened in the valley had not left him. "It was Imperials. I saw them."

"But they did not see you."

"N-no. I was fishing under the bridge early this morning. They came in over the bridge, and their commander was yelling at them. Saying they had let his enemy escape because they were afraid, and how they were worthless and an insult to his greatness, and did they remember what happened to the last troop. And then," he continued, his expression puzzled, "his voice changed, and he spoke gently, and soft, and said they were right to be afraid, because his enemy was evil, and consorted with barbarians, and probably had destroyed the Imperial city. And that her whole family was evil, and that was why their swords were dark—the evil showed that way. Then he told them to go and find his enemy, and he knew she was here because of a dream. When they left, I decided to go back to Bryddhe, because it sounded like there would be trouble, and if they came to the house they would frighten her. So I went by the hill trail, which goes by Mardah's farm. I thought I would stop and warn her, too. But before I got there, I heard…screams."

He swallowed, and his eyes brimmed with tears. "I saw them. I hid behind a tree, and I saw them. They had Mardah, and her son, and they were asking her something, and she was screaming, 'I don't know! She isn't here!' And then they took her son, and…and Mardah screamed again, and she grabbed the one who did it around the neck, and even when they killed her she didn't let go. I think he died," he said softly, tears coursing down his cheeks. "And…and then I ran. I hid, when I saw them, and ran. Everywhere, they were killing, and killing…. When I got home I put the fire out in the house, and the forge, to make it look like we weren't here, and I took Bryddhe and hid in the shed. When you came in, I thought you were one of them."

As Duanoch's tale progressed, Erith saw Ronne's face go hard as stone. When he finished, she sat immobile, and neither Erith nor Tekbeh dared speak. Edge Singing, seated at the table with them, seemed to sense the great tension in the air and likewise stayed silent.

"It is too much," Ronne said finally, her voice breaking with emotion. "How many deaths must I make an accounting for? How can I ever cleanse my name of this? I will make an end to it even if they burn me when I die!" She got up to leave, a white-hot fury in her eyes.

Erith lunged across the table and grabbed her arm. "Do, and you give him what he wants!"

She jerked her arm free and snarled at him. "You dare stop me?"

"Yes, I dare! What makes you think he will be any different when you're dead? He's mad! So are you, to think you by yourself, or even with all of us, can take on an army. When he kills you, who will defend your home? You remember, the home you said you cared about!"

"You go much too far," she said softly, her eyes narrowed. "If I strike the head from the body, the body dies. Is his army as mad as he? I could prevent all further deaths by one decisive action. He is mad, as you say— and madmen are not cautious. I could reach and destroy him."

Tekbeh coughed. "Sardis is with him," she said.

Ronne whirled from the table and strode to the fire, looking down at it with a stormy expression on her face. "How do you know this?"

"Saw one of her people at the inn. Took me a while to remember where I saw him last."

Ronne sighed, and the tension left her body. When she turned back to the table, her face was sad and tired. "She will have all the caution he lacks," she acknowledged. "Damn her Faceless."

"You know who did this," said Duanoch, his eyes wide.

Ronne looked at him. "His name is Talorgen. And I," she continued, drawing her night-dark sword and showing it to him, "am his enemy."

CHAPTER 13

Erith had difficulty falling asleep that night. The rain had turned into a storm that lashed and wailed outside, and they were all on edge, Ronne especially so. He woke from an uneasy doze to find her still watching the fire and fingering the silver dagger she had been given by those under the hill. He began to imagine it was singing to her in a high, whispery voice, like wind in dry grass. As he drifted back to sleep he began to think he could understand what it was saying.

He woke to find Ronne shaking his shoulder. "Get the others. We must leave."

The fire had died down, and through the window he could see the sky just beginning to get light. Morning. He shook his head blearily. "Wha…? Why now?" His brief sleep had not rested him at all.

"He's coming. Talorgen," said Ronne, and held up the silver dagger. Erith could hear it now, the beginnings of an angry buzz. "In that house in the valley, I felt it hum, just like this. It faded…but now it has come back. Stronger," said Ronne. A trace of puzzlement showed in her eyes as she stared at the frost-white dagger. "How I can be so certain it is him—but I am certain. And since it is too dangerous to confront him now," she added bitterly, "we must leave."

The thought that Talorgen was responsible for the ghastly skeletons they had found did not surprise him, somehow. From what he had seen, Talorgen was capable of that, and much worse. But why? What could Talorgen possibly hope to gain from it?

Zeltan was testy when he responded to Erith's urgent pounding on the shed door. "Ronne says Talorgen is coming back," Erith said, leaving out the source of the information. The Arhiia still were suspicious of anything magical. The kenjah, once they understood the danger, moved like lightning to ready the horses.

When he returned to the house, he found Ronne confronting a sleepy and terrified brother and sister.

"We must leave, and you must leave with us if you want to live," she said with obvious restraint. "He will know I have been here, and you will not be able to hide from him. If we found your house, he will too."

"But—but where are you going? This is our home. How can we just leave?"

"There is nothing left for you here," Ronne replied. "We are going to Arhi, to the city of Keris Kera. You will be safe there if nowhere else. I will provide for you, since you have lost what you have because of me. Now go! We leave as soon as the horses are ready. Take nothing more than you can carry in your arms."

She turned to Erith. "We will have to divide the supplies on the extra horse so they can ride it. Will you tell the kenjah? The load must be divided among us."

"They have split everything already. They said that's what they do in great danger, so the loss of one does not lose all."

Ronne nodded. "Very wise. We could have much worse allies in this." She was silent for a while, then continued, "Have you seen any sign of Kashan?"

He could only shake his head. He knew what she feared—this danger might be more than even Kashan could survive.

The sky was pale with the approach of dawn, but the sun had not yet risen as they rode out in the morning chill. Erith peered into the gloom, searching for any sign of danger but finding nothing. No sound disturbed the silence.

The Arhiia were comfortable with riding now, but Kemar'sto had to tie the reins of Bryddhe and Duanoch's horse to his own. Duanoch gripped the saddle tightly with one hand and held his sister close.

Ronne rode in front, the silver dagger tied to her wrist with a thong. She led them down into the valley as fast as they could go, heading for the gap in the mountains. The huddled bodies of the villagers were dark shadows on the ground as they passed by, reminding Erith of the danger that threatened them.

When they reached the crest he looked back. On the hill beside the valley they had left, where the house had been hidden, a new plume of dark smoke rose. He managed to get Ronne's attention without alerting Duanoch, and pointed to the smoke.

She gave a nod of comprehension but said nothing. She looked worried. Erith was surprised at how quickly Talorgen had found the house. They had escaped just in time. Did Talorgen have some way of sensing them, like they did for him? He urged his horse to greater speed.

They rushed through the ravine and back to the plain. The grim, driven expression on Ronne's face lightened a fraction when Zeltan spotted a black-and-white shape running through the brush beside them. Once on open ground, Kashan sped ahead, ears back.

When they left the gap, Ronne headed north along a narrow valley between two mountain ridges. He knew it must be intensely frustrating to her, to have to retreat and lose the progress they had made towards her goal. They had the advantage of speed now, and if they could outdistance Talorgen, they would be able to cut across safely.

Duanoch looked very agitated, and tried to draw Erith's attention to something, pointing to the underbrush where the snowtiger ran beside them. Erith realized none of them had warned him about Kashan. Duanoch was completely unsettled by the snowtiger's appearance, and if he had had any control over his horse at all he would have headed in the opposite direction.

"He's ours. He'll help protect us," said Erith. Duanoch was not reassured, and clutched his sister protectively. Feeling sorry for him, Erith rode beside their horse and talked with him as the pace permitted, distracting him and blocking his view of Kashan.

Ronne called a halt late in the evening, when even moonlight did not let them see their way. Erith was exhausted, and he could tell the others were as tired as he was. The horses were stumbling and uncooperative, needing constant prodding to stay moving.

The rocky cliffs went on for some distance, and Erith frowned. He would prefer more shelter than just a wall to his back for the night. Up ahead, he heard Kemar'sto say one word, then Zeltan grunted thoughtfully.

"There's an overhang," he said, falling back to speak with Ronne. "Not a cave, in truth, but deep enough." Ronne nodded, and they set up camp.

Kashan appeared not long after they had settled in. Duanoch could no longer keep silent. "Make it go away! It will eat us!"

Ronne looked up. "Kashan has been with me since he was a small cub, and in all that time has never eaten anyone. Even when provoked." There was a glimmer of amusement in the look she gave Erith, and he made a face at her in response. "He uses his teeth and claws to defend us. You are safer when he is near."

Watching Duanoch's terrified expression as Kashan approached to investigate him, Erith recalled his own reaction in the same situation, not so many months ago. Had he really changed so much? The Arhiia had changed as well. Zeltan had barely tolerated him at the start, but now even Tekbeh regarded him as one of the group, relying on him for defense and trusting him.

Bryddhe became aware that something large was moving near her. She put out her hands, feeling the air to find it. The first brush of fingertips against fur brought an expression of delight to her face, and incoherent noises of protest from her brother. Her fingers found Kashan's ears, whiskers, and huge paws.

To Erith's surprise, Kashan submitted to this examination without complaint, purring loudly and refraining from his usual rambunctious response. Somehow the snowtiger knew Bryddhe should be treated gently.

Ronne watched Kashan carefully as he approached Bryddhe. Once it was clear that he was behaving himself, she turned her attention to the silver dagger that had warned them of danger. She drew the blade and examined it. It was made of the same frost-white metal as the sheath, but without decoration. The blade itself was triangular in cross-section, long and slender.

Magic. If it was only a means of detection, why make it in the form of a weapon? It didn't have the feel of a ceremonial blade, either. She had seen enough of them to know. It was balanced correctly, the hilt well-shaped to her hand. The dagger was meant to be used.

She frowned and held the edge up to the light. There were a few small notches, the sort of thing that happened to a blade that was used and not cared for. She found a rough stone and absently began to hone the dagger.

A gasp made her look up. Erith was staring at her, horrified. She looked at her hand. The stone had been cut neatly in half, and the silver dagger was pressed against the skin of her palm. She showed Erith her uninjured hand, letting the stone halves fall to the ground.

It went through that stone like it was butter. What was it meant to be used against? Turning where she sat, she struck a blow at the cliff wall. The dagger went into the rock all the way to the hilt. The very faintest silver glimmer traced the gap it left when she drew it out.

Ronne stared at the hole, chaotic thoughts racing through her mind, flashes of memory from the hall beneath the mountain. They had not used the dagger for stonecarving, she was certain of that. *Defense—and protection.* It provided warning of danger, a weapon to use against it, and yet another means of defense, one that could be cut into stone. The instinctive understanding made her uneasy.

My feelings are unimportant, if it can defend us from Talorgen. Slowly, she stood and walked out past the fire, beyond the horses. She used the dagger to carve a solid line from one rock face to the other, enclosing the camp. No one made any comment.

Late in the night, Erith stood and stretched, looking out into the darkness. Nothing had disturbed his watch, for which he was profoundly thankful. Edge Singing, who was also on duty, had passed the time making arrows. He had no such useful task to occupy him.

He could see the line Ronne had cut with the silver dagger; it glowed at the edges of his sight. He wondered how she had figured it out. It had never occurred to him to doubt his instinct with the salve from the underhill, but Ronne trusted nothing she did not understand. He did not blame her for her suspicion of something so magical and unknown.

He looked back at the camp where the rest lay sleeping. Bryddhe had her head pillowed against Kashan's side and was clutching a wooden flute. She had played a few soft tunes before she drifted off to sleep. He had thought Ronne would object, but Bryddhe played quietly enough to not draw unwelcome attention.

Erith had been afraid Ronne would repeat her sleepless night at the house, but she eventually drew her cloak around her and closed her eyes. Her face in sleep was tired and sad. He wished there was something more he could do to help her, to ease the pain and grief he saw in her eyes. He wanted to hold her, to comfort her, but he wasn't sure she would welcome it. It had not been so long ago that she had considered the necessity of killing him.

He sighed and then found the eyes of Edge Singing on him. She looked at Ronne, and then back at him. He could feel his face reddening. He started to speak, struggling for words, but she put a hand over her mouth and winked. He managed a grin in response and turned away from the fire to let his face cool.

Ronne woke him early again, impatient to leave.

"Is it him?" asked Erith, tapping his wrist.

Ronne glanced at her own wrist, where the dagger was tied, and shook her head. "Nothing yet. But the more distance between us, the more the Face of Good Fortune will turn in our direction."

They had few belongings to pack; the horses were soon ready. Erith looked back at the camp to see what was delaying Duanoch. Bryddhe stood at the line drawn in the stone, even though her brother was trying to lead her forward.

"What is this?"

"What is what?" asked Duanoch, puzzled.

"This…wall. I can feel it!"

"Put out your hand, lass. There's nothing there," Zeltan said kindly, in passing.

She put her hand out obediently, and a wall of silver flame leaped up from the line. It was no sooner there than it vanished, those who had seen it still blinking at its brightness. "There is so something there!" she said, stubbornly.

"Whatever it is, it can be walked through," Ronne said, mounting her horse. "Now hurry."

Erith took hold of the rein. "If you don't feel anything from the dagger, why are you so worried?"

"I want to get home as soon as I can."

He waited until she looked at him. "I know you better than that. What's wrong?"

The grey danced and tossed its head, tugging at the rein he held. "I can't be certain," Ronne said at last, her voice low. "It is not Talorgen, but I feel the presence of something. Something watching us."

They traveled up the narrow valley for some time. Erith began to fear they would find it closed ahead and have to go back, but Edge Singing, riding ahead, brought back word of another ravine. By midafternoon they reached it, a steep, rocky crevice whose only appeal lay in going the right direction. They began to ascend, even as dark, threatening clouds grew on the horizon.

"I think that storm followed us," grumbled Erith. He had at least four dead enemies to worry about; he was not looking forward to more rain. Maybe they had already found him—bad things seemed to happen when it rained, lately.

"Ahh, could be worse," Tekbeh said, shrugging. "Seems like everywhere I've gone turned into a mud pit sooner or later. Least this time we won't have to walk in it." She patted her horse's neck.

Erith looked at the rocky ground doubtfully. "Mud?"

The storm continued to grow, and light flashed in the dark clouds. Kemar'sto pointed to the rivulet of water that had started to run down the ravine.

"Must be raining up yonder," said Zeltan, nodding at the clouds.

The stormclouds now covered most of the sky, building ominously and moving towards the ravine. A sudden crack of lightning startled them, and the horses tossed their heads and sidled nervously. Thunder rolled, and another lightning bolt struck the cliff above them, showering chips of rock.

Tekbeh's mount reared, its eyes rolling wildly. Another horse, without a rider, started plunging about and making terrified noises. It broke free, wheeling about and galloping down the ravine.

Tekbeh's mount made every effort to follow, but Kemar'sto blocked its way and grabbed the bridle. The other horses, while nervous, showed no disposition to bolt and instead huddled together. Erith had his hands full trying to get his horse to move again.

Zeltan gave a shout. While they had been dealing with the horses, the rivulet had expanded to a full stream the width of the ravine. Already the water was nearly a foot deep—and it was getting deeper. *How did that happen so fast? Where is all the water coming from? It hasn't been raining that long!*

Ronne stood in her stirrups, looking ahead.

"Follow me!" she shouted, and galloped up the ravine. The others followed through the growing flood. The horse beside him stumbled and nearly fell, and Erith saw a large branch go swirling by. *We have to get out of the water. It will only get worse.*

Erith saw Ronne was aiming for a promontory of rock at a bend in the ravine. It was almost halfway up the cliff, a sheer drop except for one side, which sloped steeply to the ravine floor.

"We can't get up that!" yelled Erith into the wind. Rain pelted his face with stinging force.

Ronne stopped a short distance before the slope, turning so she faced him. "Go up at a good speed, but not straight. Like so," and she made a zigzagging motion. "Lead the way for the others to follow."

"What about you?" he shouted furiously.

"The others are straggling. I'll be there soon. Now go!" She slapped the rear of his mount, and it leaped ahead, startled.

Cursing, Erith urged his horse up the slope, expecting every minute it would stumble and they would both fall into the flooded ravine. But his mount, sides heaving, made it to the top of the plateau without mishap. He turned to see if the others had followed him.

The first up the slope was Kashan, followed by Edge Singing and another of the kenjah. Then Kemar'sto emerged, leading the horse bearing Duanoch and Bryddhe. Tekbeh was close behind, but no one followed her.

Where is Ronne? Erith dismounted and looked over the edge. She was still below with the two remaining kenjah. One was halfway up the slope. The other was having trouble with his horse, which was shying away and refusing to go forward.

He looked up the ravine, and saw what looked like a moving grey wall. At first he did not understand what he was seeing. *Son of the Dark Woman, is that water?* He thrust his mount's reins into Tekbeh's hand and ran on foot down the slippery rock, yelling as he went.

"Get up here *now!*" he screamed.

Ronne glanced up at him, then up the ravine, and her eyes widened. The kenjah's horse finally decided to go in the right direction, and they raced for the slope. Ronne's mount had just started up when the wall of water reached them.

The kenjah was swept under immediately. Erith caught only brief glimpses of him and the horse as the flood took them from view. Ronne was close, and he held his breath, willing her to escape the water.

The wave did not sweep her under, but her horse stumbled and she fell, still clutching the reins. The flood pulled her as she held on desperately, but the grey remained steady once it had regained its feet.

Erith slipped and nearly fell in his headlong descent, but caught hold of the horse in time. He pulled on the bridle, urging her mount up the slope. The grey strained against the water's pull and Ronne's weight. It was agonizingly slow, but at last Ronne was close enough Erith could grab her arm.

He pulled her out of the water, and they slowly made their way to the plateau. Ronne leaned on the grey as coughs racked her body.

When she reached the plateau, Ronne took a quick look at the faces about her as she caught her breath. They were tired, and wary of the terrain that had nearly killed them, but none were so exhausted they could not continue. She nodded to herself, then cast a glance at the river. What she saw did not reassure her.

"We have to go on," she said as softly as she could over the roar of the flood.

Zeltan, who had come to stand beside her, looked down on the still-rising river and agreed. "Who's to say where the thing will end? Never have I seen the like…."

Turning, Ronne surveyed the cliff behind them as best she could in the darkness of the storm. She frowned. Something was moving up the cliff.

"What's that white…is it Kashan?"

She had thought the cliff was sheer, but now she saw the snowtiger was ascending by means of a series of ledges. Signaling Edge Singing to follow her, Ronne went to scout the path. The beginning was tricky and narrow, but ledge beyond was wider. Some sections jumped three or more feet up from the levels before them, but they appeared to go all the way to the top of the cliff.

"Can the horses go this way?" she asked Edge Singing.

The raider wiped rain from her eyes. "Some is yes, some not," she said finally. "If no, water come they float, heh?" she added with a trace of her usual grin.

Ronne wondered if Edge Singing was kenjah because of her sense of humor. *She would laugh at the Face of Death.*

They would have to dismount. The Arhiia were too inexperienced at riding to even attempt it, and it would be easier for the horses to ascend the steep path without the additional weight. *And if they fall, they won't take their riders with them.*

Edge Singing led the way, followed by Erith. "You should let someone else go last," he said, scowling. "You didn't have good luck the last time."

"You would have me wish it on someone else? Go. You are delaying us." She didn't want to argue, especially since she had a foreboding sense of trouble still to come.

They inched their way upward. The rain had increased to an impressive volume and speed, blown sideways by gusts of wind, and it was difficult to see more than a few feet ahead. The first narrow section was awkward for everyone, but after that the horses managed the trail with few mishaps. Ronne was surprised at how adept her grey horse was at scrambling from one ledge to another, with only a little coaxing from her.

Halfway up the trail, the horse carrying Duanoch and Bryddhe's bundled goods stumbled badly. A rush bag fell and burst open on the ledge. Ronne saw the wood flute hit the rock slab with a musical clunk and then roll over the side into the ravine.

Bryddhe, holding onto the stirrup, heard her beloved flute fall. Frantic, she dropped to her knees and patted the ground with her hands, trying to discover where it lay, unaware that the ledge ended mere inches away from her fingertips. Her blood running cold, Ronne snatched her up just before she fell over the edge, and swung the girl over her shoulder.

"No! My flute!" cried Bryddhe, struggling to get loose.

"It's gone, you little fool, do you want to join it?" Ronne's patience was entirely gone. "Here. Make sure she doesn't fall into the ravine," she said, depositing her burden in Duanoch's arms.

Ronne returned to the grey. *Of all the things to risk your life for,* she fumed. *And ours, in the bargain. Does she think we are out picking berries?*

The wind tugged at her as she made her painful way to the top, flinging rain-sodden hair in her face, pulling her off balance. From up ahead Ronne heard a faint shout, and she peered fruitlessly through the rain. *We're close. Either someone has fallen in, or they've reached the top.*

The wind and rain had reached such an intensity she was proceeding mostly by feel, hoping she would find the ledge ahead of her. She and the grey struggled up another jump, and she heard voices even over the storm. Putting forth her last reserves of strength, she climbed the next rock outcrop.

A multitude of hands were extended to help her up. She tugged on the reins to encourage her horse to make the leap, and grabbed a hand to pull herself to the cliff top.

The instant her foot left the ledge she heard a sharp crack and a muted roar. The reins were snatched from her grasp. Crouching at the cliff top, she saw that half the ledge had fallen away, leaving a sheer drop to the floodwaters below.

The grey was backed up on what was left of the ledge, white showing around its eyes. *Poor beast—it has nowhere to go.* The Windriders were gathered at the other end, talking rapidly and gesticulating. They dropped to their knees at the edge of the cliff and began scrabbling at the rock and dirt, using the butt ends of their spears.

Edge Singing looked up from what she was doing. "You come, make go." She made a circling motion.

Ronne was confused until she saw the raiders were digging a new step in the cliff, at the end of the ledge. But the horse had to be turned around to use it.

She whistled. The horse pricked up its ears but didn't move. She whistled again, and this time it looked up at her. Lying flat on the clifftop, she kept calling to it until it tossed its head high enough she could snag one rein. Then she coaxed and tugged until the grey shifted awkwardly on its feet, again and again until it turned.

She pulled hard, shouting at it to move, and it bucked and lunged at the muddy ditch the kenjah had dug. It slipped and fell heavily, and Ronne despaired. But it clambered to its feet again, and with another heave the grey stood at the top of the cliff, trembling with exertion. She stroked its nose to soothe it, and it dropped its head with a sigh.

The storm was abating as swiftly as it had come. With bemused eyes, Ronne watched the black clouds vanish and the setting sun emerge again. "It left like it never was here. Was it real?"

"Real enough for that man who died," commented Erith. Wringing out his cloak, he added, "and something certainly got us wet." He stopped, then spoke in a carefully lowered voice, "It stopped the instant you climbed out of the ravine. That wasn't a normal storm, was it?"

Ronne bared her teeth in something not a smile. "The watching feeling has gone as well. I begin to think they were connected."

Erith clutched a stirrup, trying to stay upright. His legs had no strength, it was an effort even to move, but he didn't have the strength to get in the saddle and ride. They were all too exhausted to go much farther that day, and it was getting dark.

He looked about. The terrain did not lend itself to shelter. It was even flatter than the Windriders' territory, the only hills far ahead on the horizon. They finally located a hollow that would at least provide a break from the wind and set about building a fire. There was very little conversation as everyone set out gear and clothing to dry.

Erith was just beginning to get warm, and enjoying the sensation, when he looked across the campfire and saw a still-tearful Bryddhe being comforted by her brother. She had borne the destruction of her village, the loss of her home, and a terrifying journey, but the loss of her precious flute had been too much. He watched them for a while, constructing a strategy, then took a deep breath and went in search of Ronne.

He found her near the top of the depression, looking out towards the west.

"When you are *alaran* of Arhi, will you be like a chief, or a warleader?"

She stirred. "The *alaran* is both. That is why they must be chosen from those of the Sword."

"Ah." He continued carefully. "Still, you will have to guide your people. Make judgments. Understand their problems and solve them. Is this correct?"

"Yes." She was giving him her full attention now.

"Not all of your people will be warriors, Ronne," he said, trying to make her understand. "Some folk are so poor they cannot replace what they lose. A chief who does not know his people's concerns will only be given the obedience of the mouth, not the heart. Had my clan supported me, my father would never have cast me out for fear of losing status."

She did not pretend to misunderstand him. "They have their lives because I took them with us, even though they burden us on our journey. What more can I do?"

He hesitated. "Even if you had nothing to give them, you could make their pain more bearable with a few words. Bryddhe knows you will give her food and shelter. But that flute was hers, and she valued it, and it's gone. Do you understand?"

She looked out into the night again, and he began to think she was not going to answer. She gave a long sigh. "Once, I think, I would have understood. Now I am dead inside, and incapable of compassion."

"That's not true. You could use more practice, though."

She almost smiled at this, but her eyes remained bleak. "And what would you do, possessed of boundless compassion?" Her voice was resigned.

"I would say I was sorry her flute was lost, and I would try to help her find another."

"You would." She gave him a skeptical look. He felt cheered by this response. Her earlier remote and emotionless manner had worried him.

"The important part is saying you're sorry. The storm wasn't your fault."

"I am not so sure of that." She smiled at him, but sadly. "I thank you for your concern. You act as a true friend, and I would not have you think I do not value your friendship. Sometimes I think it is the only thing between me and madness."

Erith blinked. "But…your people, the Arhiia…."

"Yes," she snapped. "My people. My responsibility. As are all the folk in Arhi, and I must appear calm and confident to inspire them for the battle that will come. Not a one of them must know I could howl for all the rage and pain in me. None of them," she said, jerking her head towards the campfire, "must know the countless times I have wanted to abandon common sense and travel night and day until we reach Keris Kera. The advantage the horses give us may not be enough. And I must get there before he does!"

She clenched her hands in frustration, arms resting on her drawn-up knees. He was sorry he had added to her troubles, now that he realized she had so many others. Unable to speak, his heart grieving for her pain, Erith clasped one hand in his own. Hers turned and gripped his with sudden, painful intensity, and just as quickly released it.

Ronne took a deep breath. "I have asked you more than once if you wished to leave, and each time you have refused. Yet I have never asked you why." Her voice was so quiet he could barely hear her words.

It took Erith a moment to find truthful words that he could safely speak. "This is where I wish to be," he said, just as quietly. Ronne turned her head and looked at him, her eyes widening and then fixing on him with an intensity that made his breath go short.

"I wish—"

The sound of footsteps dragging in the grass made her stop. Duanoch stood behind them, looking wilted. "I am to tell you the food is ready," he said.

Ronne got wearily to her feet and returned to the fire.

Erith lifted his face to the starry night sky and prayed. *Dark Woman, Comfort of Night, I give thanks for your gift. Grant that it is a beginning, not an end.*

Erith did his best to get the others ready to leave as soon as dawn broke the next day. Bryddhe, untroubled by the lack of light, was already prepared.

"She said she would give me her own flute when we get to her home!" she confided when he greeted her. She was greatly cheered. "She says she doesn't use it—isn't that strange?"

Erith wondered if Ronne had ever used a flute. He was glad she had not disregarded his advice.

As they got ready to depart, Zeltan squinted at the distant hills now becoming visible. "That peak yonder is a thought familiar," he said, pointing to the horizon. One hill had a small notch near the top. "When I saw it, near the Arhi border, it was northeast of me."

Ronne nodded without comment, but Erith knew she was thinking how far the border would be, and how it would take too long to get there. She was already mounted, and her horse stamped and tossed its head as if expressing the emotions that its rider refused to show.

"What delays us?" she asked, impatience in her voice.

Tekbeh came up from the back of the group, looking harassed. "Their horse has gone lame," she said, jerking a thumb back at Bryddhe and Duanoch. "It can't carry anyone."

Bryddhe was shifted without much difficulty, but her larger and heavier brother was a problem. Erith tried to think of an answer, without success—they simply didn't have enough horses. They could either abandon him or slow down the entire group.

Duanoch was looking uncomfortable at the problem he had created.

"I'll run beside you," he blurted, startling everyone.

Zeltan raised both shaggy brows in surprise. "You'd be left behind in an instant!"

Duanoch shook his head. "Not if you keep the way you have been, times when you go fast and then times when you slow down. I can keep up on foot for the slow parts, and the others I could ride with someone. Really," he insisted, seeing the skeptical looks of the others, "I am good at running."

He proved to be as good as his word. Erith was surprised at how well someone as clumsy as Duanoch could run. He kept up with the riders, aided by the curious Kashan, who followed to investigate this change in routine. Towards the end of the day he began to flag, and Ronne ordered him to ride the rest of the way.

On the second day after leaving the ravine, they reached a boundary marker. Tekbeh saw it first, giving a whoop and racing across the plain to greet it, followed by the other Arhiia. There was a wild look in Ronne's eyes when Erith and the kenjah arrived. He thought it wise to comment, in a meaningful tone, "Wait for us."

The glance Ronne gave him let him know his warning had been understood. "We are nearly three days travel from Keris Kera," she said in a tight voice, and rode on.

The first village they came to was a small one, built on the hillsides of a shallow valley with farmland below. The people came running from the fields as they approached, including the stammering, flustered headman. Erith realized this was the first village he had seen with the inhabitants still living.

Ronne questioned the man curtly. They had seen no soldiers save themselves. Some rumor of trouble "down south" had reached them, but court matters were of little interest, isolated as they were. Her audience was alternately ecstatic when Ronne identified herself, and horrified when she told them of the tragedies that had befallen the Empire and Arhi.

"The *alaran* and *he'alaran*, both killed? Who will lead us now, in our time of trouble?" asked the headman, aghast.

"You behold her," Zeltan answered, "a Sword of the first line of Arhi, summoned as *he'alaran* by Inar."

The folk responded by bowing to Ronne, one hand held before their faces. Erith watched them while Ronne warned the headman of enemies that might follow. The ordinary folk could not keep their eyes from the horses and the kenjah, and especially Kashan. Bryddhe, Duanoch, and himself seemed trivial in comparison.

This routine continued, with minor variations, at every village they passed afterwards. By the next day such villages became more numerous and larger. As they got closer to their goal, Ronne no longer had to identify herself, and the people were more aware of the dangers that now faced Arhi. Ronne gave that danger a name, and any army veterans a command to prepare to fight. With every village that she found intact, her grim tension lightened.

After they left a town large enough to support a tiny market, Edge Singing rode up beside Ronne and Erith. She was not wearing her usual cheerful, carefree expression, and he wondered what the problem was.

"How big is the ancestor house of you?" she said, almost accusingly. "We go, place of many buildings! I think, here is ancestor house. We go, we come bigger place. Still not ancestor house! This place, so big three my family ancestor house!"

Ronne looked to Erith for help. He threw up his hands, shrugging. How did he know how large Keris Kera was? The size of the towns astonished him too. If Arhi was only a minor *alar* of an Empire of many such…and this Empire had fallen. He began to understand the magnitude of the disaster.

"Tomorrow we should come to my ancestor house," Ronne promised.

The previous towns did not prepare Erith for the sheer size of Keris Kera. The city was built up against a mountain, shielded on one side by sheer cliff walls and on the other by a lake fed by a waterfall. Buildings covered the entire slope, rising one above the other, beginning at the valley floor.

Tall stone walls enclosed the city, with square towers at intervals along their length and flanking the gate. Beyond the city walls at the top of the peak, behind walls of its own, was a huge stone building. *That could be a city itself*, thought Erith, stunned. *If anyone had told me of this, I would not have believed them.*

The sun was setting as they emerged from the forested hills that edged the valley floor. It turned the sweeping walls gold and the water below them into a pool of molten metal. The people they encountered stared in astonishment as they rode by.

The road crossed a bridge over the river before approaching the city. The bridge was guarded by soldiers wearing the Arhi crest. Ronne stopped, sending Tekbeh on ahead. One soldier protested, then she recognized Ronne and saluted with a reddening face.

"Has Arhi been attacked?"

The soldier's eyes widened. "No, *na'al!* Why—"

"Double the guard here. And place soldiers on the west and south roads where they enter the valley." The soldier saluted again, too shocked even to speak.

They rode on toward the gate, and it slowly opened to receive them. The doors were massive—solid wood studded with iron bosses as big as a fist. Tekbeh had evidently spread the word as she rode in, for people were spilling out of houses and shops that lined the main road. They shouted with astonishment and joy.

Ronne dismounted and led her horse when she entered the city, and Zeltan and Erith did the same. When they saw the crowds, the kenjah were more reluctant, but eventually they too went on foot.

Ronne turned to Erith. "Follow me, to the left," she said, in a low but intense voice. "And no matter what anybody else tells you, stay with me!"

He followed this instruction to the best of his ability as they walked up the steep, winding road. The city seemed even larger from inside. Any one of the buildings they passed could have housed his entire clan, and they were almost all stone, some ornamented with columns and balconies. Some of the balconies had long grey banners hanging from them.

The buildings were so tall he could only see a section of the sky. He felt closed in, wanting more space to move, and he wondered how people could stand to live so close together.

And there were so many people there! They lined the streets, cheering and calling out to Ronne as she went by, falling silent in astonishment when they saw the kenjah and the horses. Glancing aside, Erith saw a small child clutching her mother's leg and staring at him with enormous eyes. *And what do they think of me?*

A glimpse of black-and-white fur distracted him from gawking at the city. *Kashan—is he going to be a problem?* But the snowtiger did not appear threatened or disturbed. He seemed perfectly content to follow Ronne, only flattening his ears when the cheering got too loud.

Erith's legs started to ache. *Surely we must have reached the top by now?* Ahead he saw another wall, with a gate, and he remembered the big building at the top of the hill had been surrounded by its own wall. That must be their destination.

More soldiers guarded this gate, and when the Arhiia and kenjah entered, the open area beyond was full of even more. Erith was getting confused by all the turns and entrances; he had no idea where they were. Somewhere in the big building.

The sun was just slipping below the horizon when they entered another courtyard. Across from the entrance, a dignified woman of severe beauty, dressed in grey robes, stood before a carved doorway. She was accompanied by a younger man similarly attired. They both looked familiar to Erith, and then he realized they resembled Ronne. Otherwise breathtakingly handsome, the man's face was disfigured on one side by a terrible scar.

The woman appeared oblivious to the strange cavalcade that approached, ignoring all but Ronne, who stood before her and said, "My lady mother, I have come as you bid me."

<h1 style="text-align:center">CHAPTER 14</h1>

Sardis tucked her hand unobtrusively under Talorgen's arm as he started to stumble. *Still not recovered…. How much longer will it take?* She tugged him in the direction of his tent, and for once he did not object. None of the soldiers would think it odd; Talorgen's behavior was becoming increasingly erratic, and waiting another day to march was better than having him collapse in public.

The tent was close enough, but it took a long time for them to get there. Talorgen's steps were slow and hesitant. Once they were inside, Sardis helped him to a seat at the long wooden table. She poured wine as he sat silent, sprawled in his chair. He drank deeply.

"I begin to think you were right, my dear Sardis. Perhaps feeding it three at once was excessive."

"You almost lost control of it." Sardis shuddered, remembering. Would that ever happen to her?

"I needed the power to find and stop her. It takes a great deal for such things over a large distance." Talorgen shifted in his seat. "The storm almost succeeded…but if it had, it would have killed her. No finesse…." He shook his head and drank again.

"Don't you want to kill her?" Sardis asked. She could not help the sharpness in her voice. With luck, Talorgen would not notice.

Talorgen turned his winecup in his hand, and some of the wine spilled on his fingers. "She could be quite useful, if we convince—"

"*You* convince her? Have you forgotten how she spoke of you?"

"I have forgotten nothing," said Talorgen in a dangerous voice. "Not one word. All the more reason to break her instead of simply letting her die."

Sardis kept her face blank, trying to conceal her sullen anger. *He won't give up until I show him her lifeless body. And if that's what it takes….*

"We should still attack before she has time to organize her defenses. If we move now we can reach Keris Kera before she does."

"No." He gazed off into the distance. "We will take care of the remaining *alars* first. Their leaders will recover from the surprise of

Ynduria's fall eventually, and they are more of a threat than tes Arhi's tiny force. It would be a shame to waste all the effort we put into this plan to pursue a side issue." He smiled.

"Aren't the ones you have enough for now?" She knew the question was a mistake as soon as she spoke. His face darkened, and his eyes glittered in a disturbing way. *He looks different since he used the creature last. How much control does he still have?*

"If I had any choice, I would not have let the barbarians take the southern ones. We will have to fight to get them back later. But the agreement with them was necessary to prevent even greater loss. If we had done nothing, the Empire would have vanished. No, the Empire will continue—*all* of the Empire—but under my rule."

Ronne was up before the servants had begun to stir, and armed herself with only her shortblade when she left her rooms. She could allow herself the brief illusion of peace, that she had merely returned to her family home after a journey with nothing more painful than long council meetings to anticipate.

Despite the reassuring news that Talorgen had not yet crossed the Arhi border, Ronne had begun preparations for war on the hour of her return to Keris Kera. She had sent messengers to the outlying towns, increased the fortress guard, alerted the army…she could permit herself a short time to savor the feeling of being home.

She left her room and descended the main stair. It had been four years for her, but nothing in the ancient fortress had changed. She passed by the council chamber and the Audience on her way to the lake. Catching sight of a vine-covered pillar on the portico, she stopped. The predawn light was too faint for her to see the clusters of tiny red aroe flowers, but she could smell the sweet, tangy scent.

No, there had been great changes—but they didn't show on stone. She went closer to the pillar. She barely remembered the day when her father brought the aroe vine to Keris Kera; she had been very young. It was done with great difficulty, but her father had wished to please her mother, who missed the flowers of her home.

Inar had feared the delicate plant would not survive the harsher climate of Arhi. It not only survived, but thrived, and before long had completely covered the massive stone pillar and part of the portico roof. As children, Ronne and her brothers had regarded it almost as an extension of their parents and made sure none of their more dubious escapades occurred anywhere near it, which had doubtless contributed to its survival.

Thoughtfully, Ronne fingered one of the thin, narrow leaves. Would the aroe live now that her father was dead?

Erith woke and stretched, wincing as his sore muscles knotted with tension. It made sense to put a fortress at the top of a steep hill, but that made it hard for the defenders to reach the fortress as well. Added to the accumulated fatigue of travel, the aches were almost enough to keep him in bed, but rest was not in him. There was too much that was unfamiliar for him to be at ease.

He had dreamed strangely too, seeing again the welcome Ronne had received—only this time, in addition to the warriors and townsfolk calling out and greeting her, birds swooped and darted, singing her name, and trees bent their branches to touch her. She responded with the same grave courtesy she had shown to her people. She entered the big house wearing a cape of leaves and feathers, and her eyes as she turned to him had a deep burning wildness he had seen once before. He woke with his heart pounding.

Rising, he found clothing set out for him; tunic, shirt, hose, and soft leather shoes. The tunic and shirt were satisfactory, but the hose left him feeling half-dressed. He didn't have much choice—his old clothing was ragged and filthy—but he would have felt more comfortable with trews. He shrugged to himself and left the tiny room. The interior of the fortress was quiet and deserted.

He followed a hallway to an even wider passage, which led to a broad flight of stairs. He shook his head. *How big is this place? And where would Ronne be?* Outside the main building, perhaps. That's where the soldiers had been yesterday when they arrived.

He tried to retrace the way he had come in, but knew he had made a wrong turn when he found himself at the entrance to a big, echoing room. Curiosity led him on. The far wall was open to the outside, and he saw no sign of the heavy defensive walls of the fortress. How could the builders have left such a gaping hole in the fortifications?

He crossed the room, passing a dais with a single chair. The floor was inlaid stone with intricate geometric designs, and banners flanked the dais. The banners were covered by thin grey veiling that obscured the designs but did not completely hide them. Some seemed to be missing—there were empty hooks along the walls.

The room opened onto a terrace where a line of huge pillars defined the edge. Looking up, Erith saw graceful beams, leafy vines, and pale dawn sky. The beauty seemed out of place in such a warlike setting. *Is this still a fortress?* But then Ronne had grown up here, and thought of it as her home. It was still strange to think of it as a place people lived in, other than soldiers.

Shallow, broad steps led down from the terrace to water and mist. He recalled Ronne mentioning a lake, but he had thought she meant the one outside the city. He could just make out sheer mountain cliffs on the opposite side through the mist, and realized the fortress was just one of the walls surrounding the lake. Nothing could scale the cliffs or reach the lake unless through the fortress itself.

Further out from the terrace edge the water was invisible. The mist covered it, except when an occasional vagrant silver gleam appeared only to vanish again under the white cloud. As Erith watched, a flicker of color caught his eye, and he looked up to see a dark-haired figure standing on a point overlooking the lake. *Ronne.* He continued along the terrace. The stonework narrowed, ending in a ledge that was cut out of the living rock and connected to a stairway. He started up.

The first beams of the rising sun lanced over the crags as he ascended. Long wisps of mist hung in the air, lifting slowly off the water's surface, and he paused to watch. Ronne was visible at the top of the stairs, gazing toward the jagged cliffs that rose from the edges of the misted silver water.

The mist swirled about her as it rose, caressingly. *Almost as if it had arms, reaching out…and that bit could be a head, with white hair like Bryddhe….* He gasped as the ethereal head lifted to look at him with narrow, slanted eyes and a mischievous smile. There was a faint silver glint in those inhuman eyes as it faded away, Ronne oblivious to the ghostly kiss on her cheek it gave her as it left.

Erith closed his eyes, leaning against the reassuring solidity of the rock wall as his pulse returned to normal. He opened them to see Ronne in front of him, a frown of concern on her face. "What is wrong?"

He hesitated, realizing she hadn't seen the mist creature. "I have not recovered from all that climbing yesterday." This was true enough, if not the complete truth. "What is this place called?"

"The water is An Harar—the Lake Within. This," she gestured at the pinnacle of rock that thrust up from the center of the ledge, "is called the Fingertip of the Many-Faced. It was found as you see it, many hundreds of years ago. This place and the stairs to it were here when my ancestors built Keris Kera. No one knows who built them, or when."

He joined her at the walled edge of the landing, glancing at her face as she gazed at the lake again. The tension, the rigid control in her face, had lessened; she seemed to have found a measure of peace just in being home. "Do you feel anything…strange, here?"

She smiled, but gave him an odd look. "No. But my brother has claimed there were more shadows by the Lake Within than things to cast them. He is very imaginative. Too much book-learning, I think."

Erith looked out at the lake. The mist was nearly gone from the water, and rocky cliff bottoms were beginning to emerge. "Your brother—Zeltan, and other people, talk of him as if he could never be a warleader. Why?"

She sighed. "It is the custom…it *was* the custom, to have those who served the Imperial Court distinct from those who served the army. Children of the Lineage—the four lines of a ruling house—may choose which path they take. The First Line is one step removed from the *alaran*, so one must take the sword as a potential heir, but the rest are free to choose. My elder brother and I took the sword. Alland, choosing the robe, was never taught the art of war, of command, of any military matter. He knows enough to defend himself in need, my father saw to that, but not enough to defend Arhi. This is not to say he lacks skills," she continued, "just that they are not the ones most needed now."

The portico of the fortress was no longer completely in shadow, and Erith saw people moving about. He hoped they weren't looking for Ronne. The openness of the vantage point was more to his liking than the rooms of the fortress or the cramped city, and he was reluctant to leave.

For a long time Ronne was silent, gazing over the silver water, then she drew a deep breath and turned to him. "You will need to know what is expected of a helmbearer. Many here will resent your presence, and they will use any excuse to try to get rid of you. The important rules are not so difficult; follow my orders, help me in my actions, fight beside me. In turn, I am required to train you in the way of the *tier sanas*, to protect and provide for you. The difficult part will be the social protocol."

"The what?"

She grimaced. "A thousand little rules of no real importance, but if they are broken, you—and I by extension—will look bad. Follow me through doorways. Don't interrupt me in public. If your temper gets the better of you, at least try to speak so others won't hear. Most of what you need to know you can pick up by observation, or by asking." She leaned on her elbows on the parapet and looked at her hands. "I wish it could be otherwise…I would not force you to something you have not agreed to, but the *tier sanas* are held in respect. This will give you a degree of toleration by my people that would otherwise be denied."

Erith wrinkled his brow. "They respect you. Isn't it enough that you speak for me?"

Her response was emphatic. "No. Not in this case. They will look at you and see only how different you are from them. Nothing else will matter." She hesitated, then added, "There will also be those who are envious of your standing with me, and would be even if you were from Arhi. They will resent you, even though you have done nothing to them."

Erith shrugged. "That is nothing new to me. Have you forgotten? My family feared my abilities, not my actions." Only this time, he would not let them drive him away. Only Ronne could make him leave. "I will remember what you have said. But what are the *tier sanas?* Why are they respected?"

Ronne appeared relieved at his response, and answered readily. "We swear an oath. We are bound to a code of truthfulness and honorable behavior in our fighting. If I draw my sword, I may not conceal the truth of anything I do or see done. I may not attack if there is no threat, and I must allow those I attack the possibility of defense."

Erith nodded. "I have no difficulty with that."

Ronne stirred and glanced at him. "If you have any other questions, ask them now. It is unlikely we will be able to have another private conversation anytime soon—and I must ask you not to seek me out alone."

"Why?" Erith was puzzled and slightly suspicious.

"Trust me when I say there is a reason." Her gaze was locked on her tightly clasped hands.

He agreed, but a small uncertainty took place in his mind and could not be dislodged.

They descended the stairs, and Erith waited in the big room off the lake terrace that Ronne called the Audience while she went to don her armor. He noticed now that it had tall wooden doors, folded open against stone pillars on the lake side. In the morning light he could also see a climbing vine growing from an immense urn; the vine covered the pillar beside it and much of the roof. The glossy, dark green leaves waved in the breeze.

A soft chiming noise made him look up. Hanging from the portico roof were collections of bells and metal rods, twisting and striking each other.

"What are they?" he said, waving in their general direction when Ronne reappeared.

"Ghost-traps," she said, with a wry look. "Ghosts are supposed to be distracted by the bells and things, and forget to come inside and cause trouble."

Erith was fascinated. "Do they work?"

"I have never been troubled by ghosts, so perhaps they do." She led him down the steps to the lakeside and walked in the direction opposite to the Fingertip. "Those are the council chambers," she said, indicating windows next to the Audience, "where I will be spending far too much time. And this is the bridge to the gardens."

The bridge was a delicate span that arched over the waterfall to a green area surrounded by rock walls, like a gem in a setting of crude pottery. Fruit trees, flowering plants, and a few tiny buildings formed a peaceful oasis that was almost completely concealed from the fortress. Standing on the crest of the bridge, Erith could see the whole of the valley. There was the road to the east they had come in by, the lake, and the walled city.

The thunder of the waterfall made it difficult to speak and be understood, and they headed back through the fortress.

"The army commanders will be in the inner ward. The smaller open space, where the entrance to the fortress proper is," Ronne explained, seeing his confusion. "I have many orders for them, and not a few questions."

More people were up and about now. Erith was almost getting used to the disbelieving looks, quickly masked by indifference, when they saw him. He felt more awkward than he had ever felt in his life. The Arhiia were a good bit shorter than he was, and he could feel the tops of some of the doorways brush his head. It was a relief when they left the fortress for the open space of the inner ward.

He wondered how Kashan was dealing with the close quarters, and asked.

"Well enough. I closed him in a room for now, until he becomes accustomed to his new surroundings."

Ronne headed for a building on the far side of the wall. They entered a large room, roughly furnished with benches and tables and whitewashed stone walls. A handful of soldiers were gathered about a table with a jug and a motley collection of mugs, talking loudly. Others watched one of their number who was throwing a dagger at a doorjamb on the opposite wall. It had a crude charcoal drawing on it.

Erith was impressed by how quickly they reacted to Ronne's appearance. Since her back was to the entrance, the dagger-thrower did not see Ronne and Erith enter, but the sudden activity of her comrades alerted her and she soon stood at attention with the rest.

"Bring me the commanders," Ronne said curtly to one of the soldiers, who saluted and left with speed. They waited in silence then, the soldiers seeming barely to breathe. Even so, Erith saw more than one quick glance in his direction. The silence was broken by the hasty entrance of two people, who stopped short and saluted when they saw Ronne.

"Dunand," she said to the older, barrel-chested man. "I am glad you are still with us." She looked at the other commander, a younger woman with a calm, unhurried manner. "I regret I do not recall your name."

"Finavah, *na'al.* I was a subcommander under Tanin, but after Ynduria…." Her voice trailed off.

Ronne nodded, a sharp gesture. "Then there is more need than ever for me to review the troops. Tomorrow should be time enough," she said, after the commanders exchanged looks of consternation, "but we must discuss our current situation now."

Dunand jerked his head at the soldiers still in the room, and they left without protest.

"A moment," said Ronne. She stopped the dagger-thrower with a hand to the shoulder. "Your targeting is excellent, but I would be better pleased if you spent less time with your back to the door."

"Yes, *na'al,*" the soldier gasped, and vanished as soon as Ronne lifted her hand.

Intercepting Finavah's speculative glance, Ronne introduced Erith. "He is outcast from his people, the barbarians of the plains," she added.

Dunand scowled, his bushy eyebrows meeting in his forehead. "I guessed as much," he said a little too quickly. Erith almost laughed. Who did he think he was fooling?

They sat about the table and Finavah hunted through the collection to find four clean mugs.

"What is our current strength?" began Ronne.

"Ynduria was very costly to us. We lost one phalanx and the rest are not up to strength. We have little more than four thousand able at the moment, if we count the water-carriers. In time we may have some of the wounded returned to duty." Dunand drank as if to wash a bad taste from his mouth.

A thousand is ten hundreds, Erith reminded himself. He still couldn't grasp the true meaning of the word, but he knew it was a large number. *If they have so many soldiers, why are they worried?*

"That will never be enough," said Ronne, visibly taken aback.

"What, is there action for us?"

"More than enough for you and all the rest. Talorgen tes Vaidis has taken Oguz, and has sworn to take Arhi as well. I have no certainty of the size of the army he can field. From what I remember of the strength of Vaidis and Oguz, it is likely more than ten thousand."

Dunand pursed his mouth in a silent whistle. Finavah just looked stunned.

"I did not think of it before, but a messenger should be sent immediately to Corin. I would just as soon not be fighting on three sides," continued Ronne. "Bring me word by evening of our weaponry and armor. Since we have so few soldiers, we must protect those we have. We will be fielding troops to the borders in a matter of days. From this moment," she said, rising from the table, "you are to consider Arhi to be at war."

The morning sun was bright in the inner ward, and Erith stood blinking while his eyes adjusted from the dark room. Ronne permitted herself to watch him, but not for long. *Never for long enough.* Then a thought intruded, changing the intent of her gaze. *He is such a big target....*

"You need armor," she said aloud.

Erith shrugged, looking uncomfortable. "I've done well enough without."

"The kind of combat you will be seeing is not what you have been accustomed to. And as I said to the commanders, we cannot afford to lose any of the few fighters we have. Our shields will not be adequate for your defense without armor."

Indicating he should follow, she set out across the ward to the smithy, a complex of low buildings built against the inner wall of the ward. They were full of the din of metal on metal and the smoke of many forges. The smiths within did not look up from their work as Ronne and Erith threaded their way through to the rear.

The armorer was not in sight, and Ronne grimaced. She would have to ask. She stopped at a closed door with intricate wrought iron hinges. A metal plate showed the Arhi moonrose in reversed colors—black, on a gold field.

"This is where the smiths of the darkmetal work," Ronne said, indicating the door. "Only they enter here."

"Do you have to stay out as well?" Erith was frankly skeptical.

"In theory, the *alaran* may enter," Ronne answered, pulling on the bellrope hanging by the door, "but in practice they must have a very, very good reason for doing so."

The clanging summons of the bell was answered by a man of massive girth that Ronne did not recognize. He gave a respectful bow and then waited in silence.

"Is Kelme within?"

The man nodded. "Shall I send her to you?" When Ronne assented, he added, "Finlan will want to know," looking at her uncertainly.

Ronne gritted her teeth. *Not one day back, and already it has begun.*

"This is not a visit of ceremony, but of purpose," she snapped. "My helmbearer requires arms and armor suited to his duties."

The man glanced at Erith, standing silent at Ronne's shoulder, and paled. "N-no, I mean, yes. Finlan said in my hearing he would speak with you when he heard of your return. That is all I know."

There was no point in taking out her annoyance on the smith. She would have to make matters clear to Finlan himself. She waved a hand in assent, and the man left, returning with Finlan, the master smith. He had touches of white in his dark hair and beard that had not been there the last time Ronne had seen him.

"What matter brings you to speak to me? I had only sought Kelme the armorer." Ronne hoped to defer whatever Finlan had in mind, but he was not to be denied.

"There are those who saw yester-night that you wear a weapon of curious metal," he said, tapping the inside of his left wrist.

Ronne came fully alert, giving him her complete attention, and she was aware of Erith doing the same. "What is your interest in this weapon?" she asked, keeping her tone disinterested.

Finlan paused, looking at Erith and evidently not liking what he saw. "It is a matter much in the concern of the Fifth Line, and should not be bandied about where anyone could hear."

"Erith was there when it was…given…to me, and has seen it used. He knows as much as I do, and I see no useful purpose in excluding him," Ronne said, struggling to keep her temper in check. When it looked like Finlan would argue further, she said softly, "What the eye sees may not be concealed."

Erith was not sure why Ronne had been so annoyed by Finlan's appearance, and the smith's comments had been completely cryptic. *Fifth line? Is this the same thing as the lines of the ruling house Ronne spoke of? I thought she said there were only four.* And Ronne's final response appeared to disconcert Finlan. *She has said those words before…they must have another meaning.*

While the smith was considering what next to say, there was another arrival on the scene. She was so old her hair was completely white, and she supported herself on a long, slender staff, but her face and bearing were full of purpose and her eyes gleamed with sharp understanding.

"What's going on here? Finlan! Stop standing around watching dust settle!"

"We have a matter to discuss, na'Arisaig, which the *alaran* says may be heard by this one," and he gestured at Erith.

Arisaig's quick glance darted over him. "Hmmph. Hard to miss, isn't he? Don't you think a spy would be a bit more subtle? You can practically see that hair in the dark. Brightens up the place," she added, nodding at Ronne with approval. Erith grinned. This formidable old woman wasn't troubled by him in the least. It was a pleasant change from the usual reaction he got here.

"We do not make a habit of discussing our secrets outside the line, na'Arisaig," said Finlan, his patience visibly fraying. "You know what I would speak about, tell me! Shall I tell this stranger also?"

The old woman sniffed, then turned to Erith. "Look at me," she commanded. Her tone was so resolute that he did so.

Arisaig's eyes were piercing, icy blue, and they caught and held his gaze without effort. "Why are you here?"

His thoughts were suddenly slow and indistinct, and when he spoke his voice seemed to come from far away. "To help Ronne."

"I know all the secrets of the darkmetal, from the making to the forging. Do you want to hear them?" she asked, a crafty note in her voice.

His foggy mind only produced the thought that he was not a smith, and had no use for the secrets of the darkmetal. "No."

Arisaig gave a cackle of satisfaction, then her expression changed and she snatched up his hand, holding it up to her gaze. Erith was surprised by how strong her withered fingers were.

"Well, and what is this? Look, you, and please don't tell me you have gone blind."

This last was addressed to Finlan, who looked as she bade him, frowning. Then his gaze widened in surprise and he looked, startled, at Arisaig.

"How is this possible? He is not—"

"Oho, so now I know everything, instead of knowing nothing! I haven't the least idea *how*. But if I were you I would think more of adding to our secrets and less of losing them. Don't worry about him," she said, waving a dismissing hand at Erith, "he's so honest light shines through him. You, on the other hand, are a true child of Arven the Shadowed," she said, pointing at Ronne with a stiff forefinger. "Never let anything out if you can help it, eh? Wasn't for that sword-eye, you probably wouldn't speak at all."

A muscle twitched in Ronne's cheek. "There are reasons why the Fifth Line guards what it knows. I also have reasons for keeping my own counsel," she said in an even tone.

The old woman snorted, then turned her gaze to Finlan. "You know what you saw. You heard what he said, and how he said it," she said cryptically. "It is my opinion you may trust him as you trust her. Do not forget that the world has changed around us. Many of the old ways have no purpose now. But it's your decision," she said, her formal tone changing to querulous irritability, "and you'll doubtless make a mess of it." She slowly made her way back to the hidden darkness behind the door.

A long silence fell, broken by Finlan's sigh and shrug of resignation. "If you would both follow me," he said, and opened the door of the darkmetal smiths.

CHAPTER 15

Erith caught a glimpse of Ronne's startled expression before she followed Finlan through the door. His mind was only now recovering from the numbing effect of Arisaig's gaze, but he already had a burning curiosity about what had happened. What had she seen in his hand? What had he said that was so important they would trust him with their deepest secrets?

Finlan hurried them past several rooms. Erith thought he saw an empty forge in one before it passed from view. They reached the end of the passageway and a small room with an elaborate circular pattern inlaid in metal in the stone floor. At the very center was a disc of dark green stone with several small holes in it. Finlan took a small golden sphere from a pouch at his waist and dropped it into one of the holes.

Erith had only a moment's confusion before the central disc rose on a cleverly constructed metal framework. It revealed a small spiral staircase descending below, also of metal. The stairs looked fragile, and he took a tentative step, uncertain if they would bear his weight. They did not even creak. The darkmetal smiths were skilled at more than just making swords.

They followed the stairs down to a large cave lit by torches. Finlan tugged at an iron lever on the wall, and the stone disc sank into its original position above them.

Across the cavern floor were a handful of smiths, working hard at the darkmetal forges. Erith saw no obvious outlet for the smoke, but it had to be escaping somehow. The whole cavern reminded him of the underground hall with the voices. The feeling was not a comfortable one.

"Three weeks ago, something began interfering with our forgings," said Finlan. "The nature of the interference was…disturbing. We searched through all our lore for something to prevent it, and the only thing we could find was a reference to a ring of strange silvery metal, found in this cave long ago and since lost."

"And you think the dagger might work as well." Ronne made it more a statement than a question.

Finlan nodded. "If we could have it here, to—"

"No." She folded her arms. "It must stay with me. I have need of it."

"As do we! Face of Reason!" Finlan exploded. "Do you need weapons, or not? The army won't last long without them, and we could be fighting at any moment!" He flung out his hands in exasperation.

But he doesn't need to keep it.... Erith cleared his throat. "Couldn't you use it for them?" he asked, making scribing motions.

Ronne's face cleared. "Is the disturbance occurring now?" she asked Finlan.

"Yes, worse than before. That is why—you know how to use it?"

Ronne unsheathed the silver dagger and walked to the forge area. The smiths looked up from their work, surprised. Their shock changed to confusion when they saw the master smith with her. Erith decided to remain in the shadows. If Ronne had an uncertain welcome here, how would they take his presence?

"Stand away," said Ronne. The smiths respectfully gave her room. She carved a circle in the rock floor with the silver dagger, enclosing the forges and the space around them.

"Is that sufficient?" she asked Finlan as she stood up, brushing back some stray strands of hair with her hand.

Finlan glanced at the group of smiths. One crossed the circle to the forge and picked up the piece she had been working on. Looking at it intently, she broke into a smile. "It's back!" There was relief in her voice. The other smiths lost no time returning to work. *What did she see? It looks no different than before.*

Ronne and Finlan moved away from the forge and the increasing noise, back to the stair where Erith stood. "You have not used it for this purpose earlier?" asked Finlan, amazed. "How did you know, then?"

"From the time this started, and from what I have used it for, I made a guess."

Erith drew in a sharp breath when he understood her meaning. "How could he—"

"This was made well before the existence of the Empire," she said, holding out the dagger. "How likely is it that this was made to be used against *him?*"

"Who do you speak of?" asked Finlan.

"Talorgen tes Vaidis," answered Erith. Finlan seemed startled that Erith knew the name, or perhaps at his boldness in speaking. "But why would it...have you felt him returning?"

Ronne shook her head. "No. Nothing yet. As to what this works against —something very powerful destroyed the original owners. He may have found that thing and discovered how to use it."

Erith felt a chill as he remembered the remains of the inhabitants of the underground hall.

"How did you acquire the dagger, then? Were you told anything about it?" Finlan asked as he herded them back up the stairs.

"I may have been told, but I only understood one word in ten of the language that was spoken. It was given to me in a place underneath a mountain, in…incredible circumstances by people unencumbered by bodies."

"Ah," said Finlan, with the merest trace of skepticism in his voice. "And the eye saw this too?"

"What there was to see, yes."

A small, nondescript woman in smith's garb awaited them at the top of the stairs.

"Finlan, do you know where the *alaran* has gone? I was to…oh." She stopped, aghast, when she saw Ronne ascending the stairs behind the smith.

"Kelme. I have a task for you," said Ronne, reaching the top and stepping aside to let Erith pass by. "My helmbearer requires battle armor."

"*Helmbearer?* But he's a…." Kelme cringed at the expression in Ronne's eyes, and gulped. She looked Erith up and down. "Er. Yes. Lots of armor. We, uh, we don't have anything that large in store," she said, spreading her hands apologetically.

"Not even modified?"

The smith shook her head. "It wouldn't be safe by the time it fit."

Ronne made an impatient gesture. "Then you will have to make it new."

Kelme goggled at her. "Tha…that will take me over a month, and doing nothing else!"

"Unacceptable," stated Ronne. "We may be fighting in a week. You will have to devise something by then with as much protection as possible."

Kelme just nodded weakly and left with a gloomy countenance. Erith felt a twinge of sympathy for the little armorer. He wasn't sure how well he would be able to fight in armor; it seemed a waste of effort.

"You will still need better weapons, and a shield," said Ronne after they left the smithy. "If they have nothing suitable here, we may have something in the family armory. My father and his sister were both tall."

Erith just nodded. He heard the sound of rapid motion behind them, and turned. The large man who had greeted them at the door of the darkmetal smiths was hurrying in their direction. When he reached them, he put a long, cloth-wrapped bundle in Erith's hands.

"Arisaig sends," he said as well as he could for being out of breath, then disappeared back into the dark smithy.

Erith opened the bundle. It contained a sword and harness in the Imperial style. The harness was shabby and used, but still sturdy. The sword was darkmetal, simple and unornamented.

Ronne's eyebrows rose. "You are to be congratulated. I did not know there were any of her swords left."

Erith stared at her, astonished. "Arisaig made this?"

Ronne nodded. "She was head smith before Finlan, and she made some of the best darkmetal swords before age got the better of her. You must have impressed her."

He moved the sword in the light, marveling at the dark, watered surface. *I wish I knew how I did it.*

Ronne surveyed the activity in the inner ward while she considered what next to do. Soldiers were unloading gear from a cart with a great deal of shouting and armwaving. She could hear the tension in their voices. *We have much to do—and so little time. Talorgen has no reason to wait.*

She could not devote all her time to preparation for war. As much as she would like to avoid it, the council would have to be convened, and the sooner it was done, the better. She turned back to the fortress. Erith followed, still struggling with the unfamiliar fastenings of the harness. That had been an unexpected stroke of luck—the darkmetal smiths were notorious for their independence; few would believe it was only Ronne's influence that had won him the honor.

A household servant met Ronne at the entrance, with the message that Inar wished to speak with her when she had leisure. Ronne frowned. It would not be an enjoyable visit. They had no pleasant topics to discuss, and it was another distraction she did not need. She would have to see her mother at some point. They had only exchanged a few words since her return.

"Bring me Stenay," she told the servant, who bowed and departed. "My mother will want to speak to me privately," she said to Erith. "There are other matters that should be seen to, if you would aid me." It would be best for him to avoid the fortress people in her absence.

"Of course."

Stenay appeared, dignified and soberly dressed. As a family servant, he wore a grey overrobe in mourning. He bowed and waited in silence.

"Stenay, this is Erith, my helmbearer. Go with him to the others of my traveling companions and see that they have all they need. Hear my voice in any suggestions he may have regarding them."

"*A'liata,*" said Stenay, unperturbed.

The servant had not indicated where her mother was waiting, but Ronne headed for the balcony room over the council chambers, which had always been the family gathering place. Her mother and brother were there.

It seemed to Ronne that her mother had a frozen shell over her usual calm demeanor, and some of the age that had passed her over before showed in her face now. And Alland…his handsome features had inspired the court ladies' best poems from the first day of his arrival in Ynduria.

Now his face was seamed and puckered on one side by a horrible burn. *At least he is alive.*

Inar rose to embrace her, and Ronne held her close. She was shocked by how thin and frail her mother felt. Her throat constricted, and she fought back tears. She had no words to comfort her, and at last let her go.

"It gladdens my heart that you are here," said Inar, touching Ronne's face. "I feared I might never see you again."

"It gladdens my heart to be here, Mother." Ronne took a seat on a stone bench. "Tell me how it has been for you."

Inar looked out to the view of the Lake Within, and the immobility of her face deepened. "It has been very bad," she said softly. "Death in battle…this has come before. But always there was a reason."

Alland broke in. "Do you think the fighting will come here?"

"I know it will. I feared it would be at our borders by now. There is more—the Empire was destroyed by Imperials."

A moment's shocked silence followed. "How do you know this?" asked Alland.

"My helmbearer, Erith ne'Haral, knows the customs of the Southern Horde. From the description of what happened to Ynduria, he is certain it could not have been their work."

"You have gathered a most unusual following on your return, Ronne."

Ronne was quick to hear the hidden thread of disapproval in Inar's voice. "I am indebted to all of them, in one form or another. If it were not for the kenjah and their riding beasts I would never have arrived so soon." *Or at all.*

"And the two with the strange white hair?"

Ronne hesitated. She did not want to force the full horror of the truth on those who had seen enough already. But when would be a better time?

"Their village in Oguz was destroyed, the inhabitants slaughtered. All in search of me. Since they could not remain, I brought them here, to repay what Talorgen took from them."

Alland looked at Ronne with startled eyes, breathing the name. Inar drew her robes more closely around her, as if cold.

"And when did you go among the barbarians, to find your helmbearer?" she asked, her voice cool.

"He came to me, at the outpost. He was escaping enemies and I found him, wounded." Ronne felt a flare of anger at the implied criticism. "I am nothing like Amrane, respected mother," she said softly, "and I think you would agree even she would have greater discretion."

Alland turned red with embarrassment, but Inar simply nodded and changed the subject.

Ronne emerged from the balcony room with a sense of relief. It was good to see her mother and brother, but they also reminded her of those who were gone. She had difficulty keeping her gaze from Alland's terrible scar, and it created a feeling of awkwardness between them. Still, she had given him the charge of setting up a formal Linariach meeting, and this opportunity to be of use seemed to lighten his somber mood.

She descended the stairs, congratulating herself for avoiding the tedious details of the Linariach convening. The council was bad enough—but with a new *alaran*, the Lineages would have to all be refigured to determine who would have a seat in the Linariach.

As if the thought had summoned him, Hereil tes Arhi appeared. An influential member of the past Linariach, his kinship was sufficiently close it was a certainty he would be in this one. Hoping her dismay did not show on her face, she continued to descend even as he reached her.

"Unless the matter is urgent, I must ask you to wait for the Linariach meeting," she said, interrupting his formal greeting. "I have a great deal to attend to at the moment."

"But of course…you will be having your ascension ceremony, and at such short notice! If I may—"

"The ceremony has been postponed. We will shortly be at war."

This gave him pause, but not for long. "In such a situation, just beginning your rule, you will doubtless be needing advice. Having served both Amrane and your honored father—"

Ronne gritted her teeth as his fluent speech washed over her, and continued to descend the stairs. She knew what he was hinting at, and she was going to have him on her private council when the world ended, not before.

She stopped at the inner gate, trying to think of a way to rid herself of Hereil without offending him.

Hereil awoke to the fact she was no longer moving forward. "Do I detain you? Where are you bound?"

"I must consult with the army commanders and see that my traveling companions are well."

Hereil gave a laugh, and only a severe critic would have said it was artificial. "A varied lot, I must say. And that plains barbarian, quite exotic! A fine specimen. But wouldn't it have been kinder to the poor fellow to have given him a few trinkets and sent him home? Now that you are here you can hardly have any use for him."

After considering the matter, Ronne regretfully concluded it would be impossible to kill Hereil and hide the body without anyone noticing.

He continued without pause, blissfully unaware of the direction her thoughts had taken. "I have a young kinsman who speaks of nothing but joining the personal guard of the *alaran*. If you wish, he could be here within a day."

"Arhi needs everyone willing and able to fight," Ronne said with deliberate vagueness. She saw Manohan tes Arhi approaching the foot of the stair, and she felt a glimmer of hope. There was little love lost between Manohan and Hereil, and he stiffened as she came near.

Manohan sported a streak of silver in her dark hair and wore a habitual expression of sardonic amusement. As she walked, she favored one leg, and Ronne recalled hearing Manohan had been wounded at Ynduria.

"Command me," she said curtly after bowing in greeting. "I regret I am not yet able to take the field, for I hear we shall be fighting soon. But perhaps the *alaran* can make some other use of my services."

"Indeed I can," said Ronne, forestalling any comment from Hereil. "My brother is engaged in setting up the next Linariach. If you and Hereil would make yourselves available to him, between the three of you the difficulties will be nothing and we will be able to convene without delay."

Nodding to them both, Ronne left, knowing Hereil would be delayed by Manohan long enough for her to escape.

Erith followed Stenay through the middle gate and out into the outer ward, where the Windriders, Duanoch, and Bryddhe were lodged in a small building set against the cliff wall.

"The soldiers are, of course, in the barracks," Stenay answered, when he asked about Tekbeh and Zeltan.

A number of Arhi soldiers had gathered about outside the lodging, gawking at the horses. Two of the kenjah watched the soldiers suspiciously. The horses seemed as nervous as the kenjah, tossing their heads and kicking out at each other or anyone who got too close.

When Erith entered the lodging he was besieged by questions from all sides.

"Did you bring the soft beast with you?" asked Bryddhe eagerly, reaching out her hands.

"What about Talorgen?" Duanoch asked. "Is he attacking yet?"

Edge Singing eyed him accusingly. "Why you not say, *cha'tral* great chieftain?"

No one had any complaints, but Kemar'sto said a few words to Edge Singing, who translated for Erith. The kenjah were concerned about their horses, who needed a place where they would not be disturbed by the soldiers.

"They look, hungry eyes. How we stop, they take?" Edge Singing wanted to know.

Erith left out the fear of theft in his translation for Stenay.

"There is a structure intended for the shelter of cattle during a siege. Perhaps this would be suitable?"

Erith and Edge Singing followed Stenay to the cattle shed, across the outer ward against the gate wall. It had wide doors and room enough for all the horses, and Edge Singing nodded in approval.

The kenjah lost no time getting the horses installed in the shed. Erith brought in his own and Ronne's grey. He saw Edge Singing holding her own mount's foot tucked up on her knee, and went over to look.

"What are you doing? Doesn't that hurt it?"

She flashed a grin. "Hurt if not do! See, you do same." She poked again with a carved wooden stick that had a hook at the end. A small pebble came loose from the inner part of the hoof. "Stay, no run." She let it down, then picked up another foot. Giving Erith a speculative look, she asked, "Will great chieftain say, I fight for her?"

"I think she'd be glad to have you," Erith said. Then, remembering Ronne's warnings, added, "but the ways of her people are strange to me. You should ask her."

"Yeh," she nodded. "Good merit, fight for *cha'tral.* Good to stay."

Erith scratched his horse's forehead, where it always seemed to be itchy. It lowered its head and sighed, relaxing. "You could stay forever, just by raising horses. They'd do a lot to get more."

She shook her head. "Kenjah no land, no ancestor house. *M'nes*—these old time law—say no land, no grow child, no grow horse."

"If you had land, you could raise horses?"

"Yeh. Winter place, ancestor house. No place left that way," Edge Singing waved a hand in the direction of the plains. "Some, they fight, take other ancestor house."

"Would the kenjah fight in exchange for land?"

The raider's golden eyes blazed with surprising intensity. "*Mayan!* Forever…. You hear Un'Varten words, kenjah fight with *cha'tral* for merit! Give land…." She struggled for expression. "All kenjah fight for *cha'tral* then."

He left the shelter not long afterwards and headed for the fortress, wondering if Ronne was still with her mother, and how he would find her. She would be interested in what Edge Singing had told him.

As he neared the gate to the inner ward, he heard sounds of commotion. Quickening his pace, he saw a group of soldiers surrounding something, something that made a snarling roar of frustration. *Kashan…how did he get out?*

In a burst of speed, he reached a soldier who was about to cast a spear and ripped the weapon from his hand, swinging the butt end to clear a space around the beleaguered snowtiger.

More shouts, and he realized the soldiers were drawing their swords and facing him.

"How'd he get in the gate? They must already be here!" yelled one, panicked. Erith swung the spear again, and they backed up a step. He had to do something, and fast, or someone would get killed.

"I came with the *alaran*, fool! Leave the beast alone!" he shouted. "What did you do to him?"

"He was a goin' wild-like," said one nervous soldier, spear still ready. "Broke out o' the place they was keepin' him. Bounded out like he was goin' ta kill us all!"

"He won't kill anybody if you leave him be," Erith said, exasperated. "Now give him room!"

The soldiers made way reluctantly, still keeping their weapons drawn, and Kashan slowly began to calm down. He was still too agitated for Erith to approach him, so he spoke in a quiet voice to the snowtiger until the tail ceased its lashing.

Then Ronne broke into the circle of watching soldiers, who nearly attacked Kashan again when he went to her. "Kashan is only a danger to those who attack me," she said, forestalling the soldiers. "I will keep him with me from now on."

"He says he came with you," one of the soldiers said, pointing with his sword to Erith. Ronne stared him down.

"My helmbearer accompanies me, as is the custom," she said in a freezing tone. The soldiers shifted uneasily and tried to sheathe their weapons without being noticed. Ronne looked at Erith and inclined her head toward the entrance. He was more than willing to leave.

He followed her to the fortress, Kashan padding along beside her. As they ascended the main stair, Inar appeared at the top. Her long grey robes swirled about her, pooling at her feet. She wore a gauze overrobe over her shimmering grey silk gown; it surrounded her slender form like a cloud. Lengths of delicate grey fabric hung from her shoulders, caught up in tufts held by metal clasps.

"We are preparing a feast tonight, to celebrate your arrival," said Ronne's mother in her cool, calm voice.

Erith thought he saw Ronne wince. "There is no time for such things. We may be fighting tomorrow."

"The time taken from preparation will be more than made up for by the good spirits from a proper celebration. We have not had anything to celebrate for a long time," she added softly. "Give your people that much before sorrow comes again."

Ronne looked away, then sighed. "Let it be as you say."

Ronne's council met that afternoon in the *alaran's* chambers. It was hard for her to realize she was now *alaran*, harder still to accept that her father was truly gone. Her throat tightened when she saw the familiar room without the familiar face in the central chair; the chair, now empty, that she must take.

Fear of giving way to emotion made her curt in responding to the greetings that met her entrance. It was a small gathering, consisting mostly of soldiers. *Face of Fortune permit I live to need political advice.*

When the preliminaries were finished, Ronne invited the council to give her any information from the fighting at Ynduria or after that she should know.

Dunand cleared his throat. "The barbarians began their attack early in the spring," he said, carefully not looking at Erith. "Imperial forces at the border were not up to strength and were soon overwhelmed. By the time we and the other northern *alars* could move our armies, the line of battle was just outside of Ynduria. We formed up, but nothing went right. The armies flanking us retreated early. We would have been surrounded and slaughtered except for your father's courage—Arven called Medar to him, and together they cut back through the enemy and gave us our retreat, but at a cost. Arven fell in the attempt, and our losses were high. Although we recovered your father's body and sword, Medar's body was never found," he concluded.

Medar…he should be sitting here, not me. She wrenched her attention back to the council with an effort. Finavah continued with a report on the state of the army. The numbers were much as they had reported earlier in the day, but the weapons and armor available were insufficient.

"We lost a great deal at Ynduria, and we couldn't recover what we lost in the retreat. As it is now, we have to share the heavier weapons for training, and many have no armor at all."

Ronne nodded, frowning. "That must change. Our enemy will have lives to spare. We have none." She looked about the table. "I know we will be attacked soon. Talorgen made that very clear." She recounted all that had occurred recently between her and Talorgen, omitting none of the details of the atrocity in the Oguz village or the threats made at the inn. When she had finished, there was a deep silence in the room.

"Have the scouts been sent?" said Ronne finally.

Dunand stirred. "Within the hour of your command."

"It is a pity we have only the four horses you were given," said Finavah. "They could be very useful for sending messages or scouting. Can we get more?"

"The kenjah have asked if they could fight with us," Ronne replied. Erith's information had been the one piece of good news she had heard all day. Land would be a tricky thing to negotiate with the Linariach, since they would be worried about having the kenjah close by, but she was determined to try.

The council proper broke up shortly thereafter, but a military session grew out of it. Two retired army commanders were brought in, as well as a few junior officers, and they and Ronne went over possible strategies in exhaustive detail. Ronne did her best to encourage them, but they knew as well as she did they were poorly equipped for a war of this magnitude. Their only options were caution and endurance.

"Do you think all that will work?" asked Erith bluntly when the rest had left.

Ronne rubbed a weary hand over her eyes and sighed, wishing he had not echoed her thoughts. "I hope so. What else can I do? Even Talorgen cannot produce food from thin air. He will have to withdraw to winter camps if he does not get through our defenses in the fall. We need as much of our harvest as we can get in, for the same reason. So…we fight to delay, if we cannot fight to win."

He thought for a moment. "He will have his own supplies. We should take them from him."

Ronne looked at him, mulling the idea in her mind. "Yes, that would work. How would you accomplish this?"

"I have an idea. My people did a lot of raiding."

"Good. We will discuss it next time." Ronne rose from her seat, feeling stiff. "We should take the things given to us under the mountain to the archivist. He may be able to tell us what they are."

The archivist, Temaso Conyet, was a genial cricket of a man who was rarely seen outside his precious library. It seemed to Ronne that he had always been wrinkled and stooped. He had been so in her earliest memories of him, and so he had remained. The library was dim and shadowed, every surface but the ceiling covered in some part with books, papers, and scrolls.

"So, what have you brought me?" asked Temaso after Ronne explained the purpose of their visit. His eyes were bright with anticipation. As they brought out their treasures, he grew more and more excited, rubbing his hands with glee and fidgeting like a child offered a new toy. When Ronne produced the books, he almost snatched them from her hands in impatience.

"Written records!" he breathed. "And they spoke the language of the *tier sanas* oath?"

"Much better than I."

He looked up, worried. "I taught you as best I could, from the little I knew…."

Ronne held up a hand. "I was not complaining. Indeed, I was very grateful for what I had learned. Can you read it?" she asked, as he carefully paged through the ancient tome he held.

"In time," he said absently. "The manuscripts I have are only fragments…. There is more?" This he said in astonishment, as Ronne brought out the diadem and the moonrose box.

The crown flowed through Temaso's fingers when Ronne was not touching it, even as it had for Erith. And when Ronne held the moonrose, which shed its golden light in every corner of the dusty library, Temaso could only stare at it in wonder.

"How delightful!" he said finally. "We have proof to confound the Imperial Court and that uppity Nesrin…but it's too late for that now." His face was sad.

"Is there anything you can tell us now about these things?" Ronne asked, gesturing at the collection of objects. "What they are, why they were given to us, anything." *There must be a way to find out more—these things are too dangerous to experiment with.*

"I am not certain," said the archivist, rubbing his chin. "But if I were to guess, I would say these things are for your defense. The dagger you discovered the use of yourself. And these," he picked up one of the brooches, "this is one glyph that I know. *Remalk kultoeth.* It conveys protection from evil creatures."

CHAPTER 16

I still think this is a waste of time, thought Ronne as she prepared for the feast that evening. She looked over the clothing laid out by her bodyservant and nodded approval. With the family in mourning, the layered tunics and overrobe were all in shades of grey, but the fabrics were rich—brocaded silk, with silver threads woven in the long sash.

As she dressed, she wondered how the household would find suitable garb of a size to fit Erith. They had managed once already, and very well. She smiled to herself. The Imperial styles suited him; she looked forward to seeing him in more formal dress. *And it's likely the only pleasure I will have tonight.*

The room was crowded and warm, even though it was open to the lake portico. Erith wished he could eat his meal out there, away from the noise. Hundreds of feasters filled the Audience, sitting at narrow tables set along the length of the room. One long table was set across the end, where Ronne and her family were seated, flanked by the others who had traveled with her.

He could hear some of the comments made by those standing about the hall, not fortunate enough to get a seat. Even when they were discussing him, they made no effort to lower their voices. *They must think I'm deaf, or don't understand the language.* It was an effort to keep his temper under control.

He tried to concentrate on other things, such as helping the kenjah decipher forks and the spice server. There were some things he had never seen before either, and he watched the other Arhiia carefully to see how they were used.

It was a strange feast. There was meat, but it was cut up in little pieces and covered with rich sauce or baked into fantastic shapes. He could never tell how something would taste by how it looked. After biting into what he thought was a fruit, and was instead a very spicy meat pastry, he sampled the food with caution.

The wine was stronger than he was used to, and tart. He balanced the winecup gingerly in his hand. It was so thin and delicate he feared he would crush it simply by holding it.

Ronne had placed the moonrose before her where everyone in the hall could see it, and the light from the lamps was low enough for its glow to be visible. She seemed to be alone with her thoughts. Ronne's brother Alland was seated next to Erith, and doing his best to pretend Erith wasn't there.

With no one to talk to, he watched the crowd before him instead. A voice from a nearby conversation caught his ear.

"I thought the whole idea of the war was to prevent the barbarians from coming here. Instead, she imports them herself!"

Erith glanced out of the corner of his eye. The speaker was seated along the side of the hall, a striking woman with a slash of white in her dark hair.

"You have to admit, Manohan, they are not ordinary barbarians," said the woman's neighbor.

"In my view, they are remarkable only for being here," Manohan replied, scorn dripping from her voice. "Her family should have objected."

"You know her family was forbidden to visit, or even write while she was out there. I wonder how fastidious you would be, after three years in the middle of nowhere!"

Erith became aware of a thread of another conversation. This one was directly behind him, and he could not look at the speakers without being noticed.

"…Imperial enemies, back to Amrane."

"Amrane? Are you sure?"

The first speaker snorted. "I just don't see a fighter like her letting an enemy get close enough to put a dagger in her back. And the Emperor was livid when she ignored the husband he forced her to take. I forget his name…."

Another snickered. "Amrane never knew it. Did he really think that trick would work on *her*? And then he tries it on the next *alaran!*"

Another voice added, "The joke goes further. When it was clear Inar had fooled the court and was more of Arven's mind than theirs, they ordered her to bear no more children!"

"No, they were always trying something against Arhi. Trying to get control…."

Alland regarded his plate glumly, waiting for the feast to end. Ronne wasn't speaking, the place was rife with barbarians, and he felt the eyes of every person in the hall on his scarred face. *Why did I bother to come back? What can I do?*

A server came by with a plate of *tasse*, and he forgot his troubles for a moment. The little cakes were fresh, crumbly and warm, smelling of spice. He'd forgotten how much he missed *tasse*—since they were a Northern delicacy, the court never served them. He savored the smell, holding the *tasse* in both hands, preparing to take the first bite.

The giant barbarian beside him took one and looked at it with suspicion, then bit into it. Alland almost laughed at the look on the man's face, and had a brief moment of sympathy when he looked about for more.

"They are good, aren't they?" Alland said before he could stop himself. "They never make enough."

"What are they?"

Alland was surprised at how well he spoke Middle Speech. He almost sounded like an Imperial. "*Tasse*," he answered curtly, his resentment and gloom returning full force.

The man was a barbarian, and yet he was more useful to Arhi than the *alaran's* own brother. The barbarian was a warrior, while he…what could he do? Negotiate people to death? Write insulting poems to the enemy? No one would look him in the eye for fear of seeing his ruined face. All he had been trained for was the Imperial Court—which was now a pile of charred rubble.

It might have been easier to bear if he hadn't seen the appraising glances some of the women cast in Erith's direction. Properly dressed, with his unusual gold hair tied back like the other men, it was surprising how civilized he appeared. *And there's no denying his looks, damn him.*

If Erith and Ronne weren't lovers, why was he here? Alland doubted Erith was her helmbearer because she felt a sudden need to spread the way of the *tier sanas*. *Whatever the reason, it must be a strong one to bring him so far.*

When Ronne judged she had been at the feast long enough to leave, she rose and collected the moonrose from its place of honor. It blazed at her touch, and all at the high table turned to see it. Even Bryddhe.

Her blind eyes looked at the moonrose. Ronne came closer and held the glowing flower up to the girl's face, feeling a shuddering chill pass over her. She was surprised by how little surprise she felt. More magic—around her, part of her. *Did I suspect, and refuse to recognize it?*

Like melting snow, the opaque film on Bryddhe's eyes cleared, leaving black pupils surrounded by a clear crystal iris. Bryddhe looked up at her, and Ronne knew she could see her face—and that the girl recognized her. Bryddhe showed no surprise at her sudden gift of sight. Ronne moved the moonrose away, and the clouding film began to return.

"I am taking this to the care of the archivist. I have given him other items of a like nature to study. Perhaps you would be willing to help him. I think in some of these matters you may see more than we do."

Bryddhe whispered, "Yes." She seemed both frightened and fascinated.

"Then follow me." Ronne left, ignoring the incoherent protests of Duanoch. She would not listen—she would use any means available to understand the emerging mysteries that surrounded them. Even a child.

Staring out at the Lake Within, Alland reviewed the composition of the new Linariach. He had sent the proper notification to the new councilors that morning, and now he could only wait for them to show up. Ronne would not be pleased with some of them.

The sound of soft, hesitant footsteps roused him from his abstraction, and he saw the blind, white-haired girl his sister had rescued coming forward, trailing one hand on the wall and extending the other before her.

"How did you like our revelry last night?" he asked, and she started, then smiled.

"It was wonderful! I am Bryddhe. Who are you?"

"Alland. The *alaran* has told me a little of what happened to you and your brother. I am glad you are here safe with us." He felt a certain sympathy for her. She was also an outsider, not quite certain of her place or function. Everything she knew was destroyed; she could not go back any more than he could return to Ynduria.

She shivered and held her free hand close to her chest. "It was so frightening…. But you are her brother! I heard them saying you escaped someplace too. Where the fighting was."

"Ynduria. Yes, I was there."

"Were you hurt?" she asked. He started, furious, then remembered. She couldn't see his face.

"Only a little," he replied, astonished as he realized for the first time this was true. "My face and arm were burned."

She turned to him, concern transparent on her face. "Oh no! Does it still hurt? I burned myself once, when a visitor left a lamp on the table without telling me and it hurt for *weeks*."

"No, it doesn't hurt anymore. Not like at first." He smiled at her relieved expression. "Is it safe for you to be walking alone like this? If you don't know where the stairs are you might walk off the portico into the lake."

She gave a flashing smile. "That's what my brother says! Exactly the same thing. Everybody is busy with more important things, and I can only sit still for so long. I'm very careful. I walk slowly, and if there isn't any noise you can sort of feel where the stairs and walls are. Besides, this is a friendly place. They won't let me get hurt."

She stopped short, looking a little frightened, and quickly changed the subject. "How did you escape from Ynduria? Your sister said there were many enemy soldiers, and nobody else got out."

He considered her for a moment, then reached for her hand and placed it on his arm. Her fingers were cold. "Let me take you to the garden. It's warmer, and it smells wonderful this time of year—How did I escape? By having an assignation, and a nightmare."

They reached the lake portico, and he led her along the edge. A light breeze twirled the ghost-traps without sounding them.

"What do you mean?"

"I had a secret meeting with someone who was supposed to deliver a message to me. We had arranged a time late at night, and I had tried to sleep before, but the nightmare put a stop to that and I left early." A distant part of his mind was marveling at how freely he told this stranger things he usually kept secret. Medar and Ronne had teased him about his dreams all his life.

"The night the raiders came," he said slowly. "I dreamed of a horrible creature. It was human in form, but it had small, dark, glittery eyes like a rat and lots of sharp teeth, like needles. It was…eating people. Alive." He shuddered, remembering the frantic screams, the gory thrashing of limbs. "After I managed to wake up I had no interest in falling asleep again. I went to the place I was to meet the messenger, and waited." He paused while they crossed the waterfall bridge. When the noise had faded he continued. He decided to leave out finding Narat's body.

"Then I noticed there wasn't any sound; normal sounds like the night guard pacing. When I looked, there were strangers, armed strangers inside the palace grounds. Then I smelled smoke. I had to get through the gatehouse to escape, and that was where the beam fell on me. I don't remember how I got free, or much after that, except…the pain of my burns, and running. I traveled on foot that night and the next before I met with my father's troop."

They walked in silence for a while. Bryddhe's face was troubled.

"I know what it was. That creature. It's a remalk."

"*What?* You couldn't possibly…. It's not real!"

She stopped and turned to face him. "I dream too. I see in those dreams, know things, sometimes things that exist, sometimes not. I saw that creature in my dreams the night before my village was destroyed."

He stared at her, incredulous. "Why didn't you tell anyone?"

She smiled sadly. "Strange dreams just make people frightened of you. They don't think they can be true, if there's magic in them."

"Ronne should know about this…remalk. She might believe you."

Bryddhe tilted her head. "I think she already knows."

Erith watched the group of soldiers move about the outer ward as Zeltan shouted. "What are they doing? He never seems to be satisfied with how they are arranged."

Ronne gave a muffled snort. When she answered him her voice sounded constrained. "They are drilling—practicing moving about in a large group. When we fight together like this, it is hard for an enemy to attack in a vulnerable place."

"Oh." Erith tried to imagine fighting like that, and failed. "How do they stay together when they fight?"

All traces of amusement left Ronne's face. "It is not a simple thing. It must be practiced for many months before it can be done well…and many of these here have never drilled before."

The mass of soldiers seemed identical at first glance: brown faces beneath simple helms, wearing armor over tunics. Then he saw some were without helms. More than a few had no armor at all, wearing heavy leather jerkins for protection. He pointed this out.

"I am aware," Ronne snapped.

"The smiths…."

"We have too few with armor-making skill, and they cannot make much. It is a slow process. They must also make weapons."

He began to understand Ronne's concern, and the determination in Zeltan's voice as he repeated his instructions again and again. Everyone who could fight needed to be trained, and even then it might not be enough. And with losses in battle…. A memory began to form, stories he had heard of a plains clan, poor and small, that used any means they could to preserve the lives of their warriors.

"I was told once of a crude but simple kind of armor," he said. "Short lengths of tough reed, cut in half and sewn between two pieces cloth or leather. You could use pieces of metal plate, perhaps. Easier to make, and you wouldn't need a smith for most of it."

Ronne gazed at the training army and slowly began to nod her head in agreement. "Yes, I see…simple and effective. We should attempt it; we have great need of armor."

The drill had come to a halt. The soldiers milled about, and various subcommanders came up to Zeltan to confer. Erith saw Tekbeh was among them. Ronne headed in their direction, and he followed.

"How does it go?" she asked Zeltan. He threw up his hands and rolled his eyes.

"It's only by putting the new with the old we have any order at all. Any word yet?"

Ronne shook her head. "No, and I find it strange. Have no fear, I will not keep it a secret when I do know." She turned her gaze to Tekbeh. "When you are done here, I want you to spend some time with the kenjah. Learn as much as you can of their speech, and the care of the horses. They may be fighting with us and we will need the horses for scouting. Anything you learn will be helpful." Tekbeh nodded.

"Is there no one else to send? There's none too many for the work at hand," Zeltan objected.

"She is the only one who has traveled with them who can be spared. I know your need; I do not do this lightly."

Zeltan grumbled but accepted the inevitable.

Erith's idea for armor had been acted on immediately, and within a day of his suggestion he had the first of what the Arhiia were calling steelshirts. It was large enough for him, and heavy. The sun was hot in the outer ward, and Erith could feel sweat trickling down his back underneath the leather backing of his steelshirt. He stretched, trying to get rid of the tension in his arms. He and Ronne had been sparring all morning, and he was just beginning to get used to his new armor. He preferred it to the solid plate armor—it was more flexible. He still needed to become comfortable fighting in it, however.

He rested his shield against one leg and rubbed his arm where the strap chafed. The shield was different than those of the plains—as wide as the length of his forearm and tapering to a point just below his knee. The Imperials used it actively, not just as a wall to hide behind but as a striking weapon to get an opponent off balance.

"Why don't you use a shield?" he asked.

Ronne raised her left arm, which had a disk a handspan broad strapped to her wrist. "It is called a targe. The battle armor permits this," she explained. "If you had battle armor your shield could be smaller."

"Battle armor is different than that?" Erith asked, gesturing at Ronne's gear. It was the same she had worn traveling and at the outpost, although he had a hazy memory of something different that had been loaded on the lenghur when they left.

"Very different. It is heavier, the plates are larger, and there are jointed plates that cover the arm."

He looked out at the activity in the ward. The soldiers were getting much better at drilling, but Zeltan did not let up. A few wore steelshirts now, like him.

"At least we've had some time to prepare. Almost a month."

Ronne nodded, sighing. "There is still much to be done, but I am not complaining."

Movement at the main gate caught his attention. Soldiers were picking up weapons, and one broke from the group, running towards Ronne.

"A messenger!" he shouted. "The *alar* of Corin has fallen to Talorgen!"

CHAPTER 17

In the crowd, Ronne could see wounded people with unfamiliar faces. *Prisoners? No, they have their weapons.* An Arhi soldier emerged from this group and saluted her. She was haggard and tired, her armor dusty from travel. Ronne recognized her as the dagger-thrower from when she first met with the army commanders.

"*Na'al,* I have just now come from Corin. The city of Kalmar fell to Talorgen four days ago."

Ronne closed her eyes. So that was where Talorgen had been. It was a relief to have any news, but she grieved to know Corin was in the hands of the enemy.

"Who are these with you?"

Another came forward then, a man near her own age with slightly tilted eyes above his prominent cheekbones. He seemed familiar, and when he spoke she remembered him. Siret tes Corin, a distant relative.

"Survivors, cousin, come not for shelter but to beg a place among your armed. There are few enough of us."

"You are welcome, Siret, and to what safety there is. You know the grief you left behind will follow." They gripped arms in greeting.

"We know. With luck there will be other survivors to follow us. I left word for any such to come here."

Something in Siret's tone caught Ronne's attention, and she lowered her voice so only he could hear her. "You are the Revenant?"

He nodded and answered in the same low tone. "Our Lines were sparse enough before Ynduria. There could be others with a claim, but...."

Ronne waved that aside. "Now is not the time for fine points of law." It was enough that someone with blood right could speak for Corin, could command any remaining Corinha forces.

"As you say." Then, in a more normal voice, "Edirn, Durres, and Vidin are of the Lineage and Kindred of Corin, and Tarbek and Khemis soldiers. Tallin is not of Corin," he pointed to a large and rather rough-looking fellow in their group, "but of Oguz. He warned us of Talorgen's coming. We would never have been able to put up a defense in time without him."

"He moved that fast?" asked Ronne, surprised.

" 'E runs 'is army ta th' grund," said Tallin in a deep voice. "Found one dead by th' road, not a mark o' woundin'."

The Arhiia digested this information in shocked silence. Ronne frowned. "How long were you fighting him?"

"A matter of three weeks, little more. The last eight days were spent on the siege of Kalmar."

Ronne felt a small surge of hope. Talorgen had been running his army constantly, from the taking of Oguz to Corin. *And very likely before*, she thought, thinking of the destruction of Ynduria. Even the best army could not fight for months without rest. Talorgen's forces would be at a disadvantage, if she could attack while they were still exhausted.

The council members took their seats without delay. Siret and the messenger, Kielce, were also present. Ronne gestured to Siret.

"What can you tell us? How did Talorgen attack?"

"He struck through here," said Siret, pointing at the map on the table. The commanders leaned forward for a better view. "It was a direct attack, aiming for Kalmar."

"He had the main body of his army at the city and a few smaller units on the road between Corin and Oguz. I saw no preparations for march when we escaped," added Kielce.

"Where's the most direct road from Kalmar to Arhi?" asked Finavah.

"There's a path here, in the foothills, that's the shortest. But the path is steep and none so wide, not a good choice for a large army. There is another, maybe a day's march south from the other, that is easier," said Dunand.

"Does he know we know about Corin?" asked one of the army commanders. "He might come in from the Oguz border instead."

Ronne stared at her clasped hands. "He will know some of the Corin Lineage escaped. Where else would they go? We are the only *alar* he does not hold."

An uncomfortable silence filled the room. *The best cure for fear is knowledge. He must never catch us by surprise.*

"He has a large army, you say. That should make him easy to track. We must have eyes at every point he might enter Arhi, and even further," said Ronne.

"We have no people to spare," protested Dunand. "If they are scattered to the border they won't be able to return in time to fight!"

"The horses can do it," said Erith. Dunand turned on him, scowling.

"And how many of these horses are there? No, I need a better answer."

Ronne raised her hand a fraction to stop Erith's hasty reply. "Have you found people for the roving group?" she asked him. Erith had anticipated this very problem and suggested a band of fighters that could move and strike quickly, using the horses for scouting. It also answered the question of where to make use of the kenjah, who would be difficult to fit into the regular army.

"We have a group gathered now. Some hunters, and the kenjah, and a few that know how to raid."

Some of the commanders looked at him in shock and disbelief. Dunand's face darkened. "I heard of that, but did not give it credit. A barn thief, taken from prison for this…" he spluttered, waving his hands, "raiding." His voice was full of contempt. "That may be the custom of his people, but we fight honorably, on the open field, not skulking about in the shadows! We are Imperials!"

"We *were* Imperials," Ronne said harshly. "There is no Empire now. You have said the army can spare no soldiers. If there is a thief willing to fight for Arhi, I will free him. You need not concern yourself about how Erith chooses his people."

"His?" asked one of the lesser commanders. "He is leading this band? How can you give this stranger so much, trusting him with any part of the defense of Arhi? Will he be commanding *us?*"

The resentment was plain. Ronne let her anger flare and drew her shortblade. She struck the hilt on the table with all her strength. The sudden sound made them start.

"We are fighting for our lives," she said, intensity in every word. They sat frozen, not daring to look at her. "We are fighting an enemy who will not negotiate, who thinks nothing of killing the weak and defenseless. We are outnumbered, we have no allies. If we fail, we die. *There is nowhere to run.* You do not care for this style of fighting, do you?" she said, pointing the blade at the resentful commander. "That is why he is in command and you are not."

She took a deep breath, trying to regain her calm. Kashan prowled anxiously, looking for the danger that threatened her, and she stroked his head when he returned to her side.

"Have the rovers in readiness to leave as soon as you can," she said to Erith. "When you have decided how you will post them, bring the plan to me."

Erith left the fortress full of frustrated anger. The council—it was better not to think of what the council had said. When he reached the main gate he kept going, hoping a walk in the city would calm him down. Few of the inhabitants would be out so late. It would be good to leave the city, to be in the open again, but it would not be enough. He felt restless and dissatisfied.

A muffled cry caught his ear as he passed one of the narrow alleys that ran between the streets. In the gloom he could barely make out a desperate, uneven struggle. One person was fighting like a fury against three assailants, choking one, kicking out at another even as the third slammed the lone fighter into a wall.

Erith gave a yell and charged. The alley was too cramped to draw his sword, and the combatants were too close for him to use his shortblade. One of the attackers turned to face him, and Erith saw the flash of a knife. He twisted and let the knife go past him, then grabbed the knife-hand and arm and bodily threw the attacker into the street. He landed with a thud, dropping the knife, then scrambled to his feet and ran off.

Erith turned his attention to the remaining two. They edged back slowly, then turned and ran as well. He was tempted to chase them down—the fight had been too brief to satisfy him. The target of the attack was leaning up against the wall, drawing deep, gasping breaths, and he stopped.

"Are you hurt?" He couldn't see much in the shadows. Wide eyes stared up at him from a filthy face, and rags draped the scrawny body.

He went back out to the street to see if the attacker he had thrown was in sight, but only the knife was still there. He picked it up. The person he had rescued had followed him, and there was enough light for Erith to see he was young—impossible to tell how old exactly; his eyes showed a worldly, wary wisdom at odds with his small frame. Erith guessed he might be thirteen.

"Here." He handed the boy the knife. "You can probably find a use for it."

The boy took it without a word, cautiously, watching Erith's every move, then darted into the shadows. Erith shrugged to himself and went on.

Tekbeh fastened the broken piece of armor plate firmly to the post and hung her quiver from her belt before getting on her horse. The watching soldiers were amused.

"It don't need armor! How are you going to hurt the target with a bow? They're just for folk that don't got swords!"

"This is one of their bows," said Tekbeh, indicating the kenjah.

"Looks like it's already broken!" The bows did look strange: not a single curve, but two.

"Arrows got stone points, they break on armor."

Tekbeh smiled to herself. She'd gotten a smith to make her metal points in the kenjah style, and now she was going to try them out. The kenjah bows were surprisingly powerful, and once she'd gotten used to the longer draw she could place a shaft almost as deep as they could.

She rode a good distance from the post, then turned and kicked her mount into a gallop. Her first two tries missed the post; the third glanced off the armor plate at an angle. The soldiers snickered.

Seething, Tekbeh wheeled her mount around. She'd gotten too close to the target. As she galloped away she remembered a trick she'd seen the kenjah do. Turning over the back of her horse, she drew her bow and let fly. The arrow hit true.

She rode back to the post. Kemar'sto was already there, and she saw the muscles in his arm straining when he pulled the plate away. He handed it to her, and she showed it to the now silent soldiers. The arrowhead had pierced the armor completely.

"You have learned well," said Kemar'sto.

"I have good teacher," replied Tekbeh, struggling to remember the right words. "Why not kenjah use bow, first time fight us?" They would have been slaughtered, that time on the plain. Any one of the kenjah was good enough for that, and Kemar'sto was one of the best.

"No merit to attack from far away, where they cannot strike you," he said.

She had been making progress in her understanding of their language, and "merit" had been one of the first words she had learned. It was very important to them.

"Too many enemy—we die!"

"To defend the ancestor house, all is permitted," he said gently. He glanced at the morning sun. "This we say is sun-stepping-dance," he said, pointing.

That made five different words for sunrise so far. Tekbeh hoped it didn't matter too much if she mistook sun-stepping-dance for sun-runs-through-water. They looked much the same to her.

The kenjah valued beauty, and their language reflected it. They had a different word for all the stages of the rising sun, precise shades of meaning for the clouds in the sky and the winds that stirred them, for a horse running in joy or from an enemy. She wasn't sure why she was being told all this, but when she had begun her halting attempts to speak to them, Kemar'sto had been the one most willing to help, and these were the things he taught her. It had surprised her. She had thought he was the least friendly of the kenjah; he had hardly spoken at all before.

Someone was coming across the plain towards her, a ragged, skinny boy with a knife tucked under his rope belt. He marched forward with determination, but his shoulders were hunched as if he expected a blow.

"Ert says come back, rovers gonna leave soon," he mumbled, not looking at Tekbeh.

"Who says?"

"Big man," said the boy, reaching up high with one hand, awe momentarily animating his face. Then he backed up, caution returning, and ran back to the city as if he were being pursued.

"We leave to fight," Tekbeh explained to the kenjah. They seemed pleased.

Ronne looked up from the planning map to find Erith standing at the foot of the table.

"I have plans for the scouting," he said abruptly.

Ronne almost asked for the scroll, but remembered in time. Erith did not know how to write and disliked having others write out his words for him.

"Show me," she said, and indicated the map.

"I have horses at both likely routes from Corin, and scouts along the south border." He indicated positions on the map. "They stay in place and others on horses check on them. If any sighting is reported, they will ride here immediately. I also have scouts going into Corin, to find and track the army."

"Risky."

"But necessary. I'm not sending any horses there, though."

"Good."

Erith stooped to where Kashan lay sprawled on the floor and scratched the snowtiger's head. "I'll be with the scouts on the Corin border. I'll return as soon as I have any news."

Ronne looked up. *Leaving....* "Take this," she said, unpinning one of the brooches from the underhill. "Temaso thinks it is good protection against evil magic. See him, and take more for those you are sending into Corin." Their fingers touched as she handed him the brooch, and on impulse she added, "Be careful."

Erith led the rovers out of Keris Kera early the next morning. The recently freed barn thief, Hasko, soon found his way to the front and walked beside him as he rode.

"If we're the first scouts goin' out, how do we know about this Talorgen anyway?" he asked.

"Some of the Corinha defenders escaped and returned with the messenger Ronne sent."

"Hunh." Hasko was unimpressed. "Corin don't make but scrawny fighters; big help they'll be!"

Erith just grinned and looked at Hasko's short, wiry frame. "One of them is near my size."

"Well then, the war's over! Send the two of you out, and the rest of us can catch up on our sleep. Any notables in the bunch?"

"How would I know? I don't even have the Arhiia Lineages down." He made an effort to remove all emotion from his voice. "One named Siret seemed to be in charge."

Hasko raised his eyebrows in surprise. "So, then! I've heard of him. They say he likes Herself more than a little. You have the right of it, may be a problem for you."

Erith had only known Hasko for a few weeks, but it had taken that crafty old man just a few hours to figure out most of his secrets. His only consolation was so far Hasko had refrained from telling any of the other rovers.

A ragged shadow darted at the edge of the group, and Hasko turned his head. "There he is again—you want I should send him off?"

"Leave him be." The boy he had rescued in the alley had taken to showing up without a sign, silent and wary. When Erith had sent him with the message for Tekbeh, he had found out the boy's name, Fedi, but nothing else. *He can fight, and move without being noticed. If he wants to help, we can use him.*

"How did you do your raiding?" Erith asked Hasko. The old man looked uncomfortable, and answered with reluctance.

"I'd find a likely place, not too close to any others, and watch until I knew their ways. At night I'd take what I wanted and travel in the dark to a hiding place I'd found before."

"Did you ever do this near the Corin border?"

Hasko began to look puzzled at Erith's questions. "A time or two. Raised up there, didn't like stealing from folks I knew."

This was good news. Erith knew from his own experience that knowing the terrain made all the difference in a raid, and with Hasko they had an advantage.

They had reached the crest of the hill, and Erith turned for a last look at Keris Kera. It was good to leave the city, but when would he see Ronne again?

He didn't think he had been that obvious, but Hasko remarked, "She's got you good and proper, eh?"

"What do you mean?" asked Erith defensively.

"Now don't get het up, lad, it's in their blood. Amrane was much the same, and I couldn't help myself either," he said, sighing and shaking his head. "Young Ronne's got much the look of her, but Amrane had a smile to light the night and joy in her soul. What have you been about to let her get so gloomy?" He directed an accusing glance at Erith.

"Me?" spluttered Erith. "How? I'd…." He clamped his jaw shut.

Hasko's bushy eyebrows went up, speculation in his eyes. "Some folk are going to think the only reason she keeps you near is to warm her bed. Most will think you can fight in addition. You'd have a hard time finding any who would believe she's kept her hands off you. If you'd had any sense," he added irascibly, "you'd have squinty eyes and a harelip. Save you a world of trouble. Now just keep it in mind, eh? You'd find out eventually, but this way you won't make any fuss to trouble her."

Hasko looked up at him. Erith felt stunned, and knew his confusion must be visible.

"It's all because of Amrane," Hasko explained. "Nobody'd believe one of her line could be so circumspect."

"What happened with Amrane? Who was she?"

"She was the sister to this one's father, and *alaran* before him. She, ah, loved her people. Especially if they were unmarried and male. And we loved her back," he said softly.

Erith was aware of a growing coldness spreading from the pit of his stomach. Did she only tolerate him because he could be useful? He almost began to believe the cold voice that sneered *You are not one of them—how could it be otherwise?*

But Ronne was not Amrane. Even from Hasko's description they were worlds apart. Still, Hasko's tale made clear some of the comments Erith had overheard and not understood. He sighed. It would be easy to ignore those rude assumptions if they were true.

He fingered the brooch from the underhill, pinned to the inside of his shirt. He wondered if it would work—Ronne thought it would, and she had wanted him to have it. The brooch had been warm from her body when she gave it to him, and he had kept it so ever since. It was not much of a link, but it was all he had. For now.

CHAPTER 18

A week went by before the message came, the longest week Ronne could recall living. She had known she would miss Erith, but she had not known she would miss him so badly. Each day was another day the army could prepare, but then her fear grew stronger that she had sent him into Talorgen's hands.

At last a messenger arrived from the border, riding fast. He was so fatigued he could hardly stand upright after dismounting.

"He's just started to move. They're taking the main road to Arhi," the man said, still panting as he stood before Ronne in the Audience. "Won't reach the border for three days at least."

"Were there any difficulties?"

"None, *na'al*. We were undetected."

Ronne let the wave of relief wash through her without an outward sign. *If you die because of me, Erith, I will never forgive you.* Now she had to put all personal thoughts aside. The message was clear, and she must act as *alaran* in truth and change to the Standing Court. She rose slowly from her chair on the dais and did not step down.

A hush fell over the room. She could sense the change in the atmosphere, the silent watchfulness of those present. The Seated Court was hampered by the restrictions of the Linariach, but the Standing Court was not. It meant they were truly at war, that she was now solely responsible for the safety of Arhi. The certain knowledge that there would be grief and death could not prevent her from feeling relief that she could finally take action. She drew her sword and held it by the blade in witnessing, so the eye might see what she did. "Send to the army commanders," she said. "We will march this day to meet him."

Ronne led an advance phalanx to the border, arriving well in advance of Talorgen's army. After sending scouts ahead to verify Talorgen's position, she rode her grey horse about the terrain where the road crossed the border. She didn't like what she saw. The area was flat and broad, with little in the way of advantage. They would have to go back into Arhi territory over a mile before there were any hills that could be used defensively.

She galloped back along the road, and when she passed the phalanx she called out to the commander to stop and wait. She reached the hilly region and stopped to consider it, the grey blowing and tossing its head as if it, too, was eager for action.

"Peace. It will come soon enough," she murmured, patting the sleek neck. The hills rose steeply on the northwest side of the road, but the slope was more gentle to the south. She explored a little further, then rode back to the waiting phalanx.

"Form up back there, on the hill, and angle the front line across the road."

The commander came up to Ronne. She'd expected him to remonstrate with her, but at least he kept his voice low enough to prevent the soldiers from overhearing. "But that will put them well within Arhi before we even come to blows!"

"If the Fires of Creation had not seen fit to create a boundless plain at the border, I would agree with you. We face an enemy with greater numbers than ours. With the hill behind us we may fight from an advantage. The line of battle will rotate to the left as we fight—the new recruits are not experienced enough to avoid it. If we count on it, however, it will put us with our backs to Arhi, across the road. More, they will not be able to reach our right flank."

The commander sighed and saluted. "*A'liata.*"

Ronne left him shouting orders to move the phalanx back. She did not blame him for his objections; it had taken a surprising amount of resolution for her to accept the necessity of letting Talorgen cross the border. But her goal was more ambitious than she had revealed. She wanted to win, completely and finally, so using every advantage she could find was of the utmost importance.

It was very possible that the force Talorgen was sending against them was exhausted and unwilling, and a fraction of the total he commanded. Arhi had never been one of the Empire's strongest *alars*, and she knew it was usually thought of as a sparse backwater. He would probably not think it necessary to commit his entire force. If the Face of Fortune so much as glanced her way, they had a chance of defeating him.

She continued to plan as the rest of the army arrived and took up position. She had the soldiers cut down some trees to build a rough protection for the left flank, which was still too exposed for her satisfaction. She almost didn't notice when Erith and the other rovers arrived on the field later that day, but upon seeing people riding horses she looked up. Her breath caught in her throat when she saw Erith alive and well, smiling at her. She couldn't help smiling in return, she was so glad to see him again.

"Nothing for miles," said Erith cheerfully. "He hasn't come another way."

Ronne nodded. Then she noticed the dark cloth hood he was wearing. "Is that the latest fashion?" Some of the other rovers also wore the hoods; it gave them an even more disreputable air.

Erith grimaced. "Some think my hair is too noticeable." Tekbeh, who had come up behind, assumed an expression of extreme innocence.

Fighting an urge to laugh, Ronne commented, "It has been remarked on by others. In fact, I believe the only one who has made no mention of it is Bryddhe." Erith sighed.

Ronne dismounted and directed Erith to do the same. "Take my horse as well—we need your people to ride out and warn any in the path of the battle. You are better here. The peasants would run from the sight of you." She went to the supply wagon and found the rest of her battle armor and began attaching her greaves to her boots. She had left it until she had made all the preparations she could, so the heavy armor would not weigh her down.

"You forgot your targe," commented Erith.

Ronne shook her head and reached further into the cart for her sword and harness. "No. Not for this," and she drew the blade out. The metal was midnight black. "This is Heartseeker—the sword of Amrane, the sword of Arven. A two-handed battle sword. No shield is used." And she fastened the harness about her heavy battle armor.

When Erith had gotten his first good look at the assembled army, he had thought nothing could withstand the gathered might of the Arhiia. He had never seen so many fighters in one place before; they seemed invincible in their ordered array.

But then came the even larger mass of Talorgen's army, with banners in its midst, and he remembered how Ronne had told him he had never seen this kind of warfare before. Ronne and the other Arhiia watched the enemy advance calmly, and he realized this was what they had expected. Even though they were outnumbered, Ronne was not going to retreat. This was courage of a kind he had never seen, and his respect for the Arhiia increased.

Talorgen's forces arrived the day after Ronne's, and the wait had not improved anyone's temper. Erith nearly lost his when Ronne ordered the rovers to the periphery of the fight.

"We cannot afford to lose any of the horses. The rovers may be good fighters, but they have never trained with the regular army. We have enough raw recruits that it is already a danger."

Her face was uncompromising, and he struggled to keep from shouting at her. *How can I help you if you send me away?* Arguing with her as Talorgen attacked would not help her either, so he left, seething.

When the two armies collided Erith heard it clearly, even on the outskirts. He wanted to join Ronne then, but the press was too thick and he was still not sure that one of the Arhiia wouldn't attack him before he even got to her. Then Talorgen's soldiers began to break off from the main army and attack from the flank, and he and the other rovers joined in the fight.

Judging by the sun, they had been fighting for several hours, although it seemed like an eternity to him. All the battles he had fought on the plains had been brief skirmishes, and Erith wondered how the Arhiia could take it. They had not been dislodged from their position, but the casualties had begun to mount. Ronne's people fought fiercely, and Talorgen's losses were severe, but he had more people to lose.

Erith was on the edge of the forest, engaged with the other rovers in cutting short any attempts to outflank the Arhiia, when motion far beyond the forest caught his eye. He moved cautiously in the shadows for a better view. A soldier in Talorgen's colors was moving stealthily, hunched over, following a tiny creek between the hills. Erith prepared to attack, then saw the other soldiers following in a single line. There were too many of them for him to defeat, and he had to warn Ronne as quickly as possible. He did not know how many had already slipped past.

He ran with all the speed he possessed toward the Arhi banner, knowing the commanders would be nearby. "They are moving soldiers behind us, around the hill," he gasped when he was close enough for them to hear him over the din. Ronne was there among them.

"How did they manage that?" asked one, astonished.

"Their line is longer than ours, and there is a shallow depression in that direction. If they crouched down we wouldn't notice them."

"They are following the creek, going west," said Erith, nodding.

Ronne rubbed her eyes, looking bone-tired. Her armor was streaked with blood; Erith could only hope none of it was hers. "We have no choice now; we retreat." A storm of protest arose from the commanders. "Enough!" snarled Ronne, flinging out an arm to silence them. "We will be surrounded if we stay. Now go, and bring us out of this place."

Erith was afraid the Arhiia would simply run, but their discipline held even here. The commanders dispersed to order the retreat.

"How are the rovers?" asked Ronne. "Can they still fight?"

"Well enough."

"He'll try to follow us. Take your people and do whatever you can to delay him—anything but a direct attack."

"I understand," said Erith, and went to find Hasko.

The gathering twilight aided the Arhiia's retreat. Erith and the rovers faded into the forest on either side of the road with hunting javelins in hand. The kenjah and one or two others had bows, and Tekbeh had her sling.

It seemed a long time after the last Arhiia had passed him before Erith saw any of the enemy, and when he did, they seemed more defeated than the Arhiia were. They were not in good order either, making it easy for the rovers to attack them. When larger groups appeared, Erith attacked with his sword and then ran, luring them into the woods where the others finished them off. Tekbeh never ran out of rocks, and Erith saw her make two kills with just her sling.

They did not stop and rest until late at night.

"We could use them long-legged beasties now to get home," said Hasko, collapsing on a handy log. "Seems that lot don't like our hospitality and went back."

Erith glanced back at him. "She wanted the horses to do the wasting. They can move fast enough to do the job and get out safe." He went back to his discussion with Tekbeh. "No, we shouldn't leave the road unguarded. But we should get word to Ronne, wherever she is, that the pursuit has died off."

Tekbeh shrugged. "Fair enough. Who?"

They looked about together. Hasko they passed over, his age beginning to tell in his diminished endurance, likewise Fedi. His first taste of real combat had left him wide-eyed with fear and twitchy. The kenjah still had a language barrier. They paused at a young man, one of Hasko's acquaintances who had the amazing ability to fall asleep in any position under any circumstance and was using it at that moment.

"Gotta be him," said Tekbeh, and Erith nodded.

"If we can't sleep, neither should he."

When the messenger found Ronne, the Arhiia were camped near a farm compound on the side of the hill, where she and the commanders had taken over the empty grain barn as a headquarters. She expected Talorgen to follow at first light. Since she did not want to tire her people with a long march, she had encamped at the first reasonable location.

"So," said Ronne. "None are following. How long since the last of them?"

"Uh, more'n two hour. I think." He shuffled his feet, darting a glance at her from under a tangled thatch of hair.

"Go back and tell them to keep their watch. I will send others to take their places by morning." The messenger ducked his head and left with some haste.

Ronne gave a wry smile and scratched Kashan's head where he lay sprawled at her feet. "What good are you, when you frighten my armed instead of my enemy?" Kashan just moved his head to put another itch at her fingers. Ronne had puzzled what to do with him when she left with the army, finally deciding it would be worse to leave him at Keris Kera when she might not be returning for weeks. So far the arrangement had worked out well, although she owed a farmer or two for the "prey" Kashan had found.

If Talorgen was not following, she should gather the commanders and give her orders for tomorrow. They were all present…no, one was missing. "Where is Dahade? I thought she was the rearguard commander."

Finavah looked up, startled. "She is. I haven't seen her, but I've seen those of her command."

"She stayed."

A harsh voice interrupted their conversation, coming from one of the Corinha fighters. His name was Edirn, and Ronne remembered Siret telling her that he had lost his much-loved wife in the siege of Kalmar. His eyes were empty and desolate as he came before Ronne.

"She told us when we took our position. She said she liked the view and had no intention of leaving. 'Any of a like mind could stay to keep me company,' she said, and we knew she meant to die there. I was one of those who volunteered, but she refused me, saying I would be of more value to Corin when it is restored."

"She was correct." Ronne gazed out the barn doors to the darkness outside. She remembered Dahade even from her youth as a large woman, able to dominate a room by force of personality as well as size. She was intimidating, crude in speech, yet subtle in thought. Ronne could not imagine such a vital personality destroyed.

"Did she say anything else?" she asked finally.

Edirn thought for a moment. "She said nothing more to us. But as she went to those who remained, she was singing—'We'll drink 'till we're dry, sleep 'till we're tired, and we won't go home till morning.' "

Ronne had to shade her eyes until the emotion passed. The words that Edirn had given were from a very impolite drinking song. *How fitting that her last words be those!*

Erith and the rovers kept a careful watch, but Talorgen's army did not make any move to continue the advance into Arhi. Although the battle at the Corin border was technically a defeat for the Arhiia, Talorgen's forces had been so badly mauled by the fighting he did not follow up on his advantage for several weeks.

When he did attack, the rovers were busy—Ronne continued her policy of fighting only where the Arhiia had the advantage, and of destroying anything that might be of use to the enemy when forced to retreat. People and cattle were moved; barns, houses, and crops destroyed. The rovers helped with this, as well as keeping an eye on the enemy army and its movements.

Erith could see all the effort was having an effect when he saw wagon trains bringing supplies from Corin. He was exhausted. The rovers had been fighting and running for days together, but he left at once to find Ronne.

When he reached the army encampment he was told she had gone to Keris Kera, and he continued on. Despite Ronne's efforts, Talorgen had come close enough to Keris Kera that the camp was only two days' travel by horse.

When he reached the fortress, Erith searched for Ronne for some time without success. Everyone he spoke to said she had just left for another location. He stood in the hallway, trying to think what else he could do, when he saw Ronne leave the council room and head in the direction of the main stairs. He quickened his pace and caught up with her, trying to keep hold of his temper.

"Why won't you see me?" he asked hotly. "There is news you should know."

Ronne stopped, looking puzzled. "I didn't know you were here. It is a good thing you found me—I was about to leave for the camp."

"I spoke to someone in the council room when I first arrived. He said he would take a message to you, that you would send for me when you had time."

Ronne narrowed her eyes, and a dangerous expression grew on her face. "Don't you want to talk to me?"

She looked up sharply and turned back along the hallway. "Come with me." She went out on the portico and followed the lake edge to the bridge over the falls. The roar of the water sounded loud in Erith's ears, and he had to strain to hear what she said.

"Some of the Linariach are trying to keep you away. I had nothing to do with it. Why would I want to keep you from reporting what you find? They have reasons they think are valid. I can't explain them to you."

Erith looked away from her, feeling his face go red. "I think I can guess."

He felt an air of constraint grow between them, and Ronne was silent for a while. "I thought it would be better for you not to know what they think. You do lose your temper on occasion." She tried to smile. "Your failure to understand their comments on the subject was your best defense."

"They think it anyway, so what's the purpose? Is this because of Amrane?" he asked, feeling desperate.

Ronne stiffened, then sighed. "No. Amrane gave them the idea, perhaps, but that is not why I do...all this." She turned to face him, placing a hand on his where it rested on the bridge parapet. "There are things I still can't tell you. Will you trust me in this?"

Whether it was her gaze or her touch, regardless of remembering what Hasko had said of Amrane, all of his earlier pain and frustration vanished, and he found himself answering, "Of course."

As they walked back to the fortress he told her of what the rovers had observed, and she listened thoughtfully. "This is good news. Have you thought to attack these supply trains yet?"

Erith grinned. "Our very first thought, in fact. I came to tell you they were there, and that we intend to act on them."

"Do so, and report to me at the camp. I should be there for some time." She paused, and added, "And here...you have my permission to go anywhere, enter any room, in search of me to report. I will tell Stenay this before I leave. That should prevent any further meddling."

When Ronne left for the camp, Erith went to the rovers' quarters. Even though many were out scouting, enough new recruits had been added to ensure the common room was in its usual overcrowded state. Even as he entered he heard a voice raised in a complaint to the effect there was an unknown elbow in the speaker's beer. Another voice said reassuringly, "That's part of the training, don't ya know? Thisaway, we can recognize each other in the dark, by smell."

"Eww, my elbow's all wet!"

He found Fedi standing by him, holding out a mug. When he took it Fedi darted back to the corner where Hasko was spinning some improbable tale. Erith let the familiar voices wash over him, calming his troubled thoughts as he began to plan the first raids on Talorgen's supplies.

After yet another battle in which the Arhiia had performed miracles still insufficient to halt Talorgen's advance, Tekbeh got a summons to bring the kenjah to Ronne's tent. She'd heard rumors that Ronne was going to try something new, and she had her suspicions confirmed at once. Ronne was there, and so were a few of the Linariach. Something was up; the Linariach hardly ever left the city.

"I did not forget what you said, about your people's willingness to fight for me in exchange for land. I have convinced my council to agree, and so I ask you: will you go and bring your people to fight for me?"

The effect on the kenjah was dramatic. As soon as they understood Tekbeh's halting translation, she could see Ronne had their complete attention.

"We will fight, *cha'tral*," said Edge Singing.

"But will you go and bring the others?" asked Ronne, a trifle impatiently.

The kenjah looked at each other, each apparently waiting for the others to say something. "We will send," agreed Edge Singing.

Tekbeh left the tent with the kenjah and listened as they argued among themselves about who would go and fetch the others. She didn't understand what the problem was at first. Finally, she realized none of them wanted to miss out on the glory here by leaving. It would have been amusing if their need was not so desperate.

"I ask it of you," she said in her halting version of their language. "Is there no merit in the difficult hunt, the finding of the thing hidden? Is there no merit in bringing others to…to save an ancestor house, and to start your own?"

"There is great merit," agreed one of the kenjah. "But there is great merit here, too!"

"But…." Tekbeh struggled to find the words to express her meaning. "You see how we only step backwards on the field of battle. My chief must…must stop the honorless one, and he is stronger. We need your help!" she burst out, reverting to her own language in her frustration.

Kemar'sto had been silent from the very beginning, watching Tekbeh's face attentively, his own solemn. But now he spoke. "I will go," he said quietly. Tekbeh started to thank him, only to be interrupted by Edge Singing.

"A'desam'at, you go too," she said imperiously. When he began to protest, she said, "The sun and wind know the great size of your kinship, and your words charm the listening ear. Go to the kenjah of your kinship, and tell them the words of the Great Chieftain."

He isn't the only one who can charm the listening ear, thought Tekbeh as she saw the other Windrider respond to Edge Singing's praise, and she was not surprised when he also agreed to go.

The two kenjah left early the next morning. Tekbeh watched them prepare for the journey, wondering why she felt so desolate. They were going to get help, weren't they?

They finished tying the last of the bundles to the waiting horses. Kemar'sto said something to A'desam'at, who mounted and rode away to the main gate. Kemar'sto still had a bundle in his hands when he turned away from his mount and came to where she stood.

Silently, he offered what he carried to her. Tekbeh opened it with care, not sure what she would find and half-afraid to find out. Inside was a beautiful kenjah bow and a quiver of arrows. One of the arrows had a point of carefully chipped green stone, flecked with gold, and she felt a strange sensation in her stomach.

"It's beautiful," she said softly, stroking the bow, marveling at the smooth grain of the wood, at how skillfully the horn and sinew lamination had been done. "But…why do you give it to me?" She looked up and was shaken by the expression in his amber eyes.

"You are the sun-newly-risen, the sun-glorious-departing, clear water spring in dryness time, changing as the wind in grass, straight as smoke on a still night, peaceful as the moon behind a cloud, fierce as a storm in winter. Without the sun, I am cold; without water, I thirst…."

Tekbeh clutched the bow to her as his soft, intense voice rose and fell. *He taught me all those words, just so he could say this to me and I would understand.* She watched him leave, wordless, numb with shock. She stood there even when he was no longer in sight through the open gate. *He'd better come back….*

Hasko was in his element. Erith saw a wicked gleam in his eye as he watched the lenghur string pass their hiding place. They had been raiding for several weeks now, and Hasko still retained his early enthusiasm. At his signal, the rovers fell on the endguard so quickly they had no time to cry out, and Fedi ran, crouched over beside the last lenghur, flicking his knife with careless ease. He freed six beasts from the string before stopping.

Hastily they carted off the soldiers' bodies and removed all signs of the fight, then led the lenghur away into the forest.

"Far enough," grunted Hasko, and they deposited their burdens. "Anything worth keeping?"

"They're almost as bad off as we are," said Erith, examining the dead soldiers' gear. "Take the weapons, anyway. How about the lenghur?"

"Can't tell in the dark," Tekbeh snapped irritably, but she kept looking.

"Hey, this one's got real armor!"

"Well, lad, she don't need it now and we do," said Hasko. "Get it and go, and don't deafen me with yer bellowing! They haven't figured us yet but ye don't need ta give 'em hints!"

The rover subsided with a muttered apology, and silence reigned for a few moments until Tekbeh appeared at Hasko's shoulder with a narrow leather-covered box. "Give me a light," she said tersely.

Hasko scowled, but dug out a dirty candle stub and, with a bit of cursing over the flint and steel, managed to light it. The box was full of small scrolls and pieces of parchment.

"A dispatch box," she said, sounding inordinately pleased. "If I'd been stupid enough to leave one on a lenghur, I'd be hung by my thumbs for a month. Supposed to keep them with you at all times."

She pulled out one of the scrolls and began to read it, lips moving silently and brow furrowed with effort. Erith looked over her shoulder, wondering as always how the black marks could have any meaning. "It's a list of prisoners," she said finally. "They have them…Face of Mercy." She stood up so suddenly she knocked the candle from Hasko's hand. "We have to get this to Ronne. They've got her brother."

"What, Alland? How did they get in the fortress?"

"Not Alland. Medar. The one we thought was killed. Talorgen has him."

CHAPTER 19

Erith sent Tekbeh ahead with the dispatch box while the rest of the rovers came along more slowly with the gains of the raid. Going at lenghur pace, it was early morning when they arrived in the camp.

Erith saw that Tekbeh's arrival had already roused a good deal of the camp. Soldiers milled about the rough, dun-colored tents and prepared their gear for the march. The scent of bean and bacon porridge wafted over the air. He could tell he was tired because he was looking forward to having some.

Following Arhi custom, the camp had a defensive perimeter that was always guarded. When the rovers neared the entrance he pulled his hood loose to identify himself.

"You had luck!" said one of the guards, waving to them as they came in. His companion looked disapproving, but the others in the camp echoed the welcome. Erith had noticed that the Arhiia's treatment of him had been improving as the raids produced results, but now they were almost enthusiastic in their greetings.

Ronne came out of her tent to meet him. She had already donned her armor and was hastily buckling her sword harness.

"We're going in after him," she said. "How soon can your people be ready?" She started for the main part of the camp with an energetic stride.

He held up a hand. "Wait! Where is this place? How long will it take to get there?"

She turned back, and her expression was fiercely exultant. "Not far. They were recently moved here from Oguz. We will go now with a light force, quickly. If more are needed, we will send for them, but I want your people there as soon as possible to spy out the land."

"We've been on watch since yesterday morning, and it took us half the night to get here. They need rest, especially if there will be fighting."

"We'll take carts—they can sleep in them. Some of the prisoners may be injured...Face of Mercy, just let him live!" Erith barely heard the last few words, but they were said with passionate intensity.

Erith followed her back into the tent where the maps were laid out on a low table. When he saw where the prisoners were being kept, he suggested, "We could send a few by horse now; they could keep a watch and look it over. We'd want to do this by night anyway, I think. Hit it hard and fast when they don't expect it, then leave."

"Good." A smile played over Ronne's face briefly. "A small detachment of soldiers for quickness, as well."

As he left, Erith reflected that Ronne seemed happier than she had been in months. True, she was going to rescue a brother she had thought dead, but this…it seemed like something more. It seemed like relief.

Ronne sheathed her sword without even having to clean it. If Talorgen had had time to complete the compound's defenses, they might have had a little difficulty. As it was, the palisade was not even half finished and the ditch shallow. The defenders were easily overwhelmed by her small force. *The rovers could have done it alone*, she thought, seeing their leader approach.

Erith handed his torch to her, saying "We have the last of them now. I'm going to watch the perimeter for any surprises. It's light enough for patrols to be out," indicating the near-full moon.

Ronne knew he was also tactfully taking his barbarian face out of view of the prisoners who were beginning to emerge. "Don't go too far," she said as he mounted his horse. "We will be moving swiftly when we leave, and soon." He nodded understanding and rode off.

She took her torch and walked among the prisoners, searching for a familiar face. The prisoners were still huddled together, dazed and disbelieving, just beginning to understand they had been rescued. The compound had been built around an abandoned farm, and most of prisoners had been kept out in the open weather in a fenced-in area.

Ronne saw Edirn tes Corin, also searching. Several of the names on the list of prisoners were of the Corin Lineage and Kindred. From the cries of joy she heard, he had succeeded in finding them.

The able-bodied prisoners began to leave the compound, and the aurochs carts came up to carry the weak and wounded. There was still no sign of Medar. A feeling of panic began to grow, and she made her way through the crowd to the barn, where some soldiers were standing.

"Is this all of them?" she asked, gesturing at the ragged group that had just emerged.

"The last, *na'al*," one confirmed. "They were packed in there close."

A wave of despair swept through her, followed by a jolt of fear as a voice inside the barn shouted, "There's a body here!" She entered the barn quickly, brushing by the soldiers who had gathered about what they had found.

She almost didn't recognize him, he was so emaciated and worn. His tattered clothing hung on his body like an afterthought. She handed her torch to one of the soldiers and knelt beside him.

"Medar," she said softly. "Medar, it's Ronne."

It took so long for his eyes to open that Ronne feared she was too late. But they did open, and she saw recognition in them even as a slow, painful smile came to his face. When he spoke, his voice was rough and faint. Ronne had to bend close to hear him.

"How?"

"My scouts intercepted a message."

"Soldiers here...."

Ronne bared her teeth in a not-quite grin. "Not his. Not anymore." A fierce light appeared in his eyes, reflecting her own emotions, but then it flickered and faded. "We'll get you home. Is there still a cart waiting?" she asked the soldiers. One nodded and dashed out.

Ronne lifted her brother with great care in her arms, shocked at how light he was and sensing something else, something that instantly made her say to a rover standing outside the barn, "Get me Erith. Quickly."

Sitting on the cart tail, she tipped some water past Medar's cracked lips and wrapped him in her cloak.

"So good...see you once more," he managed.

"I found you just in time. Do you know, they tried to make me *alaran?* We thought you were dead...but you survived."

"Didn't."

"You did. You *must.*" She tightened her arms around him reflexively, willing him strength and refusing to acknowledge the fear in her mind. "There is someone here who can help you, heal you."

He smiled very faintly and blinked, as if he were having trouble focusing on her face. "There is too much...but now it doesn't hurt anymore. It feels so good to let go...."

A spasm racked his body, and Ronne cried in anguish, "Where is Erith?" No answer.

She held her brother close and heard him whisper, "Oh, what a lovely day it was! How quickly it got dark...Nehneh, where are you?"

Ronne smiled through the tears gathering in her eyes. *Nehneh. That was his name for me, so long ago. What did I call him?* "Here, Darit."

"Mother's wondering where I am. I'm in trouble again, aren't I? I was climbing in the hills, I got dirty," he brushed ineffectually at his ragged clothing with feeble, clawlike hands. "You can make Alland tell Mother something so she won't get angry at me. Say you will, Nehneh, even the grownups listen to Alland and he listens to you," he pleaded.

"Oh, all right, Darit," said Ronne. She responded as her childhood self as long as Medar spoke, wandering in his mind in the memory of some long-ago escapade. She could feel tears on her face, yet her mind refused to accept the truth even when Medar's voice ceased, even when his wasted fingers just managed to touch her hand and a deep sigh seemed to empty his body.

The messenger didn't understand why he had been sent to find him, but Erith did, once he knew that Ronne's brother had been found barely living. He rode as fast as he could back to the compound, the part of his mind not involved with guiding the horse trying to figure out what he could do. It was well established that he could somehow heal wounds. He wished he knew how he did it.

He galloped into the yard, looking for Ronne. He found her, sitting on the cart holding a ragged body. He slid off the horse before it had completely stopped, and he stumbled. First he saw her face, pleading and full of grief, and then he saw her brother and was shocked into immobility. How could anyone be alive who looked like that? His bones almost poked through his skin. Ronne's voice brought him suddenly out of his trance.

"Erith. Help him," she said in a cracked whisper.

"I don't know how! I can't…."

"Just do whatever it was you did before." She locked gazes with him. The desperate intensity in her eyes overwhelmed his objections.

Uncertain, Erith extended his hand to touch Medar's face. Always before he had had some obvious wound to focus on, but where was the wound caused by starvation?

He knew something was very wrong the instant his fingertips made contact. His hand felt heavy and cold, and the sensation crept slowly up his arm. His vision began to go dark, and he snatched his hand away, gasping for air against the tightening of his chest. The darkness gradually receded, and with a pounding heart he reached out again. This time he felt nothing but dry, leathery skin, and he slowly made a chilling realization. *I just felt Ronne's brother die.*

He looked up. "He's gone," he said, as softly as he could. Ronne sat unmoving as a statue, the tracks of tears still visible on her face, holding the ragged and wasted figure as if she would never release it. The remote expression in her eyes shocked him. From the edge of his vision he noticed the other soldiers grow still and cautiously move away. Ronne stood up, carrying her brother's body.

"Let me help you."

She looked at him, uncomprehending, then said in a detached voice, "I must take him by horse, take him home. He is very ill."

Erith moved to stand in her way. "That will only make him worse. Put him in the cart."

He thought she was going to ignore him, but some of her detachment left her as she whispered, "Why won't you help him?"

Erith looked at the limp, dangling hand, the unblinking open eyes, and gathered his resolution. "He is beyond any help you or I can give him. You know this. He's dead." It hurt to see her face as she stared at him, holding her brother's body and hoping for a miracle.

A light rain had begun, a damp, constant drizzle without wind or intensity, but enough to begin to soak them as they stood in the empty compound.

"We have to leave. It is only a few hours to dawn, and we should be well away from here by then." Ronne nodded but didn't move. Greatly daring, he gently took her burden and laid it in the cart.

The Arhiia left the now-empty compound in silence. Erith rode beside Ronne's horse for the entire journey. She never said a word, her face like carved stone. When they reached the camp, he ruthlessly removed everyone from her tent, made sure Kashan was inside, and stood guard at the entrance until she emerged again.

The great gate swung slowly open, and Ronne rode through and up the winding road to the fortress. She almost welcomed the mind-numbing fatigue of the constant fighting; it meant she had no time or energy for grief or guilt. She had been glad beyond measure when Medar was discovered, glad because she could escape the duties of *alaran*, the thousand petty distractions even in times of peace. *And the* alaran *cannot marry as freely as one of the Lineage.* Now Medar's death had trapped her for the rest of her life in a position she did not want and had never been prepared for. *And my mother's heart has been broken yet again.*

The rescue of the prisoners seemed to enrage Talorgen. His attacks grew more frequent and savage and the Arhiia, although fighting fiercely, steadily lost ground. The line of battle was so close now she could operate out of Keris Kera. Every moment not consumed by warfare was devoted to the care of the teeming throngs of refugees that clogged the streets.

She could not show them her tiredness, just the same false front of confidence. They continued to hope; she could see it in their worn faces—how their eyes would brighten as she rode by their makeshift shelters in the corners and alleys. The city had not been spacious before their arrival, and now there was hardly room to move.

Ronne had to wait while a loaded aurochs cart negotiated a corner, full of the harvest that they were just now getting in. Her tactics had won them that much, at least. When she was overwhelmed with frustration at not being able to stop Talorgen, she reminded herself the situation could be much worse. They could be losing *and* starving.

She left her horse in the outer ward and climbed the narrow stone stairs to the wall ramparts. Talorgen's forces were just visible from the walls.

There was no sign of any activity toward the eastern hills. The kenjah messengers had been a long time away. She should ask Edge Singing when they might be returning—too late would be as bad as not at all.

Siret tes Corin emerged from the stairwell and came to join her. "You have changed since I saw you last," he said finally.

"It was a long time ago."

He looked out over the lake and the plain beyond. "Before you left for Ynduria. Five years. You came with your brother to Corin for Lontai's wedding. You made me think of your father's warname, the way you always stood in the shadows. All I could see clearly was the green eardrop you wore."

"Too many relatives in too small a space," Ronne responded, beginning to feel uneasy. Siret himself had made her try to keep out of sight; he always sought her out, and his friendly conversation held a thread of admiration that made her uncomfortable.

"I wanted to go and see you when they sent you to the border, but my family persuaded me it would only put you in danger," he said abruptly. "But I still thought about you."

Trying to find some way to change the trend of the conversation, Ronne became aware of a voice that had been steadily growing in volume for some time, but that she only consciously noticed now.

"What do you mean, you don't remember? I just told you! Face of Patience look at me!"

One of the fortress *taia*, face purple with rage, confronted a sentry on the rampart not far from her. The sentry stood in an attitude of boneless relaxation with a confused expression on his face.

"What is happening here?" said Ronne, coming up to the two soldiers.

"This gem of idiocy can't remember orders given less than half an hour ago! And look at him!"

Ronne did, and recognized the sentry as one of the soldiers from her father's personal guard, a solid and dependable man. He had never had difficulty with his duties or his memory before. She looked deep in his eyes and saw honest confusion behind his cloudy gaze.

"He seems ill. Take him to the healers."

The *taien* sighed and nodded, fresh worry appearing on his face. In a fortress about to be besieged, sickness was a dangerous sign.

Siret watched with a troubled expression as the soldier was led away. "What ails him?"

Ronne shook her head. "He seems confused in mind, forgetful and oblivious. And he is one of our best."

"We had something similar happen in Corin towards the end," said Siret slowly. "We thought it was some plague. It affected nearly all the soldiers, though few as bad as that. Everyone felt a heaviness in the mind, and it was hard to move or think."

Ronne felt a chill as he spoke, and instinctively felt for the silver dagger strapped to her arm. The first faint indications of Talorgen's presence had begun that morning. It was too close to be coincidence. But how was he doing it? How could she stop him?

Ronne was still thinking of the mysterious sickness late that night in Temaso's library. As promised, he had translated some of the books from the underhill.

"What have you learned?"

"This text here…it seems to be an account of an ancient war, of terrible magnitude. There is mention of 'those who host evil within' as the enemy. They are credited with amazing powers." The archivist sighed and waved a hand at the books. "It may just be a fable or legend, a real war embellished by the distance of time. Magical storms and curses added to dry fact. I made some notes on what I have translated so far…."

The hand holding the scribbled notes trembled slightly, and Temaso seemed even more bent and frail than usual. "Do not let me keep you from your rest. It is late, and we can speak of this another time," said Ronne.

"It is little enough that I can help you with; do not deny me this." His head was bent now, and his voice low.

She took the notes and clasped his bony hand. "You serve me best by caring for your health. You are the only one among us who can read these texts—if they are meant to help us, you will find it. Now go, and sleep well." He left, but reluctantly and only after extracting a promise that she would read what he had written.

When she had finished reading, Ronne stared at the dregs of her wine and wondered if Temaso was right in calling the description of the ancient war a fable. Something was clearly at work beyond the chance of fate, something malevolent and powerful. Hosting evil spirits was not something she would put beyond Talorgen, especially if he thought he could gain an advantage. He had always coveted power. Magical storms and curses…. The strange lights and the heaving of the earth when Talorgen had first found them and gave chase. The storm in the canyon that had nearly killed them and then stopped the instant they escaped. Now this plague. Three more soldiers had come down with the same confusion of mind and weakness of body, and Ronne was sure the effect would spread if nothing were done to stop it.

She drove her fingers into her braids, trying to soothe her aching head. What could she do? Every enemy had a weakness, but how could she fight something she could not see? Could magic be stopped by strength alone, or would she need to find her own magic to combat it? How would she find it?

All the treasure from the underhill was spread upon the table along with the books. The carved blue stone, the bone flute…and something else, that gleamed like frozen moonlight. The diadem that only she could hold. That only she could wear.

She turned it slowly in her hands. Something terrible had happened in the underhill, something that had destroyed the inhabitants, their culture, even their enemies. What if some remnant of that ancient conflict had survived? Why had the voices of the underhill given her the books, the diadem, the other items, if not to warn and defend against this long-buried threat?

The iridescent metal felt warm in her hands, and she froze, locked in indecision. She hated the feeling of being led blindfolded, too fast, down a path she did not know. She hated the feeling that she knew what to do without knowing what it was. It was too much like Pathwalking, the curse that others thought a blessing from ignorance of its nature. Mostly she feared the loss of control, being overwhelmed.

What choice do I have, if I want to protect my people? She took a deep breath and put the diadem on her head. She felt it settle instantly about her head, through her braids, and gasped at the overpowering sensations that flooded her mind. The shadowy library was now full of light, the candle nearly blinding in intensity. She could smell the musty parchment and acrid ink of the scrolls, even the scents of the people who had most recently been in the room: Temaso, Bryddhe, Erith….

She had to stop and breathe deeply to calm a rapidly beating heart. *All Faces grant I not meet him now!* A nameless impulse moved her from the library to the hall, where she moved silently in the cool shadows. The few folk abroad at this late hour seemed not to see her, but she did not stop to find out why. Something called her to the Lake Within.

The moonlight was bright on the silver water but somehow easy on her newly sensitive eyes. She realized she had felt the presence of the moon even within the fortress, had known its position without seeing it. She waited at the water's edge, her heart pounding, knowing something momentous was about to happen.

The lake was still; not even a breeze rippled the water. Then they came, rising from the deep lake and covering its surface like the mist they resembled, never leaving a trace of their passing on the water's surface. Even with her heightened senses Ronne found them hard to look at for long; their faint features blended with the light and water and they moved restlessly. One more solid than the rest drifted before her, its sharply slanted silver eyes occasionally obscured by wisps of what seemed to be misty hair.

"Indeed, it has been long since last I looked on the Crown of Silence," breathed the creature, floating so close to Ronne she could have touched it. She felt no desire to do so.

"What are you?" she asked finally. A stabbing pain shot through her head, but she ignored it.

"We are of the Otherworld, of shadow and the place hidden. Once the stars were not as many as we, but the Great War reduced our numbers to those which are before you, and this our only place of refuge."

"What Great War was this?" asked Ronne, even though she suspected the answer.

"You walked the ruined halls of Tak'hullus, nay, even spoke to that which remains of its defenders, or you would not wear the Crown. Did they tell you nothing?"

"I know barely thirty words of the language they spoke. The conversation was a short one."

The mist creature hissed in surprise, eyes widening. "You do not know, then, the nature of the Crown of Silence or the enemy you face." It drifted closer, its inhuman face showing what might have been concern. "The Crown is a link between we of the Otherworld and you of this. Once it was the mortals of Tak'hullus we conversed with, but they are gone. It is to you, even more mortal than they, that we speak now. The Crown is the mark of a compact between our peoples to aid and assist."

Ronne felt a small flash of hope. "Does this mean you would help us fight Talorgen?"

The mist creature's eyes grew cold. "Fight for you? No. What could we do? We cannot touch anything of this world. Nor would we if we could help it; your battles are not ours. But the case is different here," it said, coming closer and whispering in her ear. "Even as a few of our kind survived, a remnant of the evil power that tried to destroy us lay hidden for millennia. The destruction was beyond your comprehension—the war destroyed our peoples, even the magic itself broken and defeated. Until now.... One of our enemies has made common cause with yours. It is powerful; your enemy has been feeding it well. It threatens us and its mortal host threatens you. Destroy it!"

"What can I do when something clouds the minds of my people? Is this the work of your enemy? Can you stop it?"

"It is...." The creature faded, indistinct in the general mist, then reappeared. "We can shield the minds of those here. Will you destroy our enemy?"

"What is it, and where? How do I find it and destroy it?"

"You know the means," said the mist creature, pointing to the silver dagger strapped to her arm. "It will come to you, drawn even as its human host was drawn by the power welling up in you." It swirled about her, its restlessness echoed by the others drifting above the lake. "Have you paid no mind to that which is about you? The Great War drove the magics of the world down deep, where they were not destroyed. Your kind are just beginning to see them again."

Ronne lifted her face to stare at the mist creature, head throbbing. "Are you saying I have magic? Is that what the Pathwalking is?"

"You have no skill, only power," said the creature coldly. "You will never use what you have, but it makes those with skill about you stronger. And it calls to magic, draws it to you. Already two of your kind, allied to you, are strong enough to see our shadows in this world. And no, that which you fear so greatly is no magic, but part of your own mind. We cannot help you with it."

It drew back over the lake, looking down at her. "The Crown is too strong for your weak mortal strength; you should not wear it so long. Swear now to defend us against our enemy, and we will defend you in turn."

Ronne's head was a blaze of agony, but she drew her sword for witnessing and held it, hilt up, so the moonrose mark was visible. A distant part of her mind wondered at the deep blue fire that ran along the blade. "I swear to find and destroy your enemy, in return for your assistance."

"It is well," said the mist creature softly, and it sank with the rest beneath the still waters of the Lake Within. Ronne wrenched at the diadem, fearing it would not come free, but it pulled loose easily. It hung in her hand as she leaned against a pillar, fighting off collapse from the pain.

Erith searched for Ronne for a good part of the morning, and finally found her as she was leaving the fortress sickroom. He noticed her eyes were tired and bloodshot, and there were strange red marks on her forehead.

"Are you ill?" he said, suddenly concerned.

"No, I was visiting the soldiers that fell sick recently."

He knew which soldiers she was referring to. Gossip in the fortress had been running rife. "How are they?"

"Completely recovered, but with no memory of the last few days. And no others have been stricken."

"Do you think the sickness is gone?"

"It will not come again."

Ronne spoke with such conviction that all Erith's curiosity was roused. Before he could ask, an interruption occurred in the form of a nervous soldier escorted by Stenay. Ronne nodded, and the soldier said, "*Na'al*, it is a speaking delegation from Talorgen."

Ronne's gaze sharpened, and the unfortunate soldier swallowed nervously. "Where? When?"

"Uh, south road guardpost. I left as soon as we knew what they wanted. It's three of them, all according to the law."

"That will be Sardis' doing," murmured Ronne. "Well, we shall let them have their delegation. Tomorrow."

"They will regard that as a deliberate offense," observed Stenay.

"I intend it as a deliberate offense," stated Ronne, speaking with restrained force. "They will have only one topic of conversation: our surrender. Custom requires we give them a hearing, but it does not say how soon." She turned her gaze to the soldier. "Go back, but do not hurry. Tell them three may approach Keris Kera tomorrow without harm—and nothing more." When the soldier left, she looked thoughtfully at Stenay. "We should greet them in a proper manner. I would not like them to be embarrassed by any excessive notice."

"It shall be attended to," said Stenay.

"You…this is your doing! Where are the banners, the uniforms? This is disgraceful!" Hereil waggled a finger at Erith, his face growing purple. "A poor showing for Arhi to present. Perhaps you do not realize—"

"It is by my command," Ronne interrupted behind him, her voice cold, as she entered the Audience. "Stenay. Take the chair from the dais, and remove it from the room. You are overdressed for the occasion," she said, turning to Hereil. "Go, and only return in more fitting attire."

One of the personal guard silently handed Erith Ronne's helm, and he took his official position to her left. Erith could hear scandalized gasps following her rapid orders. He was still unused to many of their customs, but even he could see Ronne was breaking with tradition. To not put on a display of strength, real or not, for the enemy, to avoid ceremony, was shocking to the Arhiia.

Hereil muttered under his breath, but apparently realized the mood Ronne was in was not propitious and left with what dignity he could muster. Those remaining in the Audience were not numerous. Several of the Corinha survivors were among the Arhi nobles, and all wore armor.

"This doesn't seem very formal," Erith commented under his breath to Ronne.

"It isn't," she answered. She surveyed the room as if it were a battlefield. It seemed to him she even carried herself like she would be fighting soon.

"Will they dare to come here, only three of them?"

"Sardis knows I will keep my word, and she has never lacked courage for such a thing."

"She will come herself?" he asked, astonished.

"The opportunity to taunt me to my face will be irresistible to her, and she might not get the chance in battle. She will be here."

"I understand how Talorgen is your enemy, but why is Sardis?" asked Erith.

Ronne smiled bitterly. "Because of Talorgen. She wished for his affection, and so…she was very jealous of me. Then when I scorned him, she hated me for that. She seems to have some place with him now, but I doubt she has forgiven or forgotten what went before."

Word was brought of Talorgen's people approaching, and Ronne took her place on the dais, Erith standing behind it to the left. The others scattered themselves about the room in no particular order.

The doors opened to admit Stenay, who announced, "Those who would speak, from the enemy." Ronne gestured, and three strangers entered the room.

To Erith they didn't look much different from the other Imperials; they had the same light gold-brown skin and dark hair, although the central figure had hair a shade lighter than he had seen before. She was tall, with a sardonic expression on a handsome face scored on one side from chin to forehead by three long scars.

A memory flashed by, of Ronne, at the outpost. She spoke of an enemy, drawing her fingers up and across her face. *I marked her….* Something about the scarred woman made him instantly alert, and he watched her carefully. All three were armed; he assumed this was traditional for this kind of meeting. *It isn't as if we couldn't kill them anyway.*

Erith had no doubt that the scarred woman was Sardis. She looked about her, apparently at her ease surrounded by enemies, then turned at last to where Ronne stood with folded arms.

"I seem to have wasted my time in coming here, from the tone of your reception," Sardis said in a voice of pained disappointment, "or has the chair been forgotten? Will you not even listen to our terms?"

Ronne raised a polite eyebrow. "You must forgive our preoccupation. We have been busy for some months now with brigands and robbers invading Arhi, and it never occurred to us they would have anything to say worth hearing."

Sardis sighed with an air of resigned patience. "You have fought well, but we have the greater numbers. We will win in the end. Why not surrender now? Are you so delighted by the sounds of comrades dying in battle around you? Save them from a fate to which your pride alone condemns them."

"Go back to your master, Sardis Three-scars," said Ronne in a lazy, bored tone so unlike her Erith glanced up, startled. "He has said he will destroy us; why should I believe you, who are his creature in all things? I am not his only enemy, and your victory is far from certain. He destroys his own."

Sardis seemed startled and disconcerted at this, but she recovered swiftly and responded in a scornful tone. "You will defeat him with this ragged band? Such optimism, with so little to sustain it. Or do you count on your pet to save you?" she asked, looking at Erith with a malicious smile. "Dare you risk such beauty to the hazards of battle? But then, your standards have definitely degraded." She shook her head in mock sorrow.

"I am of the opinion they have improved beyond recognition," Ronne responded in a gentle, dangerous voice. Sardis glared furiously, and seemed about to speak, but Ronne interrupted. "You must by now have satisfied your curiosity, and I confess that I could do without your presence now. When I have defeated Talorgen, we can speak further."

"Yes, when you have defeated him! I will sit on your grave, and we will speak at length." Sardis turned to leave, saying, "Now the law is satisfied, and we will offer no terms again. We shall destroy you more utterly than Ynduria, and your people will curse your name!"

After returning to the camp, Sardis put off the meeting as long as she could, only to learn when she did seek him that Talorgen had just gone to the place set up for interrogations. She walked quickly, hoping it was just an interrogation that took him there. The other commanders thought the turf-covered root cellar had been discovered after the camp was set up, and that Talorgen simply hadn't bothered to relocate the camp. The truth was Sardis had found it well before, and made sure the camp would be located far enough that only the faintest sound of screaming would be heard.

He had arrived only shortly before her; she entered the small tent standing near the cellar door to find him changing out of his gold-embroidered tunic.

"So, what word from the pile of rocks?" Talorgen seemed to be in a fine humor; seeing his preparations and the bowl of water waiting for his return, Sardis had a sinking feeling as she realized her fear was justified.

"They are preparing for our arrival. It does not seem a matter of grave concern to them. No effort was made to reach terms."

"None?" His dark eyes seemed startled.

"None," Sardis replied, trying to hide her satisfaction. When would he realize that Ronne would never deal with him? The only way remaining ended in her death. "I saw the giant lenghur that were reported. They had people riding them. That must be how they are getting information so fast."

Talorgen shrugged and removed his shirt. "Where can they go? We have them trapped, now we'll sap their minds. How can their sneaking about help them then?" He gave a quick, giggling laugh.

Sardis turned away, trying to think of an excuse to leave that would not anger him. She heard him come up behind her, felt the strength of his bare arms about her even through her armor. Soft kisses touched lightly, enticingly at the pulse in her neck, the base of her throat, her open lips. "Come with me now," he said in a soft voice that shook slightly with emotion, and her blood ran cold as she felt the thing inside her stir. "We could share this one." She closed her eyes and swallowed convulsively, shaking her head.

He all but flung her away from him, and she felt the cold where his warmth had been. It was almost enough to make her agree, but when she thought about *sharing*, she couldn't make herself say the words.

"You keep avoiding it, when you know we need more power to destroy her! Her people should have been reduced to drooling idiocy by now, but their minds are still whole! We need another remalk like mine, strong and well fed, to be sure of bringing her down. Don't you *want* to destroy Ronne?"

"I have wanted to destroy her longer than you have," Sardis said dangerously. "I still want it more than you can know. I know what my remalk needs, and I will feed it when it hungers." Seeing him still angry, she tried to appease him. "I haven't had mine as long as you have had yours; it isn't as strong and doesn't need as much."

He looked at her more calmly then, but still displeased. "If you feed it, it will grow. Raw meat is not enough."

"I will, I will! But not now," she said irritably. *How did I get myself caught in this horror*, she thought in despair. *I thought I would pay any price for this power, and now I would pay any price to be rid of it.*

Talorgen said nothing further, but put on the plain tunic that had been laid out and left the tent, his argument with her seemingly forgotten and a small smile of anticipation on his face. Sardis saw her chance to escape and followed him out of the tent. This meant, however, that she saw the interior of the cellar when he opened the door, and she was dismayed to see one of the soldiers who had gone with her to Keris Kera bound naked to a rough wood table. As soon as the door opened he began to plead and beg, terrified. He must have heard the rumors, then. Now he knew they were based in fact.

Sardis fled, trying to move quickly but still able to hear the screams when they began, lasting an impossibly long time but at last ending in a burbling choke. The convulsions of her own demon spirit, aroused by the nearness of blood and pain, made her stumble and nearly fall. She felt like screaming herself, caught between the demon in her heart and the demon in her body. *I have done so many, many despicable things for Talorgen, why is it I cannot do this?*

She had killed many times, more than once in cruel and lingering ways, so that could not be the reason. She thought it was feeling the thing come out of her, out of her throat, watching the insubstantial mist rend the living human flesh with thousands of needle teeth, the horrible foul taste it left behind when it went back inside.

The memory was so strong Sardis had to stop and retch violently. She sent a malevolent mental curse toward Ronne when she recovered. How was Ronne resisting the demons' magic? If she hadn't rescued the prisoners, if she hadn't been so damn careful to get every peasant out of their way, at least they wouldn't have had to feed on their own people. Did she know about the demons? That comment she had made…Talorgen's demon was developing an amazing appetite. It would not be long before he needed more than one every day.

CHAPTER 20

Erith moved silently, slowly in the darkness, and the other rovers did the same. They were close to Talorgen's camp now, close enough that a wary guard would hear movement in the dry grass unless they took care to make their progress slow and even.

We should have seen them by now. He could see the tents quite clearly, but no sign of the perimeter guard. The others had stopped, looking to him for guidance. He waited, but there was still no sign of any guard, and he gestured for two rovers to follow him closer to the camp. It was too good an opportunity to miss.

When he found the thicket he knew something was not right. Always before, Talorgen's troops had made sure to clear any bushes or anything an enemy could hide behind in a wide swath around the camp. Yet here it was, big enough to hide all three of them, and close enough to see people inside the tents, moving against the light.

A solitary figure emerged from the clustered tents, and Erith quickly dropped to the ground. The other rovers followed suit with haste. He frowned, puzzled. The person moved in a stealthy manner, glancing to either side. Not the missing guard, then. The soldier left the camp and passed by the thicket, so close that Erith saw, in addition to armor and the uniform tunic of Talorgen's troop, that the soldier wore a travelsack—and the travelsack was not empty.

The escaping soldier stopped, then turned back to the camp and gestured. Another soldier emerged from the deeper shadows and followed the first out, away from the camp. The first had vanished into the night when a third soldier started out, but then there came a shout, and the sound of running feet. Erith watched helplessly as that soldier and a fourth tried to escape, but were cut off by other soldiers in a mass.

The two fought with desperate fierceness. Time and time again it seemed they would manage to break free, but they were finally surrounded with no hope of escape. Erith could see they were both badly wounded, but they still fought. Then, despair and fear plain in their faces, they turned their weapons on each other in a last burst of energy and struck hard. They fell together, hands still on the hilts of the blades they had buried in each other. *Out of friendship*, realized Erith, shocked to immobility. *They feared something more than death.*

There was nothing more to see. Erith gave the signal, and slowly the rovers worked their way back to Keris Kera. They needed to use caution, since bands of Talorgen's troops were out looking for the two who had escaped, but it was not wasted time. The rovers made certain some of those soldiers did not return to their camp.

Even in his fatigue, Erith still saw that strange, bloody scene in the camp again and again in his mind. It troubled him, and from their silence he guessed the others were equally disturbed. Try as he might, he could not find the meaning of it.

A sinking feeling in her gut, Ronne listened as a soldier gave the depressing information she had been expecting for days. When his voice ceased, a grim silence fell over the council room. She looked about the table at those seated there.

"You know our situation," she said, and she was surprised by how harsh her voice sounded. "We have one more chance to keep him from our walls. If that fails, we will be besieged with barely enough in store to survive a mild winter with all the refugees. So let us leave no opportunity for victory unexplored."

"They may do themselves in," said Erith. "If that mutiny we saw was any indication, there's some problem inside the army. A serious one."

Dunand shook his head, still astonished. "Mutiny and suicide…. But we can't count on that. How are the rest of them?"

Erith grinned. "Tired and jumpy. They either post twice as many guards from fear, or half as many from fatigue."

"They'll be ripe for panic on the field, if we plan it well," commented someone else.

"So, deceit and traps," Ronne nodded. "Give me your ideas."

When the council adjourned, Ronne remained behind, pouring over the maps, searching for any hidden weakness. The plan that she had evolved was unconventional enough to require some effort to get Dunand to agree, which made Ronne more confident that neither Talorgen nor Sardis would expect it. With so few troops, her options were limited.

If only we had more horses! The kenjah who had been sent had still not returned, and there had been time and to spare. Edge Singing could give no reason for the delay, so Ronne was forced to conclude they would not come.

She forced her thoughts away from the missing kenjah and concentrated again on the map. Talorgen could take only one route with such a large army—approaching Keris Kera from the south, along the length of the broad valley. This meant she could put traps before her front line without hindering her own people.

The line itself would be uneven. The flanks would have more soldiers than the center and would stand forward as well, forcing Talorgen's forces in toward the center. At the proper moment, the flanks would come around each side, surrounding the enemy. A group of rovers on the few horses they had would hide in the hills to the east, waiting for the flanking movement to attack the rear. She smiled to herself. And one last surprise....

When Erith returned to the council room Ronne was still studying maps and lists. He watched her for a moment, unnoticed, concerned by the fatigue he saw in her eyes. At least he had good news to give her.

"The traps will be done in a few hours. We waited until full dark to begin, and Tekbeh and the others have been rushing about with torches in a completely different place for more confusion."

"Good." She sighed and dropped the map she held on the table. "It will be soon—and with little warning when he begins. I want the rovers for the valley in place by first light."

"We will be there," he said, trying to sound confident. It would be the first time the rovers would be a part of a pitched battle, and he didn't want to seem apprehensive.

"No. Not you." She left the room as he sputtered in surprise. "Follow me."

She led him out the portico and behind one of the great pillars by the bridge. Indicating he should stay, she took the wall torch and quenched it efficiently, then replaced it. Erith watched, mystified, as she called the lone guard on the bridge and pointed out the extinguished torch.

"Go and fetch another. And be sure it stays lit!"

The man saluted and left. When he was no longer in sight, Ronne gestured for Erith to leave his hiding place, then hurried him over the bridge and into one of the small ornamental buildings in the tiny garden. It was pitch black inside.

"What are you doing?" he whispered. Ronne was engaged on some clandestine activity she didn't want her people to know about, but why? And what?

He heard a curiously familiar scrape of metal on metal, and then a heavy thud. A cold breeze went by his face, smelling dank and strange, and his hand was taken in a strong grip that pulled him down. He had only a brief moment of incredulous confusion, then Ronne's voice said softly, "There are steps here."

Puzzled and somewhat disappointed, Erith felt his way down a long flight of narrow stairs. It seemed like they would continue forever, but then they came to a level space and turned a corner. Ronne seemed to know her way quite well in the darkness.

She stopped, then he heard flint strike steel and saw a flare of light. Ronne looked at him over a candle flame.

"This is the water gate of Keris Kera, and a well-kept secret. Let Tekbeh take command of the rovers in the side valley. I will open this gate again the day of the battle. I want you to take a group of your most skilled and trusted people through here, along with the soldiers I send you. You will be the second flank attack."

He glanced about the rough rock walls, seeing the start of another flight of stairs at the edge of the light. "Where does this come out?"

"Just behind the base of the waterfall. If Talorgen discovers it, I will be forced to flood it and you will not be able to return the way you came." She hesitated, looking away from him and toward the flickering shadows cast by the candle flame. "There is one other thing you should know. From the books from Tak'hullus—from the underhill—that Temaso Conyet has translated, and from what my brother and…others have told me, the army is not the only danger. Talorgen has a creature of magic he can use against us, a remalk. He has already tried to cloud our minds with its magic. The bodies we found in that house in Bryddhe and Duanoch's village…remalks need a special kind of food."

"What do they look like?" he asked, the hair on his neck prickling as he remembered the gory scene with the human skeletons stripped of flesh.

"They join with those who use them, and have little shape of their own. Do you still have the warding brooch I gave you?"

He turned back the collar of his shirt to show the brooch pinned inside, below the neck. She nodded, looking relieved, and said, "Don't take it off. It may help keep them away."

Two long, nerve-wracking days passed without any sign of activity from the enemy camp. Ronne was glad to have the time to prepare for the battle ahead, but in some ways she wished Talorgen would not delay. The fall weather had turned unaccountably hot, and in addition to the strain of waiting put tempers on edge. Ronne stood on the wall of the outer rampart, straining to see any indication of movement in the valley. There was none.

"We'll have fights shortly," Zeltan said, shrugging in a vain attempt to shift his sweat-dampened shirt to a more comfortable position under his armor. "Have you thought to take the battle to him?"

Ronne grimaced as she descended the stair to the outer ward. "If I had known he would sit like this I might have planned differently. No, we are better here. We chose the ground and use its strengths."

"Ayeh. Is there still no sign of the kenjah, then?"

"None. Tekbeh is certain they will come, but something must have delayed them."

Entering the fortress, they passed the entrance to the library on their way to the main stair. A small white figure stood in the doorway, looking wistful. Ronne saw someone had set the broken petal of the moonrose in crystal for her use. Hanging from Bryddhe's neck, the pendant's faint glow made it just visible in the shadows. She seemed to know who they were, and put out her hand to stop them. Ronne was not certain if it was the magical light or Bryddhe's own strange talent that had identified them.

"Does Temaso wish to speak with me?" Ronne asked. Bryddhe shook her head, eyes downcast. "He tells me you have been of great assistance to him." This produced an embarrassed smile.

"I like it…he knows so much! I want to learn more. But I wish—is there anything more I can do to help?"

Ronne and Zeltan exchanged glances. What was there for a blind person to do in a battle? At last she said, "Take the moonrose and the things from Tak'hullus and gather them together. Find something that you can carry them in. Watch over them, and if there is danger I will send you word. Take them to the master smith; he will know a place of safety." Seeing her frown, Ronne added, "It may not seem a matter of great importance. But it will be one less thing to worry about, and that will aid me."

Bryddhe continued to frown, and now Ronne saw it was more in puzzlement than disappointment. "How did you know it was called Tak'hullus, *na'al?* Na'Conyet only discovered that today."

The sun was only just beginning to emerge over the horizon when Erith gave up on any further attempt at sleep and rose, carefully checking his leather-covered steelshirt for any rips or gaps as he donned it. The fortress was refreshingly cool after the previous heat.

On the evening of the second day, scouts had reported Talorgen's army preparing to march, and Ronne had given orders for the Arhiia to take the field the next morning. He found her in the Audience with Kashan, fully armored and with nothing to tell him whether she had been awake all night or not. Kashan was restless and twitchy, refusing to let Ronne out of his sight. When she stopped pacing, Kashan condescended to let Erith scratch his chin.

"Any news?" He glanced up at her, concerned by the impassive expression on her face. He knew it was a sign of withdrawal, of distancing, and it bothered him.

"He has not yet arrived, nor is there any sign his troops are moving." She began to pace again, and Kashan followed.

"Do you think we can defeat him today?"

Ronne loosed her breath in an explosive snort. "Anything is possible. His army is huge, but barely held together; Sardis is a very able commander, but he may not listen to her now he is so close to his goal. We have a chance." She turned to face him. "Can 'we' defeat him…. Are you one of us now?"

"How can you ask that?" he said, hurt and astonished. "I've been fighting for you from the beginning. Why do you doubt me now?"

She stopped pacing and stood before him, serious grey eyes gazing deep into his. "I know you fight for me, and I have complete trust in you. But would you fight for Arhi if I were gone?"

His blood ran cold and he struggled for speech, unable to imagine a world without Ronne. It would not happen, it could not. Not if he could prevent it.

"Our walls are very strong. But if they fall…I want you to save what you can. Including yourself. I have been to some trouble to ensure your survival."

"Why?" The question was torn from him. If she were going to die why couldn't he die with her? Why should she protect his life more than her own? "I don't understand!"

She smiled, a real smile that reflected in the depths of her eyes, a smile he had not seen for a long time. "Neither do I," she said softly, and took his face in her gauntleted hands. Thin steel plates covered the backs with a hard, impenetrable skin, but the palms were supple leather, soft and warm against his face, soft and warm as her lips on his.

It was not a gentle kiss, and it ended far too soon. She dropped her hands to his shoulders and shook him. "Live," she said with passionate intensity. "A part of me will be with you always."

By the time he had recovered from his astonishment she had gone. He thought to go after her, but then he heard the voices of the rovers approaching and knew it was too late. He seethed with frustration and regret. He hadn't even said anything. *I could have held her….*

A dusty, gasping messenger was all the confirmation Ronne needed. Not even waiting to hear the full message, she signaled Zeltan. "Get the troops in place now, as quickly as possible." He saluted and left at a run.

When the bulk of the army was in place, not long thereafter, Ronne led her personal guard down the winding road of the city, preceded only by Kielce, who carried the Dark Banner of Arhi. Woken by the commotion, the people of the town had begun to gather in the early light, still sleepy and confused. It was light enough for them to see the banner, and she saw their faces change. They knew what it meant. No surrender, no quarter, a fight to defend the heart of what they were. Some, especially the refugees, began cheering. Others wept silently.

They reached the plain before the city walls at last, and as they took up their positions, Ronne heard the massive gate close behind them.

The entrance to the water gate was open as promised, and Erith led his picked band down the narrow steps. "I don't like this place," whispered Fedi, even though there was no need for them to keep their voices low. The roar of the waterfall at the exit would shield them even if they shouted, but they were used to conversing in low voices.

"We won't be here long." Erith didn't mind the dark or the narrow passages, but there were others in the group who did not share his tastes. "Remember, you never saw this."

"We don't see *anything*," grumbled another rover. "Dark as the inside of an aurochs. An' why're you so cheerful, anyhow? Goin' off to get kilt like a real soldier, an' you'd whistle if you knew how!"

It seemed strange, but he *was* happy. He knew what he had to do now— win the battle and make sure Ronne didn't get herself killed. Somehow, that didn't seem as difficult as it had earlier. He sent Fedi to watch from the edge of the waterfall for the battle to begin.

Tekbeh slapped another annoying stinging insect and wondered again why she had ever wanted to be a soldier. She should have stayed on her family's farm. *Thought you were going to escape the boredom, did you? Now you've got boring and dangerous.* Her family hadn't argued with her much when she had gone. Whatever she planted would turn out to be at the wrong season, or would come down with black rot.

No, she wasn't much of a farmer. Sometimes she thought she wasn't much of a soldier, either. There were others who thought so too, and they usually didn't bother to hide it. Their families had been soldiers for generations. They had barely tolerated her presence in the army, and now here she was, commanding them.

It was bad enough that they had been hiding in the forested ravine for two days, sleeping in the open without a fire. During the day the rovers were restless and had to be kept out of the enemy's sight. Her temperament had never been calm…and the kenjah had not come.

She vented her annoyance by watching the rovers like a hawk for any sound or motion that might be noticed now that the enemy army was moving into position before Keris Kera. *If it gets much worse, they'll kill me themselves and I won't have to worry about it.*

Hasko was drumming his fingers on a log, and Tekbeh snarled softly for him to stop. The sound came again, but faint and far away.

"I told you, no more!" she whispered, furious.

"It wasna me!" He held up his hands in innocence. Tekbeh could still hear the drumming sound, and it was getting louder. They all heard it now, and several of the rovers ran to the edge of the forest by the road. A huge cloud of dust had appeared in the east, and dark shapes could just be seen within it.

Tekbeh felt a wide grin spread across her face. "They came—" Then her joy vanished, replaced by consternation. "Cruel Face, they'll ruin it! They'll run right before Talorgen and he'll stop too soon!"

"We could ride to warn them," one of the rovers suggested.

Tekbeh shook her head. "We can't get to them but by the road, and his troops can see it now." She looked around, casting about desperately for inspiration, then saw her quiver hanging from her horse's saddle. Snatching her bow and one particular arrow, she clambered up a nearby rock outcrop, taking care to stay out of sight of the plain as much as possible.

When she got to a sheltered position, she took her bow and the arrow with the chipped green stone point and took careful aim, high in the air. The arrow flew in a steep arc, landing in the road well ahead of the approaching kenjah.

A familiar dark figure sped ahead of the group and dismounted to pick it up. Kemar'sto flung up a hand to stop the others, looking toward the rock outcrop where the arrow had come from. Tekbeh waved her bow so only they could see it, and she was pleased how quickly he understood her intention. Kemar'sto left his horse and melted into the forest, and soon he stood before her, amber eyes fixed on her face with an expression she could not look at long.

"About time you showed up," Tekbeh said, scowling in an attempt to hide her reaction. "This is what we need you to do…"

To Ronne it seemed to take both forever and no time at all for the enemy troops to reach the Arhiia front line, but when they did, things happened with incredible swiftness. Talorgen attempted a charge, seeking to break the center with his larger force. The onrush was fearsome—until the first line of soldiers reached the belt of traps and pitfalls, and the stumbling and confusion destroyed the attack's momentum.

But where Talorgen's tactics failed, the Arhiia's bad fortune succeeded for him. She knew the thin line at the center was a gamble. They put up a valiant fight, but there were not enough soldiers and too many of them were inexperienced. The center broke. Seeing the bridge and the gate of Keris Kera before them, the enemy gave a cheer, thinking they had won through the weak defenses.

Now came the crucial part of her plan. Ronne shouted to the flank troops to wheel about. From her vision's edge she saw her standardbearer appear beside her in the fight. Kielce had been wounded, but not badly enough to stop her. She held the standard with grim determination as the fighting swirled about her, blood streaking her face. She had carried the banner near the center to trick the attackers into thinking the main force was there, and must have barely escaped to the flank when the center broke.

The enemy soldiers' elation did not last long as they discovered they were now under attack from both sides from a seemingly undiminished army of Arhiia.

Now for Erith and Tekbeh, thought Ronne. *If only we had more fighters! We could destroy them, the plan has worked so well....*

She looked up towards the gap in the hills. Tekbeh should be attacking, and sure enough a stream of riders poured down the gap. Many riders... more riders than they had. Still they came, riding through a familiar cloud of dust, and Ronne felt her heart lift. *The kenjah are here!*

She rejoined the conflict with a shout, and joy made Heartseeker light in her hands. The enemy soldiers facing her heard the shouts and screams behind them, faltered, then turned and ran. Some were even trampling their comrades in their panicked flight to escape. What had been a doubtful chance for Arhi was now a certain victory.

Erith and his band of rovers had an excellent view of the horde of kenjah as they swept down from the hills. He even saw Tekbeh near the front, yelling as fiercely as the rest. He grinned and waved, even though he knew she would not see him.

The rovers stared at the thundering stream of kenjah, bemused. "Whadda we do now? They're doin' our job for us!"

Erith shrugged. "Wait until they go by. We'll still have work to do. Make sure nobody gets to the waterfall."

The battlefield was complete, milling chaos. The unexpected attack from the rear threw Talorgen's troops into confusion, but the kenjah did not escape unscathed. Soon there were riderless horses, which the rovers were quick to make use of.

Erith scanned the field, searching without success for Ronne. After a few attacks, mostly from soldiers trying to escape, he found himself by Zeltan. The older man was panting slightly but otherwise unharmed.

"How are we doing? Have we won yet?" Erith pushed back his dark hood and wiped his forehead, wishing his water gourd was still intact. His throat was dry with dust and shouting.

"From my view it goes well enough, but you know no one sees a battle entire," Zeltan replied. "With the kenjah here it goes our way unless the luck is bad indeed."

Erith nodded, and started to ask about Ronne when Zeltan shouted, "Ware! Sardis!"

Nothing had gone right. From the very beginning Sardis could see victory slipping from her grasp. The Arhiia were as alert and determined as ever. *They blocked the magic somehow; it's the only explanation. But how? Tal said we had the only ones. And how did they know?*

If they had only been able to cross the bridge with the charge…but they had not, and now this seemingly infinite cloud of night-skinned raiders riding the giant lenghur was breaking the army from the rear. She did everything she could to restore order, but the soldiers simply could not be frightened any more—or were more frightened of the Arhiia than her.

Almost she despaired, but then she saw a bright gold head in the chaos of the battle. Her mind began to work, scenting a puzzle. Ronne's pet barbarian had not been on the field at the beginning of the fight. She would have seen that impossible hair or even the height of him. Yet he was on the side opposite the fortress now. How had he gotten there? *There must be a secret way! And he will help me find it.* She called some of her personal command to her, and fought her way to her goal.

A graying soldier barred her way for a small while, but a quick succession of blows and his evident fatigue allowed a small opening. She gave him a savage blow to the chest and he toppled to the ground. She looked over his body to the barbarian, who had only a clumsy short leather tunic for armor, and smiled slowly.

"Well, if it isn't Pathwalker's Pillow. How did you swim the river without getting wet, creature?" When he said nothing, she shrugged and said, "I guess I'll have to beat it out of you," and struck as she spoke.

To her surprise, he blocked her blow and attacked almost as swiftly as she had, and she laughed in delight. "She's been teaching you! And you even learned some of it! Ah, it will hurt just a little to lose such a clever pet." Another slash, which should have cut open his ribs but only sliced the leather tunic and glanced away from something harder underneath. *So, armor after all. But it won't be enough.*

CHAPTER 21

She had been fighting constantly, but at last the press before her cleared and Ronne was able to look about and see how the rest had fared. The left flank had been thrown back a bit further than before, and from the debris, the fighting had been heavy. The kenjah still fought the remnants of the enemy in places, but the largest part of Talorgen's army was withdrawing, in some cases more of a flight than a retreat.

She looked further up the river, toward the cliff near the water gate, and glimpsed golden hair above the soldiers gathered there. She felt a weight lift from her heart, an unacknowledged fear vanishing, then she frowned. Erith was still fighting. She jumped up on one of the bridge gate supports for a better view.

She could tell by his quick, defensive movements that he fought someone of skill. His opponent lunged and turned, and Ronne felt her world go cold. She recognized the move and the fighter. "Sardis," she breathed, and jumped down, running with Heartseeker in hand as soon as she hit the ground.

The sudden hot dryness of her eyes and slowing of motion around her signaled the beginning of the Path, and for the first time in her life she welcomed it and made no attempt to resist. With her last shred of sanity, Ronne gave a piercing, wordless cry of warning before the Pathwalking consumed her.

Zeltan watched the conflict through a haze of pain, amazed at Erith's skill. He had learned well—but not enough to defeat his current opponent. *Be fair, old man. It's only Herself, perhaps, that could be sure of besting Sardis Three-scars.*

Suddenly a high, keening wail cut through the air from the direction of the main gate. The cry was caught up by others, and he could hear the shouts. "Pathwalker walks! Stand away!" He could see her now, in the center of a clear space in the battle, the Arhiia behind her at a careful distance. He knew they feared she would turn and see only the weapon, not the comrade who held it.

Talorgen's forces gave way, only a few foolhardy or ignorant warriors daring to oppose her. She was relentless as a flood, and what she touched died. Zeltan had heard the tales brought back by the Arhiia who had seen Ronne walk the Path in Ynduria, and had secretly discounted much of it as a drop of truth flavoring a good tale and a night's drinking, even though he had briefly seen it himself. He was unprepared for the reality. To a warrior, and especially a trainer of warriors, every motion was achingly beautiful, so right and true it seemed impossible to do it any other way.

Yet it was a terrible beauty, inhuman and chilling in its perfection. Ronne showed neither mercy nor compassion. She made no distinction between a determined attacker and a fleeing soldier, did not hold back when faced by a soldier only attempting to defend a fallen comrade. All that stood between Ronne and her goal fell.

The sound of a blow followed by a gasp made Zeltan return his attention to the nearer battle. Erith's breathing was ragged, and cuts in his steelshirt were showing red. He wouldn't be able to hold out much longer. Sardis saw it too and flashed a predatory smile.

"The Face of Death looks at you, barbarian." Erith did not respond.

"Wrong again, Three-scars," rasped Zeltan, careless of the fire in his chest. "Herself is lookin' at *you*."

Sardis sneered, clearly thinking it a trick. Something alerted her—the flash of a descending blade at the edge of her vision, the faint sound of air disturbed by a mighty blow. She glanced aside, then spun away with desperate agility to avoid Ronne's attack.

Still gasping from exertion, Erith dragged Zeltan further from the conflict and did the best he could to staunch the bleeding. He felt an inner tug when he touched the wound, followed by crippling agony. The pain and the memory of his last attempt at healing made him hesitate, but when he gathered his courage and made the attempt, it was not successful. It felt like his energy was being deflected away, as if the wound itself was refusing to heal.

Looking more closely, he saw that the force of the blow had shattered Zeltan's armor, and in places the metal had been forced into flesh. Perhaps that was why it wasn't working—the shards of metal needed to be removed. He needed to get Zeltan off the field, get help…. He looked about for a clear way to the fortress through the chaos of the battle.

"Stay here, you can't get by her now…she's not sane," Zeltan managed to get out, clutching weakly at Erith's arm. He did not look as ghastly as he had earlier—the attempt at healing seemed to have done some good after all. Erith crouched on the ground, supporting Zeltan and holding a makeshift bandage to the hole in his chest as Ronne fought Sardis.

Erith realized Sardis had been toying with him when he had fought her, trying to get him to betray the location of the water gate. Now, time and time again she avoided certain death by some skilled and desperate swordplay, but Ronne's onslaught was such that Sardis could never go on the offensive. She seemed to realize she was only delaying the inevitable, but still she fought on, her teeth bared but her sardonic wit silent, such was her desperation. Ronne never spoke, never wearied, never slowed her attack.

Then Sardis mistimed her parry and did not recover quickly enough to defend herself from Ronne's powerful blow. Sardis cried out as Heartseeker cut deep, and she slumped to the ground, clutching the red ruin of her side. Ronne watched her fall. Only when Sardis let go her sword did she look away, as if searching for another opponent.

Erith's eyes met hers, and he felt a chill run through him. Her eyes were empty, inhuman, with no sign of recognition. They held no trace of the Ronne he knew; the haughty commander who had refused to feed him, the warrior who had grieved for the death of her armsman, the woman who had laughed with the joy of riding with the wind, the lover who had kissed his lips with fire.

"Ronne." It was a plea. His voice cracked with fatigue and fear. The empty eyes turned back to him. "Ronne! Are you…are you well?" *Are you there?*

At first there was no response. Then a faint cloud of confusion slowly showed itself in her face, and her grey eyes returned to life. "Well enough… but you are injured." Her voice was rough. Erith heard a muffled exclamation from Zeltan, and glanced to see a look of shock on the older man's face as he stared at him.

"Nothing deep. But Zeltan—he should be looked to."

The Arhiia approached cautiously when it was clear their *alaran* had returned to sanity, and she gestured to two of them to take the wounded man away. As they did, they glanced with equal amazement at Ronne and at Erith. "How did he—" began one soldier, quickly hushed by the others.

Now what have I done? Erith wondered.

I have cheated my curse once more. Ronne leaned wearily against the cliff wall, unable to lift the heavy Heartseeker again. Pathwalking always drained her, no matter how short the time it lasted. Then the terror of the first moments of return, always wondering, *where am I now? What have I done?* Erith was safe, and that was all that mattered now.

The battle seemed to have ended during her fight with Sardis. The tattered remnants of Talorgen's mighty army withdrew as a portion of the Arhiia harried their retreat, aided by the kenjah. The price was high, but it was a greater victory than she had hoped for.

A voice claimed her attention, calling her war-name.

"Pathwalker! Grant the dead a wish." Sardis had raised herself on one elbow, legs askew, scars livid in the deathly pallor of her face. Ronne turned her head, considering, then went slowly to her side. "I would make my peace with you, before I die," Sardis said, her voice fading. "My contrition gift must be my death, for I have nothing else to give that would please you…and you seem to have taken it without asking." She managed a faint smile through her pain.

Ronne shook her head. "Your death will not please me. We were enemies only because of Talorgen, and he was not worthy of it. But for that one unimportant thing we could have been friends."

Sardis looked at her, and her eyes were sad. "Unimportant…you would think so, of course. You never loved him, even as a *kalasen*…not like I did. There is no greater curse than to love someone who does not love you. You were his passion, his pride—you could not have caused him more pain than by leaving him. You," she said with her old savagery, a faint sneer on her face, "you with your family sword, your annoying honor, your fighting skill…how glad I was you were stupid enough to tell the truth at court."

Erith had come up beside Ronne while Sardis spoke, and she glanced at him. "He's really your helmbearer?" She asked without incredulity, as if she merely wished to make certain.

"Yes."

"Well, if I can't die for you, let me give your burning helmbearer a sword-eye. I suppose I owe him contrition as well, and there aren't that many of the *tier sanas* left, due to Tal's efforts." She coughed, blood staining her mouth, and when she continued, her voice was faint. "And I won't last much longer." Blood flecked her lips. Seeing Ronne's hesitation, she grinned shakily. "Well? What do you have against astounding the gossips?"

Ronne smiled. "Nothing." It was an offer of genuine value. She could not grant a sword-eye to her own helmbearer without creating a scandal, and Erith would benefit from the increase in status—even if it was given by an enemy.

She looked up at Erith. "Draw your sword, and grasp the blade." Turning back to Sardis, she put an arm behind her back to support her, and handed her her sword to grasp in witnessing. Then she drew her own to witness. "See before you Erith ne'Haral, warrior of worth, bearer of my helm." She spoke the formal High Speech phrases with care, that Erith might have some chance of understanding them.

"This I see…before me. The eye of my honor has seen…his actions. Where is the eye of his honor, that guides him so well?"

"I cannot see it, he stands too close to me. Will you show me where it lies?"

"Willingly…I show you." Sardis took her hand away from her side with a grimace. "No trouble finding my blood this time," she whispered, and touched Erith's blade below the hilt with her bloody finger.

This done, her hand dropped lifelessly and she sighed. "I would speak for your ear alone." Her voice was so faint Ronne had to bend to catch her words. Ronne tilted her head at Erith, and he backed away. Ronne looked at Sardis. Her eyes were cloudy and unfocused.

"How did you know?"

So slight was the smile she could have almost imagined it on the dying woman's lips. "Much as you respect your *samhal*, would you…walk the Path for him? And return when he called to you? I am glad it ends…like this, but want to…make right, what I did wrong." And with the last of her strength, Sardis told the ugly tale of how Talorgen and his troops had destroyed Ynduria after the barbarians defeated the Imperial army, the remalks, and the bloody conquest that followed.

When her voice faded away Ronne thought she had finished, but Sardis struggled for speech again. "Burn my body."

"What?" Ronne was aghast and wondered if Sardis was wandering in her mind, but her expression was resolute.

"Oh, I deserve it, never fear. There are…few evil things I haven't done. You have to kill the creature while it's still inside," she said, in a last burst of energy. "I wouldn't feed it, it's still weak. Hated feeding them, the screams…. Tal loved it."

"You have one as well?" Ronne asked, horrified. Now she realized that the silver dagger was sensing the close presence of a remalk, not a distant presence as she had thought. It was not as strong as she had felt from Talorgen, but it was there. *How many of these things exist?* The mist creature had not mentioned a number, and she had assumed Talorgen's was the only one.

"Yes…. You know about the demons? Promise…you must, mine isn't as bad…you will do it?" Sardis turned her head blindly, one hand scrabbling on Ronne's armor.

Mindful of the promise she had made to the mist creature, Ronne reluctantly agreed. It would look disgraceful and vindictive to those who did not know why she did it, but she could see no other way.

"Talorgen's is worse…it might not burn…so strong. They have…many teeth. So may you know them." And with these cryptic words Sardis died.

Letting her body down on the rocky ground, Ronne stood stiffly and sheathed Heartseeker. She found Erith standing beside her, some unreadable expression in his eyes. "You should see the smiths about inscribing a sword-eye for you. You are *tier sanas* now."

He paid no attention to this. "What did you do there, in the fight?" he said, his voice abrupt.

She sighed, trying to ignore the sinking feeling in her heart. She knew what he meant, and she didn't want to talk about it. His stubborn expression told her he was determined to get an answer. "Pathwalking. You saw it once before, when we fought the kenjah."

"You weren't…there, anymore. You didn't recognize me."

"No." She could identify what she saw in his eyes now. It was fear.

"Where do you go?"

It was too much. No one had ever dared ask such questions of her before. They were too much in awe of the Pathwalking; they never thought to ask the price for such ability. They did not realize the dangers, pretended they did not exist. She closed her eyes and prayed for composure.

"I don't know. I have only the faintest memory of what I do when I walk the Path, as if I see it from a distance. No, I did not recognize you. I would not recognize my mother. No, I can't control when it starts, when it ends. I never wanted it and I can't get rid of it." Her voice shook, and she fought for control. "Every time I come back, I wonder, is this the time? Have I killed someone dear to me?"

Erith said nothing, but what she saw in his face made her feel dead and cold inside. She turned away blindly and headed for the group of commanders waiting for her near the bridge. She tried not to notice that Erith did not follow.

Ronne gazed at the flames, standing at attention despite her fatigue. The soldiers were respectfully silent. She blinked and stared at the body on the pyre. *Sardis—she didn't move. It was the flames, making it look that way.* When the silver dagger went silent just afterward, she was not so sure.

A messenger made his way to where she stood, and she nodded for him to speak without taking her eyes from the pyre. "They wish to speak with you, *na'al.* From the enemy."

It was an effort to think, to care about what she should do. "Very well. Where are they?"

"The gatehouse, *na'al.*"

The body was nearly consumed, and soon the pyre would be coals and ashes. To one of the soldiers, she said, "When the fire has died, build a mound over it. Disturb nothing."

His shock was evident, but he nodded. To burn an enemy's body, and then give her a mound…the combination of contempt and respect in these actions would have confused her as well if she did not know the fierce contradiction of Sardis' life. Now it seemed fitting that even after all the terrible things she had done, Sardis had won some mark of respect for wishing to undo them at the end, and for resisting the deeper evil of the remalks.

Ronne found the envoy in the gatehouse, one of Talorgen's commanders. The enemy army, much reduced, had regrouped at the end of the valley and Talorgen was refusing to leave.

"We can destroy you," she said, slowly and distinctly. Talorgen's forces had suffered horrible casualties compared to the Arhiia. "Why do you stay? You have no hope of victory now."

"I know this," said the commander, a canny, clever-looking man with a nasty cut on his forehead that still bled sluggishly. "He refuses to leave, and speaks with anger of old wrongs. If there is a way to change his mind I would like to hear it. I tire of sending my people to die for no reason."

"Tell him I offer him a duel, if the army leaves my territory and does not return." She had to kill the remalk, if nothing else. She had given her word to the mist creatures.

Murmurs broke out among the Arhiia, which she did not have the energy to stop. They did not like it—well, she had given up on pleasing them. The depression that had threatened to consume her after the confrontation with Erith was still present, and she found it hard to care about anything anymore.

"I will tell him what you say," promised the commander.

Tekbeh kept a careful eye on the field as her horse picked its way through the debris. Not all the bodies on the field were completely dead— some were wounded Arhiia, and a few were enemy soldiers who hadn't figured out they'd lost yet. This part seemed fairly quiet, though. Everybody who looked dead, was. Far too many were.

She saw a figure she recognized up ahead, holding a bow. Kemar'sto saw her too, and he soon stood beside her stirrup. Something was wrong with her breathing—she wanted to make some offhand comment, but nothing would come out. She felt a foolish grin spread across her face. Kemar'sto also was silent, glancing at her and then adjusting one of the felt tassels on her saddle with great care.

"You came back," she managed at last. *What a brilliant observation. You've only been fighting together for hours, and you've just noticed?*

Kemar'sto looked up at her and smiled. "I return to where the sun is brightest," he said, his voice barely audible. "Is...is the sun now brighter in your eyes?"

She frowned, puzzled. He was watching her reaction with concern, his amber eyes intent on her face. What was he trying to say?

A flicker of motion alerted her, and she saw behind him a soldier from Talorgen's army rising from the ground and about to sink a long knife in Kemar'sto's side. Grabbing the crest on his head, Tekbeh pulled him towards her and out of the way of the knife. The attacker took the point of her outthrust sword in the throat.

Off balance, she started to fall from her horse. Kemar'sto caught her shoulders before she hit the ground and helped her stand.

"Are you hurt? Did that Faceless bastard get you?" He looked stunned and still gripped her, but when she craned her neck to look she saw only a small rip in his leather vest.

"*Aillaialla! Se vats'o ne Tekbe'ha corvens Kemar'sto!*" cried a voice in ringing tones. The thunder of hooves came closer and a group of kenjah soon surrounded them, talking in loud, excited voices and gesturing wildly. Tekbeh gaped in astonishment. Had they gone insane? She noticed they were pointing at her, and they seemed to be upset with something she'd done. But what? Did they think her wrong for saving Kemar'sto's life?

The Windriders' excitement made them almost incoherent, and they spoke faster than she could understand. When they slowed down they still didn't make any sense.

"You stole him, so you get no marrying-gift!"

"Yeh! We do not owe you, and we will not take him back! Have to keep," said another, grinning.

Tekbeh froze, a horrible, unbelievable suspicion growing in her mind.

"Uh, Kemar'sto? What are they talking about?"

He said nothing and avoided her gaze, and she knew she would get no help there. Now that she thought about it, the kenjah seemed to be in a remarkably cheerful and mischievous mood.

"You placed your hand on his head," explained Edge Singing, limping painfully up to them. She had a nasty wound in one leg, and was supported by another warrior. Her golden eyes danced with merriment. "His honor was in your hands. In a battle, you could have taken his blood-braid."

"I only…I was just defending him! How does that make me…us…."

Edge Singing grinned at her discomfort. "If a man wants one beside him but the families cannot agree, he can steal her if he can grasp her braid— but then her family owes him nothing. Usually it is the man who steals," she added.

"Why would she steal?" Tekbeh recognized with a shock the speaker was Un'Varten, asking his question with a straight face. "Why would the Great Chieftain and I not come to agreement on this?"

"Ah, you have seen her fight with the fire in her eye and the war-cry in her throat. So hot-blooded, how could she wait?" Edge Singing was enjoying herself.

Tekbeh felt her face burning red and wished fervently for dark skin like the kenjah that would not betray her. Failing that, her next thought was escape, and she stepped back to mount her horse again.

She was stopped by someone standing behind her, by a hand that reached for hers and held it in a gentle but firm grip. She looked into Kemar'sto's pleading eyes and found herself paralyzed by indecision. He smiled at her, and suddenly she understood what he had been asking. *Is the sun now brighter in your eyes?* It was. Something inside her snapped.

"I have him now, so it is too late to argue," she said recklessly, suiting action to words and pulling him to her side with an arm about his waist. *This will take some explaining back home*, was her last shred of rational thought. Somehow it still seemed worth it.

The kenjah whooped and laughed with delight.

CHAPTER 22

Talorgen accepted the duel. Erith was not sure it was such a good idea and said so, but Ronne and the other Arhiia disagreed. Unable to put his misgivings into words, he left the council room for the lake portico. He hesitated, thinking of going to the Fingertip, but instead crossed the bridge over the waterfall to the garden.

Tiny figures were just visible in the dusk, moving on the plain below. He stopped to watch. Looking down the river, he was surprised to see Sardis' mound. Had the fight been that close to the water gate? It had seemed farther.

Most of the soldiers were clearing the battlefield of bodies and debris, but a few were preparing a carefully measured dueling site just across the river from the main gate to the city. He gripped the edge of the stone wall, feeling frustrated and helpless. All his fear of Ronne had disappeared in the face of fear *for* her in this duel. Talorgen was unpredictable; his actions showed he could not be trusted.

What could he do? She was determined to fight him. Erith wasn't even sure he could heal her if she were wounded. His ability was not very reliable —Zeltan was still badly hurt, despite his efforts. He'd tried to help one of the rovers after the battle as well. That had worked, but it had left him weak and drained, all for a wound that was little more than a long scratch.

Best if it wasn't needed…but if it was, he'd do his damnedest. He could keep a careful eye on Talorgen. As for the Pathwalking, hadn't he called her out of it after the fight with Sardis? How, he still wasn't sure; perhaps it had been his familiar voice or, like with Kashan, he had spoken when her mood had calmed.

The next day, shortly after dawn, Ronne, Erith, and the other Arhiia left the city and crossed the bridge to the dueling site. The air was clear, with an edge of a chill, and mist pooled in hollows and drifted over the river. There was a strange absence of sound in the valley, and Erith sensed a certain hushed expectancy surrounding them that put his nerves on edge. Talorgen and his guard were waiting for them when they arrived.

Ronne wore her lighter traveling armor for better mobility and carried her longsword once again. She stopped before entering the dueling ground and unstrapped the dagger sheath on her arm, handing it to Erith.

"Take care of this for me until I finish here." It was the first time she had spoken since they had met that morning. She was withdrawn, her face an expressionless mask.

He could see why she had removed the silver dagger. Even holding the sheath he could feel it buzzing like a hornet's nest.

"Don't forget to kill him," he said, hoping he sounded sufficiently calm.

She smiled, just a fraction like the old Ronne. "I have every intention of killing him."

The dueling ground had been marked out in the shape of two overlapping triangles. Ronne and her two witnesses occupied the points of one triangle, and a sullen Talorgen and his two the other. Talorgen did not look well. Dark circles ringed his eyes, and he was unable to keep still; even when standing in one place his hands were in constant motion.

The duel began. At first it seemed to Erith to be identical to the fight with Sardis. Ronne was not Pathwalking, but Talorgen was not as skilled as Sardis. Erith relaxed, confident Ronne would have little difficulty. Then Talorgen began to do completely unexpected things; useless attacks that put him in danger, a skipping sidestep that gained him nothing. His inability to strike Ronne seemed to infuriate him. His face began working with anger and he muttered indistinctly to himself.

Erith caught a glimpse of sharp needle teeth and had to shake himself. What was going on here? Talorgen was nothing like he had been their first encounter at the inn, either in action or appearance. He took a better grip of the silver dagger.

Ronne appeared to tire of the inconclusive fight and launched a series of blows. Erith had seen her use the move in practice before; it should have deflected Talorgen's attack just enough to make it safe to impale him on the point of her sword. The instant before it touched him Talorgen seemed to twitch and pull in on himself, and instead of killing him Ronne sliced through his shoulder, leaving his sword arm dangling and useless.

Talorgen made a high-pitched, mewling cry, revealing even more clearly his narrow, pointed teeth, and dropped his sword. Ronne checked herself on the edge of another attack and stepped back to await events. Talorgen's witnesses tried to reason with him. Erith couldn't hear what they said, but Talorgen's response was more than clear.

"Yield? While she still lives? I have other weapons than puny swords, you fools!"

Patience at an end, Ronne advanced on Talorgen with such a fierce expression he took an involuntary step backward and crossed the line of the dueling site.

"The duel is over," she said in a voice like a whip, "and you have lost it. Now get out of Arhi." She turned on her heel and returned to where Erith and the others stood. Erith could see she was furious at missing the chance to remove Talorgen for good.

"Don't worry, he won't leave," he said, clapping a friendly hand on her shoulder. He was relieved the duel had ended as well as it had. Talorgen had not even touched Ronne. "You can let Duanoch drop rocks on his head when he tries to storm the gate by himself. He was very disappointed he didn't get a chance to use his sling-mills in the last battle, you know."

Ronne gave a short laugh, and some of the tension left her body. She seemed surprised but pleased at his gesture, and smiled with unusual warmth. "Very true. Without Sardis to make him reasonable we will have any number of opportunities. At the moment, however, I tire of his presence." She turned to the group of Arhi soldiers waiting by the dueling ground to give orders concerning Talorgen and his people.

Erith glanced at the other end of the field. He was surprised to see Talorgen looking at him with an expression of pure venom, his eyes more clear and focused than at any time during the duel. Talorgen reached up and pulled a short gold pin from his hair, and launched himself at Ronne with incredible speed.

Erith shouted a warning. Ronne turned instantly, but only had time to throw an arm up to block the attack. Talorgen was flung away, staggering. Suddenly Ronne screamed and dropped to the ground, clutching her arm. Talorgen recovered his balance and turned back to her, drawing his shortblade and laughing maniacally.

Intent on his goal, Talorgen did not see Erith running towards him, enraged and horrified. Erith grabbed his shoulder and pulled him around, then ripped him up the front with the silver dagger, slicing cleanly through armor, skin, and bone alike.

A horrible, inhuman scream—lasting longer than should have been possible—deafened him, and he saw a black, scummy film on the dagger instead of blood. Talorgen's body crumpled in on itself as it fell, releasing a strangely formed dark cloud that seemed to reach out to Ronne, but could not quite go far enough. The cloud vanished, and the body twitched as it shrank and dried to dust before their eyes.

Erith turned to where Ronne lay, soldiers surrounding her. "It was a thorn-of-death," one said, voice soft with shock as he held up the gold-headed pin. It was made of some dark, oily wood with a sharp point. "Poison...."

"Get her to the fortress healers. Now!" Erith shouted as the soldier stared at him in stupefaction. "And get these scum out of here." He waved at Talorgen's people. The Arhiia obeyed with alacrity.

One of the soldiers who had fought with the rovers used his head and loaded Ronne on a horse and sped toward the city. Erith followed him at a dead run.

Temaso clucked and fidgeted about the library, nervous and trying not to show it. Bryddhe could hear it in his voice. She'd always been sensitive to people's voices, since that was most of what she knew of them. But now… now she reveled in the tiny bit of sight granted to her by the moonrose. It sat on the table before her with the other treasures, illuminating her world.

She had to check her vision with the more familiar sense of touch, closing her eyes and letting her fingers tell her what she held. This was one of the treasures from Tak'hullus—a heavy gem, covered with carving, of the color *blue*. She loved color now that she could see it. The carving was very intricate, combining glyphs and tiny scenes of animals and plants, and she held it closer to the moonrose to see the detail.

She frowned, puzzled. The light wasn't helping; she could see even less now. The light was fading. She froze in disbelief, her secret senses overwhelming her with warnings. She cried, "Na'Conyet! It's dying!"

When Erith reached the fortress it was in pandemonium. People ran everywhere, shouting and crying. Pushing his way through the crowd, he found Stenay looking about as if searching for someone, wringing his hands in distress.

"Where is she?"

Stenay turned to him, relief visible in his face. "The snowtiger…it won't let us near her! Can you call it away?"

"I can try." They moved as fast as they could down the hallways and corridors, and Stenay stopped before a doorway surrounded by people. Erith made his way to the entrance and took in the scene.

Kashan paced rapidly in front of the bed, tail lashing and ears close to his head. If anyone tried to enter, he snarled and darted at them. Erith approached, wary and watching for any sign he would be attacked. What if Kashan would not let him near? As he came closer, Kashan backed away, growling softly, then sprang to the door to block the entrance again.

Ronne lay on the bed, still as stone and drenched with sweat. They had managed to remove her armor before Kashan had intervened. The linen shirt she wore underneath was stained and damp from the armor, with blood on one arm where the thorn-of-death had pierced.

His mind raced, chaotic thoughts tumbling through it in a flood of panic. *What can I do she can't die I must do something don't die don't die.…*

Through the open neck of her shirt he saw the gold clanmark he had given her at the outpost. It lay near an old scar that glanced across her collarbone, and he felt his panic subside. *She has survived before, she can survive again. She* will *survive.*

Kneeling by the bed, he pushed the sleeve back from the poisoned arm. Pale green lines snaked away from the puncture, and her hand was rigid, clawed. He held that hand in both of his. It was the poison that must be fought, but how?

He looked at her face, beaded with sweat, her breath drawn in shuddering gasps. He had so little time…and his mind, unbidden, recalled with painful clarity the horrible sensation of death when he had tried to heal Medar. Trembling fingertips touched the wound—and he felt a searing pain in his arm. He pulled his hand away, and the pain disappeared.

Without thought, almost without hope, he clasped her arm again and felt wave after wave of agony pound through him. Just when he feared he had reached the limit of his endurance, he felt a gentle tug and saw swirling darkness before him. Erith tried desperately to pull away, but the force was too strong. *She's died. My heart, I'm sorry….*

At first he thought the darkness complete. Then he saw a darker shape in grey mist and he moved forward, disoriented, stumbling on the uneven rock. He recognized the place from some shadow of a memory—or how would he know what he was walking on?

The dark shape resolved itself into two figures, two identical Ronnes— except that one was tinged with green and had many needle-sharp teeth. It was horrible to see a remalk with Ronne's features. The other figure moved with great weariness, moving her head about as if she could not see. Erith felt for the silver dagger, but he did not seem to have it here.

"Ronne!" he called. "Come back!"

She turned her head as if seeking the source of an elusive echo. The remalk glared at Erith with its mad little eyes and hissed. It held onto Ronne's arm, pulling her towards a pitch-dark cloud. Already one of her feet was invisible in the gloom.

Erith reached her and grasped her other arm, pulling her back. "You can't go, we need you, Talorgen is dead…come back!"

Ronne's face turned to him, but her eyes were blank and uncomprehending. Still, she moved toward him—only a step, but enough to bring her fully free of the remalk's cloud. It wailed, pulling harder, but Ronne did not move. Neither could Erith pull her any further. He let go, and held out his hand.

"Please," he said quietly. "Don't leave. Your people need you; your mother and Alland have had enough sorrow. You promised Bryddhe a flute…." He threw in reason after reason, desperate and hardly thinking of what he was saying, hoping he could say enough to reach her. "Kashan needs you—and I need you. And if you leave I will follow!"

A look of confusion crossed her face. Ronne's arm raised itself as if weighted with stone, her icy hand just touching his. A cold, stiff breeze whistled around them, dispersing the fog. Her hand grasped his more firmly.

The remalk screamed, thrashing about horribly like an animal in its death throes, then vanished. A sound like the very vault of heaven being torn apart thundered about them, and the breeze became a wind, then a gale.

Erith felt weightless. The ground was gone, and they were spinning, flying…. He thought he could hear voices in the wind, dry, wispy voices like they had heard in Tak'hullus. Ronne's eyes were alive now, but still confused. Most strange of all, she was surrounded by a cloud of tiny glowing crystals.

He remembered now! His dream, so long ago, when he had thought he was dying in the Spirit Mountains. The rock, the chained figure…had it been Ronne?

The wind was trying to pull them apart, and he hung on with all his strength.

"You can't have her now," he gritted, "I will never let go!"

The hurricane seemed to chuckle dryly, and Erith heard a whisper echo in his mind that said, "Very well…."

Then he was back in the room, kneeling by Ronne, his body racked with weariness. He looked at her arm. The skin was whole and unbroken, the lines of poison gone, her hand relaxed. Her breath came slow and natural.

He collapsed against the bed in exhaustion, holding her hand to his face, rejoicing in its warmth and the pulse he felt beneath the skin. On the outer edges of his awareness he could hear exclamations and hurrying feet, feel motion near him.

A touch on his shoulder and the scent of aroe made him look up. Inar was there, concern on her face. Concern for him. He had no energy left to be amazed.

"Are you well?" she inquired in her measured, cultured voice.

He could only nod. He knew he should stand, but was supremely incapable of doing so.

Fatigue and worry had lined Inar's face, and her elusive smile flickered at the corners of her lips. "It is a miracle…. How did you do it? What did you do?" He saw awe and astonishment in her eyes.

He shook his head, feeling the hot tears brimming, falling down his cheeks. He didn't care. "I wanted her to live," he whispered. "I just wanted her to live." He could say nothing more.

He heard Inar give quiet orders, and gentle hands carried him to a soft bed of oblivion.

CHAPTER 23

Voices wove through his dreams, just loud enough that he could not ignore them. Erith drifted between sleep and wakefulness for a time, fatigue like a weight on his mind. He wished the voices would argue somewhere else.

Instead, they got louder.

"…not even injured! They are all the same; lazy, no discipline…."

"He has amazing strength, but even he cannot perform the impossible without cost."

Erith smiled, amused. The second voice sounded exactly like Alland. *He has a tongue like a sharp knife when he's angry.*

"The Linariach requires his presence—"

"The Linariach requires patience. What do you hope to learn? You may not care for them, but the facts are clear."

The other voice blustered and mumbled something indistinct.

"Of course he will. As soon as he is able," the Alland-voice soothed.

Silence fell once again, and Erith dozed fitfully, unable to sleep. His thoughts would not be still. Something was not right, out of place and uncomfortable, like a small stone in a boot.

The door to his room creaked open, and he came fully awake. A line of light wavered, then grew stronger, and a head peered around the door. It pulled back when Erith moved, and a moment later two people came in, one a servant carrying a lamp. The other was Alland.

Erith held up a hand to block the light, wincing, and the servant gave him an apologetic glance before placing the lamp on the table by his bed.

"I did not mean to wake you," said Alland, looking contrite. "Only to see how you were. Do you need anything?"

Erith blinked, trying to collect his thoughts. Alland seemed concerned. He shook his head.

"How is Ronne?" he said, his voice rough with sleep.

Alland smiled. "Sleeping. She woke for a space, but some nameless fool mentioned the Linariach was meeting and she fell asleep again almost immediately."

"Wasn't a dream, then. Talking outside." Erith gestured towards the door.

"Alas, no." Alland grimaced. "The measure of their desperation is shown in their asking for you in Ronne's absence. They would still like to think you do not exist."

"What do they want to know? They can ask the commanders about the battle."

"They want not only that, but an explanation of the events at the duel. No one quite believes all that happened," he said, his voice going tight as he spoke. "The commanders are not available. Dunand died in the battle. Finavah has gone to secure the border and provide protection for those refugees able to return."

Erith closed his eyes for a moment, then sat up with a groan, swinging his legs over the side of the bed. Alland was alarmed.

"What are you doing? They can wait—you should rest. Don't worry about them."

"If I go, will they wait longer before disturbing Ronne?" Alland nodded, an arrested and thoughtful expression on his face. "Besides, I can't sleep. Not now."

He tried to stand, but his head swam so badly he staggered and almost fell. Alland caught his arm and helped him sit down again, then turned to the servant still hovering in the background and said a few soft words. The servant bowed and left.

"You have done so much, and still you wish to do more," Alland said. His face worked, and he seemed to have difficulty speaking. "I would thank you properly, for myself, for my mother…for Arhi. When I think how she…when I heard what had happened, I knew she was dead. Because of you, my sister lives. I do not have the words." He took a deep breath, and continued in High Speech. "Your friendship is gold." His face was flushed, and Erith could see the contrast with the pale scar on Alland's face. He felt awkward, not knowing what to say in return. It was both thanks and apology, his sincerity plain.

The servant returned, carrying a wine bottle and a cup. Alland recovered his composure and took the bottle, pouring a generous measure and offering it to Erith.

Suddenly thirsty, Erith drank. He choked and sputtered. "That's horrible stuff. Why do you drink it? Or were you saving it for me?"

Alland's eyes had a mischievous look, despite his straight face. "Both Good and Evil Faces are aspects of the Whole, and even bad wine has a use. It would wake a week-old corpse—which you were resembling—and if you truly wish to face the Linariach, you will need to be awake. Now, let's make you look a little more presentable…."

"Ronne, what troubles you? Are you in pain?"

"I am weary, Mother. It does not often happen that one sees the Face of Death and returns to tell of it." *I'm going mad, Mother, and what can you do about it?*

"I will have *tinsa* brought to help your rest. I know you do not need it," Inar said firmly, cutting off her protests, "but *I* will sleep the better for knowing you have had it."

Ronne tried to smile, but it was an effort. She did not want to sleep—the dreams came then, dreams of remalks. And when she was awake, she felt a presence in her mind that had not been there before. Had Talorgen's remalk transferred itself to her?

When the *tinsa* came it had not yet completely cooled. Ronne made a face.

"It tastes even worse warm. Go to sleep, Mother. I promise to drink it when it is cold." She watched her mother's retreating form as she left the room, taking the light with her. *I am so tired…but I can't spend the rest of my life in a drugged sleep.*

She felt the drinking bowl again. Cool enough. She gulped the liquid down, shuddering slightly at the taste. She heard a faint murmured exchange at her door and the sound of retreating footsteps. Exchange of guard…it must be past midnight.

She felt again at the alien echo in her mind, and tensed. It had changed direction, and seemed…further. *It must be external!* she thought, with a thrill of elation. *If I could track it down and kill it, I might survive.*

A sudden thought checked her. She had just drunk a heavy dose of *tinsa*, and when it took full effect it would be hard even to stand upright. *It could take up to an hour, though, and in that time I could do it if it is close enough.*

She pulled herself upright, feeling for her swordbelt in the dark. Moving to the window, she opened the casement with as little noise as possible and swung over the sill, holding her sword in one hand as she dropped to the portico roof. Then to the far corner, where she and Medar, long ago, had found the rough stones in the wall that made a crude stair if you rested your back against the nearest column.

She misjudged the last step and slid ten feet to the floor. She lay there until the pain receded to a bearable level, listening carefully to see if anyone had been alerted, then got up with great care.

Her sense of the direction of the echo had been lost, so she stood, eyes closed, and turned slowly to find it again. Turning, turning…*there.* A chill breeze from the lake cut through her shirt, and her hair must have been rather tousled as well.

Her lips twitched as she imagined the image she presented. *If anyone sees me, they'll think I'm Amrane returned from the dead for one last rendezvous.* Then she recalled her purpose, and she moved silently across the portico to the ancient stair and climbed.

She could see the Fingertip now, and a shadowy figure beside it. One step more…the figure turned, and she stopped, breathless, her pulse hammering. It was Erith.

He was not sure what had moved him to the terrace of the Fingertip after his appearance before the Linariach. It should, by rights, be the last place someone troubled in mind would go—exposed, chilly, dark, directly before the mysterious Lake Within. Perhaps some fragment of the legends of the Hairy Folk stirred in the back of his mind, some mention of the power of ancient rock.

What was there to worry him? Ronne was no longer in danger, Talorgen and Sardis were dead, Talorgen's army decimated and dispersed. Perhaps he feared that with the danger gone, the Linariach would persuade Ronne to make him go…but she would not, and neither would they. He had earned his place, and there were stranger folk than him now in Keris Kera. The Linariach had seen the usefulness of horses in battle, and would be reluctant to see the Windriders go.

Yet there was this niggling feeling, like a voice heard so faintly words could not be distinguished, that something was not right. He frowned. The feeling was getting stronger, the voice closer. He put the side of his face against the cool, eternal surface of the Fingertip. He was so tired…but he did not want to sleep.

The feeling he was not alone grew stronger and finally he turned, although he knew no one would be out here so late—and had to stifle a gasp at the dark shape that stood at the head of the stairs. With chagrin he realized he was armed with only his shortblade, and he could see the muted gleam of a sword in the other's hand.

The shadow came forward. The face was indistinct, but the walk, the motions, a thousand nameless details told him it was Ronne. She moved further, into the pale light cast by the sliver of moon. He noticed her unkempt appearance with surprise—her wrinkled undertunic, half-open at the neck, her loose dark hair. Another person might have thought her vulnerable, so. He knew better. The burning eyes, the predatory grace…she was very, very dangerous.

A taut silence hung between them as they stared at one another.

"Where is it?" Her voice was rough and deep, shaking almost imperceptibly. "Please do not say it is in you, for then I will go mad regardless."

He swallowed, his mouth and throat dry. "I don't understand. There's nothing here but me. What are you looking for?"

She moved closer still. "I can feel it in my mind, some alien thing," she said, with soft intensity. "Ever since I woke from the thorn-of-death it has been there, a shadow to my thoughts. My mother told me it was you who pulled me from the Dark World, thwarting the surest weapon of the Stealing Face. No one survives the thorn-of-death, there is no cure. But you...you would not let me rest, and you wove your magic yet again to heal me. There was a price.... *What have you done to me?*"

"I don't...I don't understand what I do! I found you, and asked you to come back. There was a remalk in that place, but you made it die. Do you think I'd bargain with such a thing, or leave it with you?"

Without knowing what he did, he reached out a hand to her face, to the pain he saw there. Ronne grasped his wrist to stop it.

He felt a soundless explosion shake him and his senses reeled, confused and disoriented. For a brief moment his vision doubled, but from a different viewpoint, and he saw his own face, shocked and confused, staring back at him.

Whatever the link had been, when it no longer had to cross the intervening distance between them it changed from a thin trickle of contact to a flood. He could feel her presence in his mind as clearly as he could see her, and knew she could sense him in the same way. She was a changing mixture of determination, strength, and fear rapidly becoming curiosity, with something else surfacing for an instant that was so bright he had to draw his mental gaze away.

Almost, she seemed to draw in on herself, becoming smaller, until he reached out and surrounded her presence with warmth and welcoming joy.

It occurred to him then to wonder how he appeared to her, and he opened his physical eyes again.

"It is you," murmured Ronne, eyes wondering, "but only you. It is well."

Wordlessly he extended his invitation, and wordlessly she accepted, and they held each other as tightly as fatigue and wounds permitted. A sigh of pure contentment escaped him as he buried his face in her unbraided hair, and their single shared thought was one of refuge found at last.

They stood so for some time, until Erith caught an undercurrent of Ronne's thought and looked up. He sensed, more than saw, her rueful smile.

"I need your help, beloved."

"Truly, a time of miracles...what is it?"

A chuckle shook her. "To avoid the guard at my door, I took a somewhat...active route out of my chambers. Through the window, to be exact. What with the exhaustion of yesterday, and the large bowl of *tinsa* my well-meaning mother had me drink tonight, I fear I cannot use the same way to return, and it would be best if I am not questioned about tonight's activities."

In response to his mental tendril of curiosity, she held up her unsheathed sword. " 'What the eye sees may not be concealed,' " she quoted.

Erith imagined Inar's reaction to an unexpurgated relation of the night's events, and Ronne grinned. "Ah…I see your point," he said. "But why did you…never mind. I will distract your guard, with Kashan's help. He still makes quite an impression."

She took his hand in hers and kissed the inside of his wrist. "I have every confidence in your abilities," she murmured.

He didn't understand. The Plays-with human wanted him to do something, but his motions said different things than the noises he made. The Plays-with human had brought him to a part of the Big Cave where HIS HUMAN was, he could smell her scent. He could smell her scent on the Plays-with human too. Why wouldn't he let him go to her?

Then another human with lots of fear-smell came, and the Plays-with human and him made noises at each other. They made the noise that they usually made at him, but they weren't looking at him when they said it so it didn't count. Then he thought the human could be part of a new game and pounced him, but he just fell down and was boring.

The Plays-with human leaned against the wall and made wheezing noises, which was a little interesting but not much. Then HIS HUMAN came and she made noises that sounded like when he was bad as a cub and she threw water in his face, but she wasn't looking at him. He watched carefully, but nobody got water in the face.

The boring human got up and his fear-smell was even worse. But it didn't matter, because HIS HUMAN let him go in the small cave that was her den and stay there with her. This pleased him, because he could guard her from the evil things much better than these squeaky no-claws who kept getting in the way.

CHAPTER 24

As she poked and pottered about her workbench, Arisaig glanced at Erith under her brows. He shifted his feet, picking up a dagger from the bench then putting it down. In the small space he seemed even larger, his bulk filling the room.

"A sword-eye, is it," she said, and chuckled. She could hardly wait to see the reaction to this development. It would upset any number of worthy traditionalists who never bothered to think, and about time, too.

Now where was her scriber, and the smaller hammer? If tools couldn't move themselves, how did they always manage to hide when she was looking for them? "It's customary to take the symbol of your house for your sword-eye," she said as she assembled her tools.

Erith looked even more uncomfortable. "I don't have one anymore."

"Use your head, boy!" she snapped. "You exist, eh? Therefore, you have a house. So what if you're the only member?" She noted with approval the small grin twitching at the corners of his mouth. "This simply means few will be familiar with it—or the symbol."

"I'm certainly not."

Arisaig found a stick of charcoal and scrubbed a clear space on her workbench with the heel of her hand. She looked at him thoughtfully, and then began to sketch. "I think…a flame. Like so."

"Why a flame?"

"Oh, I think it was the hair that gave me the idea," she said, shaking with internal laughter.

Erith sighed. "I shall shave my head."

"There's more to it than that," said Arisaig, relenting. "If one includes all the new folk you and the *alaran* have brought to Arhi, your house is quite large. You are not linked by blood but by similarity of nature. The *alaran* has it. You have it. A burning spirit, a fire in the heart. That is what we need now, wherever it comes from."

She brushed away the flakes of dried blood from his sword and carefully began to scribe the symbol in the darkmetal. "So there you have it—the symbol of the house Taras Dalar."

"What does that mean?"

"Fire-hearted," said Arisaig, and she reached for the gold wire.

Tekbeh stirred and stretched, deciding it was nice not to be in a constant state of warfare anymore. It allowed luxuries like sleep. *And other things*, she thought, smiling sleepily at the man beside her.

"I'm glad I stole you," she told Kemar'sto, who just smiled and tightened his hold on her until her ribs creaked. Tekbeh had been revising her earlier estimation of Kemar'sto's character. "Shy" had been the first trait to go, replaced by "subtle and tricky beyond belief." There were others, but on the whole Tekbeh was not complaining.

She was just drifting off to sleep again when she heard the sound of a slamming door below and general commotion, with Erith's voice heard over it all. Tekbeh groaned, then reluctantly got up and began to dress. "I suppose we should see what he wants," she grumbled, and they descended the steep, narrow stairs to the common room.

The rovers were perched on tables and benches, still crowding the room despite the large number missing. Tekbeh scowled, thinking how many they had lost. More in proportion than the regular army had, since they were used to fighting alone and were more lightly armed.

Erith looked remarkably happy. He would be, if the rumors were true about the thorn-of-death. Kemar'sto demonstrated his forethought and sneakiness yet again by finding a corner where they could see, but not be easily seen. She leaned back against him as he settled his arms around her.

"Good news," Erith said in greeting. "Not only has Talorgen's army gone, the *alaran* is completely recovered from the thorn-of-death." The rovers cheered and thumped tables with mugs. "We'll still have work to do, making sure they stay that way, but we have some friends come to visit that can help us." The rovers turned to look at the few kenjah who could fit in the common room.

Tekbeh translated, and they nodded solemnly. Erith glanced back to where Tekbeh stood, and widened his eyes when he noticed who was there with her. He grinned, and Tekbeh felt her face go hot. She noticed he didn't seem very surprised.

"There is one more matter," he said, turning back to the crowd. His expression changed, more serious and somber. "The *alaran* has requested, and the council has agreed, to raise a mound to those who died in the fighting here. They have asked us for the names of our people who fell, so they can be inscribed on a stela beside it."

A hush fell over the room, broken after a long silence by a soft voice speaking a name.

Erith stood by, watching as the rovers gathered about one table, wondering at the strong reaction they had shown. One of them who could write was painstakingly copying the names that were being given on the back of an old map.

"Why is a mound such a big thing?" Erith asked Hasko.

"It's for heroes," said the old man. "That our folk will be there too… well, it's an honor."

Erith looked about the room, struck by a sudden thought. "Where's Fedi?"

Hasko sobered. "They didn't tell you?

"Is he dead?

"As near to it as makes no difference. They found him late, y'see, and there's not a patch of skin as big as your hand that don't have a cut in it somewhere. It's just stubbornness keeping him alive now."

Erith was out the door and heading to the main fortress before Hasko caught up with him. "Where are you off to, then?"

"To help Fedi."

"You won't find him up there. The wounded are down in the outer ward. And what d'ye think you can do when you get to him?"

Erith slowed, then stopped. "I can do something. Sometimes." And sometimes he couldn't do anything. Why? What was he doing wrong? When it worked, his healing flowed from him without effort. Ronne's knee in Tak'hullus, Tekbeh's leg on the plains, the thorn-of-death—all were serious injuries that he had cured completely. But then he had failed with Zeltan and the injured rover.

He was missing something obvious, some important detail that would make it all clear. There had to be a pattern. A wave of fury passed over him and he slammed his fist against the stone wall, grimacing at the pain that flashed through a moment later.

"What ails you, youngblood?" asked a perturbed Hasko. "It's a shame and a sorrow, sure, but beating down the fortress with yer bare hands won't aid a one of them. Even if ye are big enough ta do it."

Despair replaced Erith's fury, and he looked at his scraped and bleeding hand, realizing Hasko spoke the truth. All his strength couldn't help now; he had only hurt himself with it.

He felt a tug at his mind, a spike of concern that was not his. He looked up and across the ward, directed by an inner pull, and then Ronne came into view. She had a very worried expression on her face. He felt a rush of relief, so strong he had to close his eyes, and he thought to her, *Help me.*

He held out his hand to her, not knowing how to put his frustration into words, trusting in their link and her understanding of him. She quickened her pace.

His battered hand began to heal. He watched, fascinated, as the broken skin became whole, the inner ache that spoke of damaged bone and muscle faded and disappeared as she came near. *Ronne.* The chaotic tumble of his thoughts calmed with sudden understanding. This was the link that was missing.

A small, incoherent sound distracted him. Hasko was staring at them both, mouth agape. He shook his head as if to deny what he saw. "You knew," he said in a hoarse voice. "You knew it was her afore she was here. An' you…your…." He pointed a shaking finger at Erith's undamaged hand.

"The wounded," Erith choked out, in response to Ronne's urgent thought. "I want to help them. It doesn't work without you." It was a disjointed request, but she understood. Without the need for speech, they left for the outer ward.

The tent for the wounded was a grim sight. Fedi was the worst still living; Hasko had not exaggerated his condition. He was a mass of bloody bandages, his chest barely moving as he breathed. Erith could sense waves of pain emanating from him. Feeling more certain, he reached to find the strongest source.

He found that he could distance himself from the healing so the pain did not overwhelm him, and mindful of the number of wounds, he did not attempt to heal each one completely, only enough to close it and start it going well. At first the healers in the tent tried to intervene, but Ronne's presence stopped them long enough for Erith to begin. Once they realized what he was doing, one of the healers even assisted him, removing bandages from each wound in turn.

He dealt with three major injuries, and it seemed to him that Fedi was looking better. The cloud of pain had diminished as well. Then the healer drew back another bandage, and Erith's confidence vanished. It was an ugly cut in the boy's abdomen, deep and ragged. Erith was already exhausted; he knew he would not be able to complete healing this wound before he collapsed.

He bowed his head in frustration. Then he felt Ronne's presence, sensed her approach, felt his strength return the closer she came. When she placed her hands on his shoulders, he felt completely restored.

"Are you sure this is wise?"

"Look at him," he said roughly. "Does somebody who fights that fiercely deserve to die?"

Ronne said nothing, but he felt her presence in his mind, supporting him, supplying her strength to supplement his. Erith closed Fedi's ugly wound, removing the infection that had already begun, and took stock.

There were a few more deep cuts, and he closed them. The rest could heal on their own now.

Ronne sent a tendril of thought to him, and he looked over to where Zeltan lay, his face grey with pain. Ronne and Erith moved as one to his side, and Zeltan looked up at them, wondering, as Erith turned back the bandages and gently laid his hand on the festering cut.

Even with Ronne's assistance, he felt fatigue returning by the time Zeltan was out of danger. Then they moved to Edge Singing, with a long cut down one leg, and a few others with dangerous wounds. Now Erith could barely stand even with Ronne's assistance, and she silently insisted he do no more.

As they left, a man who had been watching by the bed of a woman Erith had healed came up and thanked him, tears choking his voice. The healers and others who had gathered in the tent bowed, their hands before their faces in the traditional gesture of respect to a high noble.

There were several big fires near the new mound where the kenjah had gathered that night, but Ronne headed for the largest. All the kenjah rose when she and the others with her entered the circle, and Un'Varten came to meet her.

"I have this to give you," said Ronne, after greetings had been exchanged. She held out a delicate porcelain jar, lifting the lid to show the earth it contained. "Take the land beyond the Standing Stone and build an ancestor house for your people, so they will be landless no longer."

She put the jar in Un'Varten's hand, hoping the ceremonial land-transfer had not confused him. Dealing with the kenjah had taught her that many things could be easily misunderstood.

It had not confused him. He looked at what he held for a moment, then lifted it up and shouted, "*Va'tes i kenjah! Cha'tral nou corvets, mayan!*"

A vast, deafening roar erupted from the kenjah. It lasted for a long time. When at last it died down, the Windriders began to celebrate in earnest, with singing and complicated dances performed about the fire. Ronne and Erith sat beside Un'Varten, who held the porcelain jar in his one hand as if he would never let it go.

Before the festivities got fully underway, Un'Varten wove a tiny braid from his crest and cut it free, handing it to Ronne. She took it, confused. Something seemed to be expected of her in return, so she took her shortblade and cut off one of her own braids for him. From their reactions, she had guessed correctly.

"Your honor his now, neh?" said Edge Singing, back in her role of translator. "His yours. He guard ancestor house of you, you guard ancestor house of him." She grinned. "Now need be ancestors! Tek'beha, she help steal man for me!"

Erith choked on what he was drinking, coughing helplessly while he laughed. Ronne sensed amusement, but no confusion. He knew what Edge Singing referred to. Ronne was puzzled. She looked about, locating Tekbeh in the crowd…and began to understand. Tekbeh was not alone.

When she caught her eye, Ronne beckoned Tekbeh over. Tekbeh looked somewhat shamefaced, but for all that Ronne noticed she made no attempt to let go Kemar'sto's hand.

"What is this I hear about stealing people?" asked Ronne.

Tekbeh's face got even darker. "Uh, I kinda…married him. Without knowing it."

Erith dissolved into laughter again, and Ronne ventured, "You aren't sure?"

"I *think* so. I just…it happened rather suddenly."

"Is this going to cause us any problems?"

Tekbeh sighed, exasperated. "Far as I can tell, they think it is a wonderful joke!"

The kenjah did seem to be pleased. Un'Varten said something to Edge Singing, and they began a negotiation for the right to celebrate Tekbeh and Kemar'sto's marriage.

"We give four horses, we do marriage dance. Not marrying-gift! She steal!"

"Why do you need permission?" wondered Erith.

"Is for the luck," said Edge Singing. "Marrying good luck for the ancestor house, help keep away bad spirit from fighting."

Ronne pretended to think it over, then waved a hand in assent. Un'Varten inclined his head solemnly, face bland but eyes bright with amusement.

And so Tekbeh and Kemar'sto, richer by four horses, were celebrated in the tradition of the Windriders. This involved a great deal of apparently humorous song, most of which was lost on Ronne and Erith since Tekbeh was too embarrassed to translate. Edge Singing's contribution, a saga of Tekbeh's violent passion, appeared to be one of the best, judging from the kenjah's reaction. Many of the riders were reduced to wheezing spasms of laughter, and Kemar'sto hid his face in his arms.

Ronne and Erith stood at the edge of the Lake Within and watched the mist swirl about the surface of the water. Dawn had only just begun to light the sky.

"This may seem strange, but I assure you the creatures are there," said Ronne.

"I believe you," said Erith, remembering. This earned him a thoughtful glance from Ronne. He was not yet used to the subtle shades of meaning he could sense in their mental link, so all he knew was she found this interesting…and not completely surprising.

He sensed her gathering her resolution as she fingered the crown, the Crown of Silence, then set it on her head.

Erith gasped. It was almost as if he was Ronne now, he could read her thoughts as if they were his own, see through her eyes. And yet he was responding to her closeness…he became aware he had come up behind her and wrapped her tightly in his arms.

We should talk to them first, thought Ronne, amused.

Erith took a deep breath and tried to regain control. *You have this effect on me….*

It pleases me to say the same.

Through her eyes he saw shapes emerging from the mist, one more clearly visible than the rest. White wisps of almost-hair drifted before slanting silver eyes.

"That's the one I saw!" whispered Erith. He drew back, but kept his hands on her shoulders.

The mist creature hung in the air before them. "What news?" it said.

"We have destroyed two remalks. Were these all that threatened you?"

The creature hesitated. "They were the only ones active. But others still exist, dormant. They may come again."

Ronne nodded. "We will watch for them." The mist creature seemed to swirl and retreat from view. "Wait! I have a question."

"Speak."

"Erith has the ability to heal. He healed me when I nearly died from poison, and now we are linked."

The silver eyes gleamed brightly, and the slanted smile deepened even more. "Magic is returning, mortals. You would be well advised to study it, and quickly."

"How do we stop it?"

"How do you stop the wind? You do not want it, but it will seek you out despite your wishes. Those of the bloodline here have always had a stronger connection to magic. You have used the tiny trace of ability to forge your special metal."

"How can we learn, if none of us know anything of it? It is a dangerous thing to meddle with." Erith could sense Ronne's growing frustration.

"This is true, mortal. Yet you must test it to master it. Has he not done this?" The creature looked at Erith for the first time, and its smile deepened.

"You know about this magic. Why can't you teach us? Erith did not intend to create the link between us."

"Your magic is separate from you. For us, it is what we are. How can we teach what we do not know?" The creature faded, then returned. "The link you have created in your ignorance…this much we can tell you. It is in the deepest levels of your soul—to undo it, you would have to be as close to death as you were when it was made. But while it exists, you will never lose control of the gift you fear. Is that not worth the price?"

Erith felt a surge of joy pass through Ronne, so strong she was speechless. *But what is the price?* "Will…if one of us dies, will the other die as well?"

There was no answer. The first beams of the sun had touched the surface of the lake, and the mist creatures had vanished. Ronne wrenched the crown off with a muttered curse, and Erith reached up to her forehead and the pain he felt there.

"I don't know why magic has to hurt," Ronne complained. "The first time I used it, to find a way to stop Talorgen's mind-numbing magic, I thought my head would split."

"We still don't know where Talorgen found the remalks, or how he knew how to use them."

"I know." Ronne's face was serious. "They have warned us this is only the beginning. Magic is returning to the world…and we know almost nothing about it. We must learn."

"You can't be serious." Alland stared at his sister, appalled.

"Yes. Very serious."

"Um, you couldn't make it…" he lowered his voice, "unofficial?" She was so much happier…there had to be a way.

"I was under the impression that the Linariach wanted me to find a consort. I have."

Ronne looked angry again. Erith, all the way at the end of the portico, had turned to look at them even though their voices hadn't been loud enough for him to hear. Ronne and Erith had been acting like this ever since her recovery, and it mystified Alland.

"It has to be him," she argued. "It is not my heart alone saying this—I'll show you why."

She drew her shortblade, keeping it close to her, and drew one finger sharply over the edge. Erith uttered a surprised yelp.

"Which finger?" Ronne said, without turning, and Erith raised the same one she had cut. "You see?" she said to Alland.

"Er. This happened after the thorn-of-death?"

"Yes. Consider, if you please, that if our lives are linked, he must be protected."

Erith stood beside her now. He said nothing, but Ronne raised her injured hand and he took it in his own, tracing a finger over the cut. The cut vanished as if it had never been there.

It was one thing to hear about Erith's healing, but quite another to see it in person. When Alland mastered his astonishment, he managed to find his voice. "Have you even thought about what people will say?"

Ronne made a strangled snarling noise deep in her throat, and Alland started back.

"At every moment. Ever since Zeltan and the others showed up at the outpost. I—have—done—*everything* I could think of to protect Erith's reputation and honor. To our mutual annoyance, I might add." Erith looked at Ronne with an expression of dawning enlightenment. "But now they know he is more than he appears. He has risked his life for Arhi. He is *tier sanas*. And I have chosen him and he has accepted." She made a gesture of finality.

Alland felt aggrieved. "You have no idea what you are asking me to do. Hereil alone is going to have seven kinds of fit. He's been saving that idiot kinsman of his for you for years."

"I know it will be hard," Ronne said, more calmly, "but if anyone can do it, you can. I know I can't. I'm asking you, Alland. Please."

And there it was. Secretly flattered, he sputtered a little longer for the principle of the thing, but already he was forming plans. The army supported Erith, especially after the healing of the wounded. The common people liked him too, especially the women, so it was really only the nobles who needed work.

"I'll see Manohan tomorrow. She has a petition coming up," he muttered. "She'll love a chance to step on Hereil's toes."

He thought of a question for Ronne and looked up. He was alone in the room. He thought for a moment, then shook his head. "No, I'll see her now."

The End

ABOUT THE AUTHOR

Sabrina Chase was originally trained as a Mad Scientist, but due to a tragic lack of available lairs at the time of graduation fell into low company and started working in the software industry. She lives in the Pacific Northwest and is owned by two cats.

Further sordid details may or may not be available at her website, chaseadventures.com